Lumberjacks and Ladies

Lumberjacks and Ladies

EDWARD E. LANGENAU

BANGOR, MAINE

Copyright © 2003 NewChapter Publishing Company

Published by NewChapter Publishing Company
P.O. Box 2466, Bangor, Maine 04402-2446

Email: newchapterpub@adelphia.net
www.lumberjacksandladies.com

LCC2003092271
ISBN 0-9740662-0-6

Published with assistance from Griffith Publishing
Cover design by Linda Griffith
Printed in the United States of America

Contents

1: The Cabin-Raising 1
2: Violence in the Woods 19
3: Market Hunting 31
4: Wanderlust 39
5: Jacques Goes to Logging Camp 51
6: Sally's Trouble 74
7: Dietrich's Hearing 85
8: Sally's Move to Bay City 99
9: Winter Among the Pines 120
10: Jake and Thor Leave Camp 142
11: Eli the River Hog 152
12: Jake and Thor in Grafton 173
13: Jake's Loss 182
14: Sally Returns to Grafton 200
15: Summer Love 215
16: The Wedding 227
17: Jake Builds a Sawmill in Saginaw 249
18: Jake Travels to Minnesota 266
19: Sally and Jake Visit Clayburg 274
20: The Burning of Clayburg 284

About the Author 298

1

The Cabin-Raising

Sally yelled at Jacques across the wet hay field, "You gonna help build the cabin this Saturday?"

Jacques watched her seventeen-year-old figure float through the air and bounce across the field toward him like a spirit rising about the clouds. She sure had filled out during the past winter, he thought. He looked down at the hay rake and back at Sally twice before the words came out, "Me and Dietrich are going. How about you?"

"Yup. Should I bring some of my blueberry pie?"

"Yeah," said Jacques. "Nobody makes better pie than you." He scattered the hay, leveling large clumps so it would dry better in the humid morning. "See you at two on Saturday."

Like many June days in southern Michigan, the air was so thick with moisture, condensed in a combination of fog and dew, that Jacques found it hard to see. Everything felt damp. Puddles of water formed basins on the ground and hung in clouds over fields. The rain brought mosquitoes, which would become especially bad as the summer of 1872 continued.

None of this mattered to teenagers in the pioneer village of Grafton, Michigan. Jacques had more on his mind than weather or bugs. Mostly he thought about Sally Wilton. When he awoke each morning, he wondered if she was up yet and what she was doing. All day he thought about her face with its creamy complexion that always seemed so cheery. At night he went to bed thinking about the curves between her breasts and waist. Then, while he dreamed, his imagination went wild.

She had told him quite a bit about her family, one of the last to settle in the small village northeast of Kalamazoo. Sally said they'd used her grandfather's inheritance to finance their trip from Boston to Michigan. They came with fine china, silver tea sets, heavy bronze sculptures, and oil paintings. They had a secretary made from bird's-eye maple and a hutch of handsome cherry. As a child she wore dresses designed in Paris.

Jacques learned that Mr. Wilton wanted to be a blacksmith in a small town rather than a teller in his father-in-law's bank. He often rode the train on his day off to a blacksmith shop in Newton where he watched men build wood-burning stoves and wrought iron fences. Sally said he almost lost his job at the bank when his boss found a supply catalog for blacksmith tools hidden in a corner of the teller cage.

He recalled learning how the Wiltons were unwelcome at first in Grafton, mostly because other settlers had come there earlier during the 1840s. Those first pioneers pulled wagons with oxen across plains and marshes. They had few household goods other than plows, firearms, pots, and pans. In contrast, the blacksmith's family arrived by railroad in 1868, after the Civil War. Their belongings, which filled one-third of a baggage car, were carried twelve miles from the rail depot to town. Neighbors never forgot the sight of this wealthy family arriving in the pioneer village on the afternoon stagecoach, followed by a buckboard filled with fine furnishings. The family aroused suspicion because they were so different. However, people needed a blacksmith so badly they accepted the citified ways of this strange family from the east. Local folks even helped build the shop on the east end of Main Street.

Sally liked to be around men and had little interest in playing dolls or dressing up in fancy clothes. Maybe it was because her mother was too busy playing the piano or reading to pay her much attention. Whatever the reason, Sally took every opportunity to seek her father's affection, which he shared with warmth. Often he scooped her off the ground and bounced her on his knee. When she was old enough, he taught her how to climb trees and work at the blacksmith shop. She learned to stoke the furnaces and shape hot iron with a hammer.

The blacksmith shop repeatedly caught fire. Hot coals from furnaces and stoves sometimes smoldered for hours until the wood on the side of the building would catch fire. Jacques often saw Sally carrying buckets of water from the well down the street to douse flames at the shop. He also remembered how they'd met three years before at the fire.

That July night in 1869, slender orange flames lapped the walls of the blacksmith shop. Jacques and others in town formed a line to pass buckets of water from the well to the building. With boldness not common for fourteen-year-olds, she put her face close to his and said, "What's your name?"

"I'm Jacques." He blushed. "Jacques Flareau. Are you the girl who lives upstairs?" His hand grabbed too quickly for the next bucket, and water sloshed on his pants. He thought, why am I so nervous? Maybe I'm hurrying too much.

"Yup. I'm Sally Wilton. My father's the blacksmith. You're from the market hunting family, aren't you? I've seen you in town before."

"Yeah. My dad and me were taking fish to the general store. We saw the flames."

"Where do you live?"

"Out of town by the river." He tried to brush the water from his pants but it was too late—there was a dark stain from his belt to his knees.

The procession of wooden containers stopped for a few minutes, allowing flames to creep higher up the walls of the blacksmith shop.

"More buckets!" someone yelled.

The flow of wooden containers resumed. He watched the flames subside only to flare again with renewed fury. The fire seemed to have a rhythm all its own. It also created its own wind, pushing pieces of soot through the air and into Jacques's eyes. He watched ashes stick on sweaty people passing water buckets. Storefronts on Main Street were fully visible to him although the sides of the buildings were in the dark.

After several waves of bucket passing, there was a longer pause. Jacques felt awkward because the conversation also waned. Talking seemed to increase when the helpers were busy and slowed when they were idle.

Sally's eyes avoided his and darted up and down the street. He concluded that she, too, was at a loss for words. Her round face, normally cheerful and bright, looked serene. It also appeared red, as if sunburned from the heat of the fire. One of her eyebrows, shorter than the other, had been singed.

Everything he thought about saying seemed inappropriate or trite. He decided it was better to keep quiet than say the wrong thing while her family's business and home burned. Hoping to see more buckets, he looked down the row of people until they vanished in the dark.

Jacques dug his hands deep into his pocket as if some movement might break the embarrassing silence. He touched his good-luck arrowhead with a familiarity that felt comforting. Happy to have found something to talk about, he withdrew the arrowhead from his pocket.

"What's that?" she asked.

"An Indian arrowhead."

"Where'd you find it?"

"My father and I were tilling." He peered from beneath an oversized hat, hoping it concealed his large nose and long chin. "It just seemed to float to the top of the soil."

"Can I see it?"

"You sure can. It's good luck." He passed it to her.

"Was it lucky for the Indian that made it?" asked Sally.

He was proud of the arrowhead, mostly white, except for yellow-brown spots, where rubbed by dirty fingers. "Sure. I bet he shot a dozen deer with it."

She passed the arrowhead back to Jacques. Her hand pushed the hard stone into his palm. For a brief moment, their hands closed, sandwiching the arrowhead between them. His skin seemed rough, compared to hers. With much hesitation, he uncurled his fingers, leaving the arrowhead in her soft hand.

He stammered. "Would you like it?"

"Oh, no. It's your good luck piece. It wouldn't be right for me to take it." She passed the arrowhead back.

With a stronger, more confident voice, he said, "Please, take it. I think you need it more than me."

"But then you'll have bad luck."

Jacques examined the stone in his hand. She was right, he thought; it had brought good luck. He recalled the time he got lost tracking a wounded deer, rubbed the arrowhead, and found his way back to the cabin. He rubbed it before jumping in the river to save his brother, who didn't know how to swim. On another occasion, the arrowhead seemed to stop lighting bolts when he was rowing his boat on Duck Lake during a thunderstorm.

"Hey kids, stop talking. Get those buckets moving," said a deep voice in the night.

Aware that he was holding up the line, Jacques handed the arrowhead to Sally. "Here. It's yours now. I hope it brings you good luck."

The crowd seemed to be growing. Some people came to pass buckets but others were just there to watch. In case the fire spread, owners of nearby stores doused their buildings with water to squelch new flames. Then Jacques heard hissing sounds where old flames had been. Billows of smoke drifted into the sky, down the street, and smothered the crowds. The smoke, which first smelled pleasant, like odors from a winter wood stove, became acrid and stung his nostrils. Darkness returned to Main Street. Until torches were lit, he tripped over buckets, scattered wherever tired volunteers dropped them. Everything was covered with a mist of hot steam and putrid smoke.

The arrowhead didn't bring Sally much good luck. Instead, the fire caused her mother to leave Grafton. Half the blacksmith shop, with living quarters above, was lost in the fire, the last hardship that Sally's mother could tolerate. She was especially upset because many belongings, symbolic of her past city life, had been burned. On Thanksgiving Mrs. Wilton gave up.

"What a sad day," she said as her husband started to carve the wild turkey. "Here, we sit alone in the wilderness. Meanwhile, twenty-three of our relatives back home are together, sharing Thanksgiving dinner."

Mr. Wilton disagreed. "Today is a day for us to be grateful, not jealous." He cut large pieces of turkey with more force than usual. Being a portly man, he had lots of force in his arms.

"Ha! You dragged me from home to fulfill your stupid dream. This is about selfishness, not jealousy."

After grace, the family ate turkey, applesauce, corn bread, and wild onions. The white tablecloth stood out in the charred dining room. The floor, walls, and furniture were mottled with black charcoal from the fire.

The blacksmith said, "Dear, we decided to move west together. It was a joint decision."

"I just can't stand it anymore. I want to go home." She threw her fork down on the dinner plate. "I have tried and tried and tried." Tears wet the lace collar on her fine dress.

He stood at the table to make his next point, "I'm stayin' here." Pointing his finger between her eyes, he barked, "Don't expect me to go back east with you."

Sally looked like a scolded dog. She put her head on the table. She thought about speaking a few times, but the words seemed to stick in her throat, somewhere below the sobs.

Mrs. Wilton passed food around the table for second helpings. All the white meat, rare on wild turkeys, was gone. The three picked meat from the bones with meticulous care in embarrassing silence. It was hard for Sally's mother to continue in front of her daughter. Finally, she answered, "Well, then, you raise the girl by yourself."

"My God, woman! Are you going to abandon us?" He circled the table twice, pacing in deliberate strides. Sally noticed his large ears, which seemed to stick out further than usual. Thick salt and pepper hair on the back of his neck also seemed to be more visible. She'd always been embarrassed about the amount of hair on her father's arms and legs.

"Why'd you quit your job at the bank? Daddy went to a lot of trouble to get you that position."

"That was a shared decision, too. And now you want a separation?"

"That's better than divorce, which would be improper for a lady."

"What will we tell people in the village?"

"I'll pretend to be sick. You can help me act out symptoms of consumption. Then, I'll quietly return to Boston. Without the burden of a child, perhaps I'll be accepted as a lady once again." When she walked, her petite body swayed until she reached the burned coffee table. Her slender fingers slid across the wood, leaving a black stain on her palm.

"Our daughter's not a burden. She's a gift to cherish and nurture." He sat down at the table again.

"I miss my family and servants. Back home, a nanny would have helped me raise children."

"Well then, get out of here!" Breathing heavily, he clenched his fist beneath the cloth napkin on his lap. He put his glasses on the table and looked downward.

"It's settled then. I'm leaving Grafton the end of the week. You can stay here if you wish."

"I'm sorry!" Sally cried. She still had her head on the tablecloth, now wet with tears. Thinking it was her fault Mother was leaving town, in the months ahead, she would say "I'm sorry" to herself several times each day.

Lying about her mother's health was hard for Sally. Almost half the town came out to wish her mother well when she went east for a "cure." Sally was ordered to keep the family secret that the sickness was staged.

It was hard when townspeople asked about her mother's health, but somehow Sally managed. Women at church invited her to teas, where they gossiped, read poetry, and played cards. She learned to cook and sew from neighbors. Having so much responsibility at a young age made her mature quickly and fostered her desire to help others. However, not all the impacts of that Thanksgiving dinner were positive. She would have no interest in becoming a wife or mother, despite a desperate obsession to please men.

On Saturday Jacques selected his favorite axe for use at the cabin-raising, along with his cleanest shirt for the party afterward. It was still dark when the eighteen-year-old left the cabin and met Dietrich Krausse, his co-worker, on the road to Peterson's. They greeted each other before marching off in the dark with axes over their shoulders.

A mist hovered over the clearing where men gathered for the cabin-raising at daybreak. Toting axes, shovels, and hammers, they arrived on horseback and on foot. Mr. Peterson planned to build his cabin in an oak clearing, about half a mile from town. A few helpers carried jugs of their favorite whiskey, although rules prohibited drinking until all the work was completed. Men were scattered in small groups or sat alone on stumps waiting for others to arrive.

Jacques and Dietrich heard laughter when they approached the group. Almost everyone in town had heard the rumors about them competing for Sally's affection. Some of the joking may have been related to the striking contrast between the two men. Jacques, at six foot two, hovered over Dietrich, who barely measured five foot six. Jacques had thick biceps and a wide chest that stretched the buttons on his shirt, while Dietrich had a small head perched on a long, thin neck. Jacques was neat and clean-shaven with a tucked-in shirt, while Dietrich had three or four days of stubble on his face. The only similarity in the appearance of the two was the black color of their hair. Jacque's hair was thick and curly, and Dietrich's was straight and greasy.

Mr. Rice, owner of the general store, said, "Hello, boys. What a nice morning to work outside."

"Yes, sir," replied Dietrich. He stretched his skinny gooseneck as he always did when he was nervous.

A short man with white hair and a red-brown moustache asked, "Are you still going out with Sally Wilton?"

All the men in the clearing stopped talking and waited for Dietrich's reply.

"No," Jacques said. "He's not. Sally's my girl."

"Says who?" barked Dietrich.

Mr. Rice stepped between the boys. "Save your energy for swinging axes. Don't waste it fighting among yourselves."

The white-haired man spoke again. "The blacksmith's daughter must get pretty hot standing around those furnaces all day." Laughter from a dozen men filled the air.

Jacques turned toward him, ready to throw a punch. Mr. Rice pinched his shoulder and spun him around. "He meant no harm or disrespect. Crude jokes are fine when there's no women near."

Dietrich looked at the man with white hair and said, "You're right. Sally does get hot." His shifty blue eyes glanced back to Jacques.

The laughter was louder this time. It rose in volume, peaked, and then subsided as everyone waited for the next parry.

Jacques rubbed his hairy chest with oversized hands and wondered what to do. Should I punch him for insinuating he had sex with Sally? Would it be better to cut him down with words? He looked Dietrich up and down. What a sorry sight. A short frame and poor coordination.

Jacques knew he would win if there were a fist fight. Since he sensed the other men knew that also, Jacques decided to ignore his comment. "Dietrich's just daydreaming. Let's get to work." Some of the men grumbled, disappointed there would be no fight. Others congratulated Jacques on his thoughtful decision. The throng of men, laughing and talking, moved together toward a larger crowd.

Crossing the clearing at dawn was like going through an obstacle course. Jacques tripped twice over lumber and stones. He surveyed the building materials, which had taken the Petersons almost two months to gather and organize. Pre-cut boards, bought from the sawmill, had been placed farthest from the building site so they would not be damaged. Those would be used for chimney slats, door jams, and window frames. Closer to the cabin site were cedar shingles for the roof and woodshed. Raw logs, for cabin walls, were stacked according to their size. Mounds of grass and clay were strategically placed for use in chinking spaces between logs.

The Petersons had spent several months hauling rocks from the river almost two miles away. Those rocks were carefully chosen for a fireplace with a slate hearth. The family's priority for their homestead was obvious from the size of the rock pile along with its location at the center of the building site. Everyone had heard about Mr. Peterson's dream of having a majestic fireplace with a fancy stone façade and a tall, wide firebox.

The conversation shifted from Sally to former cabin-raisings. Jacques heard one pioneer say, "Mr. Peterson has sure planned a fancy cabin. When we moved here, my family lived in a lean-to with saplings for a roof."

Another man commented, "We first had a sod roof. It was covered with eight inches of grass. I replaced it six years later."

Jacques moved from group to group listening to talk about more recent cabins built with pre-cut lumber from sawmills. He watched daylight reach the ground after first silhouetting the treetops against a gray sky. Some men had worked on modern frame houses, common within larger cities on the Michigan frontier. He heard stories about parties held after the cabins were completed. Memories of dancing, drinking, and deceased friends sprinkled their conversations.

Soon Mr. Peterson walked into the middle of the talkative crowd of twenty-six males. Looking down at his dew-soaked boots, he first thanked everyone for coming to help his family complete their cabin. Jacques listened to him outline the work to be done while sketching particulars in the dirt with an oak staff. He watched him organize men into teams and give them appropriate tools.

The first team, composed of the strongest men, was told to move boulders with a rock sled to each corner of the cabin and attached woodshed. "Stack the rocks over by those sticks," said Mr. Peterson, pointing to corner stakes protruding from the ground. "We'll use the rock piles as piers to hold the largest logs."

Another team was assigned to hew timbers into squared logs for the sides of the cabin. "Make 'em nice and flat, please. Sam, you're good at that. Can you show the others how to use those broad axes?"

"Nothing to it."

Mr. Peterson walked to a cluster of men listening to Larry Walker tell stories about fishing on the Portage River. The sun seemed to jump over the horizon and turn his skin a bright yellow. Mosquitoes retreated from the clearing to the woods, as if afraid of the warming sun. "You six fellows over here will be wall makers. Lift the squared logs by hand until the wall gets high. Then you'll have to hoist them up with skid poles and ropes."

Men not afraid of heights formed a team to erect rafters for a pitched roof, which would then be shingled. Another group was told how to make a wooden floor. The best craftsmen huddled by the rock pile. "I'll work with you guys over here. We'll build the fireplace and chimney with those stones. Let's build the best fireplace in the county. I'd like to use those larger rocks near the bottom and …" It took almost ten minutes for him to describe plans for his dream fireplace.

Mr. Peterson stopped before reaching Jacques and Dietrich to organize one other team to cut openings in the wall for a single window and one door. "Harry, can you make the shutter window swing on hinges? I got some leather from old boots."

"Sure," replied Harry. "I'll make it just like the one at my place. Can I use that rope over there for the door? We can attach it to a wooden latch. Then you can tug the door open by pulling on the latchstring."

"Perfect."

Jacques felt awkward. He and Dietrich were standing alone. All the other men had been placed in a work group. "I've been saving you boys for last," Mr. Peterson said. Since you argue so much, I don't know whether to let you work together or split you up."

"We've always worked together before," replied Dietrich.

"Okay, but any fighting and I'll send you home. Go join the wall makers. You guys work with Will and Ron. Each of you take a corner of the cabin. Climb up the wall and grab the timbers they lift to you. They'll be partly notched. Just finish the notch so the logs lock together. Make sure you get a snug fit."

Jacques wondered if Dietrich was strong enough to handle a corner by himself. He knew they were both good with an axe, but Dietrich was shorter and less coordinated. What if the log slips while he's cutting the notch?

The young men walked to their respective places near the rock piles. Jacques took off his shirt and draped it neatly over the limb of a red maple at the clearing's edge. He was a hard worker and concerned about people, just like he'd been at the fire three years before. However, he was different now at eighteen, compared to fifteen. There was a deeper, more even tone in his voice, along with greater confidence of speech. His chest was broad, with a fullness rivaled only by his biceps. His muscular control was valuable in using an axe.

Dietrich had trouble climbing up the wall. Jacques watched him fumble his end of the log a few times. Dietrich's greasy black hair was so long it seemed to get in his way. When the men tried to hoist logs too quickly, the boys lost their agility. They did better at a slower pace. The two had worked as a team at several other cabin-raisings, but they had never notched corners. Usually they split logs for wooden flooring. Despite their lack of experience, they worked well together on the cabin wall.

Dietrich talked a lot when they worked. He enjoyed competition and made a contest of everything. "Lots of spaces to chink between the logs on your side," he said.

"Mind your own business," Jacques replied, hoping to end the discussion.

"What's eating you? Are you mad because Sally likes me better?"

"I said mind your own business."

They finished notching logs in silence until the wall was complete. Afterwards Mr. Peterson asked the young men to help the team working on the wooden floor. Jacques enjoyed cutting and splitting smaller logs. They had done this many times. Swinging his axe with both feet on the ground felt good.

Dietrich started to nag him again. "Slowpoke," he said. "You're way behind me." He swung his axe high, taking a solid bite from the log. A chip of wood sailed past Jacques's ear.

Jacques turned sideways at a slight angle to the log and released his axe, sending chips toward his opponent's face.

For the next several minutes, both young men swung in fury. Log chips flew through the air like bullets. Soon the ground was littered with pie-shaped pieces of wood. Between grunts and gasps, they cursed each other.

Mr. Peterson walked through the clearing, evaluating the progress of each work group. When he came by the teenagers, he said, "Nice stack of flooring, boys."

Dietrich checked his swing, wiped the sweat from his forehead, and scowled at Jacques. "My pile's bigger than yours."

Jacques shook his fist but did not reply. This is strange, he thought. A short boy with no muscles was challenging him.

Mr. Peterson laughed and walked on to examine the work of another crew.

The axe work took so much effort that Jacques failed to notice the activities beginning at noon. Women and children appeared in wagons loaded with food, tables, and chairs. Elderly men, too weak to help with cabin-raising, barbecued pork. They made fires in open pits about five feet long, three feet wide, and two feet deep. The pigs were cooked on metal grates fashioned by Mr. Wilton at the blacksmith shop.

Sally arrived carrying pies. Other ladies toted salads, vegetables, and fruits. Many of the women brought items to be tested for later entry in Fourth of July contests for cooking and baking. If people at the cabin-raising didn't like the taste of their jams or cakes, there was still time to try another prize-winning recipe.

The women looked like stagehands between acts in a play as they transformed the clearing into a picnic ground. The bright clothing of the well-dressed women contrasted with the shirtless men whose muscles and bare skin were covered with mud and bark.

When the men finished work at three o'clock, fiddlers arrived to a round of applause. Jacques watched his coworkers collect their tools and retrieve their shirts from tree limbs. For a moment, the clearing was devoid of men while they gathered around wash buckets in the woods. Laughing, they splashed each other and then reappeared a few minutes later with clean faces. Jacques was one of the last to emerge from the woods. Still mad at Dietrich, he sulked. He walked slowly, spinning the axe on his shoulder.

Sally greeted him with a wide smile and cheery face. "I brought your blueberry pie but you can't have any 'til later."

"Why not?"

"You won't eat your meal."

"Wanna bet? I'm starved."

She pointed her finger at him. "You'll have to wait 'til after dinner. In the meantime, would you like some apple juice?"

Jacques drove the head of his axe into a nearby stump and took the tin cup from Sally. He swished it around his mouth to get the most flavors from the juice, which had a snappy taste. Before he could thank her, Sally ran off and punched Dietrich on the shoulder. She chased him in circles between tables to a podium where the fiddlers were playing. Mechanically, the couple danced the last half of a polka. Dietrich asked her to join a square dance. Jacques watched every move they made. He even tried to read their lips across the clearing. His jealousy increased when they promenaded between two columns of other dancers.

As the evening unfolded, people came from all corners of the county. Jacques thought it bold to show up late at a cabin-raising after the work was done for the sole purpose of partying. Of course, maybe he was foolish, too. Why should he pout at a celebration?

The minister rang the new supper bell, mounted on the corner of the cabin as a house-warming gift from church members to the Petersons. Sally finished dancing and joined Jacques at a table for two. Apologetically, she said, "I'd promised Dietrich a dance."

"That was dumb." He felt hurt.

She fidgeted with the spoon on the table. Over the past few years, Sally teased both boys, encouraging them to fight over her. She knew it was wrong, but she liked to have men pursue her.

Dietrich pulled up a chair, which he tried to fit at the small table. "Can I sit here?" His greasy black hair swung around his head while he moved.

"No way," Jacques replied. "Sit somewhere else." He waved his arm like shooing a fly away from food.

"Dammit, what a sore loser." Dietrich moved down the row of tables, finding a spot next to three girls, where he could watch the couple.

Jacques listened carefully when the minister gave thanks for the spirit of cooperation in the village, evidenced by people's willingness to help the Petersons. Reverend Hughes always looked so composed to Jacques. His trimmed gray beard, rarely still, bobbed when he spoke. He seemed like such a happy soul, a true man of the cloth, although there were times he became so stern he was frightening. People at this celebration didn't hurry to eat. They seemed more interested in talking and drinking. Once in a while, someone would go to the food tables. Most people ate while standing or sat at small tables with relatives and friends. Young children and babies were placed on quilts spread on the ground. More than fifty people were at the picnic, and there was plenty of food.

Sally opened a package and took out the most beautiful blueberry pie Jacques had ever seen. Vents on top of the crust were exactly the same length. They were dotted with evenly spaced holes. He smiled when taking the first bite. The blueberries were soft and sweet with just enough pulp for consistency. After several bites, he offered his compliment. "Your pie is delicious. You make the best blueberry pie in Michigan." His green eyes sparkled in the sunlight.

"Thanks. I made it just for you."

When supper was finished, Jacques watched Sally organize games for the children. Many adults played, too, usually with the excuse that kids need to be entertained. Foot races were the favorite, although hide-and-seek also attracted a large crowd. Those that did not play games talked in small groups clumped throughout the clearing. By eight o'clock several pioneers began packing their wagons and horses for the ride home. Jacques, though, did not intend to leave until midnight.

He approached Sally head down and stammered, "Wanna dance?"

She took his hand. They got closer and more relaxed with each dance. When the fiddlers took a break, the couple sat at a table in the farthest corner, where there were few oil lamps. Sally deliberately stroked the back of his hand with her slender fingers. Jacques smiled. He felt a sense of contentment, mixed with excitement.

That feeling didn't last very long. Out of the shadows stepped Dietrich. "One more dance?"

"Nope," replied Sally, "we're talking. Leave us alone now."

From the tone of her voice, Dietrich seemed to know it was time to leave. He picked up his axe and swaggered off.

As more people left, their table got cozy. Jacques talked about his desire to do something more than carpentry with an axe. He shared his goal to have a large family with at least three girls and three boys. He listened with joy while Sally talked about her dream to help the elderly and sick.

For the first time he noticed how carefully she trimmed her eyebrows. "Ever been kissed by a boy?" he asked.

"No, but I've sure thought about it. A girl in town said you should always shut your eyes when you kiss."

He watched her eyes drift down, studying his chest. Embarrassed by her curiosity, he looked away, hoping she would stop staring. "I never kissed a girl, either." He glanced back and noticed her straight teeth and then her lips. Jacques couldn't get enough of the sweet smell of her chestnut-colored hair. As he leaned over to whisper, he moved forward, inch-by-inch, until his lips touched hers. They felt soft and delicate and left a fresh, warm taste in his mouth, like peaches and cream.

Sally pressed the back of his head with her hands and returned his kiss. They stood and held each other in a dark corner beside the table. His arms arched around her. He felt the warmth of her chest on his. Her soft body went limp, absorbed into his crevices. They melted together. He blushed because she knew he was excited.

Sally stared up at the moon above the freshly built cabin. Jacques noticed she was rubbing something in her dress pocket. He watched as she took out an arrowhead.

With her eyes still fixed on the moon, she said, “You gave me this three years ago. Remember?”

Jacques nodded. “How could I forget?” He, too, looked up at the summer moon. Maybe that arrowhead will bring good luck after all, he thought. Holding hands, he felt connected to Sally and knew she felt the same way.

2

Violence in the Woods

July was unbearably hot, especially for Mr. Wilton working with molten iron in his blacksmith shop. One night Sally watched him stagger upstairs. He almost fell down but caught himself by grabbing the handrail. The blacksmith's pale skin glistened from sweat and heat, and his right hand pushed hard against his portly chest.

Sally worried. What if something happened to her father? He was her workman, advisor, and friend.

"Do you feel okay?" she asked.

"I'm a bit tired from the heat." His eyes squinted from the pain that caused the side of his mouth to turn upwards.

"Maybe you should see the doctor." Sally was most concerned that he labored with exercise. She noticed that his breathing was shallow, as if it hurt to inhale.

"Tomorrow I'm shoeing his horse. Perhaps I'll ask for a tonic." He took off his glasses and put them on the coffee table.

"Please do. You've put this off long enough." There was an unusual firmness in her voice. It came from a fear that she would be left alone to deal with all the hardships of pioneer life. She recalled how sickness had destroyed many lives in Grafton. Beginning the past winter several people took sick and a few died. The illness started as bronchitis, settling in the lungs and causing pneumonia. At least Father never had bronchitis, she thought.

After dinner Sally went to Wednesday night prayer meeting where she sat with several friends. She arrived at church early so she could talk about her father's condition before the service. One friend told Sally about a woman who lived on Chestnut Ridge beyond the river. The old lady, rumored to be a full-breed, knew how to treat diseases with herbs.

Early the next morning Dr. Hollings came to get his horse shod.

"While you're here," the blacksmith said, "do you know of any tonics that might work for a person who's always feeling tired?"

"You know I won't prescribe medicine without an examination," the doctor said. "Let's go upstairs and let me have a look at you." He gave Mr. Wilton a complete physical before handing him an elixir. "Your heart sounds strong," the doctor said. "I'm not going to tell you to stop working, but I'd like you to close shop an hour earlier on hot days. If that doesn't work, we could try bloodletting."

Sally noticed her father still showed signs of fatigue even with the medicine and an adjusted work schedule. On several occasions, he fell asleep at dinner with his head on the table. He used to be an early riser, but now customers sometimes had to yell upstairs to wake him.

The fatigue continued to worsen, so Sally saddled her horse on a steamy July morning and rode the river trail to Chestnut Ridge. Even though she had been there a few times for church picnics, it took her a while to find the right path to the old woman's cabin. At one point, wild grape was so thick the horse stumbled. Thorns on black locust trees scraped her ankles.

By noon she reached the cabin, a friendly old place with a stick chimney and both front and back porches. It was one of the smallest cabins Sally had ever seen. Logs on the outside walls were round instead of square. Despite its age, the cabin was immaculately maintained. Sally surmised the widow spent a lot of time cleaning and repairing her homestead.

To avoid frightening the old woman, Sally announced herself even before she was in voice range. Several times she repeated, "Is anybody home?"

"Just me," the old woman answered. "I'm out back."

Sally walked around the cabin to the back yard, where the widow was sweeping the porch with a straw broom. The stringy white hair on her head contrasted with thick gray curls behind her ears. Her skin was as weathered as the deer hide drying nearby on a wood railing. Her native American heritage showed in her high cheekbones. Age had toned down the sparkle in her black eyes, now clouded with a milky film. She said, in a raspy voice, "Why's a young thing like you riding alone in the forest?"

"I came to see you about my father. He's very sick."

"Oh, my. I'm sorry. You must be very concerned about him. Please come inside and tell me all about his illness."

They sat at a pine table with chairs made from oak branches. Sally was amazed to see all the herbs within the large room. Bundles of dried plants with colorful stalks, berries, and flowers hung upside down from the ceiling beams. Counter tops were piled high with wooden boxes of newly started plants in black soil. Cabinets with open shelves held jars of powdered herbs and tinctures extracted with alcohol. Elsewhere were ointments, rolled in cloth, made from herbs mixed with wax and animal fat. The cabin smelled like perfume and freshly cut grass.

After a thorough discussion of Mr. Wilton's symptoms, the old woman filled a quart jar with a concentrate of boiled trefoil leaves and thorn apples. She said the blacksmith should drink one tablespoon of the mixture three times a day.

Sally couldn't contain her curiosity about the old woman. "How'd you learn to be a medicine woman?"

"My grandmother was Potawatomi. She and I used to gather herbs to make medicines. Our tribe was so gentle. We traded berries and venison with settlers for gunpowder and salt. We also traded with other Indians, mostly Chippewa. The tribe was finally forced off the land. Oh, I guess it was about 1840 when soldiers moved my people to a reservation in Iowa."

"So you really are a medicine woman, aren't you?"

"Yes, dear, but now all my people are gone."

As Sally rode home, she wondered what happened to the woman's family. Why would an Indian stay behind when the rest of her tribe moved to a reservation? Who used all the medicine she made? She reached the blacksmith shop just in time to prepare dinner.

"Where'd you go today?" Mr. Wilton asked.

"I went to see the medicine woman." She stirred a pot of stew on the black wood stove, decorated with metallic designs.

"You mean the old lady on Chestnut Ridge? Why'd you go to see her?"

"I'm worried about you. You're not well. I got a tonic for you." She pointed at the quart jar on the kitchen counter.

"I'm not drinking any Injun brew. No way."

"Please, Father. For me?"

"Well let me taste it." After swallowing, he said, "Well, a mouthful now and then probably won't hurt anything. It tastes like strong tea, mixed with spices. Okay, but I'm doing this just for you."

Sally was pleased to return to the old woman's cabin on Wednesday to share the news that her father was much improved. As before, she announced herself when approaching the cabin on horseback. "Is anybody home?"

This time the Indian woman didn't answer. Sally looked around the yard and yelled into the cabin. Nobody was there. She tethered her horse and sprawled sideways in a rocking chair on the porch. In a few moments the widow came down the trail carrying a bundle of herbs overflowing a reed basket.

"Hi little girl."

Sally took a quick breath in surprise. "Sorry for sittin' in your chair," she said. "Father's better."

The medicine woman dumped the plants on the porch and sorted them by variety. "It usually takes thirty days for the tonic to work. He should get even better."

"Thank you so much."

"I've been out making rounds on my herb trail. Want to come along?"

"Yes Ma'am," Sally replied. "I'd love to see your herbs."

The old woman got another basket for Sally. Together they walked down a steep trail through dense understory, followed by clouds of hungry mosquitoes. The first stop on the trail was near a group of plants surrounded by a circle of rocks. The bed of pennyroyal, a member of the mint family, was cultivated. The weedless soil was stirred and loose. Carefully, she plucked a few leaves from the largest plant and offered them to Sally.

"Rub these on your ankles, wrists, forehead, and the back of your neck," she said. "An oil in the leaves chases away mosquitoes."

It worked. The mosquitoes vanished. Only a few pesky stragglers remained, but they no longer bit.

"Look at the circle of stones around the plants. Those rocks are markers so I can tend my little friends. Many of the herbs occurred naturally along the trail, but Grandmother and I transplanted others. We even traded with other Indians and pioneers to get better ones."

The old woman showed the blacksmith's daughter many plants along the trail. Herbs became so interesting to Sally that she visited the widow every Wednesday to learn about plants and help prepare medicines. She also discovered her name was Lillian. That name will be easy to remember, she thought. The Indian woman is like a plant that blossoms late in life, well after its stems are thick and high. She is just like a tiger lily with bright orange blossoms that last many weeks. I'll call her Lily for short.

Sally spent most Thursdays marking herbs near the blacksmith shop, practicing there what she'd learned from the old woman. She collected red cedar bark, hoping she would never need it to treat cholera. Along the road were some blackberries whose roots she dug to make a solution for sore eyes. She also dug balsam root in the wet swamp behind Petersons' new cabin for use as an astringent.

Jacques had been busy all summer helping his father catch fish to be sold or bartered with neighbors. Since Dietrich's time was more flexible, Sally enjoyed his company on several occasions. Once they went horseback riding to an old stone church on the muddy road to Kalamazoo. They played hide-and-seek among crumbling walls and damp rooms. Another time they joined friends picking blueberries in an old jack pine burn.

She also went with Dietrich on walks through town at dusk. On one of those strolls, Sally told him about the Wednesday visits with Lily and her own collecting trips on Thursdays near the outskirts of town. He accompanied her to collect plants in late summer. Many herbs had mature leaves and seeds at that time of year. They gathered milkweed pods, asters, daisies, goldenrod, male ferns, flax, and many other plants with curative powers. Often the two returned to the blacksmith shop with sacks of plants and roots. Her home began to look like Lily's cabin and smell like the woods where the herbs were gathered. Sally continued to visit the widow every Wednesday. Her interest in herbs was becoming an obsession.

Peddlers with brightly colored horse-drawn wagons commonly visited villages north of Kalamazoo. The men were as varied in dress and temperament as the Michigan weather. Some wore tailored suits, decorated with bright ties, silk handkerchiefs, and top hats. Other peddlers dressed in baggy trousers that needed patches and washing. Their trinkets of muffin tins, pots and pans, and brooms were neatly displayed in some wagons while others, often littered with liquor bottles, were trashed with piles of books, jewelry, and clothing. The characteristic they all shared was an uncanny ability to make customers want something they didn't need and would never use.

Whenever one of the wandering salesmen arrived in Grafton, women stopped their work and surrounded the wagon. The peddlers enjoyed talking with ladies almost as much as they liked selling their wares. Since many of them traveled the same route through several states over and over again, they personally became known to pioneers and served as a source of news. Their conversations ranged from the latest theories of child rearing to new fashions in big cities.

Sally became excited when a peddler came to town in mid-August and showed her an array of unusual herbs and spices from distant places. She talked with him about herbs for almost an hour before trading some roots for his exotic barks and flowers.

Many visitors came to trade herbs with Sally during the summer. When she told Lily about her growing popularity among peddlers, the old woman was apprehensive. "Beware of strange herbs. They can hurt rather than help."

Sally replied, "Not all of 'em are strange. I've learned new uses for old herbs. You told me Indians used milkweed sap for warts. A peddler from Grand Rapids told me other uses for milkweed. It also takes off corns and makes ringworm go 'way. Ripe milkweed seeds make a salve for sores. New mothers have more milk if they drink a tea from the leaves."

The old woman's face took on the sorrowful look of a teacher whose student has just surpassed her. Lily's eyes drifted toward a cardinal outside the cabin window. "I guess you are smarter than me now."

"I'll never be as smart as you," Sally said. She patted the Indian woman very softly on the shoulder. "I just talk about herbs. You heal people with them. Father is better 'cause of you."

So much had changed in Lily's world. Here was a teenager who knew more about herbs than she did. The old woman's eyes were still fixed on the cardinal, as if she were waiting for it to disappear into the woods. She had a strange feeling that the bird would fly if she glanced elsewhere. Instead, the bird let loose with a glorious call, with perfect high-pitched notes arranged in a shrill melody.

"Want to hear about some new remedies?" said Sally.

"I'd like that very much. Meanwhile, let me show you how to collect bark from cottonwood trees. The ashes, mixed with cornmeal, make a powerful paste to get rid of boils."

The two women rambled along the trail hand in hand, as if they'd known each other for many years. Sally didn't even mind the August heat, which caused tree leaves to droop as if they were exhausted from trying to keep water in their stems. All living things in the area seemed to beg for a breeze.

Early in the morning, Dietrich rode to the blacksmith shop. Even though it was hot, he wore heavy trousers so he could walk through briars and nettles. His long black hair was so greasy that it made him look older than his age of nineteen. People were afraid of him because of his temper tantrums. Frequent fighting was one of the reasons the teacher expelled him from school after third grade. Not only did he lack self-control, but he also held grudges.

A few minutes later Sally came downstairs. Her hair shone as if she had brushed it for a long time. She, too, wore clothes to walk in brush: coveralls, a wide-brimmed hat, and her father's rubber boots.

"Where we goin'?" He pounded his right fist into his left palm, a nervous habit he'd acquired from his father.

"By the river. I need some elderberry to treat people with hemorrhoids." She surveyed the wear-holes around the knees of his baggy trousers.

"Let's go," he said. "Follow me."

Sally thought it strange that Dietrich was leading even though she'd picked the destination. He had to take the lead in everything, she surmised.

When they reached the river she sidled her horse next to his and pointed toward the elderberry grove, where bushes overflowed with purple berries atop bent stalks. Sally slid off her horse before tying it to a birch tree at the edge of a ravine. Taking a stack of tin pails from the back of her saddle, she pulled them apart and lined each with bracken fern.

Dietrich seemed irritated when she handed him one of the pails. He jerked it from her hand. They went to separate corners of the elderberry patch and put berries in their pails. He returned to meet Sally after a few minutes and compared the two buckets. "You're cutting them too far down the stalk."

"That's to stop them from turning my fingers purple like yours," she snapped back.

"My fingers are purple 'cause I've picked more berries than you."

Sally looked inside his pail. "Talk about berry stain. You've got nothing but purple mush."

"Are you sayin' I'm a sloppy worker?" Dietrich screamed, "I just picked more berries than you. The more you have in a pail, the more they get crushed." The little man lost his temper and grabbed a handful of berries. He started to throw them into his pail like a pitcher on a baseball mound, but balked instead and gently placed them in the bucket. "There," he said. "I've got the most berries. See, there's no crushed ones either."

Sally shied away from him, fearful of the way his eyes glared. She said, "Who cares who has the most berries?"

For a moment, Dietrich's anger subsided, but only temporarily. "You picked a poor place to tie our horses. The shade left. Now they're in the sun. You better move 'em, stupid."

"You can move your horse if you like, but leave mine alone."

"You better shut up, girl." Dietrich took the reins of his horse and led it to a shady spot several yards away. He walked stiffly, ready to explode with anger. His mouth was drawn tight. He bit his lower lip to stop it from quivering. Then he moved her horse, too. "Dammit," he said. "Don't tell me what to do."

Sally was afraid to talk. Everything she said seemed to anger him. The outing had lost its fun.

Dietrich tossed his head in the air. "The sun's way too hot. What a lousy day you picked to gather berries."

Sally replied, "Stop complaining. Aren't you ever happy?"

"What good are these stupid berries anyway?"

"I use them to make medicine for sick people."

"Well, I'm sick of being in the hot sun. I'm sick and tired of these damn berries, too." Dietrich threw the pail of elderberries skyward. It landed upside down beneath a clump of shrubs in the grove.

Sally froze. She didn't know what to say. Without looking at him, she marched to the overturned pail. Dietrich also walked toward the bucket. He yelled, "What the hell are you doin'?"

"Trying to save some berries."

A fist out of nowhere smashed her delicate chin. It was followed by a punch to her left eye. She felt his elbow smash into the back of her neck. Stunned by the surprise attack, she fell to the ground. Her vision became obscured from the swelling in her eye. The base of her neck ached. Curled up like a turtle inside its shell, she covered her face and waited for the next punch.

"Please stop," she begged.

The toe of Dietrich's boot slammed into her ribs. She gasped for air in tiny, painful gulps. The kick knocked the wind out of her. "No more, please!"

Dietrich's rage evaporated as quickly as it had appeared. He looked shocked, as if he didn't believe what had happened. "Oh, Sally. I'm so sorry," he said and lifted her off the ground.

She brushed the dirt from the back of her pants. What should I do now, she thought. If I run, he might chase me and beat me more. If I stay, his anger might return. Sally stood motionless, thinking. When she finally realized what had happened, she felt pure rage. "Why'd you do that?" she snapped.

"Dunno."

"What do you mean, dunno?" Sally let some of the anger out she had been holding inside. "I've been real nice to you. And, you hit me?" The rest of her rage was released like water spraying from a broken pipe. It kept gushing. "What's wrong with you?"

Dietrich shrugged. "I can't help myself."

"That's not good enough. I've had it with you."

He looked down. "I'm sorry."

"Didn't anyone tell you not to hit girls? What's wrong with you?"

Hanging his head, he appeared to be thinking hard about her question. "There's lots of hitting at home. Pa always punches Ma. Mostly on the shoulder. Sometimes on the chin. The worst is when he punches her in the stomach."

Sally put her finger on her chest. "So you punched me 'cause your pa hits your ma?"

"Maybe. Pa beats me, too. Lots of times my pillow is bloody when I get up in the morning. Blood from my lips and nose. Sometimes my ears bleed."

"That's no excuse. It doesn't give you the right to hit others." Sally sensed that some of Dietrich's anger was related to feelings of inferiority. She'd seen the other boys tease him about being shorter. Even though she knew the source of his hostility, she didn't condone it. "Stop looking for excuses. You're just a mean bully."

Dietrich put his head down. "I'll never do it again," he said. "I promise."

"That's right. I won't let you." Sally gathered the pails and tied them to her saddle. She threw two empty ones at him. "Take these!" Furious and no longer afraid, she said, "I'm going home." Her neck was sore, she was mad, and her eye hurt.

Neither spoke while they rode to Grafton. She wished she could ride faster to get more wind in her face for relief from the afternoon heat, but winced with pain whenever the tired horse jarred her saddle. Sally wondered what to tell her father. The only reasonable solution is to make up a story.

Mr. Wilton greeted the couple as they approached the blacksmith shop. When he saw her swollen eye, he asked, "What in the world happened to you?"

Sally said, "My horse tripped. Then my face hit a log."

"She took quite a spill," added Dietrich.

The blacksmith frowned. "That horse is almost seven. I've never seen him trip before."

She said, "Maybe he galloped a little before falling."

"Oh no. I told you not to gallop that stallion. He loses control. No wonder he tripped."

"I'm sorry, Father."

Mr. Wilton helped her off the horse. She put her arm around his shoulder, lifted her boot from the stirrup, and swung to the ground. Sally had used that dismount, into the arms of her father many times before as a little girl. She watched Dietrich move to her side. Trying to cover up her anger, she put her other arm around him. She hobbled between the two men into the shop. The familiar sights of home made the pain seem more intense. I can't believe I've been beaten and mauled by a friend, she thought.

She felt faint when she looked up at the stairs leading to the safety of her home. Since the three of them could not fit together on the stairway, she dropped to the floor and crawled from the first to second step and up the stairs. With a moan, she pulled the latchstring, pushed open the door, and collapsed on the floor.

The blacksmith never considered that Dietrich might have hit Sally. He believed her lie about falling from the horse. Once she was comfortably resting in bed with a mass of mud and powdered roots on her eye, Dietrich prepared to leave. He turned to her and said, "Thanks. I really mean it."

Out of hearing range from her father she said, "Get out of here—now!"

"Maybe something is wrong with me," he said. "I'm sorry. I'll never do it again." With his head down and hands deep in the pockets of his worn trousers, Dietrich turned, closed the door, and left.

3

Market Hunting

Jacques crept along the riverbank overlooking the creek bed. He tried not to step on any sticks or twigs for fear of making noise. Whenever the breeze stopped, he remained motionless for several minutes and listened for sounds of deer. He only continued when sure no deer were moving. At places with many tracks, he knelt to consider their freshness and direction. He tested the wind often, either by looking at the leaves above or by licking his finger and holding it in the air.

His dad taught him to keep the wind in his face. That way, the breezes carried his scent away from deer ahead. The October wind was from the northwest that day. It blew orange leaves off maples and yellow leaves from trembling aspen. The noisy woods were alive with the calling of jays and honking of geese in V formations high in the morning sky. Perhaps the wind was in his face too much. It sent cool bursts of autumn air beneath the collar of his jacket and down his chest. He saw his breath in the chilly air. His cheeks were red.

Somewhere a branch cracked. He tried to locate the direction of the noise without moving his head. Deer that saw him when he kept still often resumed feeding. Another branch cracked. This time he saw what made the noise—a buck with forked antlers feeding on acorns beneath a sprawling oak on the ridge to his right. Carefully he turned. It seemed forever until the buck appeared in the iron sights of his rifle. The muzzle-loading rifle went off with a thud, leaving behind a cloud of smoke that briefly obscured his vision. The buck ran thirty yards and collapsed on the ground. Jacques waited a minute to approach the deer, just in case it was still alive. While waiting, he reloaded.

Jacques touched the deer with a stick, but there was no movement. The young buck was dead. He knelt to admire the forkhorn with regal head held high, even in death. Grandpa would be proud of me, he thought. The deer died without suffering. When younger, Jacques was upset by killing. His grandpa told him how death was part of nature's plan. He learned that a well placed bullet was less painful than starvation, being ripped apart by coyotes, or many other forms of death. Now that he was older, killing bothered him less. He knew the source of his family's livelihood was supplying neighbors with food. His grandfather had taught him that the real job of a hunter was to take life quickly and humanely, without unnecessary pain. Mistakes caused wounding, which made good hunters feel inadequate and shameful. Jacques had no guilt this time, just thoughts of gratitude for a clean kill and memories of Grandpa Flareau.

After field-dressing the deer, he pulled it to the trail by a creek. The forkhorn was the third deer he'd shot that morning. Now it was time to drag the carcasses, one at a time, back to the cabin.

The last deer he dragged seemed to be the heaviest, although it was the smallest. He felt sweat coat his forehead and drench his hairy chest, now exposed to the cool air beneath an open jacket.

Suddenly he heard his dad yell, "What's the matter, son? Haven't got your second wind yet?" It was a familiar phrase he heard many times when growing up.

"I got three. How 'bout you?" Counting coup was also a familiar activity for the market hunter's son.

"Two." He pulled a field-dressed doe with ease along the trail by the north branch of the river.

Together they took five deer back to the cabin and laid them next to the woodpile.

"Can we keep 'em overnight?" Jacques asked. He was tired and didn't want to butcher the two bucks and three does until the next day.

"Nope. If they freeze overnight, they'll be hard to cut."

Jacques had learned to trust his father's advice. First he removed the tenderloins. Then he skinned all five deer and cut them in pieces. As was the practice for venison sold on the market, he kept the two hindquarters attached to the pelvis as one large piece of meat called a saddle. He cut stew meat and roasts from the front legs, necks, and ribs. Butchering took most of the evening. He walked to the river, where he cleaned his knife and washed his hands in the moonlight. Returning, he traced the lights in the big dipper to the North Star, which seemed to blink in the cold autumn air.

Pierre greeted his son at the cabin door. "Good job."

"Thanks," said Jacques. Looking around the cabin, he realized how meager a life they had for all their long hours of work.

His mother placed a pot of boiled fish surrounded by five bowls, on the table. "You men must be hungry. Come, Martha and William, join us at the table." Jacques's younger brother and younger sister huddled with them around the food.

"Dad, why'd you become a hunter?" asked Jacques.

"I never did anything else," said Pierre. "My father was a hunter. I helped him as a boy. Everyone caught their own fish and killed their own game in the old days. When more settlers came, they took different trades. Some made furniture. Others cleared land and grew crops. Some set up shops in town. With time, few settlers hunted. The Indians liked that because they traded fish and game for groceries. When the Potawatomi left for the reservation, Grandpa and I took over their business. We did pretty good."

"I thought about Grandpa today, too. He came to mind when I shot the forkhorn. It was a perfect kill."

Judy poured another bowl of boiled fish for her son. She said, "Grandpa always said a clean kill is the sign of respect. It means you praise God and love his creatures."

"Yes, I do love deer, even though I kill them. People don't understand that. Do they?"

"Maybe not," said Pierre. "But, they sure love the taste of meat."

As Jacques prepared for bed, he wondered about his schedule for the coming day. "What should I do in the morning?" He wasn't sure whether his dad wanted him to get more deer or do something else.

Pierre said, "Two quarts of stew meat go to the Solomons. They repaired our wagon wheel. Two saddles go to the Wiltons. Sell the other three at the depot. Remember to tend the smoker with fresh hickory sticks. There's forty pounds of venison inside. Then, see if you can shoot a couple more deer at dusk."

Jacques tried to review all his chores, but was distracted by thoughts of visiting the Wiltons. I'll see Sally!

All he could think about was their kiss at the cabin-raising, but he answered, "Maybe I'll shoot the deer at dawn." He planned to visit the blacksmith shop last and come home after dark.

"That's fine. Just do your work and get two more deer."

Fall was the busiest time of year for the Flareaus. While farmers were harvesting crops, Jacques and his father bartered fish and game to others in the village. Most people in Grafton couldn't afford the expensive saddles and were satisfied with roasts from the front legs. Saddles that didn't sell in town were taken to the rail depot for shipment to markets in large cities.

Jacques went to bed that evening dreaming of Sally, whom he hadn't seen for several months. He didn't sleep well. In his dreams he tasted her sweet lips. Her vision seemed so real that he awoke with a sense of loss. Has she been here with me and left?

He dressed and left early to hunt deer, arriving at the stand an hour too early, way before it was light enough to shoot. Waiting in the dark, he heard deer and turkeys moving through the woods, though they could not yet be seen. Those sounds, which used to excite him, paled in comparison to his thoughts of Sally.

When it was light enough to shoot, a large doe walked broadside in front of Jacques. He took the shot, causing the deer to drop about ten yards away. Silently, with as little movement as possible, he reloaded. He debated whether to leave his stand to field dress the deer or wait for another, but then a spikehorn appeared. He shot it quickly, dressed both deer, and dragged them to the cabin.

After hanging the deer in the woodshed, Jacques hitched his horse to the wagon, already loaded with five saddles and two quarts of stew meat. He sold three choice cuts of venison at the railroad station, a few miles north of Grafton. The depot was a busy place with several travelers waiting for the train. A few peddlers were camped in wagons that circled a fire pit at the back of the depot.

"It looks like you and your dad are having a good year," said the clerk.

"Not bad," Jacques replied.

"How much do you want for your deer meat?"

Jacques tapped his knuckles against the counter top. "Two cents a pound. Don't you sell it for three?"

"Oh no. We usually pay one cent."

"But that would only be about a dollar for all three saddles. I hear there's places where they sell for three dollars each."

"Not here." The clerk rubbed his thumb across his whiskered chin. For saddles of such fine quality, how 'bout I give you a cent and a half a pound?"

"That's the same price you've paid for the last three years," he said taking a deep breath. "Venison is worth more than that. I think you are cheating me."

The clerk's eyes sparkled. "Maybe," he said with a grin showing his teeth beneath the bristles of a moustache, "but that's my deal." He held out his hand. It held a silver dollar and a fifty cent piece.

"Sold," said Jacques. He took the coins and thought, The price of deer saddles in southern Michigan never seems to change.

"I wish things were going better for me," said the clerk. "Something's happening to our venison. Last week I sent thirty-two saddles to Kalamazoo, but only twenty-two were received. There's a shortage on every rail shipment."

"Is someone taking them off the train?"

"I don't think so," said the clerk. "The railroad unloads the correct amount, so the shortage must occur later. Look, son. You know a lot about game and meat. How'd you like to ride the train and follow one of my shipments?"

"I don't know. I've never ridden a train. Never been to the city, either."

"That would make it even better. Nobody would suspect you. They'd think you're just a boy visiting relatives. You'd have to work in secret, though."

"Oh, okay," said Jacques. "I've always wanted to see Kalamazoo. What day should I go?"

"Be here next Wednesday. That's the day I ship fish and game. I'll pay for your train ticket, get you a hotel room in town, and give you seventy-five cents for the three-day job. Remember, don't tell anyone except your parents about the purpose of your trip. You'll have to make up some other reason you're going to Kalamazoo."

They shook hands.

Just as Jacques was about to leave the depot, a peddler with a round face and red cheeks approached him. "Wanna buy some Irish whiskey?" he asked.

"No thanks. I don't drink," Jacques replied.

"Well, then, how about a nice cowboy shirt from out West?"

"Maybe. Let's see."

He accompanied the peddler to his wagon, which was painted yellow and red. Jacques stepped back while the cheery man in a silk top hat and striped suspenders lifted a wide board to expose his wares, many of which were made of tin. The blue western shirt, with pearl buttons, stood out among the tin pans that glistened in the afternoon sun. He thought it was handsome, but certainly not worth a dollar fifty. However, something else caught Jacques's attention when the peddler put the shirt back. It was a book with delicate green plants on a white cover, titled *Medicinal Herbs.* The price of twenty cents seemed just about right for the worn book with dog-eared pages.

"The shirt is too much for me, but I'll give you ten cents for that old book."

"Fifteen cents and it's yours." The peddler waved the book in front of his face.

"Thank you." He grabbed the book, paid the peddler, and offered him an explanation. "It's for my girlfriend."

His next stop took only a minute. Mrs. Solomon was in the stable brushing her horse. She nodded when he left the stew meat near her back door and pointed to the repaired wheel, which he tied to the side of his wagon. Jacques heard his horse neigh, as if to mean he was taking too long. He had a special way with Oscar, who didn't mind many people. The horse was obstinate and galloped without permission when he got near home, except with Jacques. Several people in Grafton told the young man to open a livery since he was good with horses.

Jacques was excited about his last stop. Finally, I'll see Sally!

The wagon bounced when it rolled over a rock in front of the blacksmith shop. He noticed that Mr. Wilton looked better since taking the Indian tonic. His face was no longer pale. He seemed to move around the shop with more agility and confidence.

"I've got your venison," the young hunter said. "Do you want it upstairs?" His boot hit the first step before the blacksmith answered.

"Knock first. Sally's up there." Mr. Wilton didn't look up. He was working on a fireplace damper for the Petersons. One hand held a large pincer grabbing white hot metal. He had a hammer in the other hand. Hairs on the lower part of his arm were singed.

"Open up!" Jacques said with great excitement.

"Where've you been?" She seemed aroused by his voice and yanked open the door. He gave her a gentle hug.

"I've been working very hard. How 'bout you?"

"It's been a good summer for herbs."

"So I've heard. Here's somethin' for you." He handed her the book.

"You got this for me?"

"Yeah. I bought it from a peddler at the train depot. I knew you liked herbs."

Sally looked surprised. "Come on over. Let's look at it together." She motioned him to pull up a chair to the kitchen table.

Together they leafed through the book. Taught to read by his grandmother, Jacques explained some of the text. Sally could read only a few of the small words, but seemed to appreciate the artwork. Each sketch had an herb, along with its associated parts. There were diagrams of leaves, roots, thorns, fruits, flowers, and nuts. The book also contained a full description of remedies for various illnesses and diseases. An appendix in the back listed methods to make tinctures. There were recipes for teas and techniques to prepare ointments.

"What a wonderful gift. Thank you." She opened her arms, allowing Jacques to lift her off the floor. Slowly she turned her head so their lips met. He enjoyed a passionate kiss that lasted so long he lost his balance. They tumbled to the floor, laughing together.

4

Wanderlust

Jacques' mother hummed to herself as she removed a frayed carpetbag from beneath her bed. She remembered the peg-legged soldier returning from the Civil War who traded it for ten pounds of fish filets. Judy gathered clothes from a shelf and slid them into the colorful carpetbag. She placed a small Bible, once owned by her uncle, atop the neatly folded clothes.

Judy felt nervous about the dangers her son might encounter but knew it was time for the young man to see the big city. He was almost as old as the soldier with the carpetbag. Besides, the seventy-five cents in pay from the railroad clerk would help buy supplies for the upcoming winter. Sugar was twelve cents a pound, butter fifteen, and coffee was thirty-five cents a pound. Lost in memories of Jacques as a little boy, Judy wondered, Where have all the years gone?

The rails trembled long before the massive locomotive was in sight. It came around the bend with little warning, startling bystanders with its whistle. Jacques's excitement mounted as he climbed the metal stairs leading to the last of four coach cars. He had seen locomotives come and go from the depot before, but this was his first time inside the train.

The conductor looked at Jacques's ticket and said. "Have a seat, young man. I'll be back later to punch your ticket."

Jacques walked down the aisle to the last seat. A mild sense of fear caused him to clutch the carpetbag. Would the train ride be bumpy? What would the city be like? What dangers lay ahead? His fears left quickly just as they had at other harrowing times in his life. He recalled some of those past moments, like the time a bear walked near his hunting spot. He remembered the afternoon he got lost tracking a deer and the morning he sunk in quicksand where the stream joined the river. Being afraid sharpened his senses and made him more analytical. Then the fear dissipated, replaced with a plan for action. It was time to think about the detective job he had accepted. He was proud that the clerk asked him to help solve a mystery. Exactly how would he keep track of the venison? What was his plan?

Looking out the window, he counted eighteen saddles of meat being loaded from the platform. The conductor, now at the door of the car, looked up and down the tracks, and gave a yell. "All aboard!"

The locomotive surged, dragging the rest of the train with little resistance. It moved south for half an hour until the spur met the main branch of the Michigan Central, which had connected Detroit to Kalamazoo twenty-five years before. The railroad was responsible for much of the city's growth to ten thousand residents in 1872. Of course, businessmen in Kalamazoo complained because the city had not expanded as much as Grand Rapids or Jackson. The editor of the *Telegraph*, one of two local papers, argued that the town needed to encourage "manufactories."

Jacques noticed more garbage and soot beside the tracks when the train got closer to the city. There were enough dirty factories in town, he thought. Two years before, the 1870 census showed seven hundred four men, ninety-six women, and twenty-two youths worked at one hundred and nine manufacturing firms in Kalamazoo. One of the largest was the Dodge Plow Factory, a foundry that made farm implements. Two turbine wheels were used for power at the Kalamazoo Paper Company to produce paper from straw and rags. Other companies made brooms, produced cigars, and tanned hides.

The train weaved through back yards and past tanneries and mills to downtown Kalamazoo. It was a bustling city with tall brick buildings, a state mental hospital, and branch campus for the University of Michigan. Compared to Grafton, the city's diversity shocked Jacques at first, but then became a source of wonder.

"All out for Kalamazoo!" yelled the conductor, holding a pocket watch that glistened in the sun.

Jacques hid in the shadows of the depot after de-boarding so he could watch the men unload meat. He saw venison being placed on a wagon, which he followed through city streets. It was hard for him to concentrate on the wagon with all the activity and noise. He heard sounds of horse-drawn buggies, steam engines in factories, and saws turning inside mills. It took him a while to zigzag around people in the streets who walked so fast they almost ran. Dressed in an assortment of clothes from the torn rags of town drunks to the dark suits of businessmen, they often traveled with several abreast, making it difficult to walk between them.

The biggest distraction for Jacques was the stores. Many shops displayed goods on wooden sidewalks running down both sides of dirt roads filled with horse-drawn buggies. He saw hats, clothes, candy, and tonics. His eyes jumped from storefront to storefront while still following the wagon, pulled down adjacent streets. His favorite stores were on Michigan Avenue between Burdick and Rose, where shops were in three-story buildings.

The wagon stopped at a meat market, where the venison was unloaded into a pile among several dozen saddles from other trains and stagecoaches. He watched at dusk as two figures lifted them on a hand-cranked conveyer through the shop's back door into a butchering room. Inside, he could see four men cut and wrap the meat in small packages.

Two dimly lit figures put several of the best saddles on a second wagon drawn by a pair of appaloosa horses. One man with a ponytail had characteristics of a native American. Jacques kept watching the Indian's partner, a short man with black hair. He looked familiar, but it was too dark to be sure.

Suddenly he realized this was a dangerous situation. He felt uneasy and vulnerable, like being surrounded by a pack of wild dogs. What if the men saw him hiding in the shadows?

Jacques turned the corner of the building and ran as fast as he could, swinging the carpetbag beside him through the dark streets of Kalamazoo. He ran past banks, shops, and saloons. Puffing, he raced up to the registration desk at the Burdick Hotel. "Room for Jacques Flareau, please."

The elderly clerk hadn't seen anyone with a carpetbag in years. He adjusted a thick pair of bifocals that tilted to the right because of his crooked nose. Pointing at a roster on the desk, he said, "Please sign here. Your employer has already paid your bill for two nights. Here's your key. The dining room is open until nine. Have a pleasant evening, son."

Jacques sighed and went upstairs. Before going to bed, he ate some bread and jerky his mother had put in the carpetbag. He washed the food down with water from a flowered pitcher set on a wobbly night stand. Then he used a chamber pot hidden beneath the bed and washed his hands. Despite being tired, sleep did not come easy. He rolled and tossed all night, dreaming about the two thieves at the store. The sound of music from the poorly tuned piano in the hotel bar also kept him awake.

When the sun rose, Jacques walked at once to the meat market. Seeing no activity other than the sale of three ducks to one customer, he ordered breakfast at a nearby restaurant. Poached eggs, which he never had tasted before, were hard to dig out of their porcelain cups and slippery to swallow. He thanked the smiling waitress for two chunks of bacon instead of one. Women in the big city are sure pretty, he concluded, as he admired her shapely legs.

All day the young man visited different parts of Kalamazoo but returned to the meat market every hour or so. The place that intrigued him most was the new building owned by the Lawrence and Chapin Iron Works on the corner of Rose and Water Streets. He joined a tour group being escorted through the plant.

"Our company's been in business only two years," said the tour guide, "but we just completed a new addition with one and a half million bricks. This building is three stories high with fifty thousand square feet of floor space. Several steam elevators transport people and equipment between floors."

A copula with an observation platform on the roof allowed Jacques and other tourists to look down on the city below. Some of the church spires were below his line of sight. He thought about how different this building was from the Petersons' log cabin in Grafton.

When he got back to the meat market at sunset, Jacques saw the appaloosas tied to a hitching post. Once again, he watched the two men unload deer meat, along with carcasses of ducks, ruffed grouse, and turkeys. The wagon behind the horses was piled with at least thirty saddles taken from a collection of about one hundred fifty. Now he could see the faces of the two men. The first figure was indeed an Indian, who seemed to be in command of the horses. Despite the cool temperature, he had taken his shirt off while moving venison. The second was a familiar short man with greasy black hair that swirled when he moved. It was Dietrich!

Jacques was shocked to see someone he knew in the city. Why was Dietrich, an axe man with fine skills, unloading meat at a train station?

He walked firmly toward Dietrich and stroked the head of one horse. Pointing at the tagged saddles, he said, "Some might be deer I shot."

"Hello, Jacques. What are you doing in Kalamazoo?"

"I've been exploring the city. How 'bout you?"

Dietrich said, "Me? I've got jobs all over, even here in Kalamazoo." He motioned toward the Indian. "This here's Tiny."

Like most people named Tiny, the Indian was well over six feet tall. His muscles rippled and his back was scarred, perhaps from being horsewhipped.

"Whatcha doin'?" Jacques asked.

Tiny looked toward Dietrich, signaling him to respond. "Loading the conveyer belt. We do it every night at sunset, except for Sundays."

"What about the meat on the wagon? Does it go to another store?"

"Nope, that's our pay." Dietrich changed the subject. "How's Sally?"

"Dunno. I've been busy fishing and hunting."

"Wanna have a drink with us at the saloon?"

Jacques agreed to go, mostly to get information. The two young men walked behind the wagon, driven by Tiny. They shared stories about people in Grafton. On the way the Indian stopped in an alley and traded venison to a young man for several cases of liquor. Tiny and Dietrich arrived at the saloon, took the liquor off the wagon, and carried the cases inside.

Jacques had never been in a saloon before. The sparseness shocked him. There were no tables, just a long wooden bar that crossed the lobby. It was a split log of white pine polished to a glass-like finish. Customers at the bar shared six spittoons on the floor, ringed with brown tobacco juice. Drinkers of all shapes and sizes appeared in the uneven light from gas lamps.

"Here, here!" Dietrich yelled. "I'm buying! This is Jacques Flareau from my hometown."

Courtesy of his boyhood adversary, the country hunter took his first drink. He made the mistake of rolling the straight whiskey around in his mouth before he swallowed. His gums and tongue burned as well as the roof of his mouth and inner cheeks. Then, the whiskey seared down his throat, stopping halfway. He wasn't sure if the liquid fire was going to go further down or come back up. Turning around so nobody could see him, Jacques swallowed hard, driving the fluid down into his stomach. He opened his mouth wide and let loose the same noise he heard from others at the bar. "Ah."

Many men bought drinks for Jacques. He met trappers, railroad men, and factory workers, along with those of other occupations. The only thing they had in common was a friendship with Dietrich. As liquor loosened their tongues, they all revealed involvement in some kind of illegal venture. Some cut trees on property they did not own and sold them to friends at the sawmills. Others traded in stolen paper from the mill. A few were convicts who spoke of time they spent at jails and prisons throughout Michigan.

"Jacques, have you ever worked in a logging camp?" asked one of Dietrich's friends smoking a hand-made pipe.

"No. I've never been up north." Jacques felt warm. The air in the saloon seemed stuffy. Out of habit, he unbuttoned his shirt, exposing his burly chest with furry black hair.

The logger continued talking about cutting white pine in the northern Michigan woods. "Each fall, farm boys from all over southern Michigan head north to logging camps. Others come from Maine, Minnesota, Wisconsin, and even foreign countries like Finland."

Jacques learned about methods used to log pine and laughed at lumberjack jokes. He heard about logging contests held on Sundays, when the men had time off. He joined several others and sang a ballad about the north woods:

Now boys, if you will listen,
I'll sing for you a song.
It's all about the pinewoods
And how to get along.
They are a jolly set of boys,
So merry and so fine,
Who spend the pleasant winters
A-cutting down the pine.

It got so loud in the saloon that Jacques could no longer hear the logger, whose words were now slurred. It seemed like a good time to leave and go back to his hotel. He said good night to several of the men he met, thanked Dietrich, and slipped outside. The air was cold and clear, a refreshing change from the smoke that had given him a headache. He felt like he had been in a den of thieves.

The liquor made it easy for him to sleep but hard to rise the next morning. He still had a headache and a sour stomach when boarding the early train toward home. All the way, he pondered how to deal with the situation he had uncovered. He decided to tell about Tiny and Dietrich putting meat on their wagon, but would not reveal their identities.

The railroad clerk met Jacques leaving the train with his carpetbag. "Hello. Welcome back. So, what'd you find out?"

It took a moment for Jacques to regain his composure after the trip. He flicked some ashes from the curls in his black hair before speaking. "I saw two men. They took meat off the train and put it on a wagon. I watched 'em haul venison to a meat market in town. They kept some for themselves."

"How do you know that?"

"Well, I saw them. They put some meat on their own wagon."

"Did you talk to them?"

"Yes sir. I talked to them. They told me the meat was their pay. Later, they traded the venison for liquor."

"You sure?"

"Yes, sir. That's what I saw. Yes, sir. That's what they said."

"That couldn't be right. Meat markets always pay employees in cash. Those men must be faking the paperwork to cover up." He pointed to a yellow shipping receipt. "See, look at the venison you followed. It says right here they received sixteen saddles. But, you and I know eighteen left Grafton."

Jacques looked at the receipt signed by William Tothe, one of the men he met in the saloon. "I don't know anything about shipping papers. But, I do know eighteen saddles left Grafton and eighteen got to Kalamazoo."

"Did you get the names of the thieves?"

Jacques felt nervous and shifted his weight from foot to foot. He wanted to keep the identity of the men confidential, but he wouldn't lie. He tried to act calm but he felt his face get warm. "It could have been anyone. There's a bunch of crooks in that city."

"Too bad. At least we know what they did." The clerk slapped Jacques's back. "Good work, son. I'll tell the sheriff about this Monday morning. Here's your seventy-five cents and a tip for a job well done." The clerk handed him a silver dollar.

Deep in thought, Jacques walked home through town. Maybe he told the clerk too much. What if this was shipping fraud? Then railroad commissioners would get involved. They were powerful men with connections everywhere. Tiny and Dietrich would surely be sent to jail as an example. Jacques's mind wandered even further. What would Dietrich do after he got out of jail?

When he reached Grafton, the town looked different. The country church, which always seemed so large, now appeared tiny. The stores that always crowded him now looked scattered. The people seemed different, too. Those in Grafton all looked the same in their rustic clothing, compared to the many different kinds of people in the city. Most of all, he recognized that Grafton was twenty years behind Kalamazoo.

Something had changed within Jacques, too. The trip to Kalamazoo made him want to travel. Now when he caught perch on the lake, he dreamed of seeing the ocean. When he hunted deer on the oak ridge, he pretended he was climbing snow-capped mountains in the Rockies. Going to the city had given him an itch for adventure, a trait his family termed the "wanderlust."

When fishing began to slow, Jacques inquired about working up north. He went to the general store and looked over the employment flyers sent by logging companies. He remembered seeing those notices even as a small boy. Every fall the flyers hung in the store, near a jar of rock candy. As a child he enjoyed staring at the colorless candy that looked like crystals on a string. Jacques would stare at the jar for long periods and imagine he was eating the candy piece by piece. Whenever Mr. Rice came near, he made believe he was reading the logging flyers rather than staring at the candy jar. When he got older, though, the job announcements became more exciting than the candy. He dreamed of working as a lumberjack in far off places in the north woods. One notice always caught his attention because it listed specific job openings.

Loggers Wanted
Swampers
Sawyers
River Hogs
Scalers
For more information, contact
Emerson Logging Company
Au Gres, Michigan

What were those jobs? he wondered. What's a swamper do? Isn't a hog some type of pig? What could that have to do with logging? Does a sawyer cut down trees or make boards out of logs?

As Jacques got older, he began asking questions about logging. When business at the store was slow, Mr. Rice spent hours explaining the timber business to him. Jacques made special trips to the store every fall to see if the employment flyers had arrived and what they said.

He also discovered many things about northern Michigan from the clerk at the railroad depot. He learned about the sandy ground where pines thrived, compared to the rich topsoil in Grafton. Jacques looked at maps showing the Upper and Lower Peninsulas of the state bordered by Lakes Michigan, Superior, Huron, St. Clair, and Erie.

The Flareau family needed extra money this fall because of a slow hunting and fishing season. Jacques also seemed more interested than normal in logging because of the things he'd heard at the saloon in Kalamazoo. So when the flyers arrived at the store, he asked Mr. Rice to help him submit a job application. Several weeks later, he was offered a job. All he needed was permission from his parents. One evening he got up the nerve to talk to his father.

"Dad, when you were my age, did ya ever want to strike out on your own?"

"No. I never caught the wanderlust. Maybe I was lucky to find your mother early in my life. Your grandpa had the wanderlust, though. He had it bad."

"What'd he do about it?

"He came to Michigan in search of land from a small town in New York State during the 1830s."

Jacques was attentive. He'd heard only parts of the story. "Is that when he went on the Erie Canal?"

"Yes, Grandpa took a barge down the Erie Canal to Buffalo. Then he rode a steamship across Lake Erie to Detroit. More than five hundred settlers were packed aboard the ship when a storm blew across the lake. They even threw cargo overboard to keep the ship from sinking. The steamer made two stops. All but twelve passengers got off the ship before reaching Detroit."

"That sounds like a real adventure," said Jacques. "Why'd he come to Michigan? Wasn't there much land left in New York?"

"At that time, people moved around. Some were after gold. Others wanted land. Most just sought excitement. All wanted change. People were crazy with the wanderlust."

"What did Grandpa do in Detroit?"

"He got mad about the long lines of settlers at the land office. Outlaws bought land from the government for a dollar and a quarter an acre. They re-sold poor ground at higher prices to settlers who didn't know any better. Grandpa didn't like what he saw, so he kept moving west by stagecoach to Kalamazoo on Territorial Road. There he gave the land office one hundred dollars for eighty acres of land a few miles northeast of town."

"What about you? Tell me again how you got here?"

"Grandpa went back east to get your grandma and me. He brought us here to Grafton. We lived in a small cabin upstream on this here river. Your mother lived next door. She and I grew up together and got married. You know the rest."

"Well, I must have caught the wanderlust from Grandpa." He paused, walked to the window, and stared outside. "I'd like to work up north this winter. Mr. Rice helped me fill out a job application. Now a logging camp wants me to start work in two weeks. What'd ya think? Can I go? Please. Can I go?"

Pierre rose from his chair. He took a shiny wooden box from his dresser drawer and flipped up the top, uncovering a worn leather pouch. He reached into the pouch and withdrew a ten-dollar gold piece. "This coin was your grandpa's. It was minted the year he came west." He handed it to Jacques. "You can have it. It's yours now. See the date? It's 1839." Pierre looked down at his boots and coughed. "When you leavin' for northern Michigan?"

"Soon." Jacques glanced out the window at the popple tree above the outhouse. That tree, about the same age as Jacques, was the first to get buds and unfurl new leaves in spring. Its early color also signaled the beginning of autumn. Now, yellow leaves ringed the base of the tree. Winter was on the way. Both the popple and Jacques were about to change.

5

Jacques Goes to Logging Camp

Soon the day came for Jacques to leave Grafton. He enjoyed saying goodbye to his younger brother and sister. He knuckled William's head and gave Martha one last piggyback ride around the cabin. It was harder saying goodbye to his mother. For the first time he noticed she was aging. He saw wrinkles on her forehead and baggy skin dangling from her arms. "I'll be safe, Mom. Mr. Rice picked me a good camp." He kissed her a second time for reassurance.

"Don't forget to read your Bible every Sunday. You should look for lice each night before bed." Her voice shook between sobs. "When it gets cold, check for gray spots on your hands and feet. Take care of them right away." Her tone was gentle. "Always remember, I'm here if you need me. Write if you can." She had tears in her eyes.

Jacques left the cabin and sat next to his father, who guided the horse-drawn wagon. On the way to the railroad depot they stopped at the blacksmith shop so Jacques could say goodbye to Sally. She opened the door after only one knock.

What a beautiful girl, he thought. As usual, her hair was neatly combed. She ran to him after he opened his arms. He heard her coo while they hugged. A fresh aroma, like soft soap, surrounded her like a cloud.

"Today's the day," he said. "I'm off to camp."

Sally held his head in both hands. "Oh, please be careful. We hear such terrible stories about the logging accidents."

That's strange, Jacques thought. Both Sally and Mom are worried about my safety. "I'll be fine."

"What about all the bullies? Don't let any of them hurt you."

"Of course not. I'm pretty strong, you know. I'm over six foot. Nobody picks on tall men." He stretched his arms over his head.

Jacques looked around the cabin. He saw bundles of herbs hanging upside down from the rafters. Seedlings grew in planters below each windowsill. Bottles of powders and tinctures lined the cabinet shelves. He saw a sugar bowl filled with change on her desk. Sally was doing well, he thought. She really had become an expert in making medicine. Maybe the herb book I gave her helped.

"Should I take any tonics with me?"

"There's nothing wrong with you. Just keep an eye open for lice. Make sure you watch for gray spots on your hands and feet when the weather gets cold."

That's funny, Jacques thought. That's the same thing Mom said. "I have to go." He turned to leave and gave her an awkward kiss on the cheek. It was nothing like their first kiss at the dance. It lacked the passion of their kiss in her home when they fell, laughing, to the floor. Both of them sensed that something was different.

"Oh, come on now," she said, pulling him tight to her chest. This time, the kiss was long, deep, and full of longing. Panting, she said, "See you in the spring."

He felt warm. "I can't wait. Let's start where we left off today." He took her hand while they walked downstairs. She and Mr. Wilton waved goodbye as Jacques climbed back on the wagon next to his father.

Upon reaching the depot, Jacques dismounted and tied Oscar to a hitching post. The horse glanced sideways at him as if he knew the young man was leaving. Oscar stomped his feet until Jacques rubbed the horse's head and gave him a piece of apple. He always had at least one sliver of apple in his pocket. "I'll see you in the spring," he whispered in his ear. "Be a good horse. Now, you mind Dad."

Soon, smoke from the locomotive was visible a few hundred yards away. Puffs of charcoal-colored smoke rose above the tree line like stairways to the clouds. When the engineer pulled the whistle, Jacques felt a bolt of energy pulse through his body. "Yup, I caught the wanderlust from Grandpa." He fondled the gold coin in his pocket. "Wish me luck, Dad."

His father winked. "I'm glad you can chase your dream, son. But, you be back before the suckers run!" He waved goodbye, even after the locomotive pulled out of town and headed for the north woods.

The ride seemed rough to Jacques. It was noisier than the train to Kalamazoo with more clanking and squealing. He saw burn spots where sparks from past trains had started fires beside the tracks. Everything in the passenger car had a light coating of kerosene from lamps used to provide light during evening hours. The taste of kerosene spread from his lips to his mouth. Jacques watched his fellow passengers sway from side to side in rhythm with the rocking of the train. They seemed hypnotized by the sounds and motion.

Fewer couples and families remained on the train as it proceeded north. Before long, Jacques saw only men on their way to logging camps. Some of them drank from whiskey bottles. Smoke from pipes, more common than cigars or cigarettes, stung his nose. He watched men rise from their seats and mingle with one another.

Jacques changed trains several times. They stopped often for maintenance. Tired of sitting, he left the train with other passengers during one repair. It felt good to recline in the shade of a tree beside the nearby woods. Later, he took a stagecoach from one depot to another because there was no rail service around the shore of a large lake. There was no direct route from Kalamazoo to the logging camp.

Jacques was glad the seat next to him was vacant because he was thinking and didn't want to talk to anyone. He daydreamed about things he wanted to do, like seeing Lake Michigan, visiting Grandpa's hometown in New York, swimming in the ocean, catching a fish in the Mississippi River …

Suddenly a young man in farm clothes jumped into the adjacent seat. "Mind if I sit here for a minute?" he squawked. Jacques gave the intruder a cranky glance. "Why that seat?"

"So I can talk to you." The farm boy laughed and then gulped a mouthful of whiskey from a near-empty bottle. "What's eating you, scaredy-cat? Is this your first trip to camp?"

"I'm Jacques Flareau, an axe man and market hunter from Grafton. You're right. This is my first trip to logging camp. But I'm more excited than scared, and feel more like a lone goose than a cat. What's your name?"

"I'm Eli Peters. I live in Coldwater. Our town is great! We have a general store with rock candy …" Eli rambled on about the church, school, and people in Coldwater. Not only did he talk incessantly, but he also looked funny. Eli's beard was mostly peach-fuzz. A few scraggly hairs, like cat whiskers, comprised his partly grown mustache. Freckles dotted his cheeks. The voice of the redhead cracked like an adolescent even though he assured Jacques that he was twenty-two. Jacques chuckled to himself. If I had a voice like that, I sure wouldn't say much.

Eli talked even when Jacques acted annoyed and looked out the window. "We know all about railroads in my town. Coldwater is on the Michigan Southern, the first company able to run trains from the east to Chicago. I said the first. That was in 1852."

The pesky know-it-all talked so much that Jacques heard only the sound of a boyish voice without words, beating in time to the clanking of the train and rocking of passengers. "We've got eight cows. They're pretty easy to get into the milking barn. All you have to do is …"

Jacques watched the soft light of the setting sun accent the autumn colors. Yellow and red leaves, enriched by clumps of green pine, flashed by the train windows. Jacques had supper with Eli in the dining car, returned to his seat, and fell asleep listening to the farm boy's adventures. He slept well until daylight woke all the men in the passenger car at about the same time. Eli, being an early riser, was first to use the toilet in the rear of the train. When he came back, he resumed talking.

"Good morning, Jacques."

"Mornin'."

"Last year, the best thing at camp was Saturday nights. We had lots of French-Canadians there. Everyone yelled and stomped when we sang 'Allouette.' Those Canadians are awfully loud. But they sure know how to cut pine. I watched two of them…" He continued telling tales, waking all the men on the train with his irritating voice.

Eli poked Jacques on the shoulder to get his attention. "Where are you headed?"

"I'm going to Emerson Logging Company, between Roscommon and West Branch."

"Which camp?"

"Thirty-seven."

"Well I'll be! I'm going there, too, but to Camp Eighteen. This is my fourth year…"

Jacques stopped listening and stared out the window, noting how different the landscape had become. There were only four features to the scenery: sandy barren land with smoking pine stumps, clumps of bare hardwoods that had just lost their leaves, evergreen swamps, and tiny towns. Jacques noticed that sandy vistas with oceans of stumps became more common as the train moved north. Most of the ragged stumps were scarred with soot from past fires. Smoke, with its dense odor of burning timber, hugged the horizon until the train entered another tunnel of hardwood trees or conifer swamps.

The train stopped at several railroad stations, all of which had the same box-like appearance. To Jacques the approaching towns looked like dots connected by steel rails on raised piles of gravel. Most had a hotel, a church, and a few stores. All had at least one saloon. Jacques watched gangs of lumberjacks leave the train at each successive stop. All seemed to be in a rush to report to camp with only a few hours left. He was amazed by the diversity of their fancies. Some sought food. Others wanted sleep, drink, women, or baths. However, all had a similar look, inspired by anticipation of the future and freedom from the past.

Eli and Jacques both got off the train at Roscommon. The young men teased each other about their wobbly legs, not yet used to walking on solid ground. They shared a room at the hotel to save the cost of separate lodging. After putting their belongings away, they walked to a nearby saloon. Three deep, men of all shapes and sizes lined up to the bar, with hardly a place to stand. Eli and Jacques ordered drinks. Smoke and sweat filled the saloon, along with the heavy scent of perfume from waiter girls, who spent more time talking to well-dressed patrons than serving drinks. A piano player, wearing a white shirt with red stripes and black bow tie, played briskly, but his music was overcome by waves of louder voices.

The whiskey went to Jacques's head in a few minutes. Colors in the saloon swirled together. His stomach became queasy from tobacco smoke. The music made his body throb. He looked at the patrons around him, doubting if even one of them was really happy. Some had sad faces while the glee of others seemed too shallow to be real. Jacques realized that spending time in saloons was not the life for him. He wanted something different.

Jacques had been so pre-occupied watching people in the saloon that he lost track of Eli, who was arm-wrestling a drunken lumberjack. There were several dimes on the bar between the two men. The farm boy pinned down the drunk's arm. He smiled with satisfaction, picked up his winnings, and said, "Hi Jacques. I'm buying. You know, my father was a professor of romance languages at Dartmouth before he went West to farm. He always said that buying a drink for a friend is a tribute to his presence. Now you are my friend. In fact, I'm gonna call you Jake instead of Jacques."

"But, I've always been known as Jacques. People won't know who I am."

"I know a lot about words from my father. Call yourself Jake. It will make a difference in the way people treat you. You know, I often think about my father and the things he told me. Another time…"

"I'm callin' it quits. It's been a long couple of days. They say it'll be rough walking into camp tomorrow."

"Okay, but I'm staying here awhile."

Jake walked slowly back to the hotel thinking about saloons and whiskey. He smiled at the clerk in the lobby before entering his room and undressing. His bed was inviting and felt warm. After falling asleep, he dreamed of cutting limbs from a toppled pine hung up in nearby trees. He knew lumberjacks had a fear of those trees and called them widow makers. In his dream a circle of men surrounded him while he cut one limb after another until the pine crashed to the ground. His audience applauded with claps and hoots that were even louder than those of the men in the saloon. The dream ended abruptly when Eli entered the room, stumbled into bed, and threw up on the floor. He moaned all night between bouts of the dry heaves.

At breakfast in the hotel restaurant, the two men ate without speaking, each lost in his own thoughts. Loggers gathered outside the hotel at eight in the morning beneath one of three signs. Eli, still pale from the night before, said, "It's been nice talking with you. Enjoy your first year in camp."

Jake smiled and said, "Goodbye and good luck. Maybe we'll meet again." His feelings were mixed. He was glad the annoying boy was leaving but he would miss having someone to talk to.

The longest line of men formed under a sign labeled Camp 11. Eli joined a group of men assigned to Camp 18. Jake stood behind a man holding a staff and banner for Camp 37, which seemed to have the youngest but strongest men.

A superintendent stood at the head of Jake's line and barked, "My name is Rolf Swensen. Major Swensen to you. In a few hours, you'll be shanty boys. That's what we call lumberjacks who work in the winter woods because they live in bunkhouses buried beneath snow. Welcome to Emerson Logging Company. Say goodbye to civilization, boys."

Jake thought it odd for a camp boss to have a handlebar mustache. It seemed that most men who worked in the woods had mustaches that didn't need close trimming and waxing.

Soon the recruits going to Camp 37 marched off like a column of soldiers with a dawn chill in their bones. Most men carried their clothes in a turkey or bindle, tied to a stick, first resting the burden on one shoulder and then the other. Jake lugged his carpetbag, which seemed to get heavier with each step. He wished someone in Grafton had shown him how to make a turkey.

The tote road into logging camp was filled with ruts, making it difficult for Jake to walk without tripping. Sandy areas past town looked to him like fields planted with black stumps. He smelled smoke, which drifted over and around the men, especially at turns in the road. One of the old timers toward the front of the line yelled out, "Don't worry about those burning stumps, boys. Don't worry about fires on the ground either. But look out for flames in the tops. Fires that crown are the ones that kill."

The recruits passed some older lumberjacks walking behind horses and wagons. The veterans, who were hauling supplies into camp, snickered at this year's newcomers and pointed at lumberjacks they were sure were most likely to adjust and make it to spring. They also noted those that might leave or get sick. Their comments, like forecasts from a fortune-teller, frightened the newcomers. When one old-timer saw Jake, he said, "Looky here at that big one with coal black hair. He'll never get enough to eat. That boy'll look like a walking skeleton in spring." The rest of the men laughed and whooped.

The line of marching lumberjacks came to a small clearing about one o'clock. Rumors went up and down the column that the camp was just ahead. Three cook wagons appeared soon after Major Swensen gave orders to take a break. The head cook was a balding man of fifty-seven with a wide smile that showed few remaining teeth. He and his staff, all wearing white aprons, arranged plates and utensils on a long split log. It looked like the log had been used before as a table because nearby vegetation was matted. Some of the exposed wood was stained and someone had whittled HJY deep in the surface of the massive log. It must have been a routine stopping point for lunch when lumberjacks marched into camp. The hungry recruits were orderly, fearful of offending the cooks and not being fed. They finished their stew without teasing one another.

Jake noticed many types of late fall mushrooms along the edge of the tote road. Some had brown shells that burst into clouds of spores when he stepped on them. Others were firm with bright speckled colors. Songbirds that Jake had never seen before flew overhead. He watched bald eagles soar along rivers and osprey glide over cattail marshes. Tracks of deer sprinkled the rutted road. He was often startled by the flush of ruffed grouse diving from the road to deeper cover inside the forest. Much of the conversation among lumberjacks dealt with wildlife they saw.

The temperature began to drop about four o'clock, and by then the men were tired from the long walk to camp. Some lumberjacks fell behind and lost their place in line. The supply caravan they had passed in the morning reappeared and overtook them. The snickering of veterans was even louder this time. Then, just when the men could hardly walk any longer, Camp 37 loomed ahead. It was one of the newer camps with a barn for horses and oxen, along with a bunkhouse, blacksmith shop, cookhouse, and a row of outhouses. Like many camps in the North Country, it was designed for about one hundred workers to cut ten million board feet of pine every winter—about forty-five thousand logs.

The men lined up in front of the bunkhouse, which was constructed from tree-length pine. There was no foundation because the bottom log, or mudsill, was set on the ground. Dirt was piled around the outside of the building to stop the wind from entering the inner room. Spaces in the walls between logs were blocked with split shakes and chinked with mud and straw. Doors and windows were only in the ends, below a roof of spruce poles covered with rough boards and shakes.

Major Swensen pulled a piece of paper from his back pocket. He called out names of men dismissed to find cots in the bunkhouse. "Willie Danfield, Bob Fay, Jacques Furrow . . ."

Without correcting the Major's pronunciation of his last name or announcing his new nickname, Jake entered the bunkhouse. He was relieved that his name was called and that he was in the right place. Inside were twenty bunks set up in two rows against opposite walls of a large room. He chose a vacant cot by the door. It had a bedroll on top of a cloth mattress stuffed with stiff hay. He unrolled the blankets and threw himself on the bed to try it out.

A deep voice boomed from the dark. "Better not pick dat one, shanty boy. You'll never sleep. Take one away from da door."

Jake moved to another bunk. He answered the voice in the dark with a loud retort. "Thanks." Looking around the bunkhouse, he saw several men resting on cots or organizing personal items. Towels hung from rungs above the bunks. Everything appeared neat and orderly, which was a surprise to Jake. He'd been told that lumberjacks were messy.

Men who had been in camp before told the recruits about meal schedules, where to wash clothes, and how to get a loan from the company store until they were paid in the spring. Jake rested on his cot and listened to the questions and answers, most of which dealt with practical matters of life in camp. He knew they reflected inner fears of the newcomers. For example, a redhead named Rusty from Indiana asked, "Are there any bears in the woods?"

The old-timers had fun with that question. "They're all over. You especially have to watch for them at night when you use the privy."

"You mean they'll come in the outhouse after you?" He didn't know they were teasing.

Jake had a question, too, but hesitated to share it when he heard the veterans spoofing his fellow recruits. Since Jake was a good axe man, the company had hired him to build roads through the pines before other loggers arrived. He wondered what would happen if he made a mistake. What if he cut the wrong trees and made the road go in a false direction? The edge of the forest was a thick wall of trunks, branches, and brambles. How would he know which direction to go? Would the other men laugh at him? Would he be fired and sent home?

After a lull in the conversation, he asked his question. "How do we know which trees to cut?"

Albrecht, the man with the booming voice, replied, "You and others'll walk through the woods with da road boss. Along the way, you'll put a small axe mark on some trees. Later, you'll go back and cut all da trees between marks."

The answer wasn't good enough for Jake. "How does the boss know where to build the road?"

"He lays out da trail from places with pine to the river. That's where logs will be floated to sawmills in spring. The boss got da maps from the timber cruisers. They took measurements on trees to figure how much lumber will come out of da woods. The boss uses them maps to plan roads."

"It sounds complicated." Jake lost interest in the details. Albrecht started talking about the mail in answer to a city boy's question. "They bring it every Saturday afternoon. You can read it or have it read to you on Sundays. What's da matter kid? Are you homesick already?" Everyone laughed except the young man from Detroit.

The dinner bell interrupted conversations in the bunkhouse. The sound came from an iron triangle, known to the men as a gut hammer. A long line of lumberjacks formed in front of the cookhouse. "Quite a walk in, eh?" Jake said to the man in front of him.

"Not bad. I had lots of fun teasing the old-timers. I asked one if he could still tell a white from Norway pine."

"Hey, no talking at meals," said Major Swensen.

Jake was surprised again. Eli had told him all about the laughing and singing at camp. But the men were silent as they filed into the cookhouse. Nobody was allowed to speak during meals. They sat down at picnic tables made of thick logs covered with oilcloth. For every five men there was a bowl of potatoes and a bucket of salt pork with beans. Cookees, or assistants to the cook, served hot tea and rice pudding for dessert.

After breakfast the next morning, Jake and three other lumberjacks gathered in front of the horse barn. Two of the men had built roads through the pines before. Jake immediately liked the other new man, Thor. He'd worked in New England as a timber cruiser and more recently in Wisconsin, but got lonely working by himself. This fall, he decided to try building roads to see if he liked living with others in camp.

When he first met Jake, Thor slipped around his side and lined up, back-to-back so their rumps were almost touching. He moved his hand along the top of their heads and said, "You're about two inches taller than me. I don't look up to very many men in America."

"You have an accent. Where are you from?"

"Sweden. My name is Thor Glick. I left everything behind to start a new life."

"Come on. You aren't that old."

"Twenty, how about you."

"Eighteen."

"So," Thor said. "I'm two years older but two inches shorter." He also was heavier with a stocky build, well suited to his wide suspenders and broad shoulders. He had thick sandy hair with a balding spot that started on top of his head. Thor's beard provided the most striking difference between the men. Jake had been clean-shaven, but decided not to shave during the logging season. His face was sprinkled with newly formed hairs that itched and made him scratch. Thor had a heavy beard and moustache that hid his thin lips.

Rance, the road boss, hitched a pair of horses to a wagon and told Jake and Thor to ride in back along with two other loggers. They left the horse barn in darkness and drove to the end of a bumpy trail filled with stumps, roots, and half-cut logs. As day broke, the men behind the wagon realized their supervisor had only one arm. When Rance saw them staring at his stump, he explained what had happened. "Five years ago, a pine came down on top of me. It broke my shoulder and mangled my arm. So now the company lets me plan roads, dams, and new buildings."

Thor looked thoughtful. He spoke slowly to make his Swedish accent less obvious. "Most fellers know exactly where a tree will drop. If they don't, they should be fired."

"Maybe, but how do you tell good fellers from bad."

"Give 'em a test."

"Naw. Seniority is better. Those with experience have proven themselves. There's the ones that should be fellers."

"I'd sure like to knock down those big pines. You should see me handle an axe." Thor got so excited that his full beard bounced up and down when he talked. He snapped his suspenders.

Rance got mad. "Don't worry about felling pines. The boys coming in winter will take care of that. You just cut weed trees to make the road. Don't forget that. You're not a feller."

"Yes, sir." Thor got the message. The other men kept quiet. Jake was amazed by Thor's knowledge but even more surprised by the outburst from the road boss. He concluded there is a clear pecking order among men working in the woods. Loggers who built roads, he had learned, were near the bottom.

While the wagon bounced through the woods, Jake studied the map of timber to be cut this winter. Pines extended for miles on a sandy ridge overlooking a small creek to the east and a spruce and fir swamp on the west. A new road to the south was needed for skidding logs to the river, three miles away. Jake considered the work to be done and felt well suited to his job. He and Thor were ordered to cut small trees while the experienced men took down larger trees.

Jake grabbed his axe from the back of the wagon, flipped it in the air, and caught it by the shaft below the head. That felt good. He watched the sun burst over the horizon to warm the crisp air. He felt confident because he was doing something he knew well. The first tree he toppled was a jack pine that cut like butter and dropped precisely where planned. The blacksmith had tapered the axe head just right, although it felt a bit light to Jake. The handle was smooth. Large chips fell on the ground—the sign of a good axe, he thought.

Knowing which trees to cut was easy. He stood at one blazed tree and looked ahead through the woods until they saw the next tree with an axe mark. Together, the team moved forward, cutting everything six feet on either side of an imaginary line between marked trees. Then, they spied the next blaze and continued through the woods, leaving only stumps and dried ferns in their wake. He no longer feared cutting down the wrong trees.

Thor and Jake always ate lunch together while sitting on stumps some distance from the other men. Although they usually discussed philosophy, one afternoon Thor got practical. He looked down at Jake's boots and said, "You need to spend more time taking care of those boots."

"I do take care of them. I put cloth in them overnight when they're wet. I put grease on them every Sunday." He looked at Thor's boots and saw they were immaculate, showing only spots where mud had been scraped from the leather with a stick.

"I grease mine every night. Boots are so important."

"Why's that?"

"Because that's the place we touch the ground. Your boots give you a place in the world. They're the meeting place between your soul and the earth. Take good care of them, my friend." He threw a stick toward Jake, which hit him on the side of the face. The two men rolled on the ground in play.

"See," said Jake. "Your boots are in the air now and it's your butt that touches the earth. Take good care of your backside, my friend." He laughed.

Friday was not a good day for Jake. At break time he walked around the edge of a cedar swamp, hunting for a private place. He had gotten up late and had forgotten to use the outhouse at camp.

After finding a log hidden by dogwoods on the edge of a stream, he finished his business. Walking back, he headed too far west and wandered deep inside the dark swamp. Black muck made it difficult to lift his legs. Muddy water flowed over the top of his boots and soaked his socks. Jake backed up rather than take the direct route through even deeper mud. By the time he got out of the cedar swamp, he couldn't tell which way he'd come. Water covered his footprints.

Major Swensen had instructed the men what to do if they got lost. He told them to stop, mark a tree, and place their belongings there in one pile. They should pound a hollow tree three times in rapid succession with the butt of their axe head or yell three times in a row. If it was getting dark, they were to start a fire. The most important rule was to remain by the marked tree until someone came.

Jake considered all these orders, but decided to walk a little farther before marking a tree. It's only a ten-minute walk to the road, he thought.

The trees circling him all looked the same. There were no landmarks. It was a cloudy day without a sun to tell east from west. He wished he had a compass, but the company issued them only to road bosses. Jake didn't realize he was running until his shoulder smashed into a tree. It was hard to catch his breath. Panic fogged his mind. At last he saw footprints, fresh that day, on the edge of an alder swale. He was relieved because he knew the road must be near.

Jake placed his boot in the print, noting the exact fit. Hardly anyone in camp had such a large boot. Depression replaced his elation when he realized he had just walked a complete circle. At that time he resigned himself to being lost. He marked a nearby tree with his axe and gathered some firewood.

After dropping a bundle of twigs on the ground, he heard the sound of branches snapping on a nearby trail. Is someone coming? Then, the crunching noise stopped for several minutes. It must have been a deer, he thought. He knelt to whittle some bark from a dry branch to make kindling. There's the noise, again. It's getting closer.

Thor's voice broke the silence. "What'd you do, take a nap in the woods?"

"No, I found a bear den. The sow was inside, asleep for winter." He felt his face get hot, like it always did when he lied. Jake was happy to see another person, especially Thor, who noticed his wet boots and sweaty forehead but didn't say anything. Jake took his place in line and swung his axe with pleasure. He felt proud to be a member of the team building the road. He was no longer lost.

When it was time to rest, Thor sat on a log near Jake. He brushed the dirt and bark out of his beard before lighting his pipe. "What do you think about camp?"

Jake replied, "I like working hard on a team."

"Me, too. You know I worked alone for several years.

"Yeah, I heard. My dad's a loner. He hunts and fishes by himself. He likes it. Are you like that?"

"Oh, no. I like to be around others. But, coming to America from a foreign country, I felt different." He puffed several times on his pipe, blowing smoke upwards where it trailed off in the breeze. "Sometimes it's good to be different. Who wants to play follow the leader, anyway?"

Jake grinned.

The discussion continued to get more philosophical. Thor knocked his pipe against a nearby tree, showering the ground with black ash. "There's one question that I've never been able to answer. It's liked a puzzle that can't be solved."

"What's that?"

"If God made the earth with all these plants and animals, who made Him? Who made God?" He grabbed his axe and rubbed some dried mud off its shaft.

Jake reached down and picked up an acorn. He threw it at his friend, hitting him on the forehead. "Ah ha, my friend, I got your attention that time? You know what I think?"

"What?"

"I know a lot about animals 'cause I hunt them. I think humans are too stupid to be able to understand. Many animals are smarter than us. When you die, you'll have to ask God to answer your question. Until then, you'll never know. That's what I think." He threw another acorn, but his friend ducked.

Jake liked Thor; his friendly, inquiring mind made others think. He had never met anyone like him. People in Grafton seemed so busy surviving they never took time to consider the meaning of life.

They went back to cutting trees, renewed by the rest, which gave them strength and a feeling of comradeship. Jake and Thor had become friends.

Finally Saturday night arrived. After a silent dinner, Jake and the others watched the festivities begin with a skit by lumberjacks from Maine. Six men performed a play about a logger cutting a widow maker out of the thick woods. Remembering his dream from the night with Eli in the hotel, Jake sat erect on the bench of the cookhouse table.

The actors brought several six-foot pines into the cookhouse and arranged them in Christmas tree stands like a small forest on a makeshift stage. The biggest pine hung at an angle with branches jammed into neighboring trees. One lumberjack, dressed in full gear for working outside, couldn't get the tree free. He asked a fellow logger to help but was refused.

"No t'anks. Me's got a wife and six kids at home. That tree's gonna kill someone." After much coercion, the fellow worker agreed to help when the lumberjack offered his coat as payment for work. Since the two men still couldn't fell the tree, another helped when given the actor's hat. Two more assisted when offered his trousers and boots. A fifth volunteer was given his shirt.

The six men, working together, finally toppled the pine. After it crashed to the ground, the five helpers departed, leaving the lumberjack on stage in his long underwear. A wealthy landowner, dressed in suit and tie, soon appeared and gave the axe man a sack of money. The logger went to the store and replaced all the clothing he had given away. He still had enough money for the audience to hear it jingle in the sack when shaken. At the end of the skit, the audience pounded their fists on picnic tables. They had fun even though they couldn't drink in camp. Jake realized they laughed the loudest at things that scared them the most, like the widow maker.

Singing began when the skit was over. Two men with banjos and one with a silver harmonica started a ballad. It was just like Eli said. The "Bean Song" was the best ballad of all. Major Swensen said it originated on the Manistee River in a camp owned by Louis Sand. He started it with a question, "Who feeds us beans? Who feeds us tea?"

The audience answered back, "Louie Sands and Jim McGee."

Rusty, in the back of the room, kept the ballad going. "Who thinks that meat's a luxury?"

His question got the same answer, with higher volume. "Louis Sands and Jim McGee."

A newcomer from Minnesota joined in, "We make the big trees fall kersplash, and hit the ground an awful smash."

The lumberjacks stomped their boots on the wooden floor. "Louis Sands and Jim McGee."

Two men from Detroit stood up to offer their lines at the same time. "I'm first," shouted the taller one.

"No way." The other logger crossed the room. He pulled his right arm back and punched the first man in the mouth.

Major Swensen stood in his seat, but didn't intervene. With blood in the corner of his mouth, the taller boy said, "And for the logs, who gets the cash?"

"Louie Sands and Jim McGee." The cookhouse was frenzied. Men whistled and clapped.

The Major's mustache wiggled as he led the men in singing the second stanza:

Who feeds us beans until we're blue?
Louie Sands and Jim McGee.
Who thinks that nothing else will do?
Louie Sands and Jim McGee.
Who feeds us beans three times a day?
And gives us very little pay?
Louie Sands and Jim McGee.
Who feeds us beans again I say?
Louie Sands and Jim McGee.

Major Swensen realized the men were out of control. A few threw forks and spoons across the room. He stood on top of a picnic table and yelled, "Quiet!"

Hushing sounds spread throughout the cookhouse. Major Swensen pointed at the six actors from Maine. "You easterners sing the third stanza … alone."

The six actors, with broken voices, performed to an audience too frightened to move, let alone speak.

Who gives us pay for just one drunk?
Louie Sands and Jim McGee.
When we hit the Manistee kerplunk
Louie Sands and Jim McGee.

We drink our whiskey and our ale
And sweep the town just like a gale;
Then who comes to get us out of jail?
Louie Sands and Jim McGee.

A shanty boy from Gladstone, in the Upper Peninsula, broke the silence. "Hey, now I know that song. In my town we sang it 'Bonifas and Charley Good.' Ike Bonifas came from Watersmeet and Charles Good from Nahma."

"Yeah, yeah," said the Major. "Then finish it."

The barrel-chested boy sang solo with a voice that quivered. "Who feeds us beans each blessed day? Louie Sands and Jim McGee. Who'll feed us beans on…" He froze, unable to remember the next word. His face got red.

The crowd helped him out. The men yelled, "On judgment day?" They started to clap. Major Swensen joined to encourage the nervous boy, who finished the song amidst clapping in beat to the music.

Louis Sands and Jim McGee.
And when that judgment's passed,
And we know just where we're going to be,
Who'll feed us beans through eternity?
Louis Sands and Jim McGee.

Major Swensen stood on the table again and repeated the last verse, "Who'll feed us beans through eternity*?*" He held his arms out and beckoned the group to answer.

"Louie Sands and Jim McGee." The men screamed in gruff voices. They stomped on the floor and slapped each other. The noise was so loud that logs on the side of the big cookhouse seemed to vibrate.

The song drew Jake into the group. He yelled and screamed with the others, giving him a sense of unity and belonging. The evening also made him realize that many of these men were tough. Some had done time in jail. Many had lost teeth in fights. All were rowdy individuals with strong character.

Jake woke Sunday morning at four o'clock, the regular time to rise for work, although it was a day off for most of the lumberjacks. When he wandered into the cookhouse, he realized that even the cook was off duty. Some fruits and breads had been left on the counter and there was an extra pot of tea on the wood stove. That was breakfast.

A few other early risers moved about camp. Some were doing their laundry. Others were getting ready for the church service, to be held by a visiting pastor. A few of the more adventurous men were leaving to visit saloons or friends in other camps. Most lumberjacks, though, were still in bed. Later, they would compete in contests like knife throwing, or they would play games like poker. Tobacco was the usual prize for winners in either contests or games.

Jake hoped to get his axe fixed that day because the head was too light for him. He stopped in the blacksmith shop, but only the woodworker was up that early on Sunday morning. "Come back at ten."

While waiting for the blacksmith, Jake washed out three pair of socks. He carefully draped them in the sun on a clothesline. The blue sky made everything in camp seem clean to him.

He soon returned to the blacksmith shop, now dark and foreboding, compared to the brilliant fall day. A slight man with stooped posture and a crooked jaw greeted Jake. "Can I help you with something? You'd better be quick, though. The hoss doctor is bringing over two mares that need re-shoeing. Some of us have to work on Sundays, you know."

"Yes sir, I know you're busy. I need a new head for my axe. It's too light."

The blacksmith looked at Jake and laughed. "Most men come here to get weight taken off, not added. Come outside and show me your swing."

Jake rolled a small log from a pile of firewood and placed it on top of a larger log. He swung the axe, slicing the wood into two chunks.

"I see the problem," said the blacksmith. "Come back at three. You'll have a new axe head, as well as a new handle."

Jake left just as the horse doctor appeared, holding the reins of two Belgians. Walking back to the bunkhouse, he felt leaves crunch beneath his boots. Maybe, he thought, they crumbled because of the late autumn air, much drier in the north than in Grafton. Maybe it was the pine needles, less common at home, which formed such a hard base beneath the hardwood leaves. He looked back to see if anyone was following him. Convinced that nobody was around, he jumped and rolled in the leaves.

Back at the bunkhouse, he took out his Bible and read Psalm 118. The verses seemed more real to him than ever before. The Bible made him think about his mother and home, so he wrote the following letter:

Dear Family,

I made it to camp. It's Sunday in the bunkhouse. I made a friend. His name is Thor Glick. I read my Bible today. Please give Oscar an apple for me.

Love,

Jacques (the men here call me Jake)

After sponging himself with a rag dipped in water, Jake returned to the blacksmith shop. His new axe was standing in the corner. He picked it up, went outside, and split some firewood. He swung it slowly until his muscles, tight from the cool autumn air, warmed. Yellow and red leaves glanced off his shoulder, blown there by brisk breezes. The axe head is a perfect weight, he thought. Look how the blade slices rather than splinters the wood. The handle length is an exact fit for my long reach.

It felt so good to swing his new axe that he kept it up, amazed at how the blade struck the wood exactly where he aimed. Jake removed his jacket and rolled up his sleeves while the woodpile grew in size. When he finished splitting all the nearby logs, he stopped and studied the tool in his hand. I've never had a custom axe, he thought.

Out of the corner of his eye he saw the horse doctor watching him. When he turned he noticed the blacksmith, woodworker, and four shanty boys were all staring at him.

One of the men said, "You've got quite a swing. I've never seen a man split as much firewood in such short a time."

"I'm just trying out my new axe."

"Well, well," said the blacksmith. "I think that Woodpecker from Maine may have some competition in the wood-splitting contest this winter."

"I guess so," said the horse doctor. "Look at that pile of wood. And, he's just trying out his new axe?"

Jake walked back to the bunkhouse, glad for the day off work. I'm grateful for this first week in camp, he thought.

6

Sally's Trouble

Grafton, too, celebrated autumn. Busy folks harvested crops and gathered nuts. Women were obsessed with canning and men with stacking firewood. Everyone prepared for the coming winter, forecasted to be cold and snowy.

Sally spent her time visiting the less fortunate. On one blustery day, when leaves were danced by whirlwinds, she gathered her medicines. First she stopped to see Mrs. Leeber, an elderly widow, nearly bed-ridden with tuberculosis. When Sally entered the cabin she put her hand over her nose to avoid the rancid smell of body odor, excrement, and unwashed hair.

She listened to each word, painfully spoken between coughs. "No cure…this…time. I'm ready now…ready to be…with the Lord." A coughing fit drove the widow to the floor, speckled with blotches of dried phlegm.

"Now, now." Sally spoke in a child's voice a full octave above her normal pitch. "Your cabin in heaven isn't ready yet. You'd better drink this tonic of balsam root while you wait for God to finish your new home." She helped the widow lie down in bed. Then, she took a cloth from the top of a nearby chair and dunked the rag in a washbasin. She balked because the water was gray and coated with a slimy film. She carried the basin outside and threw the filthy water into the bushes. She carried two buckets of fresh water from the spring, placed them on the counter, and refilled the washbasin. "It's time for a bath."

The widow seemed to enjoy the feel of cool water on her forehead. It had been awhile since her last bath, so it took Sally awhile to rinse the black lines from under her arms. The widow laughed when the washcloth tickled her feet. "My, my …it's been so long…since I laughed. Thank you…so much …for caring … about me."

Sally re-filled the basin once more and said goodbye.

Other visits were not as depressing or time-consuming. She stopped at the bank to give the president his fall allergy medicine. It was a quick exchange, which Sally liked. Men in suits made her feel uncomfortable. The most enjoyable stop was Lydia's room above the hardware store. Although young, she also had lost her husband. He had died in an accident on the train tracks while working for the railroad. Her baby, born last winter, was just now crawling at high speed. Sally noticed that all the furniture in the small room had been pushed to the sides of the room. She also saw a change in the new mother's physique. "My goodness, your breasts have grown so full."

Lydia shook her breasts in cupped hands and giggled. "I hope Edgar takes to solid food soon. He got another tooth last week." The two women laughed and hugged each other.

Sally left no medicine with Lydia, just some fall flowers. After lunch, she saddled her horse and rode through the woods to Lily's. It had been two months since her last visit. What an afternoon, Sally thought. It was a fine day to cheer up those in need of company. Attracted by the sound of rapids, she stopped by the river. There, she slid off her horse and lay on her back in the leaves. The sun warmed her face. The peaceful sound of water gurgling around logs and rocks caused her to drift asleep. Her nap was soon interrupted by a soft thumping noise. It took her awhile to identify the methodical beating as the clogging of horse's hooves.

Who's coming? she wondered. Lily doesn't have a horse. Maybe it's a market hunter passing by with his morning take. Probably it's just a stranger riding along the river. Sally was startled to see the rider emerge from orange and yellow leaves, riding a dainty quarter horse with tail held high. It was Dietrich.

Even in the saddle, he looked short and uncoordinated. His greasy black hair swung while the horse trotted, then stopped. "So there you are," he said. "I figured you'd be here. Are you whining about me to the old squaw?" He pounded his fist into his palm.

Feeling dizzy, Sally stood up and grabbed the reins of her horse. She mounted and spun toward the Indian's cabin. Galloping, she yelled back, "Leave me alone."

The quarter horse leaped when Dietrich's heels dug into her belly. He overtook Sally and grabbed the reins from her hands. He jumped to the ground and shoved her out of the saddle. One of her boots stuck in the stirrup until she collapsed to the ground. "No, no! Please don't hurt me!"

Dietrich tied both horses to a sapling by the trail. He removed a coiled rope from his saddle and walked toward Sally. "So, where's Jake?"

"He's at logging camp." She was so scared she couldn't get up. "You leave me alone. I'll tell the sheriff on you."

"Maybe I ought to do something then. I'll fix you this time." He threw her to the ground and dug his knee into her back. "You've never done this before, have you? Guess I'll have to show you." He stretched her arm over her head, around an elm sapling. Then he twisted the other arm around the tree. He wrapped her hands several times with the rope. Sally felt her wrists sting when Dietrich cinched the knot. "Scream all you want. We're a couple of miles from the squaw's cabin. Nobody's around. How 'bout a deal? You be nice to me and I won't hurt your father."

"What do you mean?"

"My friends could come from Kalamazoo. Some were confederate soldiers in charge of prisoners during the war and still like to torture Yankees. They're like cats playing with mice before the kill."

"What would they do to my father?"

"Isn't there hot iron where he works? Did you ever see an eyeball melt?"

Terror crossed Sally's face as he ripped open her soft canvas blouse, embroidered with flowers.

"No. Please no!" Sally struggled, trying to keep away from his hands.

Dietrich ignored her pleas. She squirmed, unable to escape his strong grip. Sally felt his hairy arm with gritty fingers reach inside her pants. She fought hard while Dietrich slid her underwear over her ankles and tossed them aside.

"No. Please no!"

Sally, now cold, felt rocks and branches dig into her buttocks when Dietrich climbed on top of her. She sighed when his arm reached down to undo his belt. "Please, Dietrich," she begged. "You promised you'd never hurt me again. You promised."

"Shut up and be still."

Sally found it too painful to fight. Her body went limp. Still, his rough thrusting made her ache. She looked at the cottonwoods above, which seemed to swirl like a carousel at the circus. "Please stop, please!" She tasted vomit in her throat.

Dietrich was belligerent, out of control, and panting with bursts of hot breath. She felt his calloused hands reach around her soft neck. The fingers got tighter and tighter. She screamed louder. "Please stop, please." Then his hands moved to her mouth and nose. He pushed hard on her face, trying to stop the yelling. Instead, she could no longer breathe. She felt the veins in her neck swell. She felt dizzy. Darkness came.

The next thing she knew, Sally awoke in the woods, naked and bruised. She tried to get up but was still tied to the tree. Is he gone, she wondered? Is he coming after me again? Oh, my back. My arms are bent and twisted. They hurt. What am I going to do?

Jake's father, who had been hunting deer nearby, crossed the river on horseback. At first Sally thought it was Dietrich returning to the area. Not again, she thought. Then she saw it was the market hunter. She watched him hold her blouse in his hand and scan the area. Then, Pierre picked up her pants and underwear. "Hello," he yelled. "Is anyone here?"

"Help. Help!" Sally's voice was barely audible above the rapids. He rushed toward the sound and found her by the riverbank, still tied to the tree. "What happened to you?"

I've got to cover myself, Sally thought as he cut the rope from her wrists. She scrambled to dress while Pierre turned his back. When she stood, her legs felt like rubber. Dizzy, she staggered and collapsed on her knees again. She struggled to stand once more. Her butt was bruised, her wrists numb, and her back ached. Slime wet the inside of her thighs. Trembling, she fought back tears. Sally's desire to protect Dietrich had vanished.

"Dietrich Krausse was here." The rest of the words stuck in her throat but eventually slid out. "He hurt me."

With the help of Pierre, Sally eased into her saddle, slumping to one side from back pain. He took the reins, one in each hand, and walked both horses to the doctor's cabin. Dr. Hollings greeted them, helped Sally off the horse, and took her inside to an examining room, which was not much bigger than a closet. Returning to the waiting room, he asked Pierre, "What happened to her?"

"I found her naked and unconscious. She said Dietrich Krausse beat her up. I think she was raped."

"I'll tend to her. Would you please fetch her father?"

Pierre jumped on his horse and spun it toward the blacksmith shop.

Dr. Hollings re-entered the examining room without looking at Sally. "Are you okay?"

Sally was silent.

"You're safe here. Can I make you more comfortable?"

It took a while for Sally to answer. She tried to speak but burst into tears.

He prompted her again. "Where do you hurt?"

Sally mumbled. The words were indistinguishable. She watched him remove a file of papers from the cabinet near the door. He reached into his shirt pocket, put on his glasses, and made some notes. Sally had seen that file many times before. She remembered when he wrote about her measles. He made notes in that file when he took out her tonsils and when she had her first period. Afraid to talk to her father, she'd run to Dr. Holling's cabin while bleeding from inside. He explained how women pass eggs each month. That was the time she missed her mother the most.

Seeing that file made her feel safe, reassured to have a listener who cared. When he finally looked at her, she noticed his eyes were filled with compassion. "I feel dirty," she said.

"I understand. You're safe now."

Suddenly, someone pounded on the door in rage. "Sally?" It was her father, accompanied by Pierre. "Sally! Are you okay?"

The doctor left the room and greeted the two men. He put his hand on the blacksmith's shoulder. "I'm sorry, Mr. Wilton. Your daughter's been hurt, maybe raped."

"Is she okay? Can I see her?"

"First, I need to examine her. With your permission, I'll start right away."

"Please do. I'll wait out here."

The doctor opened the door. "Your father's here. You can see him soon. First, we need to know how badly you were hurt. Can you undress for me? Please cover yourself with that sheet on the table?"

"Is father mad at me?"

"No, dear. He's very worried. Let's get undressed now." He left the room and shut the door to give her some privacy.

Sally took off her clothes and sat on the examining table. It felt cold. The sheet was too small to cover her and also serve as a seat. She decided it was better to be covered and have a cold bottom. Raising the edge of the sheet, she saw bruises near her groin. Dietrich lied. He said he'd never hurt me again. Dietrich forced himself inside me. This time he went too far.

Dr. Hollings re-entered the examination room and arranged the sheet like he was tucking a child into bed. "So, you feel a little dirty." He pointed at the sheet, where it draped between her legs. "Can I peek?"

"Do I have to?" She tensed when he adjusted the stirrups on the examining table.

"I'm afraid so. I promise to be gentle."

"Yes, please be easy. I hurt so much." Sally, somewhat relaxed by his professional manner, sighed. She recalled that Dr. Hollings had watched her grow up. He'd seen her naked when she first came to Grafton at thirteen, and many times afterwards.

He lowered his head beneath the stretched sheet. "You're not dirty," he said. The sheet muffled his words. "You're as clean as a whistle."

Sally was irritated that he misinterpreted her complaint. "That's not what I mean. I'm used, no longer pure."

She cocked her ear, waiting for the doctor's answer, which he seemed to choose with great care. "Lots of women aren't virgins when they get married."

"I wanted to save myself. No man will want me now." She wiped her soft brown eyes.

"You'll still find a loving husband. Not all men are like the one who did this."

Sally whimpered. "Is this a nightmare?" Tears streamed down her face. She tasted salt in the corner of her mouth.

"You did nothing wrong. Your future husband will understand what happened here today." The doctor sat on a chair near the examining table and patted her hands, still red from rope burns.

"Will I still be able to have children?"

"Oh, yes, my dear. That is not going to be a problem. Now please get dressed. I'll be back in a minute." Dr. Hollings left the examination room to tell Mr. Wilton what he'd found.

The blacksmith asked, "How is she?"

"Sally has been raped. The boy was pretty rough on her. She's got a few bruises and lacerations. Physically, she will recover. The bigger problem here may be psychological. She will need some time to deal with the shame. She may have problems if she keeps her anger inside."

Mr. Wilton scratched the hair on the back of his neck. He panted heavily and clenched his fist. "I'll kill that boy."

"Yes, I'd feel the same way if my daughter had been raped, but we've got to let the sheriff handle the details." The doctor waved the medical file in his hands. "At least we've got legal documentation that Sally was raped."

Dr. Hollings returned to see Sally still seated on the table, but now dressed. He began, "Well, young lady, you are very lucky. The boy did no permanent harm to your body. Time will heal the deep hurt you feel in your heart. You must come to realize that this was not your fault. You have to shed the guilt you feel."

She lowered her head and felt tears run down her face and drip from her chin. She could no longer hold in a sob, which soon became a full-fledged cry, and finally a wail. Sally felt the doctor's hand on her shoulder. She cried for several minutes until the tears stopped.

"How can I face people in town? They'll all know."

"Yes, everyone will know because we have to report what happened to the sheriff. You can start facing people in town by talking first to your father. I already told him you were raped. He is very sad for you, but glad you're okay."

Sally bit her lip. "You told my father?"

"Yes, dear, we all love you. We understand."

"How can I face him? What should I say?"

"Now's the time to be strong. Come back and see me whenever you want." He handed her a handkerchief and hairbrush, then left the room so she could finish dressing.

What a considerate man, she thought. He remembered that Sally loved to brush her hair. One of her fantasies was that she and her mother would someday sit together in front of a looking glass brushing each other's hair. That vision haunted her many times when growing up, but it never materialized. Now, hair brushing made her content because it symbolized her self-sufficiency. It reminded her she was able to do things for herself, despite being abandoned by her mother.

Sally opened the door on a crack and saw her father pacing in the waiting room. When he looked up, she ran and hugged him. He seemed so strong and powerful, yet comforting. "Father, I love you."

"Dr. Hollings says you'll be all right."

"Dietrich hurt me."

"Yes, I know. Let's hang that boy." Mr. Wilton repeated that several times. His words made Sally cry. She was fearful he'd hurt Dietrich and get himself in trouble.

"Now comes the hard part," said the doctor. "It's time to go to the sheriff's office and report this."

"What's so hard about that?" Sally felt angry instead of tearful. "Dietrich should pay for what he did." Her voice was strong and full of vengeance. The humiliation she showed before had disappeared, replaced with a fierce drive for retaliation.

"Let's hang that boy," Mr. Wilton said again. His ears seemed to protrude from his head more than usual. The salt and pepper hair on the back of his neck stood erect.

Even the doctor joined the fantasy. "I'll put 'natural causes' on his death certificate."

"Whoa now," said Pierre. "Let's let the law handle this." He walked behind Sally and her father toward the jail.

Sheriff Foster sat in his office finishing paperwork after the release of a prisoner. The jail, made of boards from Anderson's collapsed barn, was one of the oldest buildings in town. At first, there had been no door on the single cell, which was used mostly to hold drunks on Saturday nights. Now there were two cells, enclosed with heavy doors which were open and unlocked that day.

Dr. Hollings dropped Sally's medical record on the desk. The sheriff noted the last entry, above the signature:

> Patient has seven lacerations on back and buttocks. Both inner thighs are bruised. The hymen is freshly torn. Seminal fluid is present.

He looked up at Sally and shook his head from side to side. "Do you know the guy that did this?"

"Yes." She looked around the room, conscious that three men were present. Where's Mother now, she wondered. Oh, I wish she were here.

The sheriff seemed annoyed by her lack of attention. "Well, then. What's his name?"

"His name's Dietrich Krausse. He lied to me. He said he'd never hurt me again."

"Lying may be wrong, but it's not against the law."

"He tried to kill me. I want him arrested." She swallowed hard.

"Yes, miss. I'm sure you do." He twirled the keys to the jail cell. "Now, lots of girls tease their boyfriends. They get 'em excited." The keys bounced on the floor and rattled to a silent rest. The room was hushed. Everyone stared at the keys. "Did you do anything like that? Did you lead him on?"

Sally's father leaned over the sheriff, perched in his leather chair. "That's no way to talk to my daughter. She didn't do anything wrong."

"We need to be sure of that."

"Dietrich raped my little girl. We want him arrested."

"I'm sure you do." The reply was calm and business like.

Sally felt dizzy. Why were the men arguing so much?

Mr. Wilton grabbed the papers from the sheriff's desk and threw them across the room. "What's the matter here? My daughter's been raped!"

"A false charge could ruin the boy's life."

"What do you mean ruin the boy's life? He's tainted my daughter."

Sally moved to the corner where she leaned against the solid walls. Like a trapped animal, she squirmed, rocking back and forth. Why is everyone talking about Dietrich? Doesn't anyone care about me?

Dr. Hollings moved between the two irate men. "Sally said she bit his ear hard enough to draw blood. If you catch Dietrich now, a report noting the torn ear would make fine evidence in court."

The sheriff reached over his large stomach and picked up some of the papers. He nodded in agreement and yelled out the back door to his deputy, "Simon, go find the Krausse boy. Bring him in. The charge is assault and battery."

She felt a burning in the pit of her stomach. Assault and battery? That's what he did the last time, when I covered it up. This was worse. But, why are they arguing? I told them what happened. Doesn't the sheriff believe me?

Her father reacted the same way. "Now, hold on," he said. "Why aren't you taking this attack more seriously? Dietrich forced himself on my daughter."

"Okay. Okay. The judge will decide." He yelled out the back door again. "Charge him with the rape of Miss Sally Wilton."

Simon said, "Where do I find him?"

Foster stood up, walked toward the open door, and braced himself against the frame. He whispered to the deputy, "I'm not really sure. The last I knew, he was running with some of the troublemakers in Kalamazoo. They own a saloon. I heard rumors they hired a crooked attorney and formed a corporation."

Simon scratched his head as if he didn't believe the sheriff. "Dietrich's an officer in a corporation?"

"That's what they say in Kalamazoo County. You'd better find the saloon first. When you see Dietrich, handcuff him, and bring him here. Be official. Do everything by the book."

Yes, sir. Right away, sir." The deputy held his hat on his head and rode into the stiff breeze to find his man.

7

Dietrich's Hearing

"Train from Grafton!" yelled the conductor as the locomotive pulled into the Kalamazoo depot.

Dietrich rushed off the platform and ran, looking over his shoulder, all the way to the saloon. His greasy black hair swung while he darted through streets and alleys. After hearing that Sally had gone to the sheriff, he'd left town to seek refuge until he could organize a defense. It was Friday, the day for his weekly meeting at the saloon. He looked forward to getting advice from his friends, most of whom had been in trouble with the law and knew how to handle themselves in court. There were also some legal documents that needed his attention.

He slipped past the bar and entered a back room hidden behind a false wall. Mr. Zudman, his attorney, wearing a dark tailored suit, took Dietrich's coat and hung it on a rack by the door. The lawyer's black goatee, fringed with a thin white outline, came to a perfect point. Dietrich recalled when Billy Simon introduced him to the group after the attorney set up some illegal accounts at the bank where he worked. Now he handled all the paperwork for Dietrich's company, which bore Mr. Zudman's name.

The lawyer continued to work at Union Bank, where he embezzled funds from wealthy widows. His favorite trick was investing their money in high-risk stocks while he paid bogus interest to them on counterfeit railroad bonds. Business had been lucrative. He was a full partner in a real estate holding company, the majority stockholder in the Zudman Gold Corporation, and a board member of an investment-banking firm. Dietrich trusted him to work with the boys in the back room. He knew the attorney liked to rub shoulders with fellow criminal, even those with little education.

Dietrich smelled warm leather when he settled into the senior chair at the conference table. Relaxing for a moment, he palmed the wide armrests of his seat. The large chair made him look even shorter. He glanced at the stack of papers in front of him and stared, one at a time, at each man. How things had changed, he thought. The men used to talk business in the saloon. There the gang planned their criminal activities, shared information about cons and scams, and helped each other when they got in trouble. Now, since Mr. Charles R. Zudman, Jr. handled their affairs, weekly meetings were held in the back room, where saloon customers couldn't hear their conversations.

"Good morning, boys," Dietrich said. "I see everyone's here." The attorney had told him to use "gentlemen" instead of "boys," but he just couldn't do it.

The group answered, "Good morning."

Mr. Zudman started the discussion. "We finally arranged to buy the theater in Clayburg." He pointed at legal documents on the shiny table. "Those real estate papers need your signature. I could have signed them as your attorney, but the law requires us to first take a vote."

Dietrich looked confused. "Hold on. Dammit. Tell me again. Why should we move from Kalamazoo to Clayburg? That's way up north by Cheboygan!"

"Because there's fewer laws and city ordinances."

"The sheriff's getting onto us," added a millwright dressed in coveralls speckled with sawdust.

"That's right," said a livery worker with faded cowboy boots. "Three days ago the deputy asked me about those horses we stole."

"Any other comments?" Since nobody spoke, he continued. "All in favor of moving to Clayburg raise your right hand." The vote was unanimous. Dietrich signed the papers and asked, "Hell, that was easy. What else?"

A small man with thick lenses in tiny eyeglasses spoke next. "What do we do with the three whores upstairs?"

The men roared. Ralph, a ship-builder with a red bandana around his neck said, "Don't you know what to do with a whore?"

The man's feelings seemed hurt. He cleared his throat. "I meant, do we leave 'em here or bring the girls with us?"

A well-dressed merchant added, "Take 'em to the theater in Clayburg. Maybe they can help us move. Any muscles in their arms?"

"Just in their legs." The men laughed and whispered private jokes to each other.

"Hey," said Dietrich. "This is a business meeting, remember?"

"Shh," said the attorney, placing his finger to his lips. The sound spread as others repeated it. Voices dropped out of the conversation one at a time until there were none. The men grew silent, afraid to talk.

"What about the mill?" asked a Norwegian with hairy forearms.

The men began yelling and shouting at each other.

"Shut up!" screamed Dietrich. He rose from his chair and extended his arms, palms down. "One at a time."

He listened to his men share their views on the mill, where illegal operations generated thousands of dollars a month. His company bribed officials in key departments. A supervisor who scaled logs was paid to upgrade the quality of timber from Zudman Brothers. Mill workers who stacked lumber were slipped money to divert finished boards to secret destinations. The company even gave weekly donations to bribe one of the new directors.

When talk subsided, Dietrich sat erect in his chair. "Let's leave things alone at the mill. But, look out for the law. They're watchin' us. If you see anything funny, let me know right away."

The attorney said, "Down the road, let's consider building another mill in Clayburg, owned by us Zudman Brothers."

The men at the table agreed. Like a crowd in front of a cheerleader, they chanted, "Zudman Brothers. Zudman Brothers. Zudman Brothers."

The room was quiet again. Dietrich cleared his throat. "Boys, I've got some new business. It seems I've got a personal problem. It's that blacksmith's daughter in Grafton." He smashed his fist into his palm.

Tiny said, "The one with the boyfriend who squealed on us for the deer saddles?"

"Yeah, that's her. Sally Wilton. She came on to me. Couldn't get enough, either. Then she told the sheriff I raped her."

"Women are like that," said an older man with a beard so full it was hard to see his face. "Why can't they be honest like men? They want it just as bad as we do."

The rumble of voices returned.

"This is serious," said Dietrich. "The fat sheriff from Grafton is looking for me. Hell, his deputy may even be here in Kalamazoo."

Jack Solden, a sailor with a patch on one eye, left his chair and stood in front of Dietrich. "This talk is a waste of time. The problem is yours, not ours. You're the one in trouble because of a woman." He held his hands, fists closed, like a boxer ready to throw a punch.

Dietrich didn't stand to recognize the challenger but reached beneath the table and into his pocket. He withdrew a penknife, opened the blade, and pushed it against Jack's neck. "Sit down before I put this knife in your throat. If it weren't for us, you'd still be a drunk, a no-good panhandler. Don't forget who got you a job at the shipyard." He watched Jack retreat with cowered head and return to his seat. He thought, maybe I've been too hard on the sailor in front of his friends.

"Relax, boss," said the attorney. "I've got an idea." He pointed at Tiny. "He'll fix this for us."

The Indian asked, "Whaddya want me to do?"

"Take one of the whores with you to Grafton. Tell her to start a fist fight with the blacksmith's girl. Make sure lots of people see them argue."

"How about Sunday? In front of the church?"

"Perfect. Have the whore complain about Sally chasing the boss. Have her scream 'Stop playing around with my man!' between punches. That should take care of the jury. You'll be creating something we lawyers call reasonable doubt."

"What if the whore beats her up?"

"Oh, no. Don't let that happen. Have her throw the fight so Sally looks like the bad one."

Others at the table added their ideas. "I've got a tiny bottle of chicken blood you can use. Have the whore smear a little under her nose when nobody's looking."

"Make sure their clothes get torn."

A commercial fisherman who smelled like sour fillets said, "Well, now … I'll tell ya. Take Linda. She's young and fresh, the sweetest looking of the whores."

"I'll do it," said Tiny. He was excited.

Dietrich rose from his chair, relieved and full of enthusiasm. "Thank you, Mr. Zudman. Good idea." He smashed his fist into his palm. "Of course these plans are secret. Anyone who talks is dead. Right?"

There was resounding support. Together, the men said, "Right!"

"Meeting adjourned!" hollered the boss. He shook each man's hand as they left the back room, appreciative of their loyalty.

The last to leave was Mr. Zudman, who held Dietrich's coat open, waiting for his hands to enter the armholes. "Boss, there's just one more thing."

"What's that?" Dietrich felt annoyed. This attorney is too manipulative. I'm the boss, not him.

"Well, ah …"

Something must be wrong, thought Dietrich. Mr. Zudman is never at a loss for words. "Spit it out."

"Well, I think you should turn yourself in. It will make you look good, like you did nothing wrong." The lawyer opened the saloon door, exposing Dietrich to bright sunlight that hurt his eyes.

"Let me sleep on that one. By the way, you did a good job today." He slapped the attorney on the back and stepped on the busy sidewalk. The men went separate ways and vanished into the crowds.

At ten o'clock on Monday morning, Dietrich walked into the Grafton jail. His new pants fit well and matched the dress shirt he rarely wore. His black hair was neatly trimmed and combed so it didn't swirl when he walked. "Good morning, sheriff. I hear you're looking for me."

Peering over his glasses, the lawman sat at a tiny desk, too low for a man of his size. He didn't seem to recognize Dietrich at first, perhaps because he was so well dressed. Foster stood and reached behind his back, checking to see if his handcuffs were still on his belt. "Yes, I sent a deputy to find you. A complaint was signed against you by Sally Wilton."

"A complaint?" Dietrich threw his hands in the air. "She never said nothing to me."

"Well, she told me you roughed her up, forced yourself on her."

"My goodness, she's my girl. Of course, I get romantic at times."

Foster took off his glasses and pointed his finger at Dietrich. "Son, Miss Wilton said you made her have relations against her will."

"Oh, come on." He smirked. "She wanted it bad."

"Hmm. It looks like we've got us a problem." He threw his keys on the floor. They landed in almost the same spot as they did when Sally came to his office.

Dietrich walked around the small, clean office. He stopped near a small northern pike, mounted on a walnut board above the sheriff's desk. "Did ya ever think about moving to a bigger town? With a better office? A larger salary?"

Foster ignored the question. "To top it off, there was a cat fight between two women in town yesterday. A well-dressed lady from Kalamazoo got in an argument with Sally after church. They even slugged each other with closed fists."

Dietrich said, "Women don't fight much. When they do, one of 'em usually gets beat up."

The sheriff agreed. "You're right. Sally hurt the lady. There was blood all over her cute little face. The poor thing."

Dietrich was happy that Mr. Zudman's plan had worked. He said, "Sally hates my girl in Kalamazoo. It's pure jealousy."

"Probably, but I was surprised. I'd never seen that side of her. She'd always seemed so sweet and gentle." The tone in his voice turned the sheriff's statement into a question.

Dietrich knew his facial expressions were being studied to see if he was telling the truth. "Some of this is my fault for going out with two girls at once."

"Maybe, but I'm in a tough spot now. The blacksmith and doctor are important men in Grafton." He stood and walked toward the mount on the wall. "I caught him on the river a few years ago while reeling in a nice rock bass. The pike crossed the current to take the fish. He was small, but he put up a good fight."

Dietrich followed and walked to the mount. He, too, changed the subject. "Did I tell you we're building a new mill over at Clayburg? Lots of people will be moving there. We're gonna need a good marshal."

"Hmm, you don't say. Clayburg, huh? I hear there's pretty good fishing up north."

"I've got a proposal for you. How about locking me up for a few days. You'd be a real hero in town."

"Why would you want to make me look good?"

"Oh, it would help me, too. Let's settle this ourselves. Just between us."

"You know, I think you're right. Everyone would say I'm doing a good job."

"Yeah, and people would know I didn't do nothing wrong. Shucks, I even turned myself in."

"Hmm. So be it." Dietrich felt the sheriff's firm hand lead him into the larger cell. He was so much shorter than the lawman. The door slammed shut with a thud.

"By the way," continued the sheriff. "I never thanked you for the venison or the fine horse you gave me. Thanks."

"Now, ain't that funny. I don't know anything about venison or a horse. My men musta' donated those gifts on their own."

The sheriff smiled as if he'd been told a secret.

The next morning Dietrich saw Mr. Wilton burst into the jail, followed by the doctor. "We heard you got him."

"Yup. He gave himself up."

"Did he admit raping Sally?"

"He said he had relations with her, but she was willing. Dietrich said she was eager. These rape cases are tough."

The blacksmith walked to the cell and peered through the bars. "That's what he says, huh? Let's take care of this boy right now. We don't need much of a noose for that skinny neck."

The sheriff spoke on Dietrich's behalf. "Easy, now. The law says he's innocent until proven guilty. All we've got right now is Sally's word against his."

"Ha," said Sally's father. "The question is whether we peel off his skin before or after we hang him."

"Here's what we'll do," said the sheriff. "The traveling judge will be here on Wednesday. We'll have a hearing at three. Doc, I'll subpoena you as an expert witness. Mr. Wilton, you'd better have Sally here at quarter to three."

"We'll be ready." The blacksmith looked toward Dietrich. "We're gonna fix you good for what you did to my daughter. If the judge doesn't hang you, I will."

Dietrich couldn't hold his tongue this time. "Sally's quite a filly, but I'd hate to have you for a father-in-law. You son-of-a-bitch."

The blacksmith reached past the bars into the jail cell. "That's it." He grabbed for Dietrich's throat but missed. Frustrated, he rattled the door of the cell. "Wait 'til I get my hands on you."

The sheriff secured Mr. Wilton's flailing arms and escorted him out of the building. With a hand on his holstered gun, he waited for the blacksmith to leave. Several townspeople who heard yelling at the jail persuaded Mr. Wilton to go home.

Dietrich watched the sheriff return, move a table within reach through the bars of his cell, and pass out four cards: two for him and two for the dealer. On his side of the table, he saw an eight of spades covering a card that was turned over. The sheriff had a queen of clubs and an unexposed card.

Dietrich peeked at his concealed card and saw it was a seven of clubs. Seven plus eight is fifteen. "Hit me."

The sheriff laughed. "Are you sure? Won't it hurt?"

"Yeah, but hit me anyway." Dietrich laughed back.

Foster turned up a six of diamonds.

Dietrich yelled, "Twenty One!"

The sheriff then flipped up his own concealed card: a ten of clubs. He drew an eight of hearts. "Shucks. I'm over."

"I won."

"Yes, you win. Now, that wasn't too bad, was it?"

He went to his desk drawer, returning with two cigars and a bottle of scotch. Drinking from the same bottle, they played cards and smoked cigars until midnight.

There was no courthouse in the village of Grafton, so the hearing was held at the town hall. The large, hollow room seemed cold to Sally, even though the sheriff had started a fire in the wood stove by the back alcove. She remembered being at meetings in the hall when she was a little girl. Now here she was, in that same building, charging a childhood friend with rape. Holding the hearing in the town hall bothered her. It made the attack too public. Sally was uncomfortable because she knew the people seated behind her. When they whispered to each other, she felt guilty. That's stupid, she said to herself. Dietrich's the one who did something wrong, not me. Still, she felt nervous and uneasy.

The judge, draped in a black robe, entered the wooden room with oak chairs, perfectly arranged in rows on a varnished floor.

"All rise!" the bailiff bellowed. "Judge Harry Pickett will now consider the City of Grafton versus Dietrich Krausse." He rattled some legal documents and marched to a long table in the front of the hall where the judge now sat. "This is a hearing of discovery for Case Thirty-Seven of 1872." He stood at attention and placed his papers on the makeshift desk.

The judge nodded, waved the clerk away, and pointed at Sally. "Come up here, little darlin'. Put your hand on the book."

Sally weaved through whispering neighbors to a side table and put her hand over gold letters on a thick Bible, hearing only the last words, "nothing but the truth, so help me God."

She said, "I do."

"Now, tell us what happened in your own words. Take all the time you need, sweetheart."

After straightening the ruffles on her best Sunday dress, she licked her lips, like Dr. Hollings had recommended. All night, between restless bouts of sleep, she'd practiced a sentence the doctor told her to memorize. She also recalled the rest of his instructions to start softly, speak slowly, get louder with each word, and pause. When composed, she said, "Dietrich Krausse threw me on the ground … tied me to a tree… and raped me." She turned around and faced the audience, making eye contact with everyone in the room at least once, just like the doctor suggested.

The judge said, "Well then, can I ask you a few questions?"

She nodded.

He removed his glasses. "Please tell me the time, place, and date of the alleged attack."

"Why, it was October 19, 1872 at two-thirty in the afternoon. He pulled me off my horse down by the river, just before Chestnut Ridgc." She fought to keep her knees from wobbling.

"Did you ever say 'no' or 'stop' to Dietrich?"

"Many times, your honor. He told me to shut up and be still." She wiped a tear from her eyes.

Judge Pickett said, "Thank you, darlin'. You're dismissed." He motioned Dietrich to come forward.

Sally watched her assailant strut to the front of the room. What an actor, she thought, as he straightened his tie, primping before the audience. His black hair was neatly combed. His suit was well tailored and without a speck of dirt. He sipped water from a tall green glass on the table before being sworn in.

"What's your side of the story, son? Remember you're under oath."

"Your honor, I apologize to Sally, her family, and to the court. I lost control of my urges. I couldn't stop myself and I sure couldn't stop her." He smiled at the audience.

Sally fidgeted when Dietrich explained how their passion grew. She listened to his cold, calculating lies that she nibbled his ear, undid his belt, and unbuttoned his pants. She felt betrayed when others in the hall whispered and snickered while the judge took notes.

"Thank you, son. Please return to your seat."

Dr. Hollings was called next. He said, "Miss Wilton was brought to my office immediately after her attack.

With permission from her father, I examined her and found clear evidence of rape. I found semen."

"You found evidence of intercourse, but how do you know it was rape," said the judge.

"The intercourse was violent enough to leave bruises."

"Thank you for your expert testimony. This court is recessed for ten minutes while I go outside and consider this matter in private."

After the audience rose and then sat down upon his entrance, the judge said, "We know this couple had relations. However, we don't know if force was involved. All we have is one person's word against another. Sally said she resisted, but Dietrich said he was seduced. There's no concrete evidence either way in this case. Therefore, all charges against Mr. Krausse are hereby dropped. File thirty-seven is closed."

The blacksmith stood and asked permission to speak. "This man raped my daughter. Why are you setting him free? Where's the justice here?"

The judge pointed his finger at Sally's father. "I decide the law for this district, not you. I say there's no evidence to support criminal charges. Period."

The doctor joined his friend in objecting. "What about the bruises?"

"Maybe the young lady got excited." The judge smiled. "Case thirty eight, please."

The blacksmith took his daughter's hand and stomped off. Sally felt nauseous, just like she did during the rape. Humiliated, she wondered how this happened. How could Dietrich get away with this?

People left the town hall still arguing the case. Most of them had changed their minds during the hearing. The railroad clerk seemed to capture the attitude of many in saying, "At first, I thought Sally was raped. We've all seen that boy's anger before. But as the hearing went on, Dietrich's story made more sense."

The schoolteacher, who always carried a book, said, "Maybe his anger all these years came from being teased. Sally turned Jake and Dietrich against each other many times. You've all seen that."

"Dietrich was so polite," added a young woman with a large bonnet. "That poor boy apologized in front of the whole village. His only fault was being a healthy young man with normal drives."

"Boys will be boys," said Mr. Rice, owner of the general store.

Even the minister believed Dietrich. "Now I understand that nasty fight at church. Sally's got a mean streak."

Dr. Hollings disagreed. "Naw. Dietrich raped her. I wish we'd had a different judge."

"The issue isn't the judge," replied Mr. Renquist. "It's the lack of evidence. There's no proof the affair was forced."

Mrs. Rice said, "What do you expect when a young man and young woman are allowed to be alone in the woods? Why didn't the blacksmith keep an eye on that girl? No wonder his wife left him. He's irresponsible."

Dietrich left the town hall through the side door to avoid confrontation with Sally or her father. So had the sheriff, who stood outside puffing on a cigar. "Care for a smoke?"

"Nope. Gotta go." He kept walking. "Maybe another time. Good thing you're friends with the judge."

"Old friends." Sheriff Foster followed Dietrich while he walked. "Were you serious about my coming to Clayburg?"

"Sure." Dietrich scowled and walked faster. "See Mr. Zudman at my saloon in Kalamazoo. Be there at noon tomorrow. Oh, yeah. Add two dollars a week to your salary. Just don't forget who you're working for." He smashed his fist into his palm. "If you do, you'll be sorry."

"Yes, boss. Did you know Judge Pickett is looking for some land north of town?"

"No, I didn't." He spoke without turning around.

"I heard he's looking to buy two eighties of government land on either side of his place."

"Let's see," said Dietrich. "Two times eighty is one hundred and sixty acres. At a dollar and twenty-five cents an acre, that's two hundred bucks. Maybe we can help him out."

The sheriff, with a wobbling layer of blubber around his waist, had trouble walking as fast as Dietrich. "Hmm," he said. "He might also like some votes from your associates."

"Maybe. We'll see." Dietrich entered the livery without saying goodbye to the sheriff. At last, we have a lawman on our payroll, he thought. Clayburg will be a damn nice town. It will be my town.

8

Sally's Move to Bay City

After the hearing, people acted differently toward Sally. Villagers stared, pointed, and whispered behind her back.

Mrs. Stankey insulted her at the store. She approached Sally and said, "You should know better than tease a nice boy like Dietrich. At least the judge knew he was innocent and let him go. Maybe you got what you deserved."

Sue Crutch, who always took first prize for making strawberry preserve, criticized her at a Thanksgiving school play. She stood up and said, "Well, look who came to see the Pilgrims. It's Sally Wilton, the girl who cried wolf. She leads boys on and tells the sheriff."

Sally was no longer invited to Wednesday prayer meeting or to social teas with other ladies. Church members who used to be friends moved to a different pew when she took her regular seat in church. Neighbors crossed downtown streets to avoid speaking with her.

She went to visit her customers, hoping that would make her feel better. Sally first stopped to talk with Lydia. The new mother opened the door and said, "You look worn out. Are you okay?"

"I feel terrible. Nobody wants me around." Sally took a bundle of flowers from her basket and offered them to Lydia, who pushed the bouquet aside.

"I'm sorry you have problems." The young widow stepped into the street, forcing Sally to move away.

"People are making me feel like I did something wrong. Don't they understand?" She felt dizzy and put her hand to her forehead. "Can we talk about this inside?"

"Not today. The baby needs me now." Sylvia wheeled around and slammed the door.

Discouraged, Sally went home and cried. Everyone, even Lydia, is turning against me. How did this happen?

When I was a little girl, everyone liked me. Now they all hate me. Maybe I should leave Grafton and start over somewhere else. Nobody would know me in a different town.

The idea of running away made her feel guilty. What about Father? Who'll look after him? What if he gets sick again?

Wait a minute, she thought. He chose this life. I've got to get out of here. He'll understand.

Sally packed a few clothes and placed them in a worn trunk she found in the attic. There was just enough room on top of her clothes for the favorite doll that always sat on her bed.

She went to the bank and withdrew sixty-five dollars from her herb account. "Gotta get some new things for our place," she said to the teller. "We've had the same drapes forever. I'm tired of patching old sheets and towels. But, don't tell Father. I'm going to surprise him."

The same lie worked well at the general store, where she announced, "I'm gonna buy some new linens in Kalamazoo to surprise Father. Can someone take me to the train station?"

Mr. Rice whispered, "Sure, I'd be happy to take you." Sally had the feeling the store owner didn't want anyone to know he was helping her.

"Thanks. I'm bringing an old trunk. That way, things won't get sooty on the way home. Can we leave soon? I'd like to catch the ten o'clock train."

At the depot, Sally bought a round trip ticket to Kalamazoo. Once there, she planned to catch another train to Bay City. She'd heard about that part of Michigan from Reverend Hughes, who frequently mentioned the picturesque city on the shores of Lake Huron. He said there were plenty of jobs in the area because of numerous lumber mills, a ship building company, and several factories. It was a boomtown.

Sally's first train ride was nothing like Jake's. She took the front seat in the lead car so nobody could see her cry. She didn't notice much about the train or the surroundings.

She had no interest in watching the landscape change outside the window. Instead, she sobbed.

Gaslights at the station startled Sally when the train pulled into Bay City. The depot for the Michigan Central was a small wooden building at the foot of Washington Avenue. A porter took her trunk from the baggage car while she waited alone beside the tracks. "Which hotel, Miss?"

She felt relaxed by his gentle voice. "The nearest one with hot baths."

"That'd be the Campbell House, Miss. Three others are waiting for a ride there, too." He hoisted the trunk on a dolly and loaded it on a carriage made of lacquered wood enclosed by swirling brass. "Have a nice stay in town, Miss."

"I will." She gave the porter a shiny dime.

The Campbell House was a grand hotel at the busy corner of Water and Third Streets. As Sally was helped from the carriage, she looked up at the three-story brick building that comprised a full city block near the Third Street Bridge. She registered and unpacked before exploring the hotel shops. Saloons full of factory workers and sailors on the first floor fascinated her. She kept walking past them, staring at the noisy patrons inside. Look at all the people having fun, she thought. This is so different than Grafton.

After a restful sleep, Sally enjoyed a full breakfast at the hotel café and then strolled down several city streets. She looked at dozens of employment notices tacked on storefronts but couldn't read the words. She entered a restaurant with three different posters taped in the window, hoping there might be at least one job for a waitress.

"Can I help you?" asked the hostess, who wore a navy blue uniform with white collar and cuffs.

Sally stammered. She felt so dizzy that she asked for a table and ordered a second breakfast. When her food arrived, she inquired, "What's it like to work here?"

The dimpled girl, Sylvia, replied, "Like any other place in this city. Tips are good if you wiggle for the men—when their wives aren't looking. Want to see the boss?"

Before long she had regular hours at the restaurant and a room at the boarding house where Sylvia lived. She was glad neither of them talked about her past. That was fine. She wanted to forget her past as soon as possible. She found it easy to suppress bad memories. Whenever she thought of people in Grafton, she envisioned their mean faces and harsh words. Their shunning gestures created the most lasting visions. It was only in quiet moments that she thought of Father, recalling childhood memories of bouncing on his knee and riding high above crowds on his shoulders. As the weeks went by, there were fewer memories each day. The busier she became, the less she was haunted by guilt. The past soon evaporated from her mind like dewdrops melting one by one in the morning sun.

Every week Sally went to the bank and withdrew money. She had few staples such as sugar or salt. Only six dollars and fifty-two cents was left in her bank account at the beginning of November. She was low on groceries, needed to buy warm clothes for the coming winter, and had only half the rent due on December first.

Sally wondered about what to do. Should I send a telegram to Father asking for money? Maybe I should go home before the snow arrives? What if I ask the boss for an advance on my wages?

She became preoccupied with money while working, eating, and sleeping. It bothered her to watch wealthy people come to the restaurant. She felt jealous of their carriages, clothes, and carefree attitudes. When she thought about money, she felt a burning sensation, like a piece of hot metal, in the pit of her stomach.

Her stomach hurt so much one night she wanted to see a doctor but didn't have the money. That's when she first considered selling her grandmother's ring. The diamond ring was special to everyone in the family because the stately woman never took the ring off her finger during fifty years of marriage. On the day of her death a heated debate took place among heirs whether to bury her with the ring or pass it down to a family member. Sally received the ring, probably because she hadn't taken sides in the argument.

She took the ring from a dresser drawer and placed it under her pillow, where she prayed for several hours. The next day, Sally took the heirloom to a jewelry shop and sold it for eighty-five dollars. She bought some firewood, blankets, and other necessities for the coming winter. The money seemed to melt away. Soon it was gone.

I wish I still had the ring, she thought. Grandmother's always been with me. She's watched me from heaven. I'm sure she saw me sell the ring. Oh, if I could only have it back.

Sally felt her neck get sore when she turned her head from side to side. She noticed she was clenching her teeth. When she ran her tongue along the inside of her mouth, she detected several raw spots where she had bitten the skin. All of this happened because of Dietrich, she thought. I wouldn't be here, broke in this filthy city, if it hadn't been for him. I'd still have Grandmother's ring. Someday, I'll get back at that evil man.

Sally closed her eyes and imagined her hands wrapped around Dietrich's greasy hair. She saw herself submerge his head in the river several times. He vomited into the water and then stopped breathing. Her neck was no longer sore. She no longer clenched her teeth or bit the inside of her lip. Her uncontrollable urge for revenge had been relieved.

Her guilt about selling the ring wasn't strong enough to prevent her from hocking other belongings to pay past bills. She sold a bracelet, hair comb, and one of her better dresses. Now she had nothing left to sell and still not enough money to pay the December rent.

Sally shared her problem with Sylvia one evening on their way home from work. "Can I ask you a personal question?"

"Sure." She recognized her friend was in trouble. "What's the matter?"

"Well, I don't know how to say this." She took a deep breath. "Things in Bay City are so expensive, compared to Grafton." She wiped her forehead with the back of her hand. "I never have enough money to pay all the bills."

"Oh, that's all? Let me tell you. When I came to town, I had the same problem. It's hard for women, like us, who live alone. Everyone else has a man to bring money home. Not us, we have to earn it on our own."

"So you had money problems, too? What'd you do?"

"I got a second job, just Friday and Saturday nights. I don't talk about it. I'm not proud of it. But, I pay all my bills. Want to come along sometime?"

"Okay." Sally felt better. It was nice to talk with someone who understood.

The two women went to a saloon on North Water Street. Hot air, carrying the odor of smoke, booze, and perfume greeted them at the door.

"Hey Sylvia, who's your pretty friend?" asked a sailor at the bar.

"A girl from the restaurant. She needs a little cash."

"Then she came to the right place."

Sally watched her friend move around the bar, whispering to the men. Sylvia tickled one of them under the chin and pinched another's ear. None of them paid much attention. They were all staring at Sally. She felt embarrassed at first but then the dizziness vanished. Men find me attractive, she thought. She spun around slowly in front of the men to show off her figure and then curtsied.

The bartender took the bait. "We'd love to have you work here, Miss. Pay's two dollars for Friday night. Three for Saturday night. You keep half your tips. You'll have to work a full shift, though. No leavin' early. If you entertain customers, do that on your own time after work. That's your business, not mine."

"How much can I earn in tips?"

The laughter of men in the saloon was so loud it made her jump. Everyone listened to the bartender's answer.

"That depends on how good you are. Sylvia can tell you more about that."

"Okay, I'll take the job. Can you teach me how to serve drinks?"

"I sure will. How 'bout starting right now." He handed her a pink apron. "Think you can undo one or two of those top buttons on your blouse? You'll get more tips that way."

It didn't take long for her to learn to talk the way men liked. She enjoyed the attention and liked the excitement of saloon life on weekends. She also made friends with other barmaids. Even with the extra money from her second job, Sally didn't earn enough to pay her expenses. When she asked the other bar maids how they afforded to live alone, most just smiled and told her things would work out.

Sylvia finally told her, on the way home from work, how most of the girls made ends meet. "Gentlemen at the saloon will tip you better if you spend time with them after work."

Sally asked, "Why would men pay me to serve them drinks after work?"

"They expect a little more than that, my dear." She explained the other side of getting tips.

Sally was disgusted by details on ways to satisfy men. "How could you possibly do *that?"*

"Why not? To make money, you've got to give customers what they want. Surely, you know what these men want. Besides, what's wrong with having money?"

"Don't the men hurt you?"

"Of course not. They take good care of their women. Most come back to be with girls they know and trust. In fact, one of my regulars is coming for a visit tomorrow. Would you like to meet him? He's a big tipper."

"Maybe. Can I just talk with him? I don't want to do anything. Just talk."

"Okay, I'll introduce you right before closing. You'd better talk in his hotel room. Don't ever bring men to your own room."

Sally kept watching the door while working Saturday night. Only three newcomers had entered the saloon—a mousy man with wiry hair along with two sailors who staggered so much they were asked to leave. Just before closing, she saw a man wearing a well-tailored suit burst through the door. He held a silver-tipped cane, which seemed more like an actor's prop than a necessity for the broad-shouldered man with firm gait. She watched several regulars nod toward him while he slipped along the rear wall to the table where Sylvia waited. Sally was intrigued by the way her friend and the man interacted, like brother and sister.

Soon Sylvia signaled her to join them and said, "This is the girl I told you about. Her name's Sally. She works here with me on Friday and Saturday nights. We work together at the restaurant, too."

Sally inhaled a heavy aroma of cologne surrounding the newcomer. "Nice to meet you," she said.

"Hi. I'm Ralph." He spoke precisely, with authority and distinction. "Please join me. Sylvia will get us something to drink. What would you like?"

"Brandy would be fine, thank you." She was fascinated with the eagle carved on top of his cane. He appeared to be both powerful and gentle. He seemed like the kind of man that she needed—someone to take care of her, help pay the bills, and make her feel wanted. Still, she realized he was a man. Will I ever be able to get close to another man after what Dietrich did to me?

Sylvia returned with their drinks just after last call. "It's closing time. I've got a big day tomorrow. Is it okay if I say good night?" She winked when Ralph wasn't looking.

"You do look tired," Sally said. "Go home and get some rest. We'll be fine."

After Sylvia left, Ralph talked non-stop about his travels in Europe. In turn, she told him about Lily and the herb business. She appreciated the way he treated her. He seemed to care about her feelings. Thinking about the contrast between him and Dietrich Krausse helped her relax.

Her fear about getting close to another man seemed to vanish as their conversation continued.

Sally's heart pounded as he put his hand on her arm and asked, "How'd you like to continue this discussion in my hotel room? It's more comfortable. Besides, I fear we'll soon be asked to leave."

"Okay, Ralph, I'd like to talk more, too."

They left the saloon and walked into the lobby of the Fraser House, where she sat in an upholstered chair surrounded by ornate furniture and fixtures that dazzled her eyes. She watched Ralph talk to the clerk at the registration desk. A chubby black man then escorted them upstairs and opened the door to a room. He ushered them in and stood, smiling, by the dresser. The lawyer gave him a quarter for his service.

Sally scanned the stately suite with a drawing room covered in red wallpaper. Delicately carved chairs were arranged on a Persian rug. She thought they looked much too fragile to support a person of average build. Beneath a chandelier with dangling crystals was a velvet love seat, placed purposely to center one's attention. She sat in the left corner, leaving a wide area for Ralph.

"Come dear, give me your shoes." He knelt and replaced them with slippers furnished by the Fraser House.

"Ah," said Sally. "These are so comfortable. And you're very thoughtful."

He sat next to her and talked about a show he'd seen at the Opera House earlier in the week. "Something about Uncle Tom's Cabin justifies all the sacrifices of the Civil War. Perhaps it reminds us that the real issue was not state's rights but human rights." Each time he spoke, he slid closer to Sally until their bodies touched.

Now she paid more attention to his presence than words. "I love the smell of your cologne," she said.

He lowered his head, inch by inch, until it rested on her shoulder. She felt a kiss on her neck. It felt soft and delicate.

At first Sally resisted his advances. He backed off and did not persist, which she appreciated. Without being forced to follow the lead of a man, she could set the pace of their touching. She felt confident again, at least with this man. But she also realized she was no longer pure. Dietrich had shattered her dream about being a virgin for a future husband. So, she thought, I might as well enjoy the moment. Everything feels right. He's attentive and oh, so gentle.

Sally slid down in the love seat and relaxed. She felt his hand reach beneath her blouse. They caressed each other with soft, delicate touches until their passion built. Later, he guided her to the bedroom, where they had sex twice. She enjoyed his power, like that of a stallion, but also appreciated his patience. He was slow and deliberate.

Ralph left in the morning before Sally awoke. When she opened her eyes, all she saw was a rumpled pillow with a lingering scent of cologne. She dressed and collected her belongings. Just as she started to leave the room, she saw a two-and-a-half dollar gold piece on the dresser. Sally first considered leaving the money, as if that would erase what had happened. Instead, she took the coin, looking over her shoulder as she walked out of the hotel.

Sally continued to entertain saloon patrons after hours but was careful to avoid those who appeared angry. Sylvia gave her tips on how to fend off men who might be dangerous. She soon had enough money to pay her bills. Many of her customers returned on a regular basis, which gave her a sense of security and familiarity. Most men paid her two dollars. She made enough money to rent a tiny crib, not much larger than the straw mattress it contained. Like neighboring cribs, designed in rows beneath the basement of the saloon, it had quick access to and from Third Street. She had over a hundred dollars in the bank within a few months. Her money problems were over.

Sammy Renkowski, one of Sally's favorite customers, had just been hired as an unskilled laborer at a sawmill. He was a young man in his early twenties whose family came to the Saginaw Valley from Poland. Like many of the men who worked at the mill seventy-two hours a week, he drank heavily and enjoyed easy women. Sally charged him only fifty cents a visit, far less than the normal two dollars.

She liked his build as well as his simple ways. Sammy had dark brown hair, always clean, that curled behind his ears. His jaw was square, like many Polish men, which seemed to match his thick neck and broad shoulders. His upper arms and back seemed to move together, despite pronounced muscles. Even when it was hot, there was a sweet, pleasant odor to Sammy's skin. It was the kind of smell a woman could discretely sniff.

After the saloon closed one Saturday night, they talked in her crib. Sammy said, "Don't ya know. What comes. In spreeng?"

"No. This'll be my first spring in Bay City."

"Shanty boys. They've been to logging camp. All long in winter. You, then. Won't see me. Too busy you'll be." He pulled his pants up while lying on the mattress.

She also dressed. "Things are good for me. I don't want to get any busier."

"For you, yes. For others, no. Times are tough. Strike at mill. Everyone got fired. Boss hired all new men. Like me. From Poland. That's how I got job."

She listened as Sammy explained how the owner, Mr. Sidney B. Rutherford III, saw the strike as a threat to all lumbermen, especially absentee owners. Many timber barons lived back east, like he did, and visited their mills four or five times a year. They took finished boards from Bay City and sold them in eastern lumberyards. Sammy told her that the rich owners didn't care about laborers at the mill who earned just over a dollar a day for twelve-hour shifts. When the workers went on strike, Mr. Rutherford fired them. Since they were no longer mill employees, their bills at the company store were due at once. Many were evicted for failure to pay rent in company-owned boarding houses, infested with rats and insects. Sammy told her that Mr. Rutherford then hired Polish men because they were willing to work for low wages. He said that even Mr. Henry W. Sage, who owned the large sawmill in Wenona, across the river form Bay City, was beginning to hire Polish immigrants.

As a result, Sammy explained to her, workmen were mad at wealthy timber owners and there were numerous fights between laid-off workers and Poles. Sally began to understand why business at the restaurant and saloon had slowed.

"Bay City. Will be better in spreeng. It needs money from shanty boys. They drink and whore. After camp in the north woods. Some home to go. Others stay. Work in sawmills all summer too long. Just wait. You'll see."

Sally didn't like the idea of entertaining drunken lumberjacks on binges. She liked regular customers who made her feel safe and secure. "Maybe spring is a good time to visit Father."

Suddenly, she realized she'd crossed the line. Sylvia had said to never discuss her personal life with customers. She finished dressing and took a silver fifty-cent piece handed to her by Sammy. "Well, I'd better go home. Tomorrow's communion at church. I go to the Old Hen. That's the Presbyterian Church on Washington Avenue."

She noted faint light of dawn in the east as they stepped from her crib into the street. Sally locked the door and said goodbye to Sammy without a kiss. She knew waiter girls never kissed a customer.

Sally didn't have to accept every offer to entertain men because she had income from other jobs at the restaurant and saloon. Her experience with Dietrich taught her some customers might be dangerous. Sylvia had given her pointers about how to predict men's behavior and how to negotiate fees. She made only one mistake in early May, when she was outsmarted by a shanty boy from Grand Rapids. He sat alone at a back table, which was usually the sign of a shy person. Sally noticed he used "please" and "thank you" when he spoke. She thought he would be a compliant customer with good temperament.

He seemed pleasant when served drinks and asked, "What time do you get off work?"

"One more hour."

"What's the tip if we leave together?"

She tried for the maximum fee. "Five dollars, but no overnight."

"See you in an hour." He winked.

Back at the crib, the lumberjack seemed affectionate until she undressed. Without warning, he stuck two fingers in his mouth and whistled. The locked door burst open, splintering wood by the jam. Nude and helpless, she felt a gag stuffed in her mouth.

The dirtiest one waved a knife at her and said, "Do all four of us ... the way we want ... or I'll split you wide open."

The waiter girl in the crib next door heard the commotion and entered the room with her half-dressed customer, armed with a pistol. He fired a shot and hit the knife-wielding man in the shoulder. The four men fled, leaving a trail of blood from the mattress to the door and out into the street.

Sally screamed. She felt warm blood on her neck that had been splattered from the wounded assailant. Touching the hole in the wall left by a bullet, she yelled, "Run! Run!" The words, like the scream, seemed to come from someone else.

Sally grabbed her clothes, dressed quickly, and led the way into a complex maze of tunnels beneath the building. She'd used the escape route before and knew how the hallways connected to dank caverns. The brick corridors beneath the buildings served not only as a hiding place during raids, but also as an entry to saloons for respectable gentlemen who didn't want to be seen on the streets above. While walking through the catacombs, she noticed some of the poorer whores without cribs being fondled in dark corners.

The three huddled together in the shadows for nearly an hour. Hearing no police, they moved to a smaller cavern and then into the street. Sally returned to her crib, where she washed puddles of blood off the floor. Nothing was left at the scene other than her memories of men like Dietrich.

One day after the church service, Sally went home and fried a trout she'd purchased from a French Canadian fisherman.

Someone banged on the door. "Miss Wilton?"

She moved the drape just enough to peer outside and caught the glimpse of a policeman's uniform. Oh, no, she thought, it must be about the shooting. She straightened her dress and tried to recall distinguishing features of the four assailants.

"Police. Open up."

Sally opened the door. "Can I help you?"

"Are you Miss Sally Wilton?"

"Yes, sir. That's me. What do you want?"

The officer smirked. "Miss Wilton, you're under arrest for prostitution within the city limits. Come with me."

She felt her arms pulled behind her back and her wrists pinched by cold metal handcuffs. "But I haven't done anything wrong." Sally was shocked. She'd heard about waiter girls being arrested before, but at home on Sunday afternoon? "What about my fish dinner? Can I take a change of clothes with me?"

"The city will be buying your meals for a while. They'll give you clothes, too. You whores always look so pretty in stripes." The policeman shoved her out the door and closed it behind them.

Sally was lodged in the new jail overlooking Battery Park. She was glad female inmates were housed on the third floor just above the sheriff's residence. Still, it was hard for her to sleep because the cell had no mattress or pillow, just a cold cement bench for a bed. The damp blanket she pulled over her head smelled like cucumbers. All night she heard women sobbing in nearby cells. A guard walked by every hour and dragged a metal rod across the bars to arouse and account for every inmate.

In the darkness of her cell, she thought of Dietrich. All of this is happening because of that evil man. She tried to stop her neck from tightening by rubbing it, but could not control the spasm. She put her thumb between her teeth but was unable to stop her jaw from clamping shut. This time she saw Dietrich hanging by his neck with a frayed noose twisting his head to one side. When she saw his limp carcass swing, her neck got soft and her jaw relaxed. The pleasurable feeling spread throughout her body until she fell asleep, content that the uncontrollable urge for revenge had been satisfied once more.

Well after midnight, she awoke and had to use the outhouse. Sally's efforts to summon the guard did little but wake women in adjacent cells. She finally gave up and urinated on the floor, fearful that she would be reprimanded in the morning.

The voice of an irritated prisoner echoed up and down the hollow corridor. "Now shut up, girl, so we can sleep. If you get ninety days, you'll have more to worry about than taking a pee."

Sally fell asleep, shaking beneath the damp blanket.

On Monday morning, she was taken across the street to a yellow brick courthouse with slate shingles. Sally was led down the hallway on the first floor, past county offices, and then prodded to climb a wide stairway. She sat in a pew by the second-floor courtroom next to several other prisoners, all in handcuffs.

When it was her turn, two guards yanked Sally into a cavernous room illuminated by tall windows. About thirty people, hoping to be entertained by the public forum, waited in the hundred-seat courtroom.

The judge peered over his glasses and growled, "Miss Sally Wilton, have you offered sex for money within the city limits?"

"Well, your Honor, sometimes men give me gifts in return for my company." She was surprised by her feelings of pride about being a waiter girl.

"Yeah, yeah. We've got just the lawyer for your type. I hereby appoint William L. Paine to be your defense attorney. If you provide fifteen dollars in bail, you're free to go. Otherwise, you'll be remanded to city jail. Your trial will be at ten in the morning on February 18, 1873."

Sally paid her bail and left the courtroom tired, dirty, and hungry. She went home and bathed before visiting Sylvia for advice. When her friend opened the door, Sally noticed a policeman's uniform draped over the sofa.

The man who'd arrested her peered through a crack in the bedroom door. He said, "Now, Sally. Don't get angry. We had a quota to meet. This month, they made me arrest three waiter girls. You were one of them. Sorry. There's nothing I could do."

"You knew I was a friend of Sylvia's. And you still arrested me?" Sally slammed the door and walked to her room. She wondered if Sylvia had turned her in.

Everyone at the restaurant knew what had happened because Sally's name was listed in the police reports in Tuesday's newspaper. Her boss said she was innocent until proven guilty and refused to fire her, despite complaints from several customers who asked for another waitress.

Sally went to work at the saloon Friday night and served drinks without soliciting after-hour customers. She didn't want a second count of prostitution added to her current charge. It felt good to be in a familiar place with boisterous singing that lifted her spirits. She watched lumberjacks dance with each other. Men who danced as females wore colored scarves around their arms. That tradition, common in winter camps, was also accepted in saloons. The festive mood was so different from the depression and bitterness she had seen among inmates in jail.

As Sally put on her waitress smock and scanned the customers, a familiar face appeared. The lawyer she'd met when new to Bay City was swinging a beer mug in time with the music. She winked at him and he waved back. When it was time for her break, Sally sat at his table and told him about her arrest. She shared her speculation that Sylvia had reported her to authorities. Ralph said he was in town for business with city officials. When he heard about her problem, he suggested, "Let me represent you. The judge is a friend of mine."

"Please do. I'm in a terrible mess. I need all the help I can get."

The next morning Sally and Ralph entered the judge's chambers. The men shook hands, lit cigars, and told stories about their escapades in law school. Without speaking, Sally sat on a couch in the rear of the office.

"Well, what should we do with this young lady?" asked Ralph.

"I take it she's a client of yours? And you are a client of hers?" The two men laughed.

"Well, your Honor." He waved his cigar and winked. "My client pleads guilty to a charge of solicitation, but not prostitution. That way, the city will save the cost of a trial and you'll still get credit for discouraging this dirty business." He bowed.

"Done." The judge summoned the clerk who prepared some papers for Sally to sign. When leaving the building with Ralph, she thought about freedom in a new way, common to those who've had it withdrawn. I'm free to make choices in life. But then, I'm responsible for things that happen. That's what it means to be free.

"Now," said Ralph, interrupting her meditations. "Do you think we should request the Chief of Police to include Sylvia in next month's quota?"

Sally took a while to react. "Oh no. I want her to be my friend."

"Dear me, you are so naïve. Okay. If it makes you happy, we'll leave her alone."

Ralph spent the night with Sally at her room rather than in the crib, even though Sylvia had advised her never to take a customer home. She felt something special when they had sex. Sally liked Ralph's power and gentleness. She'd seen those traits combined in very few men. Feeling content and safe, she leaned over and kissed him good night. She remembered Sylvia's warning never to get personally involved with a customer. But, she thought, Ralph is more of a friend than a customer.

She fell asleep and dreamed of running through a cherry orchard, leaping and soaring among trees aligned in perfect rows, while blossoms fell on her shoulders. She was free.

Sally thought spring would never arrive. She'd been used to shorter and milder winters in southern Michigan. By March she was tired of snow and cold temperatures. At least her routine kept boredom away. She worked at the restaurant six days a week and at the saloon on Friday and Saturday nights. On Sunday, she went to church in the morning and to Bible study in the evening.

April brought warm afternoons that melted snow banks, leaving black and brown gravel. The season's accumulation of shoveled snow mixed with dirt was no longer covered with periodic blankets of white powder. Instead, the sun gave snow banks a pockmarked texture. Streams of water ran in crevices between mounds of frozen ice into streets that became quagmires.

It seemed to Sally that everything in the city slowed down during mud season. It was quiet since no mills were running yet. There were no boats on the partly frozen waters of Saginaw Bay. Few people ventured downtown except for necessary supplies.

Several customers at the saloon placed bets on when the first train full of lumberjacks would arrive in town. According to the rules, it could have no empty seats but had to be completely full. Even Sally put her quarter in the oversized pickle jar, hoping the date would be April 7th. For a newcomer, her guess was close but not good enough to take half the pot of 264 quarters won by Penelope Brigham for her April 13th estimate. The saloon took the other half.

Bay City seemed to Sally like a different town in spring. She noticed how fit the men looked, tempered by winter work, as they came off the trains. Most, though, were filthy with unkempt hair, wild beards, stained clothing, and torn Mackinaw coats. Some of the passenger trains had broken windows smashed by drunken lumberjacks. Quite a few of the men left the train with black eyes and bloodstained faces. She was fascinated to watch the boys shed their winter personalities.

Many of the stores sent runners to give wooden nickels to lumberjacks coming off trains. Those tokens could be redeemed at saloons, restaurants, and other businesses. Clothing stores sold many bright-colored shirts, new trousers, and dress shoes. Most men back from camps went to barbershops where they lined up to get haircuts and shaves.

Sally took a walk one morning before church. She noticed how the city had changed during spring. The air smelled of burned wood from steam engines at dozens of sawmills along the Saginaw River. Their whirling saws could be heard twenty-four hours a day during spring and summer. Soot and sawdust littered the ground, rarely seen near the riverbank where lumber was stacked several stories high. Even the water in the Saginaw River was stained brown and matted with bogs of sawdust. Perhaps, she thought, rowdy shanty boys damaged the city less than greedy businessmen.

She also became aware of the marked differences in Bay City neighborhoods. Unskilled laborers lived in ethnic communities, each with their own church and school. She walked along the river, past shacks owned by French Canadians, the poorest group in town. Sally turned onto Third Street from Water and went south on Washington

Avenue. On Center Street, she strolled past mansions with gingerbread designs and castle-like dormers. Most of the ornate homes of wealthy timber barons had ballrooms on the third floor. Twirling in circles, she pretended to waltz.

Sally saw a young man on the other side of the street walking toward her with a confident gate. He looks tall enough and has thick black hair, she thought. Maybe it's Jake!

Suddenly, her knees wobbled. She felt dizzy about seeing her old friend. Wouldn't it be wonderful to run her hands through that thick hair on his chest? Her heart beat faster until it seemed to rattle against her ribs. Her lips felt warm and wet. The young man was closer now, his face coming into clear view. Oh no, she thought, it's not Jake.

"Good morning," said the tall man. He smiled and flipped his hand up toward the rising sun. "What a beautiful day."

"Oh yes," she said. She smiled back and tried to hide her disappointment that the man was not Jake.

Continuing her walk, Sally saw more modest houses owned by merchants and professionals on Fifth Street. She kept going along Washington Avenue, past Eighth Street, where the Germans lived, to Twelfth, the Irish neighborhood. She walked south toward Portsmouth, where Polish immigrants were just getting out of church.

Seeing all the homes and families made Sally think about her father in Grafton and mother in Boston. Her thoughts were interrupted by the chiming of the clock in the town square, reminding her she had only thirty minutes to get to church.

At night Sally watched the lumberjacks fill saloons and cribs along Third Street where she worked. One of her best spring customers was a shanty boy who'd worked in a camp near Harrison. He returned to visit her every night for six days. On the first night they met, she asked, "How's it feel to be back in civilization?"

"Haven't you heard?" He laughed and slapped his thigh. "This isn't civilization. This is Hell's Half Mile." He told her about the area's reputation throughout logging camps in northern Michigan. He said many shanty boys talked about buying a train ticket to Hell so they could visit the infamous catacombs where Sally worked. "This place is a legend."

So, Sally thought, here I am a waiter girl in a famous logging town. Hundreds of lumberjacks a day come off these trains. Next winter, they'll tell stories about this boomtown around the camp wood stove. Those stories won't concern the town's stores or buildings. Instead, she concluded, the tales will be about the ladies of Bay City. Perhaps, the shanty boys will tell stories about me. Maybe, I'll be a legend, too.

9

Winter Among the Pines

Jake worked hard up north while Sally was getting established in Bay City. He'd finished his first assignment in early November when the four-man crew cut the last road through the pines. He was honored that the camp superintendent was personally inspecting the team's work. Jake was thankful for the adventure his job provided. He felt proud to be part of a successful team that met its mission.

Walking the road with Major Swensen gave him a chance to review his personal experiences during the past fall. As he passed special places where he'd cut trees, he remembered early mornings and long days. He rubbed his fingers against his palm, recalling that the hard yellow calluses were once watery blisters.

When the men got to the river, Thor stood on a stump, which accentuated his stocky six-foot build. He breathed in to expand his wide chest, stroked his full beard with his hand, and then tugged on his suspenders. He spoke slowly so his accent wouldn't be too obvious. "See how wide we made the rollaways? There's plenty of room for horses and sleighs to turn around."

"Good work," said the superintendent. "By the end of winter, logs will be piled to the sky here. They'll be ready to shove in the river when it swells with melting snow. You and Flareau did a nice job." He walked toward two other road builders and put his arms around their shoulders. "Of course, you had two experienced men to show you the way." Continuing along, he pointed at Rance who was leaning against a tree. "And you had a good boss."

The superintendent accompanied his men back to the bunkhouse where he was scheduled to greet newcomers. Jake was startled to see all the new lumberjacks. He watched the camp boss tweak his handlebar moustache.

"My name is Rolf Swensen. Major Swensen to you. Say goodbye to civilization boys. Welcome to Emerson's Logging Company." Jake smiled because he'd heard the speech before.

The major called off the names of men to find their cots in the bunkhouse. "Dick Craft, Harry DeFray, Sam Holden ..."

Jake smiled again. He remembered being in line outside the bunkhouse waiting for his name to be called. When he went inside to change his shirt, he felt crowded because he'd been used to a near-empty room shared by the smaller autumn crew. Now, ten new bunks had been added along a back wall to accommodate the winter staff. At least he had a cot away from the door. He was glad he'd come to camp early.

A skinny man who claimed the bunk next to Jake asked Thor, "What's that accent? Where're you from?"

"Wisconsin, and New England before that. But, I was raised in Sweden."

"Why'd you leave?"

"Isn't this the land of golden opportunity?" He took off his boots and carefully wiped them with a greasy rag.

"So they say," said the skinny man, who looked at Jake. "How 'bout you. Where's your home?"

"Grafton. Over by Kalamazoo. And you?"

"I'm from Lansing." The newcomer straightened his belongings. He copied the way Jake had organized his things.

"We've been here since early fall building roads."

"Did 'ya like the extra pay?"

Jake sat on his cot. "This was my first time in camp. I learned a lot."

The recruit seemed to care most about money. "I get thirty-seven fifty a month. I'll leave here with two hundred bucks. That'll buy me a hundred and sixty acres of farmland."

"I'm moving west with my stake," said another newcomer.

Someone else added, "I'm buying a clock shop in Flint. Then I'll be my own boss."

The talk shifted to camp routines. "What time do they serve meals?" Everyone looked at Jake.

"Four-thirty in the morning and six at night. This fall, we took lunches with us to the woods. We ate whenever we wanted." Uh oh, he thought, they're treating me like an old-timer.

As he left the bunkhouse to meet his new boss, Jake heard a boy from Ohio ask, "Any bears in these parts?" He winked at Thor because he remembered past questions about bears from recruits. On his way out, he heard his friend's answer. "You gotta watch for them when you use the privy at night."

The logging foreman, Harry Shield, wasn't as polite as Rance, his old boss. He said, "You'll be a skidder on Flanigan's crew. Meet him at two this afternoon. He'll tell you what to do."

"Okay. I'll be there."

"You won't give us any trouble, will you?"

Jake felt resentful. The boss doesn't even know me, he thought. Yet he thinks I'm a troublemaker. I'd better stand up to this guy.

"No sir," he said. "I do my job and keep to myself."

"That's what all of you boys from southern Michigan say."

In the afternoon, Jake went to meet Fred Flanigan, who explained his new job. He was excited because Thor had already met with him and been assigned as a head feller on the front lines, where he would cut the tallest pines.

After shaking hands, Flanigan said, "We picked you to be a skidder because you're good with horses and can move fast. Rance says you've got large, strong hands."

Jake didn't like looking at his boss because tobacco juice had streaked his white beard with yellow stains. "What will I do?"

"You'll fetch pine from sawyers who cross-cut logs. You'll put a tight chain around the belly of the log." Some wet pieces of tobacco wobbled on his lip when Flanigan spoke. "Then, you grab a line from the horse's harness. Its gotta a metal hook on the end. You set the hook into the chain. Got it?"

Jake raised his voice. "Set hooks? I want to use an axe. I can cut trees like a razor slices whiskers."

"Now hold on, son. The hard part of your job is snakin' logs through brush while steering your horse. If your logs get hung up on small trees along the way, you yell for a swamper. They're the ones with light axes to cut brush."

Jake's feelings were hurt. Here I've worked all fall, he thought, and just been praised by the superintendent. Now they give me a lousy job with a cranky foreman and stupid crew chief. This'll be a long winter.

He raised his voice even louder, and said, "Why can't I cut big pines like my friend Thor?"

"That takes years of seen-your-ity. Those fellers on the front line are top dogs. You're new in camp. You gotta pay your dues." A piece of chewing tobacco fell on his shirt. "We need lively boys like you to be skidders. You young ones can move fast when the logs slide. You'll see. Those logs weigh several hundred pounds. We've had men crushed before. Look out when the damn things come downhill. You need to dodge horses, too. Just do as I tell 'ya and you'll do fine."

In early December a few lumberjacks worked in the woods, but most couldn't do their jobs until logs could be skidded on snow. Swensen assigned the men to do maintenance on buildings just to keep them busy. That's when Jake felt anxious. He didn't like waiting for snow. He daydreamed about climbing Mt. Everest, wandering in the Sahara Desert, and visiting other exotic places. The wanderlust was strongest when he was bored.

Other shanty boys enjoyed the free time and easy work. Steffler, who was lazy, began teasing Jake. "What's da problem, kid?"

Jake always avoided Steffler because he smelled bad. His breath, which could be detected almost ten feet away, smelled like a mixture of hot metal and moldy cheese. The odor seemed to come from his black gums, which bled frequently.

"I came here to log pine, not caulk the cookhouse. And I'm not a kid. My name's Jake Flareau." He jumped to the bunkhouse floor from his cot. "I can't stand sitting around with nothing to do."

The lazy slacker jumped down from his cot. "I like dis quiet time. Soon, I'll put da logs on top of da sleighs to my friend Schmitt over dar. He piles logs on rollaways. He's da head banker in dis camp."

Schmitt didn't smell much better than his friend. Grease dripped from his hair and stained his collar with dark oil. Globs that looked like orange candle wax clung to his ear hairs and smelled like sour milk.

Schmitt jumped from his cot and said, "Ya, we like this time before the snow comes. What'ya think about that?"

All the lumberjacks in the bunkhouse got off their cots and formed a circle around the three men. They cheered when Steffler threw the first punch. Jake felt cold knuckles smash his jaw. Schmitt grabbed him from behind and held his arms back. The lumberjacks cheered again when the loader punched him in the stomach. He doubled up in pain and had trouble breathing. A right uppercut caught him between his nose and eye, causing blood to flow down his face and drip from his chin. It tasted warm.

Shield ran into the bunkhouse after hearing the commotion. "What's going on here?" He grabbed Jake's collar and threw him on a cot. The boss said, "Stop by the van tomorrow morning after breakfast. I'm telling Major Swensen you got in a fight. He'll wanna talk to you."

Jake knew the headquarters of the camp was called a van, which included Major Swensen's office, a company store with candy and tobacco, and the desk of a scaler, who kept records on the size and number of logs cut. The Major made frequent reference to logging statistics while talking to his lumberjacks. The measure of performance in camp was the number of board feet cut per day by a two-man team. Most knew a board foot was a piece of lumber twelve inches wide, one inch thick, and one foot long. On a good day, with nice weather and accessible trees, a team could cut ten thousand board feet of pine. Teams that cut more were rewarded and those that cut less were often disciplined.

"Yes, sir," said Jake. "I'll be there in the morning."

"Yes, sir," repeated Steffler with a smirk. "If you make it through the night."

Jake didn't sleep well. He tossed in his cot, fearful of being attacked in the dark. He also worried about the pending meeting. Will I be punished for fighting? Fired? Ridiculed in front of others? Finally, after a long night, he got up for breakfast but barely ate.

When Jake entered the van, Major Swensen sat at his desk shuffling through papers and didn't look up for several minutes. He pointed to a wooden chair in front of his scarred oak desk. "Have a seat." He shook his head in disgust. "That's quite a shiner you've got. What a shame you went bad. You did such a good job building roads."

"Shield didn't give me a chance to explain what happened. Steffler and Schmitt started it."

"You've been wound up like a clock spring."

"Maybe I am a little … bored."

"We've decided to give you a reason to get up at four-thirty again. Both Rance and Flanigan say you're a good hunter. Is that so?"

"Yes, sir. My dad and grandpa taught me how to hunt." He felt better just thinking about his family.

The Major took a rifle out of the gun cabinet behind his desk. It was so old that the bluing was gone from the barrel, leaving a shiny silver surface. "Most lumberjacks are lousy hunters because they move around too much. Hunters need to be still." He handed him the rifle and got another, which he tossed through the air as if catching it was a test. The gun smacked Jake's palm as it landed in his right hand—a hand used to catching firearms in mid-air.

Swensen said, "Try both of these rifles at a hundred yards and pick the best. Then, get some meat to feed our camp through winter."

"Yes, sir, but I'll test 'em at fifty yards. That's where I shoot most of my deer." He left the van and set up a make-shift target range.

His activity attracted a small crowd of onlookers. "What'd the boss say?" asked one of the newcomers.

"He told me to shoot game for camp."

"He gave you those rifles?"

"Yup." Jake dragged a slab of pine and set it on a stump. With his penknife, he scored a circle in the board around a silver dollar. Then, he dug chunks of wood from the circle and formed a cream-colored target. Jake paced off fifty yards and fired five shots that created a cluster of holes about three inches in diameter. Next, he replaced the slab with another board and repeated the process using the second rifle, which had a shot group of about six inches.

Thor walked toward the group when he saw his friend. Trying to hide his accent, he asked, "Hey, how'd you get that shiner?"

"Steffler and Schmitt ganged up on me. I wish you'd been there."

"Major Swensen's a smart man. He gave you the guns for a reason. Now, the loader and banker won't mess with you again."

"Maybe, but the camp does need meat for winter." Jake looked at Thor's steady shoulders and piercing eyes. "How about you? Did you ever shoot a rifle?"

"No. Only the rich hunt in Europe. It's not for common men."

During the next hour, the two friends shot dozens of rounds. When he felt satisfied Thor could kill a deer, Jake went back to the van and got permission to keep both rifles, with the understanding that Thor would be his assistant. He gave the more accurate rifle to his friend. The two men then went to the camp blacksmith and got the barrels blued so their shiny surface wouldn't spook game.

Deer season, which was closed during the summer months when does nursed fawns, opened on September 15th. However, Major Swensen always waited for cold weather to get camp meat so it wouldn't spoil. Jake enjoyed being paid to hunt and did his job well. On his best day, he shot three bucks and four does. He also got some turkeys, ruffed grouse, and snowshoe hares for the cook. Getting up early and spending time in the woods with Thor made him less irritable. Nobody picked on him anymore.

Christmas in Camp 37 was a sad day. Major Swensen tried to make the holiday festive with singing and games, but the melancholy men lay on their cots reading mail or daydreaming about home. The younger shanty boys, like one found by Flanigan crying beside the Christmas tree, suffered from homesickness the most. Even men in their late twenties and early thirties brushed tears from their eyes once in a while during the day. The lumberjacks wished Christmas would just go away and be forgotten. They were tortured all day by pocket watches with hands that seemed stationary.

Saddened by memories of past holidays, Jake missed his family. He thought about the many Christmas traditions at his home, church, and town. Since being in camp, he'd received two letters from his mother and a Christmas present he hadn't opened. He re-read the letters with news about neighbors. In the first letter, he read about the chimney fire in the Peterson's new fireplace. A paragraph in the second letter told about Mrs. Leeber, found in her cabin two weeks after she died from tuberculosis. The next part, about Sally, confused him:

> News about the Wiltons, too. Sally got herself in trouble with Dietrich. Remember him? He was the angry boy whose father beat him with a hoe. Dietrich won a fight in court with Sally and the town turned on her. She ran away from home. Nobody knows where she went. Most people say she went to Boston to be with her mother.
>
> William is helping father split firewood this year. He doesn't have much strength, but …

Jake read the part about Sally again. What kind of trouble did she have? Why did she go to court? I wish I could get more information, he thought.

He folded the letters slowly so they wouldn't rip and put them in his Bible. Then he opened a cigar box containing his gold coin. Jake wondered how Grandpa spent his holidays.

Amidst the arrowheads, a turtle shell, and a bear claw, he uncovered the present. He removed the canvas wrapper, exposing a small wooden box with a note that said, "Merry Christmas from your family. Love, Mom, Dad, William, and Martha." Inside the box, he found a tiny carving of a lumberjack cutting down a tree. He'd seen his father whittle such carvings and his mother paint them. Holding the figure close to his eyes, he was awed by the detail. The tiny figure held a miniature axe notched in a tree with the perfect shape of a white pine. It must have been hard for Dad to carve this, he thought. He always wanted me to be a market hunter. I'll have to tell him how I shot game for camp.

Several kinds of meat graced the picnic tables of Camp 37's cookhouse for Christmas dinner because of Jake's prowess as a hunter. The shanty boys appreciated the feast, even though they could not talk during meals. In the middle of dinner, Steffler raised his hand and requested permission to speak. After being acknowledged by the Major, he said,

"Maybe dat boy from Grafton is okay." He pointed at Jake and continued, "T'anks to him and Thor, we got good eats dis Christmas day."

The men applauded, almost as if it was Saturday night. Major Swensen said, "Quiet now. Yes, these hunters did well. But, remember, this camp runs on teamwork. And what's our mission?"

"Board feet!" they all yelled.

"That's right. Board feet. Merry Christmas, boys."

The day after Christmas brought relief to the men in camp. Everyone felt good when the gut hammer rang to announce breakfast. There seemed to be more pre-dawn talk in the bunkhouse as if loneliness had strengthened bonds between the shanty boys.

Snow started to accumulate on the ground at the end of December. The first few days after a blizzard the men threw snowballs and wrestled in the fluffy powder. Each morning when the lumberjacks rose, they hoped the camp boss would let them log. Finally the day came on January 3rd, when Major Swensen woke the men at four instead of four-thirty. After breakfast, he lined up the shanty boys like soldiers in formation and gave them assignments for the first day of logging. He stressed the importance of safety by telling horror stories about men killed and maimed in other logging camps. That morning, he seemed to be more of a coach and less of a drill sergeant.

Jake grabbed his axe and made it to the horse barn just in time to jump on a sleigh with three other skidders. They tied four horses to the back of the sled and left camp in darkness, amidst flickering lanterns and echoing voices. At the edge of a trail filled with stumps and holes, they talked and smoked pipes while waiting for daybreak. Overhead, the moon silhouetted two sentinel pines that towered over smaller spruce with snow on their limbs.

When the sky lightened, Jake heard Shield yell, "Let's cut some pine, boys!"

All shanty boys in the area echoed his yell. "Let's cut some pine!" It was time to start logging.

Jake took a few days to learn his new job as a skidder. At first he had trouble with Amy, a sixteen hundred pound Belgian horse. She calmed down when he stopped using reins after a log was chained to her harness. It was best to guide her with soft words in quiet tones, just loud enough to be heard above the harness bells that signaled her location. He'd forgotten how well horses hear, especially in the cold. She also seemed to do better when he used her name. After a few hours of working together, Amy seemed to sense when to turn left or right and when to slow down or climb. Jake enjoyed her company as he called to her while walking beside logs dragged along the skidding trail. "This way, Amy. Here, Amy, over here. Whoa now, Amy."

Jake had to learn how to work in snow, now reaching the top of his boots. Hooking and dragging heavy timber seemed hectic because everything was in fast motion. Men and horses around him never stopped moving. Sometimes, when he hurried too much, he slipped in the snow. Lumberjacks limbing and crosscutting fallen trees often yelled at him to move faster, especially when he stood motionless, wondering which way a cracking pine would fall. Even Thor, who felled trees nearby, hollered at him a few times.

Jake also had trouble hand digging tunnels beneath logs to attach chains and hooks. Sometimes, he placed a chain too close to the end of a log and it slipped off when pulled. It was also difficult for him to first place the go-devil beneath the front of a log to be transported. That forked piece of hardwood served as a sled to keep the front of the log from digging in snow or dirt. He envied some of the experienced men who had skidding sleds designed by the blacksmith.

After a few days he'd learned how to stay clear of falling trees and crosscut logs. He jumped at the right time and place to position chains and hooks. There is a rhythm to being a skidder, he thought. It's like dancing.

He also learned to keep logs in motion when dragged by horses. Success came from moving at a constant speed, not too fast and not too slow while trying to avoid snags in the skidding trail. In order to protect Amy, he never pulled more than one log from the lower trunk of a pine.

When logs got stuck, it was a slow process to free them. At times he had to summons swampers to cut the brush free. They cut and cleared skidding trails from the places where tall pines lay to the landing sites. When a log snagged, it took several minutes to calm Amy, who was startled by abrupt stops. Several times each day he thought of Major Swensen's Christmas speech about teamwork. Even Amy seemed to sense the importance of working together.

Jake watched in amazement the first time he saw Thor fell a white pine. His friend was on the right side of a tree that was three feet in diameter and more than one hundred feet tall. He undercut a notch a quarter of the way through the trunk. A co-worker on the left side of the tree made the final back cut leaving a narrow hinge of wood above Thor's notch. Jake saw a small piece of red cloth placed in the snow about twenty-five yards from the pine. Thor yelled "Teember!" as the tree fell on the red marker. The sound of the trunk smashing the ground and of limbs shattering seemed to linger, along with the odor of fresh pine.

After much clapping and hollering, a team of two sawyers rushed to the fallen monarch. First they axed limbs from the trunk, beginning at the base of the pine, and then bucked the remaining shaft into sixteen-foot logs with a two-man saw. Jake had been told that larger camps had feller crews to down trees, chopper crews that limbed, and sawyer crews to buck logs. He realized that the names of all these jobs varied by region of the country, the type of tree being cut, and the size of the operation.

The thing that shocked him most about sawyers was their weight loss over winter. For example, the previous year, one sawyer from Pennsylvania came to camp weighing 175 pounds and left at 144. In the bunkhouse, they always complained about sore arms and backs. At the start of the logging season, many sawyers had trouble lifting their arms to use knives and forks at the supper table.

After watching his friend work, Jake ate lunch with Thor in the middle of a clearing. A sleigh from the cookhouse delivered the mid-day meal of hot tea, frozen biscuits, and a slab of pork. When they finished eating, Thor prepared a smoke. His accent seemed to be more pronounced when he held a pipe between his teeth. "Do you have a girlfriend?" he asked Jake.

"I used to. Her name was Sally. She had legal problems and left town. Nobody knows where she went."

"Women like that don't make good wives. You want to marry a responsible lady…unless you're just having fun. You know." He took a stick and knocked a clump of pine needles from his right boot. "Have you ever done it?"

"Done what?"

"You know, slept with a girl." He blew a cloud of pipe smoke in the air.

"No, but I did kiss Sally a few times." He stroked his black beard, now well established.

Thor nodded his head, causing a pine needle to fall. "You've got some growing to do. Maybe you should forget about her."

"Maybe." Jake lit his pipe after filling it with long-cut tobacco. "What about you? Do you have a girl?"

"Not any more. I like blondes who speak Swedish."

"There's not many of them in these parts."

His eyes twinkled. "Next best are country girls who work hard. You know—responsible."

"Why is responsibility so important? What's wrong with good-looking women and nice figures?"

"Maybe," said Thor. He winked.

Jake liked Thor's view of the world. Unlike most people he'd known in Grafton, he was an observer and thinker who analyzed life. The two friends talked more about women until it was time to put out their pipes and go back to work.

Thoughts about Sally caused Jake to work harder than usual that afternoon. He guided Amy to the log landing several times on the long trail. On one trip, he almost collided with a skidder who pulled logs through cedar swamps using an ox named Willie. The animal had iron shoes on either side of his cloven hoof, a loud bell around his neck, and copper caps on his horns. Willie was stronger than Amy but much slower. His master, who was called "Toad" because of the warts on his face, said, "You go first. Willie only goes about one mile an hour."

"No," said Jake, "I've made enough trips. I'll take a break." He released the chain from Amy's half-Sweeny harness so she wouldn't get a sore shoulder. He threw some oats on the snow for her and lit his pipe.

He knew he'd worked the horse too hard because she was tottering and losing her balance when feeding. She seemed dizzy and disoriented. This is a good place to give her a rest, he thought. Meanwhile, Toad steered Willie to the landing site, where he dropped his log among a dozen others and left in slow motion.

"Build her up." Shield pointed to an empty sled just pulling up to the loading site.

"Here she goes," replied the loader as he and a coworker slid the first log on the sleigh. Each successive log was carefully selected until the first few rows were firmly wedged on sled bunks using crowbars. The men used long poles with hooks to pull and seat the logs. Decking lines of light chain, pulled by horses, were used to build a pile of logs on the sleigh. The last timbers completing the pyramid of up to eighteen logs that could weigh more than twenty tons. After they checked the load for stability and balance, Jake heard Shield whistle twice.

A teamster hitched a Clydesdale and a Percherons to the sled and climbed on top of the pile. With reigns in his hands, he barked, "Giddy Up!"

Jake noticed that the horses pulling sleighs had sharp shoes, allowing them to bite ice. He looked at Amy's shoes and saw the blacksmith had made hers blunt, like other skidding horses.

Suddenly, the sleigh heaved once and slid down the trail, iced earlier by a horse-drawn sprinkler which sprayed water into ruts dug during the fall. Those main roads, unlike narrow skidding trails, had been built to handle sleighs that were twelve feet wide. Jake met few shanty boys from the sprinkler crew because they worked at night and slept during the day. They tended to be the heaviest men in camp since they ate throughout the night to fend off cold temperatures. Once a water tank was filled, the crew had to keep the sled moving or it would freeze to the ground. When that happened, the men got out and used a hammer to free the runners from the frozen track.

Lumberjacks called "road monkeys" kept the icy tracks clear of debris and horse manure. They also placed sand and straw on steep hills where teams had to be slowed down before they tipped over and killed horses or men. Chains, which served as brakes, were tied to sleigh runners. Still, accidents occurred, especially when loads went faster than horses on the icy track.

Jake saw another empty sleigh pull up to the landing site. Six sleighs ran the ice track from the landing site to the river, so Shield tried to keep a half-hour between each load. I need thirty minutes, too, he thought. It will take me that long to get back to the others. Putting out his pipe, Jake put the harness back on Amy and dropped his log, now first in a new pile. He said, "Back, Amy. Back."

As he walked, he envisioned rollaways at the river where he'd built so many roads the past autumn. He knew that loaded sleighs were met by bankers, who transferred logs from sleds into two parallel lines of timber perpendicular to the riverbank. The log nearest the riverbank was held in place by chocks, or short blocks of wood, that could be removed in spring to allow the entire stack to roll into the swelling current. Someday, I'll get to see all those logs splash in the river, he thought.

The camp scaler often measured logs at the rollaways. When he did, he used a yardstick to gauge the diameter of each log, which he used to calculate board feet. Everything in camp had to do with board feet, thought Jake.

He turned the last bend in the trail and saw three of his coworkers with hands on their hips. One said, "Hey, Flareau, where've you been? You're the last skidder in."

"I gave Amy an extra break. She did more than her share of work for the day."

"That was smart," said Shield. He seemed to notice that Amy was tired. "All of us had a big day. Let's head back. Tie the horses on and jump in." They turned toward camp just as darkness fell and the temperature started to drop.

On the ride home, Jake looked at snow on tree limbs in the forest. He thought about all the different kinds of snow he had seen during the past few weeks. Wet, heavy snow was the worst because it would slip off tree limbs and melt down his neck. It made branches bend downward, leaving little space to peer through the forest. Powder snow was the best because it did not stick to boots or logs. He also liked sugar snow, composed of small pellets, because it didn't bog down his stride.

Jake hated crusty snow because he never knew if it was thick enough to support his weight. He could walk on top when it was thick, but he broke through when it was too thin, often causing him to trip and fall. He found the best way to move through ice-covered snow was to raise one boot high in the air and bring it down hard to shatter the surface. He also had to firmly plant his boot on the ground without letting it slip beneath the snow or his ankles would chafe and bleed.

When the snow reached his waist, he learned how to walk and even run on snowshoes. Amy was also issued a pair of snowshoes specially designed for workhorses. Everyone seemed to enjoy watching the tall man with a black beard bounding atop snowshoes, followed by a frosty-mouthed Belgian horse with cupped hooves.

On Sundays, some of the men left camp to visit friends. Jake was sharpening his axe one bitter February day and held the axe skyward to look for nicks in the blade. Suddenly, he saw the face of a redheaded farm boy with freckles. He knew it was Eli before he spoke. "Let me tell you about my trip into camp on that snowy tote road. There was water under the snow down by the creek. At first, I didn't know …"

Jake interrupted. "Hello, my old friend. How are things in Camp 18?"

"Fine. I usually go to the saloon in town on Sundays, but I wanted to see you. You know, there are several…"

Jake spoke before Eli finished. "It's nice of you to visit. Watcha been doing?"

Eli said, "I'm a sawyer now. I trim limbs from big pines. How about you?"

Jake shrugged his shoulders. "I've had three jobs: road builder, hunter, and now I'm a skidder."

"You know there are two ways to get ahead in this logging business." Eli's freckles seemed to move when he talked. "You can do all the jobs in camp in order to become a foreman. Or, you can pick one job and do it better than anyone else. That's what I did in Camp 18. When I first got there, I …"

Jake tuned him out.

Sunday lunch was informal and open to visitors, although few ever came. Jake introduced Eli to Thor when they entered the cookhouse, but they couldn't speak at lunch. After eating, they talked and smoked outside.

Thor seemed to like Eli. He smoothed his beard with his hand, shaking some bread crumbs free. "What are the saloons like around here?" he asked.

Eli paused for a moment. After deciphering the Swedish accent, he answered in a voice filled with excitement.

"Well, there's music, drink, and women, but never enough money to pay the bill."

Thor leaned over and said, "If you ever need company, just let me know."

That was all the encouragement Eli needed. "How about next Sunday? How about you, Jake? Want to visit the outside world?"

After a brief discussion, the men agreed to meet at a road junction between camps 18 and 37 at seven o'clock the following Sunday.

All week, Jake thought about the saloon in Roscommon. He remembered when Eli had the dry heaves. Why am I going? he wondered. Maybe I can keep them out of trouble. Yes, I'd better go as their chaperone.

Jake was surprised the road was so clear. It was a nine-mile hike from camp to town for Jake and Thor, but even farther for Eli. There was more traffic back and forth to the camps than he had expected. Perhaps it was the supply sleigh or visitors that kept the trail open. There was only a trace of new snow on the well-traveled road, but about a mile from town a storm started with flurries that became blowing snow. Soon there were three inches of fresh snow on the ground.

By the time they reached town, snow was driving sideways into their faces. A heavy layer of caked ice drooped from their eyebrows. Icicles formed on their beards in small circles around their mouths. Jake could no longer tell the road from openings beyond. Looking through the snow, he saw a white building loom ahead. Smoke from a wood burning stove made the building even more alluring.

When they reached the building Jake opened the door. Inside, it was warm and dry. He saw more than fifteen people sitting in pews. They had walked into church during Sunday service. The preacher didn't seem to mind; neither did Eli or Thor. The three friends picked a pew in the rear of the church and sat down still covered with snow. Quietly, they removed their hats and gloves and wiggled out of their coats.

The preacher asked the congregation to sing Hymn 247, "Rock of Ages." The men felt more comfortable as the congregation stood. Eli and Thor shared a hymnal, but Jake fumbled with his book trying to find 247.

It wasn't long before Eli was singing so loudly that people looked back to see who had such a precise tenor voice. "Rock of Ages, cleft for me, let me hide myself in Thee."

Thor, not wanting to be outdone, chimed in with a deep bass, complete with a Swedish accent. "Nothing in my hand I bring, simply to the cross I cling."

Jake looked at his two friends and back to the cross. Here I am, he thought. I looked for a saloon and found a church. The congregation softly sung the final hymn, "Until We Meet Again."

The lumberjacks said goodbye to the preacher and left the church. The storm had stopped, leaving five inches of fresh snow. As they walked, Eli broke the silence. "Now on to the saloon."

Thor looked down at the ground and made a circle of compacted snow with his boots. He said, "I want to get back to camp."

"Me, too," added Jake.

"Well then," said Eli, "perhaps we'll try again some other Sunday. As for me, I'm going to the saloon. It's been too long a walk for nothing."

"Goodbye then—until another Sunday," said Jake. He and Thor headed back to Camp 37 while Eli went to the saloon. On the way, Jake talked with his friend about the day, hardly characterized as a long walk for nothing. They also talked about their past. Both the exercise and company were good.

The end of February brought cold temperatures. It was often below zero when the men went to work in the dark. The first bitter morning was 16 below zero. It was so cold that the horses did not want to leave the barn, despite strong urging of the men.

The camp superintendent inspected each crew member as they left camp to ensure they had proper clothing. In two cases, lumberjacks were sent back to the bunkhouse. One logger had forgotten his hat, and the other had no gloves. The foreman also ordered the cook to put more hot drinks on the lunch sleighs. Anyone with numb ears, nose, fingers, or toes was instructed to come back to camp with the lunch sleigh. The men were shown how to inspect their extremities for skin spots. Crews were told to keep their morning fires going all day. Men were permitted to warm up at the fire whenever needed.

Jake was amazed at the sounds the forest made in the sub-zero temperature. He thought the lack of animal activity would keep the woods quiet. Instead, the freezing of sap inside the tree trunks made a sound like a small-caliber rifle being discharged. The men were lucky because the temperature rose quickly with the sun. By ten in the morning, it was four above zero, comfortable for logging in the white-pine woods.

One lumberjack seemed to take advantage of Shield's generosity. He kept going back to the fire to smoke his pipe. It didn't take the men long to notice his laziness. A sawyer came back from the cutting zone to get warmed by the fire. He said, "What's the matter, sissy? Are you a little cold?"

Before the shammer could answer, the sawyer pulled off the lazy man's coat and threw him to the ground. Within a minute three other lumberjacks joined the hazing. They took off his shirt, trousers, and boots. The lazy lumberjack was dressed only in socks and underwear. He lay face down in the snow while the men draped his clothes on the sleigh.

"Are you ready to get back to work, or should we take off the rest of your clothes?"

"I'll work. Give me my clothes. It's freezing." He walked to the sleigh, gathered his clothes, and got dressed.

Stories about the fate of the lazy shanty boy spread through the camp. There was never a problem again with a logger taking unfair advantage of Shield's concern with safety in sub-zero temperatures. The men in camp also saw the northern lights that evening when Woodpecker, who'd seen the display above the privy, woke others in the bunkhouse. The sky was filled with white, yellow, green, and blue streaks that pulsated. The colors, accentuated by a fresh snowfall, seemed to move from one part of the sky to another.

March brought the men even closer in male solidarity. They held more contests of strength outside the bunkhouse, especially when Major Swensen wasn't looking. The lumberjacks often played a game called "Putting a Man Down." The victim was held, stomach down, over a log while one lumberjack held his head and another his feet. A third opponent spanked him with a bootjack until he surrendered. Sometimes the pause was just a temporary time-out, after which the victim retaliated.

The men also liked to challenge each other outside to see who could throw a knife closest to his opponent's boot. When he saw dangerous games being played, the Major stopped the contest. In extreme situations with repeat offenders, he would quarantine the lumberjack in solitary confinement for a week or even dock his pay. The games, however, continued in secrecy. Jake noticed that the contests forged a bond between the men and reinforced their pecking order that never seemed to change. Secrecy made that bond stronger.

The snow started to get rotten in early March. There were days that the sleigh could not make its run to the decking bank because warm temperatures made the runners stick. By mid-month, the men were covered with bark and mud. Each day Shield told the men to work a little longer because there was more daylight.

Only a few of the men realized how many hours the camp worked at the end of winter compared to the rest of the season. Several men got bad colds from working too long in the melting snow.

The men talked about leaving camp. There was much discussion about where they would go and what they would do with their pay.

Jake said to Thor, "I keep hearing Dad's words to be home before the suckers run. I'm worried I might be a little late."

Thor wiped a clump of mud from the top of his left boot. "Didn't you say William was going to help your dad this year?"

"Yes, but that doesn't give me the right to disobey my dad."

"I wish I had a place to go. I'm not spry enough to work the river drives. Running saws in the mills is too dangerous for a daydreamer like me. What do you think I should do?"

"Dunno." Jake looked out into the woods. The trees showed little evidence of new leaves. There were spots of bare ground and puddles of water in low spots between trees. "Hey, why don't you come home with me? Dad could teach you how to fillet fish. Nobody in my family likes that job."

Thor jumped up and down in the melting snow. "I hoped you'd ask me to go. I've heard so much about Grafton. Thanks." He grabbed Jake's arm and twisted it behind his back. Then he tickled him. The two men laughed and punched each other in jest.

Camp 37 was officially closed on April 3. Within two days all the lumberjacks were gone. Jake and Thor boarded a train headed south. Thor gambled for about an hour but gave up when he lost eight dollars. Jake sat alone while his friend played cards. He was thinking about his family. He fondled his gold piece. It had been a good winter in logging camp. He was glad he'd had the wanderlust.

10

Jake and Thor Leave Camp

The filth of an industrial city compared to the cleanliness of the wilderness shocked Jake as he walked with Thor away from the Bay City's train depot. The next connection to Kalamazoo didn't leave until noon the next day. Jake had heard so much about the city; he wanted to spend the evening there and see Hell's Half Mile. Thor, always game for excitement, seemed happy to keep his friend company.

Jake watched many kinds of people leaving the station. He saw a new breed of lumberjack with different clothes. These men, known as river hogs, were gathering to work on river drives. All the pine cut in logging camps throughout the north woods would soon be shoved into waterways swelled by melting snow. He noted some obvious differences between the river hogs and shanty boys returning from the winter woods. They had clean summer clothes, compared with the dirty Mackinaw coats and winter boots of men back from northern camps. River hogs wore calked boots with quarter-inch spikes so they could cling on logs in water. The boots splintered wooden sidewalks in town and dug up saloon floors.

Jake walked the city streets ahead of Thor to find a hotel for the evening. Ladies passing in swishing dresses excited him. The smell of perfume tickled his nose as well as his imagination. Store signs with bright colors startled him because he was used to green pine, white snow, and black logs. When he peeked through restaurant windows he saw lace tablecloths covered with dainty napkins and sterling silverware.

He was amazed by the energy of children running in circles around their parents and became captivated by their emotions, clearly displayed in their facial expressions. They seemed to have their own communication system with each other. The children also noticed Thor and Jake. They studied lumberjacks carefully, perhaps empathizing with the men's reactions to the sights of Bay City.

Jake watched a streetcar on trolley tracks pulled down the middle of the road by a horse. He and Thor jumped aside and ran to the next stop where they climbed aboard the car. He knew Bay City was one of the first towns in Michigan with a street railway system. The streetcar fascinated Jake, who waved and pointed at people walking beside him on the road. Two men, a driver and a conductor, manned the tiny cars with four wheels. He rode the full length of the line from Third Street in Bay City to Thirty-fifth Street in Portsmouth, where the horse was unharnessed. A fresh animal pulled the car on the return trip to Third Street.

Jake and Thor talked about riding the streetcar again, but decided there were too many other attractions. They stopped in two hotels to inquire about the cost of a room but found the prices too high. They agreed to share a room in a third hotel, where one evening cost them each a dollar and ten cents plus twenty cents for a bath. They left their belongings in the room, gathered towels and clean clothes, and headed for the bath. Jake poured warm water in the wooden tub. It was big enough that he could submerge his entire body under water. There was plenty of soap, too. The men spent almost a full hour in the bathhouse, which had eight tubs separated by heavily varnished walls leading almost to the ceiling. Although they had washed with wet rags in logging camp, they hadn't bathed in months. Alone in the bathhouse, Jake and Thor spoke freely.

"What do you want to do?" asked Thor.

Jake replied, "I'd like to get a new shirt. How about you?"

"I could use some new soles on my boots. The leather on top is fine."

Jake laughed. "I hate this dirty, torn shirt. I need a haircut, too. Maybe I'll have the barber shave off my beard."

"Not me," said Thor. It's too much trouble to shave."

The men walked from the bathhouse to the shoemakers. They sat in wooden chairs overlooking the street while Thor's boots were repaired. The young men then stopped at several stores, where Jake bought a colorful shirt and some souvenirs for his family. As they approached the barbershop, they shoved each other to see who would be first in the door. Thor won.

All customers in the barbershop were visitors to Bay City. They talked about where they had come from and where they were headed.

One of the barbers, answering a question from his customer, said, "There's lots of work at the mill this year, but only for Poles. Everyone else got fired. The Poles are the only ones who'll work for low wages."

The customer said, "We hear the rich owners don't want to help the town. All their money goes back to New York State."

"Dunno. The lumbermen have their own barbers. They don't come in here. Neither do the Poles. If they did, I'd cut their ears off instead of their hair." After a few minutes of silence, he finished snipping, collected his fee, and yelled, "Next!"

Thor, with his hair and beard still wet from the bath, sat in the barber's chair. "Just cut the hair, not my beard."

"Yes, sir," said the barber, who took a fresh scissor from a jar partly filled with alcohol.

"My accent is Swedish, not Polish," volunteered Thor.

"Are you looking for work?"

"Nope. I just got out of winter camp. I'm going home to Grafton with my buddy."

"Next," said the other barber.

Jake climbed into the adjacent chair. "You can shave my beard and cut my hair."

The first barber asked, "Are you boys finding everything in town you're looking for?"

Several other customers stopped talking and reading, curious to hear Thor's answer. "Almost everything. The only thing missing is a nice Swedish girl. Do you know where I can find one?"

"At the catacombs," answered the other barber. His bow tie pinched his neck into two long creases of skin. "But you'd better keep your wallet in your socks and keep your socks on your feet." Laughter filled the barbershop.

"You'll find a four-block area with several saloons, liquor stores, and hotels. The catacombs itself is in a three-story building on Water Street."

"And the women are there?" Thor's voice got louder and his accent more pronounced.

"Yeah, they don't hang around on the streets. They're inside."

"What's it like?" asked Thor.

The first barber smiled. "Don't you know?"

"No. We haven't been there yet."

"Well. There are three stories in the building. The top is too rich for my blood. I went in there once when half drunk. I even paid the five-dollar admission. It's just a fancy dance hall and theater with waiter girls. They're all dressed up and smell like flowers. When I went, they did a play about a man with a dream to have two girls at once. They did it right on stage for all to see."

Jake grimaced. "That's too vile for me."

"There's other variety theaters in town with box seats. Whatever takes place between a man and his waiter girl is in full view of everyone."

"What else is in the catacombs?"

"There's a wine room off to the side on the third floor. Lots of ladies take their men from the theater into the wine room. You can imagine what that place is like. It's just a big orgy room." The barber lathered Jake's face and honed the razor on a leather strap.

"What about the other floors?"

"The second story has several saloons where waiter girls mix with customers. It's not as depraved as the top floor and has no cover charge. That's the floor you enter from the street. It has a long bar surrounded by dozens of tables. But you have to be careful of the drinks they serve. Some drunken shanty boys have been drugged, robbed, and thrown into the street below."

"And the bottom floor?"

"That's the worst. It's just a maze of dark, sectioned-off rooms in the basement, tiny cribs where women do whatever they are asked for pay."

"Whatever they're asked?"

"You know. Men have tastes for different acts. If you really want to find a nice Swedish girl, don't look here in Bay City. All the nice girls left here twenty years ago."

A lull came over the barbershop. Jake broke the silence. "Towns with money may have growing pains. But they also have good schools, libraries, police protection, and fire control."

Several men joined the conversation to discuss the social pros and cons of economic growth. In addition to good conversation, the young men got fine haircuts. As they left, Jake watched the barbers sweep a pile of thick sandy hair from beneath the first chair and curly black hair from the base of the second chair. Noting that the pile of hair beneath his chair was larger than Thor's he said, "I win. I grew more hair this winter than you. So, you buy dinner."

"That's not fair," said Thor. "Your pile is bigger because some of that hair is from your beard."

"Nope. I grew more hair at camp than you did. You buy."

"I give up. But nothing fancy. Just a plain meal."

After supper the men wandered into several saloons or dives. They started from the hotel and walked toward the catacombs. Three old men were talking about the weather at the first bar they entered. It was so boring they left after one drink. The second bar was the opposite: two wait ladies for each man. Lumberjacks and sailors were playing poker, singing ballads, and telling jokes. Before long, a fight started at the rear door of the bar. The bartender left the counter and threatened the troublemakers with a club in his hand. They agreed to move the fight outside.

A shot rang out in the alley a few minutes later. Jake went outside with others to see what had happened. A lone man covering a bloody chest with both hands was sprawled on the street. He grimaced a few times, convulsed, and died. Most of the men moved to a door leading into a basement. There, underground tunnels connecting saloons provided many hiding places. Jake and Thor stayed with the crowd in the street, watching in disbelief as the bartender blew a whistle. In a few minutes, a policeman in a freshly pressed uniform dragged the man to the front of the store where a coroner's wagon waited. The body was removed without any fuss as if it was a common event. All that was left of the drama was a small pool of blood in the alley.

Life is certainly fragile, Jake thought. He felt numb as they moved to the next saloon. After a quick drink, he'd seen enough. "I'm going back to the hotel."

"Not me," said Thor. "I'll be back later."

Jake walked to the hotel in deep concentration. He tried to sleep but had nightmares of the dying man. Finally he drifted to sleep in the fluffy bed. This is so nice, he thought, compared to my straw mattress in camp.

It was almost midnight when Thor came into the hotel room and yelled, "Get up! Get up! I've got some news!"

Jake tried to focus on the big form at the foot of his bed in the dark. "What kind of news? How could anything top that murder?"

"I met a Sally. I think it's your Sally. She came from a pioneer village north of Kalamazoo." His accent made the name of the city hard to understand.

"Did you tell her your name or mine?"

"No. You never tell prostitutes your real name."

"Sally wouldn't be a prostitute. You're just drunk."

"Her father's a blacksmith. It must be your Sally. Come on. Get out of bed. I told her I'd bring you back. Come on. Let's go."

Jake dressed with deliberate care. He wondered if he was having a dream. So much had happened since he left camp.

He and Thor walked into the saloon on Third Street, a business bursting with customers. Sailors and lumberjacks lined up at the bar. He spied a waiter girl serving drinks to four men at a corner table. Even in the dark, he recognized her creamy complexion and chestnut-brown hair. Thor was right. It was Sally.

"Oh, my. It is you," Sally said when she came to take their order. "I couldn't believe it when your friend said he was traveling with someone from Grafton."

Thor said, "See, I told you it was your friend from Grafton. How about a Scotch for me and a beer for our friend?"

Sally returned with the drinks and pulled up a chair. "My boss said I could take a fifteen-minute break."

"So will I," said Thor. He left and paced about the saloon, apparently hunting for excitement. He finally sat at a table with three other men and joined their poker game.

Jake studied her figure. It was even more stunning than he remembered. Her complexion had the same purity he recalled. Her teeth were perfectly straight and her hair had the same sweet smell. There was something different about her, though, but he couldn't quite determine what it was. "You look great. I can't believe you're here in Bay City."

Sally and Jake shared stories about where they had been and what had happened to them. She said, "Nobody in Grafton knows I'm here."

"Not even your father?"

"Especially my father. Please don't tell anyone you saw me."

"Why'd you run away?"

Sally looked at the clock on the wall. The fifteen minutes were passing quickly. "Dietrich raped me." It was easy to tell Jake. He was like a brother.

"What? He forced you to have sex?" Jake came partly out of his chair.

"I kept telling him to stop. But, he didn't listen." She wiped a tear from her eye and shook her hair from side to side.

"That evil man. Wait 'til I get home. He'll pay for this."

"He tied me up and abused me. It was terrible."

"Oh, no." Jake stood up and pushed his chair from the table.

"Then we had a trial at the courthouse and the judge said I led Dietrich on."

"He got off?"

"Yes. The whole town turned against me. They made me feel like I'd done something wrong. So I ran away."

Jake felt nervous. He wanted to say something but couldn't think of the right words.

She stopped speaking for a moment, which gave him a chance to organize his thoughts.

Jake said, "Thor told me you're a prostitute. Is that so?"

"Let's talk about that some other time. I do have lots of friends here in Bay City. Some are men."

He looked at the girls working in the saloon. "Do you charge for your friendship?"

"Sure. But I don't sleep with men for money all the time. Just once in a while."

"Oh, Sally. How'd you get in such a mess? Was it because your mother left?"

"Money is quite a distraction."

"So that's it. You're doing this for money?"

"Partly. I've also learned what kind of man I want to be with for the rest of my life. I want a husband who cares about me."

"But what a way to find that out—by trying different kinds of men? That's like trying on dresses at the store. If you've really learned what you want, why are you still seeing customers?"

"I told you. The money's a distraction."

"I feel sorry for you. Maybe it's time to go home."

"I can't. The people in town were so nasty to me. I can't ever go back to Grafton."

"What about another town with another job?" His voice had a gently pleading tone that became more authoritarian as he continued. "You can't live like this. One of these men is going to hurt you."

"Please, Jake. Just understand me. Please don't try to change me."

He sat back in his chair as if defeated. "Oh, all right. I'll keep your secret. I won't tell anyone where you are or what you've done. But if you ever want to come home, please let me know."

"Thanks for your friendship." Sally stood up to leave. They hugged each other and said goodbye.

Jake and Thor walked back to the hotel past the saloons on Third Street, stepping around men curled up on the street. The lucky ones were sound asleep, wrapped in blankets. The less fortunate had torn clothes, covered in vomit, urine, and even blood.

Thor said, "So Sally's a prostitute?" He accented the last syllable.

"I'm afraid so. We're to keep her whereabouts a secret."

"Then you'd better forget about her completely."

"I agree. I asked her to come home with us, but she's not ready yet." At that moment Jake tripped over something on the ground. Looking closer, he could see the form of a large-framed man wearing a torn Mackinaw.

Thor stopped. "I think this poor fellow's dead." He rolled the body over to see if the man was alive or not. There, lying on the wooden sidewalk was Eli. He could recognize him by his bright red hair and the peach fuzz on his chin. His hands were weather-beaten and chafed.

Jake leaned down and said, "Is that you, Eli? Are you okay?"

Eli looked up at Jake and Thor with his deep blue eyes and moved his body into a sitting position. "No, I'm not okay. I went to the catacombs and had too many drinks. The bartender must have drugged the last one. It tasted bitter. Then, my head started to swim and my stomach burned. The waiter girl must have set me up. She and I had just come upstairs from her crib. She must have seen all the money in my wallet and told the bartender to spike my drink." Eli continued the story in his usual detail.

"How'd you get outside?" asked Jake.

"Dunno. When I came to, I was in a tunnel under the catacombs. It was like an anthill with many rooms and passages. I reached for my wallet and found it was gone. Then, two men came and dragged me outside into the street. I didn't have enough strength to fight them off."

"Come on back to the hotel with us," said Thor. "We'll pay for your room tonight and buy you a ticket to Coldwater. Bay City sure isn't the fun place they told about in camp, is it?"

Jake and Eli answered at the same time. "No way."

The train station at Bay City smelled of wet wood, stacked in great piles along the tracks. After raw logs were floated to mills in Bay City, finished lumber was transported by ship to ports along the Great Lakes and the Erie Canal. The highest quality lumber was sent by rail to large cities. Jake kept looking at the clock in the train station. At exactly one-fifty in the afternoon, the conductor allowed passengers to board.

Jake said goodbye to Eli, who was taking a different train. Thor added, "Maybe we'll see you next fall, eh?"

Eli answered, "Thanks for helping me out."

Talking with Sally the night before had made Jake think about home. He was anxious to see his family and excited about fishing with his father. After a long ride, he and Thor left the train and walked from the depot toward his cabin. Jake was pleased to be going home before the suckers spawned. His dad would be proud.

11

Eli the River Hog

Eli stared at the train ticket in his chafed hands. Once I'm in Coldwater, how am I going to explain that I have no money left after the long winter of hard work? Should I tell my father about the prostitute and about the bartender who robbed me? No, I can't do that, he thought; my father would never forgive me for being so foolish.

After much thought, he traded his ticket for one to the Au Sable River near Oscoda. He decided to head back up north to work a river drive where men were paid from two to five dollars a day. That way he could accumulate some cash and never have to tell his family what happened to him in Bay City.

Eli found a wanigan, a floating barge with tents, that followed the river drive to the mills. It was owned by Royston Lumber Company and had a cookhouse, company store, office, and cots on board.

"Got any work?" he asked. "I've had experience in winter camp, where I..."

"Shut up," said the clerk. "We've got more work than men." He pointed at a paper on his desk. "Sign your name above the line. You'll sleep in company tent twelve, a mile west of here. Go see Silas Remke, foreman of the jam crew."

"Thanks. What other crews are you working on the Au Sable?"

"Our company has driving crews to keep logs moving and sacking crews to collect stray timbers. You're agile enough to work on jams."

To Eli, river drives didn't seem very well organized. They weren't anything like regimented winter camps, which were run like military units. Rather, men just showed up at the river and were hired on the spot. There was less planning and little paperwork. Even daily work schedules were more flexible because of changing weather conditions.

Eli followed a well-worn footpath along the riverbank to a group of tents pitched on a plateau beside the rapids. He walked toward Silas Remke with some hesitation. The foreman sat on a log by a campfire where he yelled at two of his men. When he saw the stranger approach, the foreman barked, "Hope you're here to work. We've got a big mess to clean up."

"Yes, sir. I'm Eli Peters. I'm here to work jams." He held out a weatherbeaten hand. The bright yellow sun glistened in his red hair and made the peach fuzz on his chin more noticeable.

"Good." Silas got a peavey from the tent and handed it to Eli, who fondled the combination hook and spear for several minutes. Although the farm boy had seen many kinds of mechanical implements, he had no experience with tools used by river hogs. The peavey, five and a half feet long, was used to pull logs into water with the curved hook mounted on its side. It also had a spike at the end of the tool for pushing logs into the river. The peavey was different from the pike pole he had seen before. That tool was about fifteen feet long and had a twisted point but no hook. It was used to push logs midstream or pull logs once speared through the bark.

"Take this peavey and go downstream of jams," said Silas. "Snag logs with that hook. Then pull them off the jam. Make sure they're free. They'll float down the river." He wiped his dripping nose on his shirtsleeve."

"Yes sir. Where's the jam?"

The three men laughed.

"Two miles downstream. Put your things in tent twelve." He wiped his dripping nose again. "Go with these fellas. This is Sam and that's Ernie. They'll show you what to do."

The men followed Eli to his tent where he left his clothes on a cot. He put on his new calked boots but found the laces bit into his ankles more than he liked. The quarter-inch spikes stuck in the ground and tripped him twice when he walked. He'd seen a few men wear boots like these in Bay City and remembered how they splintered wooden sidewalks. He also recalled a saloon fight between two river hogs who kicked more than punched. Loggers' smallpox, he thought. That's the name given to skin marks left by a kick from calked boots.

The three men walked downstream on a muddy path. Eli was bothered by swarms of small gnat-like creatures that rarely bit during the heat of the day. He noticed one or two black flies that flew at noon near his eyes, ears, and nostrils. As the afternoon temperature dropped and there was more shade, black flies gathered in larger groups. When the sun set, the pests got nasty. They bit him around the ankles and wrists, where his skin and clothes met. The bugs flew into his face, got stuck in the wet corners of his eyes, and invaded his nostrils. Their bite was painless but left a small red circle that soon became an open sore. The black flies seemed to be the thickest in areas where logs got stuck on sand and gravel bars, where creeks fed into the main channel of the river.

The Au Sable River had a spirit. Each bend showed a different personality. In some areas, Eli watched the water flow through high sandy banks where birds nested in fist-sized tunnels. Elsewhere banks were low and filled with so much tag alder that it was difficult to see the water's edge. There were special places, almost holy to some river men, where water flowed through century-old cedars. Marsh marigolds dotted the banks in flat grassy spots and watercress wavered in the current of small pools. Pink lady slippers and white trilliums carpeted the forest floor where it sloped upward from the river to the ridge above. Clouds of mayflies hatched along the banks. They hovered in clusters while darting toward one another. He saw otters, beavers, and muskrat. Osprey flew the river curves with agility and grace.

Eli saw crowds of people when he reached the logjam with his two co-workers. Some were company men scrambling on a huge pile of logs, several acres in size. He walked downstream along the bank to the head of the jam. The logs looked like a cabin wall in some places, organized as an orderly array of flat timbers. Elsewhere it was a twisted mass of jagged sticks protruding in all directions. At the deepest point, it looked to Eli like the jam was at least ten logs thick. He saw open water at the upstream head and downstream tail of the woodpile. Men removed sticks in the middle with little apparent success. The pile kept getting larger and thicker as more logs came down river.

Sam stopped near the bottom of the jam. He looked at Ernie and said, "Yup. This is a big one. We'll be here several days."

"Maybe several weeks," said Ernie.

Eli was amazed at the size of the jam. "How'd this happen?"

Sam said, "The company does everything possible to avoid these pile-ups. Silas always releases the first two or three rollaways of lower quality logs to grease the drive, or fill spots in the back bays. That keeps the remaining logs in the main channel."

Ernie added, "River hogs also cut sluiceways in places where the river's shallow. They built dams on feeder streams. At just the right time, they busted those dams to raise the water level. They removed tree limbs and boulders that might stop the flow of logs. In some sections, the river itself was completely dammed. That way, logs can be floated from one pool to the next. It's kinda like a ship lock for pines."

"Men were stationed on river bends to keep logs moving in places they'd get stuck," said Sam. "Still, there's so many logs coming down the river from winter camps all over the north woods. There'll always be jams."

Eli looked at all the people on the riverbank who'd traveled to the Au Sable as part of a spring tradition to watch river hogs free stacked logs at rollaways. He watched the spectators walk up and down the riverbank or gather in small groups around bonfires.

Sam pointed to the crowds and said, "They come from all over to see the spring drive. Being at a jam is a real treat for them. Local residents sometimes come and join these visitors when there's a jam. You can hear the logs comin' downstream about two miles away. When there's silence on the river, it means there's a jam somewhere. That's when people run or gallop horses upstream looking for piled up logs. If there's silence on the river for two or three days, shop owners even close their stores so they can hunt for the jam."

Ernie pointed to a spot on the bank and motioned Eli to enter the river. "Don't get in the water near tree trunks. You'll fall in the deep holes. Climb in by the outer side of river bends. The water is shallow there. Be careful, though. Sometimes the sand is soft."

Eli tried to step on a moss-covered boulder. Even with spikes on his boots he slipped, leaving him seated in the water up to his waist. He felt stupid.

Sam reached out his hand. "You'd better stay wet. If you change into dry clothes, you'll get a cold."

Eli thought he was trying to be funny. He said, "Seems the opposite. Won't I get a cold if I stay in these wet clothes? Shouldn't I walk back to the tent and get some dry clothes?"

"No. Let 'em air dry. Many of us even sleep in wet clothes. When you throw off a blanket in the morning, steam will rise in the cold air. You'll get used to it."

The foreman saw the three men talking and said, "Look out. We're using dynamite to free the logs on this jam. We've tried everything else. You guys better duck behind that boulder."

Eli watched a man in the distance remove some dynamite packed in a paraffin container inside a wooden box.

The employee uncoiled some fuse. He'd heard that the men who handled explosives, called powder monkeys, used new fuse because it burned at a predictable rate of about thirty feet per second. Old fuse might burn faster or slower, and either way that could be dangerous.

Peering around the boulder, Eli watched the dynamite go off. Water from the explosion sprayed his face. Splinters of wood rained down on him and sprinkled his red hair. It took several minutes for the ringing in his ears to subside so he could hear again. Looking upstream, he saw little change other than a few wet spots and some splinters on the woodpile. The explosion had little apparent impact. So he again began pulling logs from the downstream end of the jam.

When he hooked a log and yanked it free, Eli's shoulders and forearms hurt. His cold hands were shriveled in the wet gloves. Before long he learned how to guide logs over sandbars, boulders, and brush. He steered timbers with his peavey from still to fast water. He learned by trial and error to shove logs so they drifted into vees formed by the river current. Logs would surge there, increase their speed, and then disappear downstream.

He wasn't the only river hog who was wet. Most of the men had fallen into the river by lunchtime. The noon meal was served under a tent on the riverbank by a company cook and three cookees. Hot soup warmed him.

He asked Ernie, "Where you from?"

"Upstream," said his partner. "The past doesn't matter here. Just stay alert and watch out for others. Sam and me are partners. The boss paired everyone up. We've got a buddy system to keep us safe. You're just assigned to us for training. Later you'll be paired with someone else."

Eli didn't like Ernie's attitude. "I know that. I said, where are you from?" The two men's faces were only inches apart.

Sam intervened. "I'm glad they bring two lunches a day. The next meal will be here in about two hours."

"Well, then," Eli continued, "I'll tell you where *I'm* from. My hometown is Coldwater. We have a big picnic at haying time…" Eli kept on with the boring details.

After lunch Sam taught Eli how to ride logs. "Bend your knees a bit so your feet are flat. That way your spikes will dig into the bark without shifting too much weight from side to side."

Eli was soon able to walk up and down a log without causing it to spin. It's like walking the railroad track in Coldwater, he thought. By the time the second company lunch arrived, he felt comfortable jumping on the back of a log to drive the nose up and over brush in the water. He even tried jumping from one log to another, but fell in twice. The secret to jumping logs, he found, was getting a good take-off from the first log, without spinning his body, and landing flat-footed in the center of the second log. Holding the peavey sideways seemed to provide the most balance.

Eli and the other men worked for six days without success. One afternoon Ernie was helping him shove away a thick sixteen footer near the back of the timber pile. His partner yelled, "Look out! Henry's putting a charge on the key log by your starboard!"

He looked on both sides of the log because he forgot the difference between starboard and port. Why do these river men think logs are ships? he wondered.

Suddenly Eli noticed a wire twisted between several logs, one of which sported three sticks of dynamite bound together in a bright red wad. Sam had already told him that Henry had a reputation for being careless in his use of explosives. Some of the men said the powder monkey was crazy because he loved to blow things up.

Eli dived into the water, expecting the worst. He felt his body heave as it flipped in the river. Water spouted up his nose and into his ears. He lost his grasp on the peavey, which disappeared in the current. The explosion drove a piece of wood into his calf. His leg felt cold and wet. Was it blood? Did he still have a foot?

Before he had time to assess his situation, a second charge exploded. This time a wall of water pushed the logs downstream. Pinched several times by logs smashing each other, he tried to get his head above water. It was hard to know which direction was up. He gasped for air whenever his bobbing head surfaced before the current pushed him underwater again.

The wall of water at last subsided. Eli climbed on top of a log, sitting with his legs beneath the water. He kicked his feet and legs, pleased to see the water splash over his limbs, glad they were still there. Before him were thousands of logs floating downstream amidst pieces of bark and men. People were running along the shore throwing ropes to river hogs too tired to swim or walk on logs. Next to him in the water was a dead man floating face down. Upstream he saw Ernie's dead body pinched between a raft of splintered logs. One of his legs was missing. The right side of his face, scraped and peeled, looked like raw meat.

"Ernie's gone!" yelled Sam, standing on the riverbank. "He's upstream coming down toward us." He threw a rope.

Eli grabbed the lifeline, slipped between wet timbers, and climbed onto shore. He shook the water from his red hair. "Let's go get Ernie. We'll have to fish him out ourselves."

"Yeah. I think he took a direct hit from the dynamite. Let's bring him in."

The two men waded in the river and retrieved their co-worker. As they placed the body on the riverbank, Eli watched several river hogs help injured men out of the water. He glanced down at Ernie's torn skin and shredded flesh. The panicked face, mashed by logs, bothered him most.

In the distance he spotted a group of men with a rope around Henry's neck. Five or six of them led the powder monkey toward a tree while two others pushed him away from the crowd. Eli heard yelling but couldn't make out the words. Perhaps, he thought, they are arguing about whether to hang him or not.

Three river hogs swung a rope over a sturdy tree branch. Henry struggled and punched one of the men in the stomach. The largest man pushed him to the ground and tightened the noose around his neck. Another pulled on the rope draped over the branch. Slowly, they lifted his body until he stood on tiptoes, screaming. All three men now pulled on the rope, yanking the powder monkey off the ground. His legs bounced up and down several times and then dropped, motionless. Henry, suspended in air, wailed once and went limp.

Silas blew his whistle. Men ran toward him from all directions, forming a circle around Henry, whose tongue protruded from the side of his mouth. Eli and Sam were the last to reach the group because they were carrying Ernie's body, which got heavier with each step they took in the spring mud. When they finally reached the group, Silas had already started his speech. "You guys are damn stupid. I know Henry was trigger-happy. But, you had no right to hang him. You aren't the law. Now, look at this mess. How will I explain this to Mr. Royston?"

The men sat in a circle without talking. They all stared at the dangling body.

"Now you'd better all be saying the same thing," Silas barked, swinging a stick in the air. "Everybody's got to have the same story. Now, go around and say what you saw. If anyone saw something different, speak up now before the sheriff comes."

Each man explained where he was, what he saw, and what he heard. Only two men spoke up to correct their fellow workers. Silas called roll, revealing there were sixteen men safe and accounted for. In addition, three were dead, one hung, four injured, and one missing. All but two men had lost their peaveys. Four coats, some boots, and six hats were missing.

Silas assigned a detail of men to transport the bodies and injured men to the wanagan. The rest were dismissed for the afternoon to return to their tents. Eli and Sam had trouble leaving Ernie in the care of others. Even though he was dead, they still felt responsible for him.

After that logjam was broken, Eli worked on a sacking crew. His group of river hogs was told to bring up the rear or gather scattered logs. Some of the logs got trapped in tree roots on the riverbank while others got stuck in feeder creeks away from the main flow of the river. Eli waded shallow portions of the river and hooked lost logs with his new peavey, pulling them back into the main current of the river.

A cloud of mosquitoes followed Eli wherever he went. He slapped the annoying pests when they stung the back of his hands—a good place, he thought, for their smashed carcasses to remain. The ones that attacked his forehead were harder to kill. He listened while their buzzing got louder and waited motionless to locate the source of the hum of one of the insects. When he detected the position of a blood-sucking pest, he jerked his head before swatting, and this often allowed them to escape. An unexpected sting followed, usually on the neck or other part of his body left unprotected. A lump that begged to be itched soon appeared. The easiest mosquitoes to kill were the greedy ones that had already fed and flew as if drunk because they were so full of blood. Eli caught those in his hand, squished them with a satisfying smile, and flicked the carcass through the air with his middle finger. Then came the best part, licking the blood from his palm and hoping it was his own.

Eli knew that bringing up the rear was a chaotic, difficult, and uncomfortable situation. Sometimes it took a full hour for men to reconvene after working different sections of river. They always waited for the full crew to return. River hogs sometimes got lost while wandering up tributaries off the main stream. It took a while for them to realize their mistake and wade back to the main branch. When a man was late, others wondered if he was hurt. Several men broke their legs in tangles of brush. Some got caught in the current and smashed their heads on stones or logs. Others drowned in deep pools. He saw several hand-made crosses tacked on trees or shoved into the riverbank where someone had died. He also noticed a pair of calked boots nailed to a cedar in memory of a river hog.

Sam told him the company sought scattered logs to reduce theft. Logging companies each had their own special brand hammered into the butt end of white pine logs with a special log-marking tool. There were hundreds of brands used on the Au Sable. Eli learned that individual logs were sorted near the mouth of the river in booming grounds, a series of corrals partially enclosed by timbers and chained together. Those areas were not just small impoundments but stretched across the horizon of large rivers and lakes. Many booming grounds were dotted with several dozen men holding long poles to steer logs into their respective company corral. Branded logs were sorted and counted to determine how much each logging company was paid at the end of the drive. Sawmills were often located near booming grounds. Logs were frequently collected in a boom and tied together into rafts. Some of those rafts included only a dozen logs, but others, on large water, were two to three acres in size. Pilots steered the large rafts with over-sized oars to sawmills along the Great Lake's shoreline.

After two weeks on the job, Eli ran into a band of log pirates. He was bringing up the rear, working a shallow, gravely part of the river that ran through a dark cedar swamp. In order to watch spawning fish shimmy in the spring sun, he climbed on a cedar limb that hung over the river. The female was laying eggs in a small shiny spot that she swept clean of debris. He recalled that the fish nests were called reds. Eli watched two male fish dart across the red and sprayed milt on the eggs. He got so excited he almost fell from his cedar perch.

Whenever the wind blew from the west, he heard human voices mixed with the babbling of rapids among cedar roots. He slid down the tree and sneaked through the woods at some distance from the riverbank.

Eli hid behind the trunk of a hemlock and watched three men working on the riverbank. They cut off a small portion of a log, thereby removing the log mark. A fresh brand was hammered on the end of the log, set free in the current.

Eli considered his next move very carefully. If he confronted the three men, they might kill him and make it look like an accident. Yet he knew he should report the theft of timber to someone. While pondering his options, he studied the men's clothes, physical appearance, and other characteristics that might help him identify them later. When one of the men stood up to scratch his head, Eli knew he'd seen him before. Did I see him in logging camp last winter? Or was it back home in Coldwater? Wait, I remember. I saw that man in the catacombs of Bay City.

The other two men were not quite as visible, so Eli sneaked through the dense forest to get a closer glimpse of them. As he moved, he tripped on the root of a cedar tree.

"What's that sound?" said one of the men.

"Look! Someone's on the ground over there," another said. Let's get him." The three men ran toward Eli, who bolted but was tackled.

"There—I got him!" said one of his assailants.

Eli's face hurt where it was pushed into the mud.

Two men held him down while the third spoke. "What are you doing here?"

He tasted mud when he talked. "I'm looking for stray logs along the riverbank."

The man from the catacombs appeared to be the leader of the group. He relaxed his grip on Eli and reached out to help him stand. Then he shook hands. "Allow me to introduce myself. My name's Bruce Royston. My father is president of the company that pays you. We, too, are looking for stray logs. We're also analyzing the river flow in this area. Our company may purchase twenty sections of land a few miles from here."

Eli spat some mud and wiped his mouth on his wet sleeve.

The young man continued. "My father asked us to see if this river can handle the volume of timber we plan to cut next winter. If not, he may move logs on a narrow gauge train instead of floating them downstream."

Why's the president's son pirating logs? Eli wondered. Maybe it was just the fun of doing something mischievous. This man has unmistakable breeding and a good education. I've heard that rich people often do stupid things, like stealing things even when they have money.

"Excuse us for tackling you," said another man in the group. "We saw you watching us. We thought you might try to rob us. We have no guns or knives, you know."

Eli knew something was wrong. He'd watched one of the men cut a branch with his sheath knife. "Well, I'd better catch up with the rest of my crew before the sun sets," he said, wading into the river.

Bruce said, "I'm glad we met. Be careful of the loose sand on the next river bend."

"Goodbye, gentlemen."

Now Eli was puzzled about what to do. The three men had been polite, shook hands, and even apologized for tackling him. Still, he'd seen them illegally cut the end off a white pine and stamp the butt with another company's mark. For some reason, they lied about having a knife.

Eli had lots of time to think while walking along the riverbank and in shallow water. I'm fortunate to find spring work. I can't turn in Mr. Royston without more convincing information.

After working another week on the river, Eli had a Sunday off. He walked to town and visited the local saloon where he joined discussions about politics, religion, and the timber business. He asked, "Any news about Royston Lumber Company?"

One of the men at the end of the bar answered. "They're having a fight with Simmons Incorporated. Both companies made a claim to the same twenty sections of pine near the Au Sable River. That's more than twelve thousand acres!"

"Why the fight?" Eli pretended to be only mildly interested. Inside, he was bursting with excitement to find out what was happening.

"The Lands Office hasn't finalized the sale yet. The company attorneys claim there were mistakes in the land survey."

"What kind of mistakes?"

"Someone cut down the witness trees on section corners. A market hunter saw the culprit. The sheriff's got a good description."

"Maybe they'll catch him."

"Even so, the Lands Office doesn't know which parcels of public land are for sale."

Another man in dress clothes, obviously not a river hog, added, "There's some investment bank from Detroit involved, too."

The bartender pointed out another aspect of the dispute. "There's a company trying to sell the narrow gage locomotive to Mr. Royston. The whole deal's political."

"Yeah," said Eli. "I'm glad I just catch stray logs for Royston. I hate politics. You know what the big problem is in Washington today…" Eli soon had a group of six men listening to him. In spite of his words, he was thinking something else. He was analyzing the crime he witnessed. It should be investigated, he concluded.

A foreman told Eli to report to Mr. Royston's wanagan on Monday afternoon. Just as he climbed aboard, he saw a deputy sheriff leave with a prisoner in handcuffs.

"What'd he do?" Eli asked one of the office clerks.

The company employee answered, "He works for Simmons Incorporated. They caught him pirating logs. He fits the description of the guy who cut down witness trees. Because of that, the Lands Office couldn't record the deed."

"Can they buy the land now?"

"Nope. There's still some problems. Mr. Simmons is a silent partner in The Detroit Trust Company, a bank that controls all our company accounts. Nobody knew that before. Now the funds to pay the Lands Office for the twenty sections have been frozen by the bank's headquarters in Detroit. The Lands Office will only wait until the close of business on Thursday. If the funds aren't released, the land will be sold to Simmons Incorporated. This is a nasty legal fight."

An accountant on the wanagan said, "There's more. The Fitzgerald Railroad Company is experimenting with narrow gauge trains. They put pressure on officials at the Lands Office to sell the twenty sections to Simmons Incorporated because they were willing to try hauling logs by rail instead of by water. We hear that a federal legislator may be involved."

All the pieces fit together. Bruce Royston had re-marked logs to frame the competition. If Simmons Incorporated were charged with illegal pirating of logs from Royston Lumber Company, the transaction involving the twenty sections of pine could at least be delayed, if not cancelled. So, Bruce used log-marking tools with the symbol of Simmons Incorporated to pirate logs. That way Royston Lumber Company could file a legal complaint against Simmons for illegal logging. That's why a man of Bruce Royston's status spent several days in the wilderness re-marking his own timber with a competitor's log mark.

Bruce walked from his office to greet Eli. He said, "Want a cigar?"

The men lit their cigars and wandered around the wanigan.

Eli said, "What a wonderful aroma. This is indeed fine tobacco." He pretended to be knowledgeable about cigars although he'd smoked only one before.

With the poise of a minister, Bruce asked, "Is there anything on your mind that you'd like to talk about?"

"Of course. I'm a curious fellow." He brushed tobacco from the thin red moustache above his lip.

"Anything specific?"

"Well, I did see you and your friends mark some logs with another company's symbol."

Bruce blew smoke in Eli's face. "Yes, we thought you might have seen us."

"Now, I hear you're turning in someone else for that."

"So, what's your question?"

Eli moved away from the smoke. "Why'd you frame that poor man?"

Bruce, like most powerful men, appeared to enjoy Eli's directness. "The person we framed was a known trouble maker from Simmons Incorporated. He murdered one of my men in Bay City. The prosecuting attorney could never prove the murder. Our landlooker found that white pine first and we made a proper claim at the land office. We have rights to that timber, despite the illegal tactics of our competitor."

"Is that so?" Eli puffed his cigar. He shook the tobacco ash from his weather-beaten hand. "What's a landlooker?"

"That's a man whose paid by a timber company to find pine. They work in teams of two, living in the wilderness for two to three weeks. They study maps, land surveys, and even climb trees to look for pine. When they find it, they rush to the nearest Lands Office to make a claim, usually in the name of the company that pays them."

"What if two landlookers from different companies find the same pine?"

"There may be a race to the Lands Office. That's not the situation here, though. We registered our find. Simmons didn't. Our company did everything right."

"Is that so?" repeated Eli.

"I've got to protect a staff of over two hundred men. I also represent thousands of stockholders. We take care of our own justice here in the north country."

Eli puffed several times on his cigar. "I'm sorry, sir, but I know nothing about justice in northern Michigan. If you are truly avenging the murder of one of your employees, I applaud you with deep respect…" Eli seemed to have found his niche. His talkative nature seemed well suited to the Ivy League mannerisms of Mr. Royston.

For his part, Bruce knew how to cut off a man like Eli. He threw his partially smoked cigar into the river. "You worry about gathering logs in the river and I'll take care of the competition and stockholders. Now get back to work."

Eli smiled. Since he liked Bruce Royston, he did what he was told.

He worked hard that spring breaking logjams and gathering up the rear. Eli learned how to ride logs without falling in the water. He knew where to hide when dynamite charges went off.

When the river drive ended, he was paid in a lump sum. After subtracting what he owed at the company store, he had one hundred and sixty-five dollars left to show his father when he got home. This time when he traveled home, he didn't take a train through Bay City.

Eli arrived in Coldwater just in time for the second haying. That seemed like such easy work, compared to logging, but the heat near the Michigan-Indiana border bothered him. He also got a bad case of sunburn from working long hours in the scorched fields. He told everyone in his family he was happy to be home for the summer. Secretly, though, he missed northern Michigan. He also missed the comradeship of other men his own age.

His boredom vanished when he received a letter at the Coldwater post office in early August. It read:

> Dear Mr. Peters:
>
> I am writing as a representative of Royston Lumber Company to inquire about your interest in an executive position with our firm. We are currently interviewing for a manager at the Bay City lumberyard. Mr. Bruce Royston, Vice President of Timber Operations, provided your name to our office as a potential candidate for the opening. If you are interested in being con-

sidered for this position, please respond by the 17th of September so we can arrange an interview.

Sincerely,

Tracy M. Boyd

Personnel Director

Eli was delighted that he might be able to work up north for a timber company. He wrote a letter back, in his best cursive, stating he would like to be considered for the position. At the end of the month, the company wired him some money for travel expenses to the job interview.

He met the personnel director at the Bay City lumberyard in a shed filled with stacks of lumber that smelled like turpentine. Mr. Boyd didn't ask the usual questions about former jobs, career objectives, or references. Instead, he said, "Why does Mr. Bruce Royston want you to join our firm?"

Eli wasn't prepared for such a direct, personal question. He quickly organized his thoughts while he spoke in polite, elaborate phrases. "I suppose he wants diversity in the staff. My background in agriculture might augment the business skills of others in the company." Eli continued to discuss the importance of diversity in business organizations.

At the conclusion of the brief interview, the personnel director offered Eli the job with the stipulation that Mr. Howard Royston, president of the company, first approve the appointment. Eli was asked to report to the president's residence for dinner at seven o'clock.

The Royston estate was one of the majestic homes in Bay City. Eli stopped at a wrought iron gate with stone lions on both sides. He gave his name at the guardhouse to a uniformed employee, who swung open the massive gate. He walked toward the house, set back on a thick green lawn, accented with lush gardens. A high fence, topped with sharp iron points, surrounded the property. Eli stared at the house's fine wood with gingerbread design.

A butler met him at the front door and announced the entrance of a dinner guest. The farm boy removed his hat, exposing his recently cut red hair, and handed it to the servant. As Eli followed the butler through the parlor, he noticed that some of the artifacts were from Asia and Egypt. They included fine oil paintings, some four by eight feet in size, on the walls.

Mr. Howard Royston rose from a well-carved French Victorian chair while the ladies remained seated. "Welcome to our home. I understand you spent the afternoon at the lumberyard." Mr. Royston was a slim man with stooped shoulders and pure white hair that formed a horseshoe around the back of his head. He wore three rings, gold cuff links, and a jeweled stickpin in his tie. A pocket watch with fob dangled across his belly. He was clearly an aristocrat.

"Yes, I enjoyed meeting some of the staff. Thank you for the courtesy of inviting me to your home." He was glad he had gotten a haircut and had the peach fuzz shaved from his chin.

"Mr. Peters, I am honored to present my wife, Louise."

Mrs. Royston rose and extended her hand, palm down.

Eli kissed her hand. "I'm very pleased to meet you, ma'am. What a beautiful home you have."

"Thank you. We so enjoy our time in Bay City. Of course, our permanent home is in the Finger Lakes Region of New York State."

Mr. Royston then introduced his two daughters. "These are my daughters Rose and Marie." The girls stood when he motioned to them and curtseyed like well-rehearsed actresses. "Please have a seat," he said.

The butler responded briskly to the cue. "What kind of cocktail would you like, sir?"

Eli noticed the ladies had some kind of red drink and Mr. Royston's glass contained a thick yellow fluid. "Could

I have bourbon and water, please?" He felt quite at home dealing with the privileged class.

"What do you think of Bay City?" asked the host.

Eli had already thought of a topic he planned to introduce in conversation. "I'm surprised by the need here for community funds. The city lacks adequate fire and police protection, the schools are in need, and there is a noted lack of cultural amenities, like museums and art galleries."

"Yes," said Mrs. Royston. "The editorials in the paper blame that on Mr. Rutherford. They say he refuses to support the town with additional taxes from his mill."

"What foolishness," said Mr. Royston. He stood and walked about the parlor with his hands in his pockets. "Why do these western towns always seek charity from business? There is only so much profit after the stockholders' share. The excess either goes to the workers in wages or the community in taxes."

"Yes," Eli added. "It would seem we need more voluntary giving rather than mandatory taxation."

They continued the discussion over dinner. When they were finished, Mr. Royston excused himself and Eli for a smoke in the library. The ladies retired to the music room where Rose sat at the piano and played a delicate piece of music from the classical era.

Mr. Royston sat down close to Eli. "Could I ask a personal question?"

"Certainly, sir."

"Mr. Peters, why does a man like you with a farming background have an interest in the timber business?"

"Because, sir, I love northern Michigan, I understand logging, and I respect your son, Bruce."

Mr. Royston finished his after-dinner crème de mint at the same time he finished his conversation, "Well, there are few human traits more worthy than love, understanding, and respect. Please report for duty at the yard on October 1. Thank you for your long journey here to visit me. Welcome to our company."

That was it. Eli hurried home to Coldwater to pack, say goodbye to his family, and start a new life. In one sense, he'd come a long way from a destitute lumberjack on the streets of Bay City to a manager in a lumberyard. Of course, he knew his new job was payment to keep quiet about seeing the son of a timber man pirate logs on the Au Sable River. His rise from poverty to wealth was a polite form of bribery. Eli also knew it was time to be careful about what he said and did.

12

Jake and Thor in Grafton

Jake welcomed the hot sun beating on his shoulders as he walked with Thor from the train depot to Grafton. It seemed much warmer here in southern Michigan than in the pinewoods. The bare and brown ground looked strange after a winter of snow. He skipped in the mud puddles and splashed water on Thor. Like brothers with spring fever, they were soon coated in mud.

He looked at the chunks of clay stuck in his friend's beard and was thankful he was now clean-shaven. Jake had enjoyed having a beard during his stay in camp, but now he was happy he'd had it removed by the Bay City barber.

A gray thundercloud raced across the sky to replace sunshine with drizzle. Jake felt tiny raindrops dot his face and arms while he marched through the mist. Before long the drizzle changed to a spring downpour. Rain cascading straight down was so heavy it stung the top of his scalp. It drenched his hair with sheets of water that slid down his curly bangs. When the rainwater reached his lips, he tasted a mix of fresh earth, hair, and sweat. A constant stream of cold water soaked his sideburns and flowed down his collar. He peered through wet eyelashes at his friend who seemed to be standing beneath a waterfall.

"We don't have to worry 'bout mud any more," said Jake.

Thor tried to grin, but his face was contorted. He didn't like being wet because water dripped down his beard to his chest. "There's no evergreens in your southern Michigan. These hardwoods are bare in spring. There's no place to hide from this rain."

"Why hide? We'll get a free bath and smell better than sweet fern."

"Look at my boots!" He tried without success to scrape the heavy clay from the bottom and sides of his boots.

Jake pointed to town, barely visible in the mist. "There's Grafton—the place I grew up."

"I see a blacksmith shop." Thor snapped his suspenders. "Is that where Sally lived?"

"Yeah." He began to daydream, recalling the time he saw her at the Bay City saloon. How could she be a prostitute? Could I have said something to make her come home?

"Which way to your cabin?" asked Thor.

"It's only a mile or two to the river." He shivered. The wind took away all the sun's warmth. "I hope Dad has a fire going."

Jake remembered how tiny Grafton looked when he returned home from his first trip to Kalamazoo. Now the town looked even smaller. There were only a few buildings. Why had he remembered more? Where were all the people?

Seeing the blacksmith shop and general store made him feel welcome. He saw the church had a new bell, but everything else looked the same. Maybe that's good, he thought. There should be places that never change, especially childhood homes. He recalled picnics, cabin-raisings, and parades. He remembered sitting at his desk in the schoolhouse, fighting Ronnie in the village square, and fishing with his dad. Then a vision of Sally flashed before his eyes. He saw her creamy face, smelled her scent, and tasted her lips. He recalled the first time he kissed her.

"So, this is the village I've heard so much about," said Thor.

"Yup, but we're too wet to stop anywhere. Besides, I want to see Dad. Let's keep going."

Jake could see a large black cloud moving quickly to the east. He wrung the rainwater out of his hair. Sunlight shone in long streaks through the mist. Even though the rain and wind had vanished, he was skeptical that the sunshine would last.

Thor scanned the horizon, turned in a complete circle and, with the sun at his back, peered off in the distance. "There it is. I see it!" Jake followed his finger, which pointed at a thick rainbow with bright colors perfectly separated in discrete bands. It made a full arch, spanning from one side of the sky to the other.

Thor looked fascinated by the colorful display. "Did you know, there's a pot of gold at the end of that rainbow?" His Swedish accent was heavy.

"No, that's an old wives' tale. Reverend Hughes said rainbows are a promise from God that he'll never again try to destroy us. Don't you know about Noah's ark?"

"Naw. A rainbow means you're about to achieve some kind of success. It's not always gold. It could be love, health, or whatever you're searching for. A rainbow is a symbol of opportunity."

"I like the way you notice things that others don't see. You make me think about life. You're a good friend."

Thor grinned. He leaped in the air and landed in a puddle, which showered Jake with water and mud. "I'm glad you're my friend, too."

He punched Thor's shoulder. The next thing he knew Thor had him in headlock, which squished his ears. He felt himself flipped, like a pancake, into a mud puddle. The two friends wrestled playfully in the soggy soil. Grunts and groans rose from the ground beneath the rainbow.

A few minutes later they reached the cabin. Jake pounded on the door. He heard his mother humming.

"Isn't this your cabin?" said Thor. "How come you're knocking? Don't you live here?"

His mother, Judy, opened the door before Jake had a chance to answer. "Is that you, Jacques? My goodness, look at you. You're filthy!" A wide smile exposed her perfect, white teeth.

"Hi Mom. Please call me Jake. That's my name now."

He leaned across the doorway and kissed her, pleased that even after her kiss there was no mud on her clothes.

This is just how it used to be, he thought. When Jake or his dad returned dirty from hunting or fishing trips, they often kissed her on the other side of the doorway. She didn't want dirt in the cabin and they didn't want to stain her clothes. She always seemed so bright, clean, and pure.

Judy leaned out the door to kiss him again. "It's wonderful to see you. I worried about you. Now, you're safe with us. We missed you so."

"It's been a long winter." He dropped the carpetbag, returned with a bit more wear, along with a heavy coating of mud.

"I don't know if I'll be able to call you Jake. You've always been Jacques to me."

"Please try, Mom."

"You look different. Stronger. More sure of yourself. More like a man."

His face turned red. Jake looked at his friend, who had a slight grin on his face. It was a small enough gesture to go unnoticed by Judy, but big enough to send a message to both young men. The grin made Jake feel awkward.

Two heads appeared in the doorway on either side of Judy. Martha and William clung to their mother's dress as if their brother was a stranger. Then they saw how muddy he was and began to laugh. Martha said, "Haven't you had a bath all winter?"

Jake relaxed when everyone chuckled. He said, "This is my friend Thor. We worked together at camp."

"Welcome," said Judy. "Where's your family from?"

"I come from Sweden, on the other side of the ocean. I'm pleased to meet you."

"Oh my, I love your accent," she said.

Jake asked, "Can he stay with us this summer?"

"Let's talk later." She hummed a few notes from a familiar church hymn. "First, go down to the river and wash that mud off. I'll send William with clean clothes. I'm so happy you're home." She leaned out the door to kiss him again.

Jake led his friend along the path to a familiar pool. He undressed, grabbed a rope tied to a tree branch, and swung into the river. Within seconds, he scurried up the riverbank out of the cold water.

"That wasn't very smart," said Thor. "Now you have to stand there shivering until William shows up with your clean clothes."

"I know. I was just so happy to be home and see the old rope. I didn't think much." He was pleased to see William arrive with towels, shirts, and trousers. "Hurry up! I'm freezing."

Jake used a towel to blot cold water from his shoulders, belly, and legs. He slipped into his warm clothes, which felt soft and clean. While dressing, he watched Thor's nude form swing in a circle over the swimming hole several times. A splash signaled that he had let go of the rope and was in the water. Jake took the other change of clothes from William.

Thor gasped for air and paddled water with his hands, as if that might speed up his retreat from the frigid river. Jake smiled as his friend slipped on the muddy soil, splashed back into the river, and climbed up the bank again. Nude on the shoreline, Thor's body turned blue with small goose bumps that speckled his hide.

Jake said, "What'd you say about being stupid?"

"Okay, I give up. You win. Gimme my clothes."

In the distance someone whistled a tune. It was too far north for Jake to make out the tune, but he knew it was his dad. He often whistled, especially after a good day of fishing. Soon he made out the notes to "Onward, Christian Soldiers."

"Well, it's about time you got home. The suckers just started to run." Jake's dad lugged a full stringer of fish over his right shoulder. His left hand, crossing his chest, was red with streaks of white around the knuckles. The scent of fish penetrated Jake's nostrils. Pierre dropped the heavy suckers and extended his hand. "We missed you, son."

Thor didn't wait to be introduced. He felt comfortable being himself in the company of men. "I'm Thor. Your son thought an extra hand might help this spring." He stared at the fish with round, puckered mouths.

Pierre shook his hand. "Any friend of Jake's is a friend of the family. There seems to be an accent in your voice. Where are you from?"

Jake thought it strange that both his mother and father asked about the heritage of his friend's family. "His family's from Sweden. Can he stay with us a while?"

"We'll see. You boys gather your old clothes and bring back the fish. I already gutted them to lighten the load. Just toss 'em in the smoker."

"Yes, sir," said Thor.

Pierre left with William on his back. The boy reached for tree branches along the trail during his piggyback ride.

After dinner Jake carried his muddy carpetbag into the cabin and placed it in on an oilcloth in front of the wood stove. "Martha, come over here. I've got something for you," he said to his sister.

Everyone in the cabin took chairs near the stove while he carefully opened the carpetbag so mud would fall on the cloth, rather than the cabin floor. Sliding his hand inside, he felt the crumpled paper that concealed her present. He watched Martha's eyes open wide with excitement as he guided the prize from the muddy bag.

"Is that for me?" She unwrapped the bright purple paper like removing the skin from an onion. Inside was a tiny rag doll, no more than three inches in length, with a painted face. He'd bought it in Bay City, at a store not far from the restaurant where Sally worked.

"Yes, that's just for you. Nobody can play with it unless you say so."

"Goodie, goodie! Thank you."

William peered into the carpetbag. "Oh, yes, I got something for you, too." Jake withdrew a leather pouch and handed it to his little brother.

The boy loosened the pouch string. Reaching inside, he pulled out a green marble with yellow spackling. There were two more marbles in the pouch. One was red and white; the other was burnt orange.

"They're made from polished agates. I got them in trade from a lumberjack who found them on a yoopee beach on Lake Superior. U.P. is for Upper Peninsula, way up in northern Michigan."

Jake removed a carefully folded dress and presented it to his mother. She went to the bedroom and returned in a flowered dress he also bought in Bay City. Everyone stood and applauded as she spun in circles showing off the beautiful present.

She leaned in front of the warm stove and kissed Jake on the cheek. "Thanks. This will be a special dress for special occasions."

His father's gift had been the hardest to choose. Jake wanted to get him something that would represent their relationship. He wanted to find a gift that would symbolize his dad's sacrifices as a parent, his guiding advice, and his well-earned authority. However, all the gifts he saw seemed to come up short. Finally, on his way home, he met a lumberjack sitting near him on the train with a holstered pistol. It was the kind of pistol carried by union officers during the Civil War. He had heard his dad talk about those pistols many times.

When Jake expressed interest in the pistol, the lumberjack offered it for sale. The young man had foolishly wasted his winter's pay on booze and women. He'd sold many of his possessions to conceal his mistake. Jake was pleased to buy the pistol because it was the perfect gift for his dad.

Everyone's eyes were on him as Jake inched the firearm above the lid of his carpetbag. "Isn't she a beauty?" He passed the pistol to his dad.

Pierre fondled the firearm. He aimed it at the fireplace and turned it over several times, admiring the craftsmanship. "This is a real work of art. Where'd you get it?"

“I bought it from a lumberjack on the train. He said he won it in a card game.”

“It is a perfect gift. When I look at it, I’ll always remember you and your first trip up north. Thank you.” He winked. “And I’ll always remember Grandpa and the wanderlust you inherited from him.”

Jake was glad. His dad’s excitement meant he had picked the right gift.

Thor led the group in singing a loud rendition of “For He’s a Jolly Good Fellow.”

After a few minutes of talk and laughter, Jake pulled out a final present for the entire family. It was a roll of bills totaling eighty-two dollars. “I tried hard, Dad. This is what I’ve got left after all my expenses.”

Pierre counted the money and handed it to his wife. “Good job, son. These are tough times. Not many people have cash. This will help all of us. Thank you.”

Thor stood and walked around the stove. He put his hands out to be warmed. Then he reached into his pocket and withdrew some money. “I’d like to pay for my summer room and board now.” He gave Pierre two twenty-dollar bills and put the rest back in his pocket.

Jake’s parents looked at one another. She nodded. Pierre said, “Good enough. But you’ll have to work hard and stay out of trouble.” He gave one of the bills to his wife and returned the other to Thor.

“I will,” he said. “Thanks.” He lifted Martha in the air. She locked her legs around his waist, and they danced about the cabin.

Before bed the family talked about things that had happened in town since autumn. They talked of people who had died in winter and of the two big snows that kept everyone in their cabins for three days. They finally spoke about Sally, although Jake was hoping to avoid that topic.

“Too bad about your old girlfriend,” said Pierre. “Some say she went to the Potawatomi reservation and became a medicine woman. One of the customers at the general store told Mrs. Rice she saw Sally working at a bank in Grand Rapids. Nobody really knows where she went."

The two young men glanced at each other. He couldn't tell his parents that he had seen her. He had to keep his promise to Sally.

Jake said, "Too bad. We always had so much fun when we were little." He changed the subject. "What about the church steeple? I saw it had a new bell."

"A butcher moved into town and died within a week. His family gave the church the new bell. I hear it came all the way from Allentown, Pennsylvania. That was his hometown. His widow's a nice lady. She buys lots of deer meat from us."

Thor listened to the discussions while cleaning his boots. When he finished rubbing them with a greasy cloth, he stuffed the boots with cloth so they would dry better. He looked at the Jake's brother and sister and asked, "So what'd you do this winter."

Martha told about the snowman she built, complete with pine knot eyes and nose. William explained how his friend Randy Kauffman fell through the ice and almost drowned. They shared some interesting things they learned in school, especially about space. Their tales of stars and planets soon led Thor to share some ghost stories.

"One night at camp," he said, "we were sound asleep at two in the morning. Everyone woke to the sound of pots and pans banging in the cookhouse. When we went to see what was making the noise, we saw huge footprints in the snow. Our visitor was Sasquatch, a huge beast who lives in the north woods. He looks like a giant ape." Thor repeated the word, Sasquatch, using his best Swedish accent.

That night, Martha and William hid under their blankets without sleeping very much. In another corner of the cabin, Jake slept the best he had in several months. His cot felt warm and soft with crevices in all the right spots. It was his bed. He was home.

13

Jake's Loss

Thor was surprised by how quickly he learned to catch fish in the rivers and lakes around Grafton. He took the most fish during peak periods that varied by time of day, wind, water level, cloud cover, rain, and other factors. He learned to work when fish were most active, which often meant being on the river at daybreak or in a boat after midnight. What pleased him most was bringing Pierre large quantities of fresh fillets.

Thor expected to be bored with poles and nets. Instead, he enjoyed the peaceful activity, especially the quiet time between fishing peaks. He sang when fishing was slow. He remembered many songs, some from his native country and others he learned in logging camps. Many were French-Canadian ballads passed down from generations of voyagers who carried beaver pelts in oversized canoes. Sometimes Thor's verses echoed across the water and seemed to be joined by distant voices from the past. Whenever the fishing kept him busy, he stopped singing.

Thor was good at catching fish. He and Jake processed more than a thousand pounds of fillets during the first month they were home. The family business prospered and soon had more fish to sell than people were buying. One day Pierre said to Thor, "I've got an idea. You're good with people. What if Jake catches fish and you sell them?"

"How would I do that?"

"By being a salesman. That's a person who makes you want to buy something."

"But exactly how do I make people want to buy fish?"

"First you make friends with them. They'll buy your fish because they like you. It might work better than throwing away fillets. Let's try it."

"Okay. What should I do?"

"You're good at telling stories. People have to listen closely because of your accent. So, put emotions in your tales. Make people laugh and cry."

Thor listened to Pierre and did what he was told. During the next month Thor played cards in the general store and told stories in the village square. He found that Jake's father was right. People bought more fish when the story was good and fewer fish when the story was poor. He tried to make his stories better to sell more fish. He elaborated them with more vivid details and contagious emotions. Before long Jake couldn't catch enough fish to meet the new demand. Even Pierre had to catch fish after an especially good tale.

This public exposure also helped Thor fit into the community. People appreciated his friendly mannerisms and kind ways. In turn, he got to know many town folk in Grafton. They made him feel welcome. They laughed at his Swedish accent, especially when he misunderstood the subtle meaning of words or phrases. His smile disarmed everyone, even the crankiest residents in town. Thor learned about politics, too. He always recognized dignitaries, like the minister, bank president, and sheriff. He identified them to his audiences as positive, helpful leaders.

Thor made sure the residents of Grafton ate lots of fish during the summer of 1873. Since few people had cash, the Flareau's root cellar overflowed with fruits and vegetables. They had promissory notes for firewood and furniture.

Soon it was time for the young men to once again head north for logging camp. The morning they left, Jake's mother said, "Please take care of yourselves. We hear terrible things about logging accidents. Make sure you watch for gray spots on your hands and feet when the weather gets cold."

Jake smiled and gave her a hug and kiss. He had heard those words before.

Thor replied, "Thank you for letting me stay with your family this summer. I feel like this is my home now."

Judy leaned over and kissed him on the cheek. "Please come back and stay with us next summer."

"I will. Thanks." He took her hands in his. "You made me feel so welcome."

Thor did return the next summer and for several summers after that. He enjoyed his new life of working in logging camp in winter and returning to Grafton in summer. Both men prospered. Jake was even assigned to be a head feller at logging camp, along side of Thor. The men were paid well because of their experience in the woods.

The Flareau's market hunting business also grew. Thor became famous in the Grafton area as a storyteller. He also tutored students that the teacher referred to him for extra help in summer. People in town were always excited when the two young men came back from up north and they were saddened to see them leave in the fall.

The best year for fishing in Grafton was three years later, in 1876. The Flareaus took in enough money that year to add separate rooms to their cabin. Judy and Pierre shared a room, as did Thor, William, and Jake. Martha had her own room. That was also the year when Thor was invited to the Centennial Celebration.

The mayor of Grafton passed along the invitation in public after Thor told one of his stories in the village square. "I have a special announcement," said the mayor. "The City of Kalamazoo asked me to give you this note." He patted Thor on the back and read part of the text. "It is my honor to request your presence on July 4, 1876. Please join me and other guests of our city in celebrating the one hundredth birthday of our nation. I have allowed you between five and ten minutes to tell one of your best stories. I look forward to meeting you."

The audience cheered. Grafton seemed proud to have its first celebrity. The guest of honor was humbled. He replied, "I love this country. Here I am a foreigner in a strange land. Yet, I have been asked to tell a story about your independence from Great Britain. This is not only the land of opportunity, but also of hospitality."

Thor and Jake arrived in Kalamazoo on July third. All day, thunderstorms drenched the city's streets and buildings. Oh no, thought Thor, people will get wet at tomorrow's ceremony. Maybe some of the guests will stay home. Perhaps the parade will be cancelled.

A rainbow appeared in late afternoon when the rain stopped. Maybe, he thought, a better day will come tomorrow. At six that night, a gun was fired to start the celebration. Firecrackers and band music followed.

The Fourth of July began with a national salute, fired at sunrise to recognize the Centennial. Most people in town rose early to hear guns and firecrackers welcome the day. Thor also heard the ringing of bells from homes, churches, and businesses.

People began to gather at eight o'clock for the parade. Thor and Jake left the hotel at nine. Walking toward town, Thor was amazed at the number of flags he saw flying on houses and shops. Many stores had streamers hung from third-floor windows to the sidewalks below.

Beginning in April, the local newspapers had invited residents in seven counties to the Kalamazoo celebration. The marketing approach worked well. There were 15,000 people in the streets by ten o'clock.

Colonel G. Edwin Dunbar, Grand Marshall, led the parade. Behind him was the fifteen-piece Cornet Band of Constantine. Next came the Kalamazoo Light Guard with a drum major, four Prussian snare drums, and thirty-six men. The loudest applause accompanied a horse-drawn float that carried a lady for each state surrounding the Goddess of Liberty. Other organizations in the parade included Grange Societies, the Odd Fellows, and several businesses, such as the Kalamazoo Knitting Company.

Thor had never seen such excitement. He was thrilled by the crowds, tall buildings, and bustling activity. The things people talked about fascinated him: commerce, government, family and many other topics. He and Jake tasted several kinds of food they bought from street vendors and in shops.

As the parade ended, people gathered by the courthouse near Colonel F. W. Curtenius, Master of Ceremonies. Thor climbed the stairs of a gazebo, leaving Jake behind in the crowd, and introduced himself to the colonel and Mayor. He listened to more band music, a prayer, and "America," sung by The Grand Chorus. Then, it was his turn to be introduced by the colonel. "Next in our program we have a story from a man who has spent many days and nights in the forest, both in this country and in his homeland of Sweden. He now lives in Grafton. I am pleased to introduce Thor Glick."

Thor stood at the podium covered in red, white, and blue ribbons. He looked out over the large crowd. He started his speech with enthusiasm. "Thank you for inviting me to your birthday celebration. My story is about a great black bear that lived in the woods. He was so large that all the other animals in the forest feared him. When he was hungry, he made the rabbits get his food. The bear forced raccoons to bring him water. All the animals were slaves to this great bear who lived a life of luxury. Onc day a tiny squirrel, who worked very hard to bury nuts all fall, was told to bring the bear an unfair share of his hidden acorns. The squirrel refused and organized all the other squirrels into a renegade pack of guerilla soldiers that fired nuts at the bear from the treetops. 'No taxation without representation,' they chattered. The bear, insulted and injured, felt sore from the lumps on his back and head. He gathered his relatives and formed an orderly brigade of disciplined troops to fight the squirrels. Even though they were stronger and better armed with spears and stones, the bears were defeated by the squirrels who loved freedom. We are gathered here today, one hundred years after this nation's independence, to remember that the desire to be free is the most powerful weapon in any arsenal. Happy Birthday America, the Land of Opportunity."

The Honorable Germain H. Mason read the Declaration of Independence after Thor finished his story. Next, Ara H. Stoddard read a poem. "We hail with pride as well we may, with joy and exultation, this glorious and immortal day, the Centennial of our nation…"

A benediction and intermission followed. Crowds returned to the site when the Constantine Band resumed playing the "Grand Chorus" and "Sweet Home." The keynote speaker, Foster Pratt, M.D., spoke on the history of the Kalamazoo area and the band ended the program with an energetic rendition of "Auld Lang Syne." Thor looked at the sea of faces from his seat of honor on the gazebo and waved to his best friend, Jake. It had been a great day in the big city.

The young men also continued to have some memorable experiences in logging camp. Not all of the situations were good. One winter, Jake was felling a tall pine that had two trunks welded together near the forest floor. He heard a worker nearby yell, "Help! Come quickly!"

Jake ran as fast as he could, sensing the urgency of the request. He saw two men trying to free a sawyer pinned beneath a pine. Jumping into the snow beside the injured man, he worked his axe with wide swings that became smaller as he neared the injured man's face. Dark blood, filled with foamy bubbles, sprinkled the snow. Jake remembered the different kinds of blood from hunting deer. Bright red blood was from spurting arteries. Darker blood was from veins. He recalled that foamy blood came from lung injuries.

The limb pinning the man at last came free of the tree trunk. He pulled it hard to the side so it would not scratch the face of the man in the snow. He recognized the lumberjack who looked like he was sound asleep. It was Franz Heimer from Grand Rapids.

Jake leaned down and spoke directly in his ear. "You're free now."

There was no response. Jake put his head down so his ear was in front of Franz's nose. He heard breathing but it was labored.

One of the swampers said that Franz should remain flat until he regained consciousness because his neck might be broken. The men left him where he was. They sat by his side and waited for some sign that he was awake. Franz finally opened his eyes, which darted from side to side without any movement of his head. His speech was slow and barely audible. "I can't move my head."

A sawyer asked, "Can you wiggle that finger by Jake's axe?"

"Oh my God." He paused. "I can't move my fingers." He paused again. "My hands won't move either."

"How about your toes?"

"Nope, I can't lift my feet or move my legs." Foamy blood flowed from his nostrils and leaked into his mouth. "I taste blood. Am I bleeding?"

Jake stayed with the injured man while the two swampers went for help.

Franz asked, "How bad is it?"

"I can't tell. I don't want to reach inside your coat to find out. You need to stay warm."

"Thanks for cutting the tree off me. What will I do if I'm paralyzed? How can I make a living?"

Jake avoided his questions. "We'll have to wait and see. Do you need anything? Would you like my coat to keep you warm?" He noticed Franz was getting pale. His lips were turning blue. When he spoke, his breathing was shallow.

"Franz. Franz. Are you okay?"

The injured lumberjack gurgled.

Oh no, thought Jake. His eyes aren't moving.

He gurgled again and kicked his feet.

"Franz, speak to me. Please." He shook him.

There was no reply, no movement.

"Please don't die, Franz. Not here."

He stopped breathing. Franz was gone.

There wasn't much for Jake to do while he waited for the men to return. He thought about the way Franz died. It didn't seem to be much different than the way deer died when shot. Why do people have a soul, but not deer? Where is the soul found inside the body? He had field dressed too much game to think it was in the heart or brain. It must be something that escapes at death rather than being left behind.

The sight of the returning men broke his concentration. A sleigh appeared on the horizon, loaded with almost a dozen shanty boys.

"How is he?" asked Shield. He jumped off the sleigh and ran to Franz.

"He's gone," said Jake.

"What do we tell his parents? His father is a township supervisor, you know." Shield seemed to be panting.

Jake reached up and put his hand on the shoulder of his boss. "Tell them he died peacefully, without pain. I know. I watched him leave this earth and go to heaven."

Four men loaded the warm, limp body into the sleigh, which bounced on the icy road back to camp. Franz rolled and slid, leaving behind streaks of blood.

Mr. Swensen organized a service after dinner for the men in the cookhouse. Franz's body was placed on a picnic table. Major told the men to form a line and walk by his body. "If there was something you always wanted to tell this boy, do it now. His body is being sent to Grand Rapids in the morning."

The procession of sobbing lumberjacks moved slowly in the hushed room. Some men stopped to kneel and say a prayer. Others touched his face or put their hand on his. One shanty boy tucked a note inside his pocket. Another placed a twig with white pine needles on his chest. When it was Jake's turn, he whispered, "I'm glad you had no pain."

Major Swensen ended the service with a short eulogy. "Lord, take this man to your great camp in heaven. Give him a job there that will please both you and him. Amen."

Death also visited Grafton one summer. Thor told stories to children on Thursday afternoons in the village square. Mothers brought toddlers and infants from miles around to hear his tales. He liked to blend Grimm's Fairy Tales with Swedish folklore and often created his own special endings. He tried to send the children home happy, carrying images of good witches and silly animal characters in their memories.

Thor told one of Aesop's Fables on a hot Thursday in July. "Once there was an oak tree," he said with a twinkle in his eye. "It was so tall its branches almost reached heaven. They spread so much they got to be thin twigs near the edge of the sky."

Bobby said, "Does the sky really end somewhere?"

"My daddy told me the universe goes on and on," said Sam. "It never stops."

"Shh," said Bobby's mother. "Let's be quiet and listen."

Thor continued. "A thunderstorm brought lightning, thunder, rain, and wind. The great oak tree was so top heavy from trying to reach heaven that the wind blew it down."

"I've seen that!" screamed Mary. "A big tree fell right down by my cabin. Yes. I've seen that."

Thor smiled. "Well, this tree fell into the river and floated away. It kept going and going until it reached a lake. It rested there in a bed of reeds along the shoreline."

"What's a reed?" asked Patty.

"Oh you know," said Bobby. "They're little twigs that stick above the water near shore."

"Be still," said his mother.

Thor walked inside the circle of children noting their wide eyes and curious gazes. "The tree spoke to the reed. It said, 'How come you are so puny but survived the great wind? How come I am so tough but am broken and dying?' What do you think the reed said back?"

"That's silly," Harry said. "Trees don't talk."

Thor knelt on the ground so his face was right in front of Harry's. "Some stories are make believe. Let's pretend trees and reeds do talk. What would the reed say?"

"I know! I know!" said Jake's sister. "It would say, 'I lived because the wind could only blow on my tiny neck. The rest of me was under water. You died because the wind could blow your whole body.'"

Thor laughed. "Good guess, but that's not quite what the reed said. Anyone else?"

Bobby waved his hand. When acknowledged, he said, "Big tree, your trunk is too thick. The wind pulled you to the ground 'cause your trunk's too heavy. I'm a reed. I have no heavy trunk to make me fall."

The children and mothers clapped.

"Nope," said Thor. "The reed didn't say that either. But, what a great guess. Does anybody else have an answer?"

"We give up," said Linda. "Tell us what the reed said."

"Okay. It said, 'It's better to bend than to break.' The strong oak fought the wind with all his might and was blown down. The little reed just bent when the wind blew and was saved. Sometimes, the best way to fight is by giving in."

The children and mothers strolled toward their wagons after the story was done. Thor felt the children tug on his trousers while he walked. Many wanted to stay with him rather than leave. He peered down at their smiling faces, full of appreciation and excitement.

Suddenly he heard a scream from Herman's mother by the hitching post. Her son was lying on the ground.

"Wake up!" his mother yelled. "Please open your eyes. Wake up!"

Everyone ran toward the boy. Thor screamed, "Quick, Alice, get Dr. Hollings!"

Soon the doctor ran from his office, which was only a block away from the village square. Dr. Hollings pushed past the crowd of bystanders to examine the boy. He took the stethoscope from around his neck and placed it on Herman's chest, beneath his shirt. The boy appeared motionless. He didn't seem to be breathing.

The doctor whispered something to the mother, whose scream became a wail. He carried the boy, lifeless and limp, back to the office. The crowd followed until the doctor waved them away. Thor would always remember that image of the doctor carrying the dead boy while his mother stumbled behind.

Dr. Hollings announced that he would make a public statement about Herman's death at three o'clock. People gathered in front of his office a full half hour before the appointed time. There was much speculation by townspeople about the cause of death.

"Herman had that telltale look of cholera," said Mrs. Rice. "His face was lead-colored with a brown tint along the hairline. His sharpened and elongated face was drawn, without expression."

Bobby's mother said, "I was there and saw it all. It was cholera. I touched his little body to say goodbye. Herman's fingers and toes had no warmth at all. The boy's hands and arms were colder than his chest."

Lydia added, "I was there, too, listening to Thor's story. Herman had the smell of cholera—sour bowels. He stunk like an outhouse."

The crowd gasped.

She continued. "When the doctor rolled the boy over, he had brown stains on the back of his trousers. He surely died of cholera."

The office door flew open and the doctor appeared with eyeglasses drooping low on his nose. He spoke solemnly in a loud voice with clear diction. "Herman Swanson passed away at the children's storytelling hour. I have completed my examination and find that he died of ague, not cholera."

The crowd sighed, as if relieved.

"I took a stool specimen from the boy and peered through my microscope at the sample. There was no evidence of *Vibrio cholerae*, the bacteria producing cholera. Instead, I found *Coccidia* and *E-coli*, both fairly common, but not often deadly."

"Then why did he die? asked Mrs. Rice.

"His mother told me he's had severe fever and chills for two weeks. She thought bringing him to story telling would lift his spirits."

Everyone turned and looked at Herman's mother, who was seated on a buckboard. Three ladies moved toward her to offer comfort.

"The ague had weakened Herman's body and produced diarrhea, with symptoms very similar to those of cholera."

The crowd moaned again and began to disperse. People walked past Mrs. Swanson and offered their condolences. When it was Thor's turn, he said, "I'm sorry about little Herman. I feel responsible since this happened at my story telling hour."

"Oh, don't be foolish. This wasn't your fault. In fact, your stories gave Herman many happy moments. Thank you."

Thor and others in Grafton were pleased that the boy hadn't died from cholera. He'd heard about the cholera epidemic of 1832 in Kalamazoo. Thor remembered stories in logging camp about cholera epidemics in Chicago during two periods, 1849-1855 and 1866-1867, both of which claimed thousands of lives. The lumberjack telling the story said sewage dumped in the Chicago River tainted water supplies. A water tunnel extending two miles into Lake Michigan was built in 1867. There were no more deaths from cholera by 1870. Thor's strongest memory of the story was the shortage of coffins in Chicago. There were so many dead persons, it was said, that families of the deceased couldn't locate coffins. They buried their loved ones between boards.

Thor learned that ague, although not as deadly as cholera, was still a serious disease. During the next two weeks, the doctor made at least a dozen house calls on people in town with ague. Once again he announced a town meeting would be held on Thursday after Thor's storytelling hour.

The doctor was more animated at this meeting. He said, "Many of you seem to be in a panic about the epidemic that is claiming lives here in Grafton during this long, hot summer. I want to reassure all of you that this disease is not cholera. It is ague."

"You told us ague is rarely fatal," said Mr. Rice.

"Most patients have chills, followed by fever and intense sweating. There are many types of ague, such as chill fever, dumb ague, shaking ague, and other varieties. The disease itself is not fatal. People in Grafton have died from complications such as pneumonia or influenza. For the most part those who have died were already weakened by other medical problems."

Mrs. Rice asked the question on everyone's mind. "Is it contagious? Will I catch it from someone who is sick?"

"No." The doctor removed his glasses and spoke with his hands for emphasis. "Epidemics, like this one in late summer, don't seem to be contagious. The disease strikes all types of victims: young, old; men, and women. Some say it's like malaria, which may be carried by mosquitoes."

People argued when they left the meeting. It seemed to Thor that the doctor had lost some of his respect. Most people, he thought, fear we have a cholera epidemic in Grafton. They think Dr. Hollings is hiding the truth.

Jake's mother was the first one in the family to contract the disease. William then became listless, rare for a hyperactive boy. Martha got a fever so high that perspiration dripped from her hair. Judy attended to both the bedridden children until she fainted while trying to walk.

The doctor prescribed quinine to help the Flareau family. He told them to take it as a gel, not in tonic form, so it would enter their bloodstream faster.

Thor was confused. In my country, he thought, we take quinine, too. But, we hide the taste in coffee. Some people put the gel inside the ooz from boiled bark of slippery elm. Others put it in raw egg whites. But nobody eats the gel off the blade of a knife like they do here.

Regardless of the method used to take quinine, it didn't work for the Flareaus. All three family members got worse after nine days of taking medicine.

Thor helped Jake and his dad take care of the sick family members. He was on duty one night when Jake was fishing. Pierre stared out the window into the darkness. Jake's mother, soaked in wet clothes, sat near the fireplace, where flames blazed despite the August heat. Martha and William snuggled nearby under homemade quilts. The Flareaus spent most of the day in the same position and rarely talked. All Thor could do was carry food and water, stoke the fire, and help patients to the outhouse. That's when he thought of Sally. Didn't Jake say she knew herbal medicine? What if I go to Bay City and fetch her home?

Meanwhile, Jake stopped to see Mr. Rice on his way home from fishing. He handed him two fish. "Hello, Mr. Rice. My family's got troubles. Can I talk to you for a minute?"

It was hard for Jake to ask for help. He was raised to be independent and to solve problems without relying on other people. Both of his jobs, logger and market hunter, were solo activities, pitting himself against nature. It was difficult for him to continue. "My mother and brother and sister all have the ague. Father and I don't know what to do."

Mr. Rice asked, "Are they taking quinine?"

"Yeah, from Dr. Hollings."

"It tastes awful. Are you sure they're taking it?"

"Yes sir." He grimaced the same way people did when swallowing the bitter medicine.

"How's your dad?"

"Not good; he just stares out the window."

"All right, Jake. You go on home and I'll stop by tomorrow after breakfast. You are eating, aren't you?"

"Most days. Thank you, sir." Jake left the store and returned to his cabin.

Mr. Rice, Dr. Hollings, and the minister went to visit the Flareaus in the morning.

Jake threw open the door when they knocked. "Come on in."

The cabin was in disarray with dirty clothes scattered about the room. Blankets and quilts were draped on top of chairs. Dishes were piled in the corner along with a bucket of ashes someone had forgotten to take outside.

Reverend Hughes put his hand on his forehead. A stern frown replaced his peaceful smile. "These poor people. Look at this. Satan has been here."

The doctor moved quickly between the three patients with ague and probable depression in the father. He identified William as the sickest, given his high fever and severe congestion. The little boy's chest was so full of fluid there was barely enough air entering his lungs to keep him alive. His breathing was shallow with a crinkle like the rustling of cellophane.

Although Dr. Hollings never talked about his medical experiences during the Civil War, it was obvious he was trained in setting treatment priorities. Thor knew combat physicians were under orders to pick which patients to treat first, second, and last. Military surgeons treated those most likely to die last. That's why it bothered Thor when the doctor moved away from William to examine Judy. She looked terrible. The fever had filled her mouth with open sores that oozed yellow puss.

Dr. Hollings gave orders as if he were on the battlefield. He pointed at Mr. Rice and said, "You empty the bucket of ashes." The minister was told to get fresh water from the river and Jake was asked to wipe his mother's forehead with a wet rag. "Quick," he said to Thor. "Get more blankets from the shelf over there."

Meanwhile, the doctor moved on to examine the little girl whose teeth chattered with chills. Martha's lips, as well as her toenails and fingernails, were bright blue. Like he had done with William, the doctor shifted attention away from her to Pierre. Noticing beads of sweat on his forehead, the doctor seemed to recognize that Jake's dad also had the ague, although he'd concealed his symptoms from the family.

Thor suddenly watched William drop to the floor and convulse. His little body thrashed and heaved, twisted, and rolled.

"Quick, stick a wooden spoon in his mouth," said the doctor.

Thor ran to William's side and held him down while Jake put a stick of kindling wood between his teeth. He suddenly felt the little body stop struggling. A tiny gurgle came from deep within his lungs. Thor watched the boy's eyes peacefully stare at the ceiling and lose focus.

Dr. Hollings pushed his fingers inside the William's mouth. He turned the patient over and rested the boy's head on crossed wrists before pushing on his back in a rocking motion. Next, he yanked his arms back and forth.

"It's not working," he said. "The artificial respiration is having no effect. It's been unsuccessful."

Judy raised her head. "What do you mean? Is my little boy dying?"

"I'm sorry," said the doctor. "There's so much fluid in his lungs I can't get air to enter or leave." He pushed the boy's eyelids down. I'm so sorry."

Reverend Hughes cleared his throat. Everyone turned toward him and listened. "Let's all stop for a moment. It's time to pray. Let us come before the Lord." He lowered his head, and the others followed. "Lord, take this boy to be with you now. Help to cure this family of pestilence. In Jesus' name we pray."

Thor watched the sick mother and father crawl toward William and wrap him in a blanket. Pierre rocked the body in his arms. With tears streaming down his face, he said, "Father, take care of this little boy in heaven. He was a good boy who did no wrong. Please watch over him until I get there."

Judy sat in silence and stroked William's hair.

Thor shuddered when Jake ran from the cabin and vomited by the woodshed. It was time to do something. There were still three sick people in the family. He went outside and said to Jake, "I'm so sorry, my friend. It's time for me to go for help. I'm going to Bay City to get Sally. Maybe she has something better than quinine."

Jake wasn't listening. He seemed to be lost in thought. "I remember when William fell out of a tree and landed on the ground. After a while, he awoke. Maybe it's like that this time. Perhaps he'll wake up again."

"Listen, Jake. Do you hear me? I'm gonna bring Sally back. Maybe she can save your sister and parents."

"It's too late for William. He was such a happy boy." Jake's eyes were wet. "Why? Why did God take my little brother?"

Thor shook his head and couldn't answer. He choked when a lump formed in his throat but went back in the cabin to say goodbye to Jake's parents. Judy sat on the floor next to William's corpse, now wrapped in a blanket. Her face was bright red in the yellow glow of the fire. Her blonde hair, although dirty and wet, shone in the flames. He went to the stove and boiled water. Handing a cup of tea to Judy, he said, "I've got to leave now. There's someone I know that may be able to help."

She said, "I don't know what's happening here, but I do know this is God's work. He had a job for William in heaven. He may call the rest of us, too. If he does, we should be happy to serve him."

Thor smiled. "I'll be back soon. I promise." He emphasized the word promise with his Swedish accent.

"Nobody can blame you for leaving this place of sickness. Go now. We'll be fine. Hurry, now. Leave before it's too late."

14

Sally Returns to Grafton

Thor sat on a bench in the dark and waited for the next train to Bay City. He listened for the sound of a whistle in the distance or humming in the tracks. This is the second dead end spur I've been down, he thought. Busy railroad officials must have directed me to board the wrong trains. Here I am, tired and hungry, somewhere in mid-Michigan, waiting. It's so hot and muggy.

He scratched his beard where he'd developed a rash beneath the thick sandy hair. When the mosquitoes swarmed about him, he walked up and down the wooden platform and then returned to his bench where he stared at the bright silver moon. He shut his heavy eyelids and drifted in and out of consciousness.

Soft chugs, progressively louder, awoke Thor from a nap. A few minutes later, he watched a locomotive and two passenger cars come to a rest. Only four people got off the train, leaving both cars empty. He stared at the engineer with a blackened face.

The conductor spun a red lantern with bright yellow flame and yelled, "Are you coming aboard, sir?"

Thor jumped up. "Oh yes, I've been trying to get to Bay City for two days. Can you take me there?"

"Yup, this is the right train. We should arrive there by late afternoon. How did you ever get on this spur to the old tannery?"

"I guess I got turned around."

"You sure did. Well, climb aboard, sir."

Thor didn't remember the rest of the journey because he curled up on the back seat and fell asleep. When he arrived in Bay City he had no trouble finding Sally's saloon. That's funny, he thought. It took me three days to get to Bay City, but only a few minutes to find Hell's Half Mile.

Sally wasn't at the saloon because it was Thursday night. He'd forgotten she only worked there on weekends. Rather than spend the evening alone in his hotel room, he decided to join a group of millwrights drain a freshly tapped keg of Canadian beer. As the evening wore on, he heard stories about their work in the more than forty mills around Bay City. He noticed there seemed to be a pattern in their stories. The men were all overworked and underpaid. No wonder, he thought, so many of these men loved to drink, fight, and whore. Those are releases from routinized lives once filled with dreams of success in frontier towns and sawdust villages.

Thor began telling logging stories after his fifth beer. He repeated some of the tales he'd heard before and made up new episodes. As the alcohol further loosened his tongue, he began telling children's stories with an intentional Swedish accent. He frequently leaped into the center of the audience and snapped his suspenders to drive home a point. The millwrights at first scoffed at his silly animal tales. Soon more than two dozen men, who laughed and punched each other like the children in Grafton, surrounded him.

When he was half way through "The Dog in a Manger," one of the town bullies entered the saloon. Thor noticed that everyone shied away from the man with a bushy beard, muddy pants, and torn shirt. The bully strutted around the saloon and intimidated smaller men, many with terror on their faces. He pointed at Thor, circled by millwrights. "Are you new here?"

"Yeah," said Thor. "But I've seen the likes of you before."

The bully moved toward Thor's table, swatting several men on the back of the head as he strolled around the saloon. "Wise guy." He rolled up the sleeves of his shirt, exposing a large scar on his forearm.

A waiter girl tried to stay out of his way but got trapped behind a chair.

The bully kicked her and said, "Wench."

The millwrights scattered. Thor thought they were coming to her defense but soon realized they were moving to allow room for the bully and him to square off without interference. Other men in the saloon also jumped up, cheering the fight on from a safe distance near back walls.

With little fear of the man, Thor said, "Only sissies hurt women."

"Look out for him!" hollered one of the men. "He's been jailed dozens of times for fighting. Even the police are afraid of him. He's killed three men with his bare hands."

"So why's he kick women?" Thor blocked the bully's punch and thrust an elbow beneath his rib cage.

The man wobbled. His eyes seemed to pop out of their sockets. He couldn't seem to catch his breath.

Soon the two men were wrestling on the floor. Thor saw blood on the floor but couldn't tell which one of them was bleeding. They smashed chairs, turned over tables, and threw beer mugs, one of which cracked the mirror behind the bar. Onlookers, pinned against the wall, cheered and placed bets.

Thor felt angry when he saw the man holding the bets had a thicker wad of bills for the bully than for him. He leaped on a table and shouted, "I can lick him. Come on. Put more bets on me."

His tactic worked. Soon the man holding money had more bills in both hands. His plea also caused men in the saloon to choose sides. Those betting on the bully moved toward one end of the saloon while those betting on Thor moved to the other. The arrangement sparked some pushing and shoving until another round began. This caused a free-for-all between dozens of men in the saloon.

Nobody seemed to notice when the bully pulled a knife on Thor. He saw the blade twinkle in the gas light. I've got to get that knife, he thought, and lunged. He twisted his opponent's arm until he heard a crack, followed by whining.

"It's broke. You broke my arm."

"Yeah, and I'll break your neck if you don't get out of here." Thor folded the knife and slipped it into his pants pocket. He looked around the saloon, which was in shambles. Chairs and tables were turned over and broken. Splinters of glass from shattered bottles littered the floor.

"I'll remember this," said the bully. He escaped out the side door.

"You better." Thor left through the front door and walked to his hotel.

The next night when Thor entered the saloon, he was met with cheers from the bartender. "Bravo! Here's the man who beat Gustav last night. One round of drinks on the house!"

Thor was not interested in drinking beer. He was looking for Sally. "Any waiter girls around?"

"Hold on," said the barkeeper. "Just the drinks are on the house, not the whores." Laughter filled the saloon.

"I'm serious. Does Sally Wilton work tonight?"

"Yeah, she's outside on break, talking to Sylvia."

Thor watched Sally return and noticed she looked much older and tired out. Maybe, he thought, she's had enough of this life and will come back to Grafton to help Jake. He approached her and said, "Do you remember me? I was here a few years ago with Jake Flareau."

Sally's face showed no expression. "I'm sorry, all you men look alike. But, I do remember the night Jake came."

"I'm here because of Jake. He's in trouble. His brother just died of ague. His sister has it, too. So does his mother and father." He reached out and took her hand.

She squeezed his fingers until they turned white, then blue. "William is dead? That couldn't be. He's so young and cute."

"Yes, he was. He's gone now."

"Are you sure?"

"Yes, he died of ague."

"How could that be?"

"There's an epidemic in Grafton. Will you come back home and help?"

Sally's face was still blank. "I left Grafton because the people were mean to me. Why would I go back now?"

"Because Jake needs you." He stared at her until she blinked.

"Jake and I were childhood friends. That was a long time ago. Besides, Dr. Hollings can treat them. He's better than me."

"His quinine isn't working. I told you William is dead. Please come with me."

She stroked her hair, which circled her painted face, heavily covered with makeup. "I'm sorry. I can't go with you. Now, let me get back to work. Look at all these thirsty men."

Thor collapsed into a chair and ordered a beer. I came all this way for nothing, he thought. I've failed my friend.

When his beer arrived, he waited a minute for the head to settle. Staring down in the mug, he felt thick fingers pinching his ear. Thor looked up and saw the bully with his sore arm in a sling. Gustav reached to his side with his good arm and withdrew a knife from a sheath on his belt. "I'm going to cut off your ear as a trade for my broken wrist."

Customers stopped talking. Thor noticed everyone was watching him, waiting to see what he would do next.

Sally ran to the table and said, "Gustav, leave him be. He's a friend of mine. Go pick on someone else."

"Yeah, come fight me," said a millwright with a stump on his right arm just below the elbow. He held up the other arm, tipped with a glistening hook.

The bully, still holding the knife, ignored him and kept his eyes fixed on Thor. "So Sally's one of your friends?" He slapped her across the face, splitting the skin in the corner of her mouth. "There, that's for last night."

Men in the saloon groaned in unison. Yet, they all seemed too afraid of Gustav to assist Thor.

Sally dropped to the floor, stained by a spreading pool of bright red blood. She covered her head and thought of Dietrich. The puddle of blood grew in size. All of this is happening because of Dietrich. Her neck got tight and seemed to shrink inside her collarbone, making her strained muscles sore. Her teeth ached from a clenched jaw. She thought, am I going to have another vision?

Closing her eyes, Sally imagined herself whipping Dietrich with a leather belt studded with steel spikes that ripped his unclothed back and buttocks. He pleaded for her to stop. She felt her neck relax and her jaw open. Her uncontrollable urge for revenge had been satisfied again. She felt better.

Thor snapped. "I told you not to pick on women." He circled Gustav and smelled an odor of stale whiskey that tainted the bully's breath.

Thor's ears rang with the cheering of drunken lumberjacks. He looked down at Sally and saw her hair matted with blood. He struck out of instinct, like a cat pouncing on a mouse. "Didn't you learn anything last night." His punch was blocked by the bully's forearm.

"I told you I'd come back and kill you." Gustav slashed the air with his knife.

Thor grabbed the bully's good arm by the wrist and twisted the knife from his hand. It fell and rattled on the saloon floor. Both men groveled for it on the dirty floor. Thor snatched the bone-handled blade from beneath the rung of a nearby chair and quickly stood. "Now I've got two of your knives. Go away now."

Gustav started to leave but returned. He lifted a chair and prepared to smash it over this opponent's head. The bully was too slow for Thor, who landed a punch in his opponent's belly. "I said to leave me alone." He followed with a right uppercut that smashed against Gustav's jaw. It was a powerful punch, delivered with the force and precision of an arm used to swinging axes. The large man tumbled to the ground and lay still.

Sally tried to get up but collapsed. Thor reached down and extended his hand but she was too weak to stand, even with his help. Thor lifted her limp body and placed her in a chair near the table. “Are you okay?”

“I don’t know.” She looked at Gustav. “You knocked him out.”

“Yeah, he deserved it.”

Thor smiled as the customers cheered. “Are you okay?”

“I think it’s just a little cut by my mouth. Facial wounds bleed a lot.”

“Let me see,” said Thor. He held her head beneath the gaslight. “Yes, you’re right. It doesn’t look very serious, just a lot of blood.

“Nobody’s ever protected me like that.” Her gaze had a peculiar mix of shock and delight.

He touched her soft hand. “Let’s go. Please leave with me for Grafton.”

She shook her blood soaked head. “No. I can’t go back there.”

Thor crossed his arms on his chest and shook his head. He stared at Gustav, who moaned.

Sally said, “You’d better get out of here before he comes to.”

Thor left the saloon with his head down. He needed to take a walk and sort things out. Soon he saw the Third Street Bridge where several drunks circled a campfire. He slipped into the group as if he had been there all night.

Rats scurried nearby amidst piles of garbage and debris. The odor of human waste was strong because the city had never pursued a recommendation to install a privy at the east end of the bridge. He also saw some ferrets that had been released to control the rat population.

The rodents triggered memories from camp. He recalled stories about the rats in Bay City. One sawyer from Flint told about contests in a saloon where men bet on fighting rats that tore each other to pieces before gamblers. There was also a rumor about a man who climbed into a pit with dozens of rats. He fought them with knives and hammers while drunken lumberjacks tossed him dimes and quarters.

Thor left the campfire and went to the railroad station. Since the next train wasn't due until six in the morning, he tried to sleep on a bench using his luggage as a pillow. Several other men slept nearby.

At about five in the morning, he sensed someone was near him. Through half-open eyes, he made out the form of a lady with dark brown hair.

"Who's there?" he asked.

"It's me, Sally," a voice replied. "I changed my mind. You came all the way from Grafton to find me. You protected me. The least I can do is help you and Jake. You're right. If the village needs me, it's time to go home."

"Thank you. Jake's family really needs help."

"Let's hope they're still alive."

They boarded the train a few minutes before six. Both were happy to see Bay City fade in the distance.

"Hold your horses!" yelled Mr. Wilton. "We don't open until eight on Tuesday mornings. I'll be down in a few minutes." Despite his plea, the banging on his door continued. Angry, he yanked the door open. When he saw Sally standing there, suitcase in hand, he said, "Oh, my dear little girl. You've come home." He hugged her and pulled her into the room. Thor jumped inside before he shut the door.

"Where in the world have you been?"

"I've been living in Bay City. It's a beautiful place the minister told me about." She looked around the room, which hadn't changed much.

"What did you do there?"

"I got a job in a fine restaurant overlooking the river. You know, I told you in my letters. It was so nice of my friend Sylvia to write down what I said. Some of my friends have been teaching me to read and write, but I'm still not very good."

"I never got any letters. Nobody in town knew where you went. We were all very worried."

"Well, I'm here now."

"How'd you meet Thor?" He ran a hand through his salt and pepper hair.

"He came to get me." Sally looked down at the floor. "He told me Jake's brother died."

The blacksmith took Sally's suitcase and put it near her room. He stared at Thor. "You knew where she was and didn't tell us?"

"Well, ah…well..." He didn't know what to say. Should I lie, like Sally did about the letters? Or, should I tell the truth?

"Ask Jake. I just did what he said. He told me to go to Bay City and find Sally. You'll have to ask him how he knew she was there."

Sally tried to change the subject. "Oh, Father, none of that matters. I'm home now." She pointed at her suitcase. "Can I stay in my old room?"

"By all means. It's so nice to have you home." He hugged her again.

She put a kettle on the stove and made some tea for her father and Thor. They sat and talked for almost an hour about Bay City. She never told him about her work at the saloon but talked mostly about the buildings and businesses in the city. Thor noticed that Mr. Wilton was especially interested in the ironworks used in mills and other factories.

After they finished their tea, Sally said, "I've got to visit the Flareaus to see what kinds of herbs might help. Will you come with Thor and me?"

Mr. Wilton said, "Sure. I'd like to come along." He went downstairs and saddled three horses.

Jake was carrying water to the cabin when they arrived. "I found her. Sally's here!" Thor shouted.

Jake ran to greet his old girlfriend. "Well I'll be. I can't believe you came all the way from Lake Huron just to see us."

Sally remained polite but distant. The circumstances didn't seem appropriate for a welcome hug or passionate kiss. "Thor said your family's sick," she replied. "How could I stay away?"

"Yes, we lost my brother." Jake glanced down.

"I'm so sorry. We all loved little William."

"Did you bring medicine?"

"Not yet. First, I need to see your parents and your sister. Are they okay?"

He shook his head from side to side. "They're not good. They have chills, fevers, and more chills. It's terrible. Even quinine doesn't seem to work. Come on in. See for yourself." He waved at the blacksmith and Thor to join them.

The cabin was neat and organized this time, although the patients looked worse. Thor could barely hear Pierre's voice when he said, "Hello."

Martha's blankets were soaked with sweat, which dripped from her forehead.

Jake's mother was the only person to rise. "Is that you, Sally? Have you come back home?" She wobbled to the table and rested for a moment before speaking again. "Everyone was so worried about you. We didn't know what to do."

"Yes, my daughter's come home," said the blacksmith. "I'm sorry about little William."

Sally put her hand on Judy's head and wiped the lady's face with a handkerchief. "You know why I left Grafton, don't you? Do you remember my trial? The whole town turned on me."

"Not now," said Judy. "We don't need to talk about this now."

Sally kept wiping her forehead. "Everyone said I was to blame. But Dietrich took advantage of me." Tears dripped down her cheek. Her voice quivered. "He hurt me, remember? That's why I ran away."

The blacksmith knelt next to Sally, now seated beside Judy at the table. "How could we forget? We can talk about this later, my dear. These people are sick and need medicine. Let's tend to them. We can discuss your situation later at home."

"I disagree," said Judy. She grabbed Sally's hand. "This girl's been carrying a big burden. She and I are going to talk about this now. Come, Sally, let's move to the corner so nobody will hear us."

Jake, Thor, and Mr. Wilton left the cabin while the two ladies talked. Pierre, too weak to leave, shivered beneath a blanket on the other side of the room.

Thor put his ear to the wall of the cabin. He heard sobbing between muffled words. Jake's mother is probably crying for her dead boy, he thought, and Sally for being attacked by Dietrich. He and Jake looked at each other several times, wondering if Sally would admit having worked as a waiter girl in Bay City. They walked toward the river to join the other men.

Thor threw rocks across the water. Round rocks skipped only two or three times, but flat ones bounced seven or eight times. One, thrown side arm, hopped on the surface over two dozen times.

Mr. Wilton sat on the riverbank next to Jake. He scowled at him and said, "How'd you know where my daughter was?"

Jake stammered. "Well…I met her there on the way home from camp." He cleared his throat. "She was so afraid of people in Grafton she asked me not to tell anyone. I had to keep her secret."

"Why didn't you tell me? My goodness, I'm her father." Mr. Wilton looked hurt.

"You need to ask Sally about this. She's the one who ran away. She made me promise not to tell where she was." He stared at the blacksmith, waiting for some sign that he understood.

Suddenly the door of the cabin swung open and Sally joined them. "Let's go."

"Can you wait 'til we finish talking?" asked Jake.

"No." She marched down the trail. "It's time to leave. I know which herbs to fetch."

She left quickly, followed by her father.

Jake waved goodbye.

Thor yelled in the distance, "See ya! Thanks!"

The next morning Sally knocked on the door of the cabin, opened this time by Pierre. She was accompanied by five churchwomen holding heavy baskets of food. The women scurried around the cabin, tidying up anything out of order. When all the cleaning was done, the women made breakfast. Then they washed Judy and Martha and left a bucket of hot water in the woodshed so Jake's father could bathe.

Sally opened a packet of yellow birch bark and sassafras root. She poured the medicine into a large pot of boiling water on the stove. "Everyone listen," she said. "All of you must drink a pint of this tea every four hours, even at night." Sally left a dozen unopened packets near the stove for future use.

Each day Sally returned with a procession of ladies who stopped at several homes. More than a dozen people in town had ague or complications associated with the illness. The churchwomen visited many families and gave them packets of Sally's tea.

Jake's parents got better, as did many people in town, but Martha got worse. She continued to have blue lips and fingernails, along with alternating chills and fever.

Sally asked Thor if he would accompany her to see Lily. He agreed to keep her company along the path that had grown even thicker with grape vines. Without warning, she slowed her horse near the river and said, "This is where it happened. That's the tree Dietrich tied me to." She eased in her saddle and sobbed.

"That evil man." Thor pulled his horse next to hers. "How could he do something like that?"

Sally dismounted and knelt by the tree, where she prayed. "God, let me forget this place. Help me to be a better person because of what happened here." She smiled. "But," she added, "if you catch Dietrich in a moment of weakness, strike him down. Make him suffer for what he did."

"Aren't you Presbyterians supposed to forgive and be forgiven?"

"I can forgive my mother for leavin' and my father for wantin' to live on the frontier, but I can't forgive Dietrich." She climbed on her horse and galloped off toward Lily's cabin.

Less experienced with horses, he followed at a slower pace. As he turned the last curve in the trail, he saw Sally knocking on the worn cabin door. He heard her yell, "Anybody home?"

Soon the old Indian woman opened the door. Stooped and fragile-looking, she reached out and grabbed Sally's hands. "Hello, little girl. How wonderful! It's been so long since you've come to visit. Come in. Please come in."

"This is my friend Thor. Can we sit and talk? I've got so much to tell you."

Sally explained that she had left Grafton but returned because the Flareau family needed help in overcoming the ague. She told the old woman about the tea she had prescribed, which seemed to be curing Jake's parents but not his sister. She explained that the church women gave her steel dust, spirits of niter, and pills made from cobwebs. Even the doctor had given up, suggesting that Martha, like William, might not survive the epidemic.

The Indian woman listened carefully and then opened a cabinet near her sink. "First, try blood wort tea," she said. She handed her a packet of ground herbs. "If that doesn't work, then you'll need to give her this smelly mixture." She reached in the cabinet to the back of the lower shelf and handed Sally a jar with tiny packets wrapped in paper. "This is my strongest cure. I've mixed it with a few special herbs and formed it into a long, thin roll. Then I cut the roll into pills covered in flour to make them taste better. Each is wrapped in a small square of paper. She should take a pill every two hours. It will purge her. Then, after three days, ask the doctor to put her back on quinine for nine more days. That's all we can do. The rest is up to the Great Spirit."

Sally and Thor said goodbye to Lily and went back to the Flareau cabin where they started Martha on the special cure. The doctor agreed to try anything to save the girl and began her second course of quinine three days later. Color soon returned to the little girl's fingers and toes. The fever and chills stopped on the fourth day. She was out of bed by the sixth day. It was hard to keep her inside because she wanted to go out and play by the river. On the last day of her treatment, Martha lost a front tooth.

Everyone in the family laughed when she announced it was the cause of her illness. "Lookie here at this tooth. It just got loose and fell out. That's why I was sick. Now, I'm all better. I didn't have the ague, just a loose tooth!"

The next morning when Sally came to see how the family was progressing, Jake finally welcomed her home. He said, "Martha is better today because of your medicine. Thank you so much for coming home." He leaned toward her and kissed her cheek.

Sally wrapped her arms around his wide back. "You're welcome. I forgot how good it feels to be useful, to help someone else." They kissed and held each other.

Suddenly, Judy burst through the door, carrying a pile of freshly laundered clothes.

"Hi, Sally. We're all feeling so much better, thanks to you. It feels good to be up and about."

"I'm so happy for you and others in town who are feeling better," Sally said. "We should be thankful for the old Indian woman on Chestnut Ridge. She's the one who deserves praise."

"You're right. Maybe the women in town can take her some food and the men some winter firewood."

Sally was not only a hero to Jake's family. The church-women gave her medicine to several others who also recovered. Even the doctor used her teas and special cure. As a result, people seemed to forget about the trial and Dietrich Krausse. She was invited to social events where dozens of people thanked her for fighting ague. They also told her about different ailments and purchased other herbs. Sally's business once again prospered, especially when peddlers trading herbs returned to Grafton.

Thor resumed his job of telling stories in the village square to sell fish. Of course, he often reminded people that he was the one who had brought Sally home.

15

Summer Love

Sally talked to almost everyone in town. She knew who was sick, who was pregnant, who had financial hardships, and who was grieving the loss of a loved one. It feels so good to be home, she thought. People really like and appreciate me. They seem to have forgotten about Dietrich and the trial. At least they don't know what I did in Bay City.

The minister gave her more lessons in reading and writing. At first Sally liked books about plants and medicine but then she was more excited about romance stories. With guidance from other women, she sewed, gardened, and was active in the women's circle at church. She continued doing favors for people, such as taking meals to the sick. Working with others helped take Sally out of herself and gave her a sense of purpose.

Her greatest feeling of success arose from helping the Monotas, a poor family that lived in the country. The oldest daughter, Matilda, had ridden to town to summon Dr. Hollings. He visited the family twice, but his cures had no effect. Six of the eight children were sick as well as the mother and father. The doctor told Sally about the family in need and gave her directions to their cabin.

Sally left immediately when told about the family. She guided her horse into the front yard of the cabin and was appalled by the family's poverty. Chickens and pigs roamed everywhere, an old milk cow stood near a falling barn, and strong-smelling goats urinated in an area where the children played.

Matilda greeted her when she came near the cabin. "Are you the lady doctor?"

"Kind of. I've come to bring you some medicine. Can I see the sick patients?"

The oldest daughter stopped for a moment and stared at Sally's turquoise blouse. "They aren't patients. It's my mom, dad, brothers, and sisters."

"Yes, I'm sorry. I didn't mean any disrespect. Dr. Hollings said you're very concerned about your family. Can I see them?"

"Please come in."

Sally recognized the signs of ague. After leaving the appropriate herbs along with detailed instructions, she said, "Now, if you feel sick, be sure to take some of the medicine, too."

"Thanks for coming all this way." Matilda waved goodbye. "I'll do exactly as you say."

Two weeks later Sally returned and found some signs of improvement. Three of the sick children were playing in the yard. "Where's your big sister?"

"Out back hanging up the laundry."

"Are your parents better?" She tied her horse to the hitching post.

"Oh yes, only Cecile is still sick. Everyone else is over the cold."

A cold, Sally thought, while walking to the back yard. Ague is much more serious than a cold. "Hi Matilda. Let me help you with those clothes."

"Sure. But, please call me Mattie. That's my nickname."

Sally spent the rest of the afternoon with the family. She visited the Monotas often and became friends with the oldest girl, who taught her much about country life. She learned how to prepare beans and tomatoes and other vegetables and store them for winter in large glass jars. Mattie also showed her how to can apples and make jellies and jams from strawberries and blackberries. One of the girl's favorite pastimes was embroidering, which Sally picked up quickly.

Mattie was in charge of the younger children, as well as the cooking and laundry. She was one year younger than Sally and had a nice build, creamy white skin, and long blonde hair, which she usually wore in braided pigtails. Her fair skin was bronzed from the summer sun. Sally noticed she was always barefoot, even on rainy days, and that all of her blouses were embroidered with butterflies or flowers. When she spoke, Mattie couldn't hide being a poor girl with lots of responsibility but no knowledge of social graces.

One of the times when Sally came for a visit, they teased each other about men. "I bet Jake Flareau would be a good man for you. He's so strong. I bet he's good at making babies. Your kids would likely have brown eyes."

"Yes, I like him. What about you? What kind of man do you like?"

"Do you know his friend Thor? I listen to his stories in the square whenever I can. I take my little brothers and sisters along so I don't look out of place. He is beautiful."

"Beautiful? Men aren't beautiful; they're handsome."

"Not Thor."

Sally didn't mind the playful joking because she liked Mattie. She could talk to her about anything, except her former job in Bay City. She even mentioned her secret desire for Jake. "Once I was washing dishes and began thinking about him. I felt dizzy—overcome. In my fantasy, I ran my fingers through the hair on his chest. I rested my head on his belly."

"Why don't you just have sex with him?"

"Maybe I will," said Sally. She shoved her friend and tickled her. The girls giggled.

Sally didn't tell Mattie that once those feelings started they often became unbearable until she was in bed at night. Then she pretended he was beside her on the mattress. When she dreamed of him, they made love on sandy beaches of secluded islands and in fancy hotels with room service. Of course, she never told her friend the details of those dreams.

Sally invited Jake and Thor to dinner above the blacksmith shop at least twice a week. Her father seemed to enjoy talking with the young men about politics and business. She noticed Jake seemed more interested in speaking with her than with Father or Thor. He seems to enjoy my company, she thought.

While walking home after one of those dinners, Jake confided his feelings to Thor. "Sally's sure fun to be with, isn't she?"

"Yup." He smoothed his beard. "Are you starting to like her again?"

Jake took a moment to answer. "I'd sure like to be with her. Do you know what I mean?"

"Of course," said Thor. "I get those feelings a lot."

Jake hung his head. "Before going up north, I used to get excited when I saw her dressed up."

"Yeah, she's got a nice figure." He stopped for a moment to listen more intently.

"Now it excites me most when she's playful."

"Maybe that's 'cause you're older. When you were younger, you thought desirable women should look mature. Now you can see the real Sally when she plays and has her defenses down. The real Sally is quite a woman."

"I think about her all the time."

Thor laughed and punched Jake in the arm. "So, you still haven't done it, have you? Maybe Sally will show you how."

Jake picked up a stick and playfully stuck it into his friend's chest. "You better not tell anyone how I feel about her. If you do, I'll fix you good."

The two young men raced to the Flareau cabin by the river.

The end of August was hot. Sally found a place to bathe a mile and a half from town, where the river entered a small lake. The cove had a bottom of sugar sand, freshly deposited each spring. The mixture of hot sun and cool runoff kept the water at a perfect temperature. Breezes that danced above the rapids blew away any mosquitoes and biting flies. Thanks to thick trees near the shore, it was secluded and provided a place to undress. The secret spot also had a view, in case someone walked by.

Sally went to this bathing place at least two times a week without seeing another person. She didn't know Jake fished the same cove in late summer when brown trout came to spawn.

When she first saw him there he was staring into the water. She wondered whether to be still and hide or to say hello. It would be a good place to talk to Jake in private, she concluded, because the cove was so secluded.

Even though naked, she called to him. "Hey Jake. Come on in. The water's fine."

He walked to the shore where her clothes lay and answered, "Do you see any trout out there?"

"Oh, silly boy. Aren't you interested in me? I've got nothing on."

Jake looked awkward to Sally. His face had a mixed expression of curiosity and embarrassment. Fantasies filled her mind. I'll bet his chest is muscular from logging. He has such large hands. They would feel oh so good …

"You're the one who's silly," he said. "I've always been interested in you." Jake stood on the shore and started to unbutton his shirt, but stopped.

She sensed his hesitation. "What's wrong? Are you nervous?"

"Maybe."

"Afraid of being naked with a former waiter girl?"

"Not really. I know all that's in the past."

"What's wrong then?"

He stammered. "Well…no girl has ever seen me naked. What if you think I'm funny looking?"

"Oh, Jake. I just invited you to swim. Nothing more. Come on in. Join me." She dove purposely to expose her milky backside. Sally submerged her long hair, then shoulders, rear, and feet. She hoped he recognized her gesture as a signal to follow.

Jake took off his clothes. He stood in his underwear on the bank and appeared unsure of what to do next. When

Sally submerged again, he slipped off the last of his clothes and joined her in the cool water. Underwater, she was glad to hear the splash and swam toward him. Here he is, she thought, my fantasy's come true.

They broke the surface of the water together. He inhaled hard. "You're right. The water's perfect today."

She swam closer. Both their heads were above water, a few inches apart. Sally said, "I didn't know you came here."

"Just in fall after browns. Sometimes they're so thick the water looks dark. I never swam here, though."

Sally didn't want to hear boring talk about fish. Doesn't he care for me anymore? Here I am without clothes and he's talking about trout. Maybe I should let him see a little more of me. What if I push backwards and show him my breasts? Before she had a chance, Jake put his arms around her neck. She felt his lips touch hers. It was a playful little peck rather than a strong kiss. But she liked it. Suddenly, his heavy arms pushed her underwater. When she sank, her hands fondled his chest. I was right, she thought. It's firm with rippling muscles. She swam underwater to the other side of the cove.

Now she was able to complete her plan. Sally broke the surface on Jake's side and waited until she was sure he was watching. She leaned her head back and allowed her hair to spread in the water. Pushing up and back, she broke water with her chest floating above the surface. She saw him gazing at her breasts bobbing in and out of the water's surface. It seemed such a happy, childlike gaze.

Jake swam toward her like he was in a race. He swung his arms around her body and whispered in her ear, "You are so beautiful."

She turned inside his arms and kissed him. The rubbing of their bodies excited him. She felt the kisses shift from her lips to neck. He does like me, she thought.

He swam away and climbed out of the water with his backside toward Sally. Jake slowly turned.

Sally's mouth opened. There on the shore of her secret place was the most perfect man she'd ever seen. Dark black hair covered his massive chest. His stomach was flat and firm. Beneath that, he was swollen.

She was glad her plan had succeeded. He likes me a lot, she thought. The brief glimpse ended when he spun around and stepped into his clothes.

Jake said, "I've got to go. How 'bout meeting here again tomorrow at noon?"

Sally thought about climbing on shore, too, but decided to remain underwater with only her head exposed. "I'll be here." She wished his kiss had been longer, more serious than the little peck. "This cove will be our secret place."

"Okay." He vanished behind the trees.

Sally waited all morning for time to pass. She wondered whether she should seduce Jake. It would be wonderful to make love with him in the cove. But will he think less of me then? What should I do?

She purposely arrived at their secret place a few minutes late to make sure Jake was already in the water. Sally slowly unrobed while he watched. She thought his gaze was more relaxed this time and full of longing. Neither spoke.

Sally swam toward him until they grabbed hands in the calming water. They bobbed in circles about each other until Jake pulled Sally to him. He guided her to a shallow part of the cove where the water was only up to their arms. His nude body rubbed up and down against her thighs. Her breasts pressed hard against his chest while she wrapped her legs around his buttocks. When their lips touched, she didn't want to break the seal. They kissed gently, all the while wiggling against each other under water.

"Let's wait," said Jake.

"For what?" She felt awkward arguing with a man who didn't want sex. That was a new experience for her.

"For the right time," he said. Jake turned away and walked toward shore.

She followed, feeling rejected. “Don’t you want me?”

“I sure do. But, I’m uneasy. I’ve never done it before.” His face turned red. Together, they climbed out of the water and dressed. He said, “Thanks for the kiss, though.”

Thor came home from town, sat by the river, and smoked his pipe before dinner. Jake joined him, excited to get some advice about Sally. He said, “I could have done it today.”

“Done what?”

“I went swimming with Sally. We were skinny dipping.”

Thor puffed several times on his pipe. “So you think she was willing?”

“Definitely. I was the one who stopped it.”

“How come?”

Jake hung his head as if ashamed he’d failed his friend. “I dunno. Maybe I was scared.”

“What scared you? Are you sure it wasn’t something else?”

“Well…she’s had hundreds of men with more experience than me. Maybe I can’t measure up.”

Thor blew a smoke ring and watched it drift in the evening breeze. “My friend, making love is not a contest. It’s a way of showing affection. You need to think more about Sally and a little less about yourself.” Gray ashes floated to the ground when he tapped his pipe against a tree.

The two men walked back to the cabin and talked about ways to catch perch in the heat of summer.

Sally hurried to visit Lydia. When invited into her home, she asked “How do you like being a mother?”

“It’s lots of work, but much joy. I feel like I’ve been given a gift from God.” She gathered some dirty clothes and put them by a washtub. “But I wish I could find another husband.”

“You will. You’re young and pretty. Hey, guess what? I’ve got good news. Jake Flareau is courting me.”

"I know him. He brings us deer meat and fresh fish. So, you like the tall ones, huh?"

Sally blushed. "He is tall. I especially like his strong muscles."

"Well, be careful. With your past trouble in town, it would be better to wait until you're married."

"Wait for what?"

"To show him your affection." She took a handful of baby clothes and dunked them in the tub. "People in Grafton are nosey. You don't need any rumors going 'round about you and Jake." She added some soap to the water and rubbed a bib on the washboard.

"I don't care what other people think," Sally said. "I only care about Jake."

Lydia dunked the bib in the soapy water a second time. "That's what I mean. You'd better be careful."

The women talked a while longer about the baby and Jake. Sally walked home that afternoon in deep thought. Maybe Lydia is right. I'd better not have sex with Jake. Someone in Grafton will surely find out. What a shame, though. It would be so nice to…

All the way home, she recalled the image of his naked body, slowly turning toward her on the shore.

Later in the week, Jake and Sally met at the cove. They undressed without inhibitions in front of each other. The couple swam and splashed each other for several minutes before kissing underwater. Sally slipped her hand down his chest. She reached even further down and touched Jake. They bobbed up and down in the water and kissed some more.

Soon she felt his arms beneath her back and buttocks. He lifted her out of the water, carried her to shore, and put her down softly on the grass. They rubbed against each other until she finally spread her legs. He entered her with ease and power. The hot air dried their bodies, which swayed together in the breeze. Sally shuddered first, followed by Jake. Afterwards they kissed again, rolled over on their backs, and stared up at a thick cottonwood tree.

Just then, a strong wind came down the river corridor. It formed whitecaps on the lake and knocked a limb of the cottonwood tree to the ground between the two lovers. Sally broke a twig and two leaves off the end of the limb as a keepsake. These two leaves represent the two of us, she thought. The leaves are fastened to the twig by the same God that holds us together.

"That twig will always remind me of today," she said. I've always loved you and always will. I'm going to keep this twig forever as a sign of our union."

Jake replied, "I've always loved you, too. I'm glad we shared ourselves with each other."

"Me, too. So much has happened. I was afraid to love you. You might lose respect for me. Now I feel different. I want to be close to you. One with you."

"I feel so content, at peace, loved."

They dressed quickly, as if someone might be more likely to catch them dressing than making love.

Sally and Jake spent the rest of the summer together. On occasion they made love at their secret cove or in the nearby clearing. They told Thor and Lydia that they were in love but kept word of its consummation to themselves.

One afternoon, on the way home from the cove, Jake felt confused. His conversation with Sally shifted from one topic to another. Finally, he spoke what was on his mind. "I've been thinking a lot about you and me. Ever since I met you at the fire, my life has been different—full, more meaningful. When I'm with you, everything seems right." He kicked a rock, which tumbled across the trail and landed in a puddle. "I'd like to spend the rest of my years with you. I'd like to make a home with you. Have a family with you. Take care of you." She felt his eyes reaching deep into hers. "Sally, will you marry me?"

Sally thought of her mother and father. What if I marry him and we grow apart, like my parents? On the other hand,

I've been with so many selfish and dominating men. Here is a person who cares about me and wants to have a family. Besides, I enjoy his company. He's also a wonderful lover and friend. Yes, I'll marry him, yes.

She locked her eyes on his. Without looking away or blinking, she said, "Yes. I'd like to be with you forever. Yes, I'll marry you."

She felt a soft kiss, followed by a tight hug. Her cheek felt damp. The next fifteen minutes were filled with non-stop talking about the when, where, and who's of the June wedding.

Jake went home and wrote a letter to Major Swensen to explain he was getting married and wouldn't be coming to logging camp. Sally told everyone about the good news, which spread quickly around town. Although people seemed excited and happy for her, she had a feeling that nobody was surprised by their announcement.

Thor gathered his belongings from his corner of the Flareau cabin while Jake's mother baked bread. His re-soled boots looked brand new. He said, "Thanks for letting me stay here this summer."

Judy replied, "You're welcome. If it weren't for you, I'd have died from the ague. Thanks for bringing Sally back from Bay City. And now, she's going to be my daughter-in-law. All because of you."

"Well, Cupid did more than me." He smoothed his beard with his hand.

Pierre entered the cabin after he finished splitting his morning's quota of firewood. "I see you're packing up to leave. Are you goin' today?"

"Yes sir, I'm leaving right now. It's time for me to cut some trees."

"Good luck. I hope you'll come back and stay with us next summer." He brushed a piece of wood from his shoulder.

"Thanks. I'll be back."

"Just get here before the suckers run."

“Yes, sir.” Thor snapped his suspenders. He tied his belongings to a stick, swung the turkey over his shoulder, and headed out the door. He tickled Martha as he left and said, “Take care of your doll. Keep her warm this winter. I’ll be back when the snow melts.”

Thor met Jake in town at the blacksmith shop. After he said goodbye to Sally and Mr. Wilton, he and Jake rode together on one horse to the depot. They dismounted and waited in silence for the train, which arrived with a burst of four whistles.

Thor climbed the stairs of the passenger car and stopped on the top step. “Don’t forget to invite me to the wedding.”

Jake replied, “You’ll be the best man.”

“You can count on me. See you in the spring.” He waved once and vanished into the train.

16

The Wedding

February brought snowstorms that kept townspeople in their cabins. The temperature remained near zero after the first squall, which dropped six inches of snow on the ground. Then, a two-day front added three more inches. One afternoon a blizzard arrived with wet, heavy flakes that stuck on people's coats and in their hair. By sunset, the soggy snow changed to powder, blown into drifts by fierce gusts.

The next morning the pioneer village was a winter fantasy. Snow flowed in curved layers from the rooftops of cabins to surrounding trees and fences. The virgin snow was unmarked by boot prints. Tiny specks of ice crystals in the powder shone like diamonds touched by rays of the rising sun. Smoke circling from chimneys gave Grafton a snug, safe feeling.

The first people to appear outside were children making snow angels by lying on their backs and waving their arms and legs. The snow was too light for making snowballs or snowmen. Next, bands of teenagers left their cabins to shovel snow. They created white mounds in front of stores and homes while bounding between jobs to play tag. Some of the older residents offered pennies to the teenagers; others paid in cookies and hot drinks.

The knee-deep snow kept most adults inside their houses until late afternoon when some ventured outside to feed and water their livestock. Many people took advantage of the storm to read books, write letters, or take naps. Preparing meals was the most absorbing job, aside from keeping the fireplace stoked with dry logs.

Sally was worried about Jake because he had been delayed by the snowstorm. When she finally heard his knock on the door, he was almost an hour late.

"It took me two hours to trudge through snow banks," he said. "The drifts were really deep along the river."

She hugged him, glad he'd arrived safely. "I was worried. There are only a few boot prints in the new snow. Thank goodness you're here."

The couple spent the afternoon talking about their wedding plans. They envisioned a small gathering of family and friends in their home. The hardest decision was what to do about Sally's mother. Jake said, "She ran out on you. Why invite her?"

Sally disagreed. "Mother will be at peace to know I'm getting married. She probably won't come anyway. Let's send her an invitation…in care of my cousin in Boston."

"It's your mother. Do what you want."

"Thanks. Let's send her an announcement but hope she doesn't come."

The couple laughed so loudly that Mr. Wilton came out of his room to see what was happening. He said, "Why don't you go outside and use some of that energy to clear the snow in front of the shop?"

Sally said, "Father, we want to tell you about our wedding. Would it be okay to have the ceremony right here?"

"Of course. Most people get married in their homes. Only people in the big cities get married in churches. Besides, church weddings require high dress. Nobody in this town has those kinds of clothes."

"What's high dress?" She didn't realize her father knew about fashion.

"That means no bare necks. Arms must be covered to the elbow. See, a wedding in our home would be better. You can get married in a dress and veil, rather than a fancy gown."

"Oh, father, I'm so excited. Come Jake, dance with me." The couple took a few waltz steps and laughed together.

Just as Mr. Wilton was about to return to his reading, there was a knock at the door. "Who would visit in a snowstorm?" She swung open the door, surprised to see the minister. "Please. Come in."

The Reverend Hughes shook hands with everyone and took off his coat. "I was just over at the general store. Mr. Rice said he had a letter for you from Thor, but he couldn't leave the store to deliver it. He's very busy. People are stocking up on staples in case there's another blizzard." He handed the letter to Sally, who ripped it open.

After a few minutes she said, "Will you read it to me?"

"Of course," said Reverend Hughes.

Dear Friends,

I got to camp 37 and was offered Flanigan's job. He was transferred to camp 18. Now, I may grow a handlebar moustache in case they offer me Major Swensen's job!

Thanks for inviting me to your wedding. I am honored to attend and be Jake's best man.

I'll be back before the suckers run.

Praise this land of opportunity,

Thor

"He'd better be back in spring," said Jake. "We sold a lot of fish because of him last year."

The minister added, "I'm glad he'll be at the wedding. Is there a day you want me to reserve the church?"

Sally felt embarrassed. "We'd like to be married right here, above the blacksmith shop."

"You can't do that." Reverend Hughes marched over to Mr. Wilton. "There's too many people in town that want to come. Sally saved many lives during last summer's epidemic. Your daughter must be married in the church so people can show their gratitude."

Mr. Wilton scratched the long hair on the back of his neck. "You do have a point there. But people here don't have the right clothes for a church wedding. There's never been one in Grafton."

"Don't be foolish. We wear our best clothes to honor the Lord in his house, even if our best is not quite Victorian."

Mr. Wilton turned to Sally. "I think he's right. Why don't you plan a church wedding? Then we can have a picnic afterwards."

"Yes, father," Sally said. "I'd like that." She grabbed Jake's hand and danced around the room."

Two days after the storm Sally rode her horse along the river to Jake's cabin. Judy helped her with details of the church wedding. Hoping for good weather on June second, they got permission from town officials to have a reception in the village square.

Mrs. Rice, an accomplished seamstress, offered to make a gown for Sally and dresses for Mattie, the maid of honor, and Lydia, the bridesmaid. Women in town were so busy making new clothes for the occasion that the store had to place extra orders for fabric, ribbons, buttons, and lace from their Kalamazoo distributor. Sally was glad they had decided to be married in the church. See, she thought, women in Grafton will come in high dress.

It was one of those years with a short spring that went right from winter to summer. Mud from the traffic of horses and people covered everything. It coated wagons and carriages, formed clumps on wooden sidewalks, stuck to people's boots, and speckled everyone's trousers. Just when the service berry started to blossom, temperatures rose quickly. Trilliums soon surrounded the cabins. Even the robins nested two weeks before normal that spring.

Thor also came home early because it was too muddy to log pine in the north woods. Sally was glad to see him when he knocked at the blacksmith's door.

"How'd the winter treat you?" he said. He dropped his turkey outside the door and kissed her gently on the cheek.

His beard was scraggly looking, in need of a trim. His suspenders were stained with tea and gravy. Even his boots were scuffed.

"Wonderful." She returned his kiss. "I'm glad you made it back from logging camp. It was a long winter without you."

"It seems like yesterday I left Grafton."

"It sure does. We've been busy getting ready for the wedding."

"That's right. It is very soon, now. Where's your fiancé? Is Jake here?"

"No, he's at his cabin. They're making a new bed for Martha, who outgrew her bunk. Have you seen Mattie yet? She's missed you something awful."

"That's my next stop after seeing you and Jake. Please give my best to your father."

"Maybe you should get a bath and haircut before you see Mattie. If you like, I'll wash your clothes and get the stains out of your suspenders."

"Oh, Sally, there will be plenty of time to clean up. I want to see everyone first." He picked up his belongings and left for the Flareaus.

When Thor went to open the cabin door, he was greeted with laughter and happy giggles. Martha was jumping up and down on the new bed made by Jake and his dad. Judy had made a straw mattress. Everyone in the family clapped as she bounced higher with each attempt. "Thor!" yelled Martha. "Look at my new bed. I'm a big girl now!"

"Yes, you are." He put his turkey in the corner of the room and grabbed Martha just as she leaped through the air and wrapped her legs around his waist.

"Welcome home," said Jake's mother. She appeared apprehensive about his dirty clothes, but still kissed him. Judy started humming and walked back to the kitchen before he had a chance to reply.

Thor shook hands with Jake, who said, "You look like an old man. It must have been a tough winter for you in camp. That's what you get for being a foreman instead of a feller."

"Is that how you greet an old friend? I am older than you. Remember? I'm two years older, but two inches shorter—and wiser, stronger, and smarter."

"And still a bragger," added Pierre. "Are you ready to tell some stories and sell more fish?"

"Yes sir. Is it okay if I stay here again?"

"Sure," said Judy. "Our home is always yours." Her smile showed a row of perfect, white teeth.

"Thanks. Have you seen Mattie?"

"Oh yes," said Jake. "Wait 'til you see how she's changed her hair. She said she did it just for you. Whenever I see her, all she talks about is you. 'Thor this, and Thor that.'"

"That's my next stop." He moved his turkey into his old room, combed his hair in the looking glass, and walked toward the door. "I'll be back soon."

Jake closed the door behind him and chanted, "Thor this, and Thor that."

Thor ran the last half mile to Mattie's place. He heard the laughing and screaming of children as he entered her yard, strewn with family belongings. He darted past her brothers and sisters and pounded on the door, crooked with wear. "Mattie, Mattie. It's me, Thor. I'm back!"

He watched the door open on a crack, revealing a blouse embroidered with butterflies. Two bare feet pushed the door open a little wider. Finally, he saw her face.

Thor lifted her off the floor and hugged her. He reached beneath her rib and tickled her. "I missed you so."

She giggled and said, "I missed you, too. The days seemed so long without you near."

Thor kissed her and said something in Swedish.

"What's that mean?"

"Absence makes the heart grow fonder."

She smiled. "I'm very fond of you, Thor. I missed you terribly. Fortunately, I had lots of work to do taking care of my brothers and sisters and keeping the cabin clean."

"We are so much alike," he said. "Both of us are hard workers, practical…and responsible."

Since Mattie's mother was in the next room making beds, they kissed again, hurriedly.

"When can I see you again?" asked Thor.

"Well …"

"Alone. Just you and me."

"Tonight," she said. "Let's meet at the village square. I'll tell my parents that you and I are going to sit on the park bench under the lights so I can hear some of the stories that you made up at winter camp."

"I can't wait." Thor left Mattie's cabin filled with lust and desire. They would be alone, tonight. All alone, he thought.

That night they met at a lean-to he'd made to keep them warm in the nippy spring air. It was the first of many evenings they shared together—alone and in love.

Sally hadn't mailed a wedding invitation to Lily because she wanted to deliver it in person when the weather got milder. One April day she thought about the old Indian woman and approached Jake. "Will you accompany me to Chestnut Ridge? I'm still afraid when I go there alone."

"Oh, dear," said Jake. "Do you still think about that terrible day?" He held her hand.

A single tear formed in the corner of Sally's eye. "Yes, I'll remember that day for the rest of my life."

"Come on now. Let's be happy about our wedding plans. Yes, I'll go with you to see Lily. Let's saddle our horses and go this afternoon."

They stopped and sought shelter twice along the way from a driving rain that made it hard for the horses to keep their footing. Even though she had a large-brimmed hat, water dripped from Sally's head and wet her shoulders. A stream of water ran down Jake's back and left a puddle on the back of his saddle.

When they got near the cabin, Sally announced herself. "Is anyone home? It's me!"

There were no tracks leading in the mud to the cabin door. "I hope nothing's wrong," Sally said.

"Things don't look good. There's no smoke coming from her chimney on a wet, cold day. Maybe she got the ague."

They peered in the window. Sally looked from one side of the room to the other, past bottles of medicine and clumps of drying herbs. Finally, she saw Lily's body, slumped in a chair next to the table.

She said, "Jake look, by the table. She's not moving." Sally feared the worst because the Indian's head rested motionless on her chest. She knocked at the door several times, but there was no answer. "What should we do?"

Jake pushed open the unlocked door and they went inside. Lily sat in the sunlight with a pale green face and filmy eyes that stared into space. Sally smelled a strong odor. "She's been dead for several weeks, maybe months."

"Yes, I'm afraid so."

"The poor woman. I hope she didn't feel any pain."

Jake touched her body softly. It seemed stiff. "I don't think so. It's more likely she fell asleep and never woke up."

Seeing her fiancé touch the body gave her courage to reach out and stroke Lily's hand, which felt cold and hard. "Jake and I are getting married," she said to the corpse.

He knelt. "She can't hear you."

"Oh yes, she can. She knows we'll be happy." She felt warm tears drip down her cheeks. "Let's go tell your dad about this. He'll know what to do."

The couple ran toward the Flareau cabin as fast as they could in the slippery mud. When she saw Jake's dad in the doorway, Sally screamed, "Help, help! Lily's dead." Her knees wobbled before she collapsed on the ground.

"Let me help you inside," Pierre said. "You're both soaked and covered with mud. Come, have a cup of tea."

After sharing details about what they had found, she headed for Lily's cabin, followed by Jake and his father. Maybe it was all a dream, Sally thought when they approached the door. Perhaps Lily will greet us.

Disappointed, she looked inside the cabin and saw the body still in the chair near the table.

Pierre said, "Let's bury her now. There's no need for a funeral. She'd want to stay right here."

Sally watched him leave the cabin and walk to the edge of the field, where he dug a narrow trench in the soft soil.

With Jake's help, Sally placed the body on a piece of pine, twenty inches wide that they found in the woodpile. Each took an end of the board and marched to the freshly dug grave. Along the way, Sally noticed the herb garden she'd first visited and saw piles of carefully stacked rocks marking special plants. Pierre is right, she thought. This is how Lily would have wanted it. She'd like to be near her herbs.

The three held hands above the grave, after lowering the woman to her final rest. Pierre said, "Lord take this weak body, from which a strong soul has escaped. Let her be with her family and friends. May the Great Spirit be kind to her and to us. Amen." He stooped down, shoveled several loads on dirt on top of the body, and bowed again.

Sally took the shovel from his hand and spread more dirt on top of Lily, now barely visible beneath the soil. "Thanks for being my friend and teaching me so much about plants and life." She knelt and wept.

Jake picked the shovel off the ground and filled the hole. He piled some rocks on top of the fresh earth and erected a cross of ash sticks, tied together with rawhide he cut from his bootlaces. Dozens of Bible verses flashed through his mind, but he chose to say the Lord's Prayer. "Our Father who art in heaven…"

The next job after the burial was to clean the cabin. Jake threw out a bucket of dirty water and swept the floor. Then he scrubbed the chair where the old lady died, using a mixture of soap and lye. Sally opened the windows so that fresh air could replace the odor of death.

While they were working, Pierre saw something on the fireplace mantle. "Look at this," he said. "There's a letter here. The envelope is addressed to 'anyone who finds this note.'"

"Read it then," said Jake. "You're the one who found it."

"I'm sorry. I don't know some of the words."

Jake took the letter and read the following:

To whom it may concern,

Having no family or relatives, I leave this cabin and its belongings to Sally Wilton from Grafton who brightened my life with her visits. She loves my herbs and will take good care of my affairs.

Sincerely,

Lillian Piquany

Sally asked, "Do I really get this beautiful old cabin?"

"We'll have to see. If the Indian woman had no heirs and the title's in her name, everything would seem proper. Of course, you may owe back taxes."

Sally dried her tears with the back of her hand. "What a wonderful gift!"

"This place is worth quite a bit," said Pierre. "You must have been very special to her."

"I'd rather have Lily at my wedding than own this cabin." She knelt by the fireplace and cried.

Jake sat down beside her on the hearth and said, "Let's take our wedding announcement and put it under a rock by the cross on her grave." He helped Sally stand.

"Okay. I'll put a piece of pennyroyal there, too. That was the first herb she taught me about. She'll know it's from me."

The wedding day was gray and rainy in the morning, but the skies cleared by noon. Judy asked Sally to be there by noon and requested the rest of the wedding party to arrive by twelve-thirty. She stood in front of the church wearing a new hoop dress and waited with Martha to greet each guest. Jake's sister wore an ivory-colored dress with silk underskirt. Typical for little girls, she wore an extra wrap that was short enough to show two to three inches of her dress.

Sally came first with the maid-of-honor Mattie followed by Lydia, the bridesmaid. The three girls giggled while showing off their clothes and hairdos. Sally wore a white satin gown with a long train cut full and round. The other girls were dressed in pink, with gold combs holding their white veils. Mrs. Rice, who made the dresses, had worked hard to duplicate fashions common in large cities.

Judy said to the girls, "Stay in the small room next to the minister's study. Don't let anyone see Sally in her wedding gown. None of you should leave the room. Don't even go to the privy. Do you understand?"

Mattie spun in a circle. The pink dress accentuated her blue eyes and fine blonde hair. "What about our clothes? Aren't they beautiful, too?"

"Yes, they are. Now hurry. Into the room. Don't leave until I come for you."

Jake and Thor came next. The groom looked confident in his new suit, although his tie was crooked. The silk hat, a foot above his forehead, made him look older than he was.

His mother straightened his tie and said, "God has answered one of my prayers today. I always hoped to be here when you got married. This is a very special moment for me."

"I'm glad you're here, too. Thanks for liking Sally. I love her. Is she here yet?"

Judy winked. "She's here with Lydia and Mattie. But you'll have to wait to see her. No peeking."

Thor did his best to dress appropriately, but wore his boots instead of shoes. His silk hat was tilted on his head. Feigning a heavier than normal Swedish accent, he asked, "Can I see Mattie?"

"I suppose," said Jake's mother. "She talks about you all the time. I'll get her." She went to check on Sally and returned with Mattie.

Thor's girlfriend ran up to him and said, "You look beautiful."

"Beautiful? Bah! That's for girls." He threw his hands up in the air. "How 'bout handsome."

"Nope, you're beautiful. Just look at your well-trimmed beard and clean clothes."

"There's no sense arguing with you. I never seem to win. But, you're the one that's beautiful. The dress makes you look so good. I can't wait to hold you and dance with you."

"Nobody's looking. You can hold me now if you like."

Thor hugged her carefully so her dress wouldn't wrinkle.

"That's enough now," said Judy. "You'll have plenty of time to dance later." She stared at Mattie and said, "You'd better go back to Sally now."

Mr. Wilton rode up on a horse and tied it to a hitching post. Jake's mother greeted him with a kiss on the cheek. "Welcome. What a special day for us." The generous words didn't match her expression of disbelief that the bride's father was wearing a cowboy hat much too large for his head and completely inappropriate for a wedding. Of course, it did minimize his protruding ears and hairy neck.

"I'm very happy for our children."

Jake shook Mr. Wilton's hand with apprehension. "Are you really going to wear that Stetson to our wedding? All the other men will have silk hats."

"Of course. I've always dreamed of wearing a cowboy hat to my daughter's wedding. Grafton is still on the western frontier, you know." He removed his glasses and clutched them in his hand.

"Yes sir," said Jake. "Everyone knows we're pioneers. Especially you blacksmiths."

Thor laughed with the other men and shook Mr. Wilton's hand. "Congratulations, sir. Weddings are a time for dreams to come true."

"Ah, yes." He looked skyward for a moment. "Mine came true when I moved here from Boston. Now my daughter's dream is coming true."

"America is definitely a land of opportunity," said Thor. The two men nodded.

A carriage pulled up to the church. Everyone watched as the driver opened the door for Eli Peters, the groomsman. He wore an expensive wool suit, silk shirt, and a tie with perfect knot. A ring worn on the outside of his white gloves, told everyone he was an aristocrat. Although it was getting warm, he wore a Prince Albert coat, neatly buttoned. Not a red hair was out of place, and he no longer had peach fuzz on his chin.

Jake, who hadn't seen his friend for some time, greeted him with a handshake. Then he twisted Eli's arm behind his back. "So you're a timber man now. I see you even wear gloves like a girl. No more farm boy, huh?"

"Ow, let me go!" When his arm was free, Eli pulled the sleeve of his suit to straighten the wrinkles. "I'm happy for you, my friend. What a beautiful little church. Did I ever tell you about the church in Coldwater? It has stained glass windows and…"

"Shh," said Jake. "Let me introduce you around." Everyone smiled when they met Eli because they'd heard so many stories about his gift of gab. It didn't take long, though, for them to discover his annoying ways for themselves and avoid him as he prowled looking for new victims to bore with his long-winded prose.

At five after one, Reverend Hughes rang the church bells, which echoed up and down the streets of Grafton. Almost sixty people in pews watched the wedding party in front of the altar. Sally waited with her father at the rear of the church for the music to begin. She looked out over the audience and saw a sea of women's hats in all shapes and sizes. Most had some kind of floral arrangement on their bonnets. Several hats had cock feathers pointing upward—in contrast to the bare heads of men and children.

Her father whispered beneath his breath, "Look at all the people who have come to wish you happiness."

She squeezed his hand. "Yes, father, I love this town."

"And they love you, my dear."

When the organist began the music for the wedding procession, Sally floated down the aisle, hand in hand with her father. Everything seemed to be in slow motion. Seeing Jake and Thor at the altar relaxed her. She fixed her eyes on her future husband and drifted toward him, wiggling her hips a bit more than she needed to.

It seemed forever before she stood with her father in front of the minister with her back toward the audience. She felt a kiss on her cheek as her father turned and left her standing beside Jake. The groom caught her hand just as it reached her side after being dropped by her father. That's the real meaning of the ceremony, she thought. It isn't the ring or legal sanction, but the transfer of hand holding from father to husband.

The best part of the service for Sally was the wedding vows. She'd heard the words before but never paid much attention to their meaning until now. The gravity of the commitment struck her when she repeated the minister's words: "Until death do us part."

I already died once, she thought, when living in Bay City. Then, Thor rescued me to help Jake and his family. Thanks to Jake, I've got a better life. Of course I'll stay with him forever. Of course.

"I now pronounce you husband and wife," Reverend Hughes said. His soft words and pleasant smile spread from the altar across the pews. The audience seemed hypnotized by his happy soul. "You may kiss the bride."

She felt her husband's soft lips touch hers, gently, like a feather on skin. She recalled their first kiss. She felt that same sensation of heat rising from her feet to make her face blush.

The couple turned toward the audience to be greeted by a standing ovation of loud clapping. Several of the young men whistled even though they were in church. Sally watched children jump and dance in the aisles.

Martha came forward and placed a bouquet in the bride's hand. The bouquet had already been divided into two bundles, one of which contained a special ring. Blindfolded, Sally pulled one bundle of flowers from the arrangement and tossed it in the air. Lydia rushed forward and caught it with ease. Then the bride flipped the second bundle skyward. It seemed to float into Mattie's waiting hands. Both girls dug into their bundle of colorful blossoms, searching for the prize.

It was Mattie who found the ring, a symbol of who was to be married next, buried deep within the flower stems. She shrieked a second time and said, "It's me. It's me." Everyone in the audience turned toward Thor, who quickly looked down at his boots.

A gaggle of screaming girls ran toward Mattie and surrounded her. They patted her on the back, and whispered in her ear.

One of the girls said, "Oh dear, what man would be good enough for you?"

"There is one, but just one."

The girls giggled and laughed while talking about boys.

A feast was held at the village square after the service. Mr. Wilton furnished several kinds of meat, vegetables, and fruit. Children at the wedding spent hours mixing peaches and cream in a container surrounded by ice and salt. When it got hard to turn the handle, several high-pitched voices let everyone know the ice cream was done. Sally and Jake cut the cake after everyone tired of the children's chant, "Dessert time. Dessert time."

Thor toasted the couple. "Jake has shown himself to be a good market hunter and excellent logger." He stopped talking for a moment and struggled to dig some notes from his suit pocket. Finding them, he continued. "He'll make an even better husband. Sally, keeper of the herbs, knows all our secret ailments." He stuffed the notes back in his pocket. "Now she plans to fill Jake's lonesome heart. As best man, I wish this couple many years of happiness and health."

Eli rose to speak after the applause died down, but Thor interrupted him and said, "Not now, my friend. The toast is the responsibility of the best man, not the groomsman."

The bride winked at Thor, thankful the guests would be spared a long oration from Eli.

The village band played quiet background music while the guests enjoyed the wedding cake.

When people finished dessert, the music changed to a waltz. Sally and Jake took the dance floor to start the festivities. Alone on the patio next to the gazebo, the couple soared in perfect motion to the beat of the music. The clapping of the audience grew louder as the couple bowed and curtsied.

Sally searched out her father, who was talking politics with a group of men. She said to him, "Here you are hiding from me. It's time to dance with your daughter."

"See," said one of his friends. "The state of the nation's economy can wait. But, your daughter can't."

While they danced, she whispered in his ear. "Dad, I have finally found a place to be and a man to share it with. My life is now complete."

Sally's father had not danced in more than twenty years but was still graceful and moved in time with the music. "Yes, dear," he said, "he'll make a good husband. You'll be a good wife, too. Maybe God will even let you be a mother." He took off his glasses and put them in the pocket of his suit. "It's too bad your mother isn't here today."

Sally felt a twinge of sadness when recalling that her mother had not even acknowledged the wedding announcement. Feelings of abandonment, which she had not felt in several years, returned. She wondered, why doesn't mother care about me? What did I do wrong?

Then she perked up, realizing how fortunate she was that her father was still alive. Lily saved him, she thought. I should be happy for the people at my wedding rather than pine over those not here.

Eli approached Jake and asked if he could talk business for a few minutes. When the groom agreed, the timber executive said, "I've been watching the development of sawmills in the Saginaw River Basin for several years. There's still room for another well-managed plant. Would you be interested?"

Jake seemed bored talking business. "I don't know. Are you offering me a job?"

"Oh, my. We already have enough employees. I'm talking about starting your own company."

"Whadaya mean?"

"Why don't you build a mill? My associates would be silent partners. The company'd be yours."

"What's it cost to build a sawmill?"

"About $5,000."

"Where would I get that kind of money?"

Eli pulled a piece of paper from his hip pocket. "Here's what we're offering." He went on to explain the conditions of the note and interest rate to be charged by his company, along with the share of future profits expected.

"How much would I need to put up?"

"In the neighborhood of $1,000. Do you have any cash or property we could mortgage?"

"Maybe," he said. "Let me worry about getting my thousand dollars. You worry about the other four thousand.

I don't want to talk about this any more on my wedding night, but let's get together next week."

"Fine." Eli pulled out a money clip and gave Jake twenty dollars. "Here's an advance for you to come to our Bay City office next week."

"Oh no," said Jake. He returned the money. "If this is going to be my company, I'll use my own funds. I'd also like to have Thor be my assistant."

"That's okay with me. Give me a date and time, and I'll ask Bruce Royston to join us."

"How 'bout next Thursday at eight in the morning. Is that too early for you?"

"I'll check and let you know. Good luck to you and Sally."

"Thanks."

Eli put the bill back in his thick money clip. "You know, I owe you one for getting me out of Bay City."

"Let's talk about the future and not the past." Jake shook hands with Eli. "The only thing you owe me is one dance with my wife. Let me introduce you."

"Jake, my friend, I already know her."

"How could you?" His face paled. "Oh…you met her before? In Bay City?"

"Well, there was lots of liquor and lots of waiter girls…I'm not sure."

Jake started to get mad and then relaxed. "As I said, let's talk about the future and not the past. Anyway, she really does like to dance."

The men moved toward the gazebo where the band played, and found Sally dancing with Pierre. When the music stopped, she approached Jake, who said, "Sally, I'd like you to meet my old friend Eli Peters." He swung his arm toward her. "And this is my wife, Sally Flareau." It was the first time he'd used her new last name.

Eli said, "I'm very pleased to meet you."

"Have we met before? You look familiar."

"Perhaps." He glanced at Jake who raised his eyebrows. "But probably not. I'm from Coldwater. Have you ever been there? Our village square is much like this one, but…" He motioned to the center of the room. "Can we dance and talk at the same time?"

"Thank you," she said. "I'd love to dance with you." The rest of the wedding party joined them in a spirited polka.

Sally worried all the while she danced about the next part of the wedding when she was to open her gifts. Although guests were not expected to offer presents, it was customary for the bride's mother to announce her gifts, usually personal items for the bride. Since her mother was in Boston and had no interest in her wedding, she had expected an awkward moment after the wedding party finished dancing and before the guests were invited onto the dance floor.

Much to her surprise, a group of her women friends from church stood on the platform in front of the band. The tallest of four girls said, "We women of the Wicker Circle would like to announce the wedding gifts we are giving the bride."

Sally couldn't contain her excitement. Her shrieks of joy brought laughter from the audience.

"Our main gift is a new mattress along with sheets and blankets. We also made a nightgown and some other comfortables for the bride."

Sally ran up to the stage and hugged each of the four women. Under her breath, she said, "Thank you. God be with you."

"And with you and your new husband," replied one of the girls.

Judy walked up to the platform and addressed the audience. "I have a gift for my daughter-in-law, too. You've all heard the adage, 'Something old, something new, something borrowed, something blue.' My gift is something old, a used article from a happily married woman to bring good fortune to my son's marriage." She motioned toward Martha, who carried a quilt to the platform and handed it to Sally.

The bride hugged Judy and whispered in her ear. "Can I call you Mom?"

"Yes, dear. Welcome to our family."

Once again the audience cheered. Guests took their places on the dance floor when the bride and groom started to waltz.

Thor and Mattie had left the reception and slipped into the woods unnoticed. The June afternoon was warm enough to be comfortable but not yet hot. Brushing the mosquitoes that stung the back of their necks and buzzed around their ears, the couple sat on a log beneath a maple tree.

He said, "I've enjoyed dancing with you so much. I always feel so happy when I'm with you."

Mattie blushed. She swatted but missed a mosquito that buried itself in Thor's thick sandy beard. "Oh Thor, you're the first man I've liked. Maybe I'm too critical, but other men have too many flaws."

Thor took both her hands in his. He took a deep breath and said, "I know I'm from a foreign land and may have different way, but I'd like to share life's opportunities with you. Will you marry me?"

"See, the ring in the bouquet was for me! Yes, Thor. Yes. I'll marry you. You're beautiful."

He picked a piece of grass off the shiny surface of his right boot and stuck the green shoot in the corner of his mouth.

She pulled the grass out of his mouth. "Don't eat grass. Especially when I feel like kissing."

Thor put his arm around her shoulder. Her blonde hair draped over his elbow. She turned toward him until their lips met. The kiss lasted for several minutes and got wetter with time. "Wow," he said.

"More." She begged. "Let's kiss some more." They spent several minutes kissing and petting. Suddenly, they heard brush move a few yards away. Peering out, Mattie saw Pierre urinating on a stump. "Uh oh," she whispered, "we chose a bad place to sit. Let's get back to the square."

After Pierre fastened his pants, the two left the woods separately so people wouldn't know they'd been together.

Townspeople started to leave the party at nine. After saying good night to the last guests, Sally and Jake rode to their cabin past Chestnut Ridge. The couple would spend this first night together as husband and wife in their own home.

Jake opened the door and lifted her across the threshold. After they kissed, she lit an oil lamp, which shone yellow light on the walls. Sally had never seen so many shades of wood before. Lily must have intentionally gathered maple, birch, oak, and other woods to decorate her cabin.

The couple undressed and got into their night attire. Jake sat in the large chair by the fireplace while Sally took the rocker. He said, "Today was the best day of my life."

"Me, too. Would you like some sassafras tea? It would be good to settle our stomachs before sleep."

"Sure." He stood and rubbed the well-oiled mantle over the fireplace while Sally poured water in the kettle. She watched him move slowly about the cabin. It's so nice to be with my husband in our own home, she thought. She was surprised when he squatted on the floor by the base of the fireplace and rattled a floorboard.

"Well look at this," said Jake. "This board needs to be re-seated. I remember how Dietrich and I used to cut these boards a few years ago."

"I don't want his name mentioned in our house." Sally ran over to Jake as he knelt by the fireplace. "Don't ever say that name again. Do you understand?"

"I'm sorry, I wasn't thinking. I was just looking at this loose board and remembering how we worked together on puncheon floors. I won't mention him again."

Jake removed the loose board and turned it over several times. "That's different. This board has never been properly attached. I wonder why?" He reached down into the hole left after the floorboard had been removed.

Sally watched him withdraw a furry sack tied with a thin piece of rawhide. "What's that?"

"I saw a pouch like this once before. A peddler at the train depot had one. He told me it was made from a bear paw. Indians used to keep special trinkets in them."

"Open it up." Sally was so excited she ignored the boiling water in the kettle.

Jake carried the sack to the table, sat down, and untied the cord. He stretched the mouth of the sack and dumped the contents on the table. A dozen jewels spilled out on the oak table. There were two large diamonds, along with several rubies, sapphires, and emeralds.

"Where did the Indian woman get these jewels?" asked Jake.

"She traded many things with other Indians. She told me she'd bartered for perfume, silk, lace, and gold nuggets. Relatives who had died had left her furs, rare feathers, and beads. Maybe she inherited the jewels. She never mentioned them to me."

Jake put the jewels back in the bear-paw sack. "I think these are worth some money. I'll get them appraised tomorrow. Should we keep them or sell them?"

"You never had enough money to get me a diamond ring for our engagement. What if we take the big diamond and have a ring made. We could sell the rest."

"I think Lily would like that. In fact, I've been thinking about building a sawmill up north. Can I invest the money from the jewels to finance the mill?"

"Whatever you think. Husbands take care of finances. That's your job."

The couple drank their tea and spoke about their future. Sally talked about ways to keep selling herbs and still raise a family. Jake shared his ideas about building a sawmill on the Saginaw River.

Their lovemaking that wedding night was spectacular. They enjoyed each other twice. Afterwards, they fell asleep, happy to be Mr. and Mrs. Flareau.

17

Jake Builds a Sawmill in Saginaw

The pleasant days and nights with Sally slipped by too quickly for Jake, lulled by the bliss of early marriage. He lost all sense of time until he was due to visit Bruce in Bay City. He didn't want to leave his new wife but was excited about the prospects of running a sawmill. Several days before his appointment, he went to the bank, withdrew a thousand dollars in crisp new bills, and met Thor at the depot. This time, his friend knew exactly which trains to take to avoid the errors he'd made on his last trip to Bay City.

At seven thirty on the morning of their appointment, Jake and Thor took a carriage from the hotel to the offices of Royston Lumber Company. There they met Bruce and Eli in a conference room. Jake felt a bit awkward wearing a tie to the meeting but was glad he did when he saw that the timber men dressed in business suits.

Eli welcomed them. "We're so happy you came here to meet with us." He turned to his boss. "Bruce, please meet my friend Jake Flareau and his assistant, Thor Glick." He put his arm around his boss's shoulder. "This is Mr. Bruce Royston."

"Welcome to Bay City and Royston Lumber Company. Please have a seat."

The four men sat before a stack of papers on a table. Jake noticed that the legal documents, printed on heavy paper, had several places already marked where signatures were required. Eli said, "Gentlemen, we're gathered here today in celebration of the first meeting of Flareau and Company. Let's spend a few minutes and introduce ourselves. Mr. Glick, would you start? Just tell us something about your past so we can get to know you better."

Thor leaped from his chair and strutted around the table while he told a story about cutting spruce trees in Sweden. With his sandy beard, stocky build, and bright red suspenders, he looked like a hawker trying to get people to enter a circus tent. He ended his story with a tribute to the country. "Above all, I am thankful for all the opportunities in America."

Jake remained in his seat while introducing himself. He reviewed some experiences he had in logging camp. At the end of his introduction, he said, "My time in the woods taught me the importance of teamwork."

Bruce left his seat and walked to the window, where he began his introduction. "Our company has a social responsibility to the town of Bay City." He looked at Thor. "We must keep an active economy to support both the long-term residents and new immigrants in town." Then he turned to Jake and said, "My father feels that the company must be good to its neighbors." His gaze shifted to Eli. "We must protect the people who depend on us."

As Jake expected, Eli talked too much about his upbringing in Coldwater. "Let me tell you about the values I grew up with in my home town…" When he saw that the men were no longer paying attention, he switched the topic. "Our second order of business is to collate funds. Jake, you agreed to invest one thousand dollars in the company and Mr. Royston four thousand dollars. Do we have those funds?"

Bruce placed a certified check on the table made out to Flareau and Company. Jake counted his money and put cash on the table.

Jake recalled how fortunate he was to have sold the jewels in Kalamazoo for eighteen hundred dollars. He'd paid thirty dollars to have the large diamond set in a nice gold band for Sally's ring. The transaction left him more than enough cash to invest in the sawmill without having to mortgage the cabin.

Eli initiated the signing of papers after the cash and check were placed in an envelope. Jake and Thor signed at least ten different documents that had been prepared by the parent company's attorney. They passed the documents to Bruce for his final approval.

Bruce didn't sign the papers at first. He placed his pen on the table and started to say something, but paused. The other men waited patiently for him to continue. He said, "There is one thing that is bothering us."

"What's that?" asked Jake.

"We better all be honest," added Thor.

"Well...your sawmill will be built on the Saginaw River, but your home is in Grafton. That's a long way from here. Will this project put undue stress on your families or loved ones?"

Jake stood and paced around the room before answering. "I'm recently married, but my wife has only one family member in town. Perhaps she could join me while we build the mill."

"Who is this one family member?" asked Bruce. He motioned Jake to sit down.

"Her father. He's a blacksmith."

"Is he well and able to care for himself?"

"Yes." Jake sat back down at the table.

"Here's what we'll do. My company has its own housing for mill employees and a few nice homes for visiting executives and their families. You and your wife can have one of the houses with an extra room for your father-in-law, if needed."

Jake felt embarrassed to admit what he was thinking. "Will it be expensive?"

"Oh, no. That's part of our investment in you and your mill. There will be no charge."

"Thank you very much, sir."

Bruce looked at Thor. "What about you?"

"I'm single, but am very attached to a country girl named Mattie."

"Will the separation be a problem for you or for her?"

"No, sir. This building project may be a good test. If our love is real, it will last."

"Okay. The company will provide you with a room in a boarding house. But no women are allowed. Do you understand?"

"Yes. You are very generous. Thank you."

Bruce lifted his pen and signed the documents. "It's a pleasure doing business with you."

With the finesse of a politician, Eli withdrew a bottle of champagne, popped the cork, and said, "Now, here's to the success of our new partnership."

The men drank one glass of champagne and talked about the mill's location, selected by Eli. Thor emptied the bottle into his glass, raised it, and said, "To America, the land of opportunity."

After the meeting Eli stopped at the bank where he deposited the funds in a new account created for Flareau and Company. He mailed an advance to a construction firm from Buffalo, New York, that he had chosen to build the sawmill. Jake agreed with the choice because the firm had built many mills throughout New England, Michigan, Wisconsin, and Minnesota.

By the end of the week about two dozen men had set up tents at the site of the new mill. Jake and Eli met with the managers and foremen in a field near the river to discuss specifications for the building. Jake was impressed with the knowledge of the company officials and fascinated by the sketches they brought with them. He peered at the tiny lines depicting doorways and walls. Another drawing showed the position of saws and other equipment to be installed. A third illustrated land boundaries, showed where the river would be diked to make a millpond, and depicted where finished lumber would be stacked.

When Jake looked at the detailed sketches, his mind drifted into the future. He heard the whining saws and envisioned scores of men bustling throughout the yard and building.

One of the foremen pointed at the third sketch and asked, "Well, Boss, what do you think? Do we need a shed for fire-fighting equipment?"

Jake glanced across the vacant field and realized he had been daydreaming. "No. We need that space for lumber. Let's just put a dozen shovels and six pick-axes in the corner of the entrance."

"Are we done?" asked the foreman.

"Yes. These are good plans. I've never seen such detail in sketches. These diagrams are works of art."

"Yes, sir," said the senior project manager. "The men seem to work harder if they can see how their jobs all fit together."

"Randy's built twelve mills in five states," said one of the other foremen. "He ought to know."

"Well, build us one just like that model," said Jake.

"I believe we will," replied Randy. He hollered at his men. "Let's get to work!"

Jake was amazed at the speed of the workmen. Within a few days a two-story structure was framed. It's like other sawmills I've seen before, he thought. They all look the same. Maybe that's because the same companies build them.

Soon the workmen had constructed a powerhouse with a tall smokestack. They added boards to the side of the mill and attached a tin roof. Another crew built a conveyer belt with a toothed bull chain to yank logs from the millpond that was just starting to fill with river water.

During the week he watched several machines delivered on oversized wagons. Whenever some new equipment arrived, men left their work sites and gathered to inspect the circular saws and log-holding carriages. They spent almost thirty minutes probing the used steam engine, purchased from a mill in Maine that was going out of business because all the adjacent timber had been harvested. Just when they were about to return to work, a boiler arrived. Sawdust and scrap wood would be burned in the boiler to power the hundred-horsepower steam engine with a cast iron flywheel.

Jake and Thor were so busy that they slept only five or six hours a night. Since Sally had not yet arrived in Bay City, Thor stayed with Jake in the company house.

Sally arrived on a Thursday afternoon. Jake took time off work to meet her train, which was two hours late because of fires next to the railroad tracks in southern Michigan. When he saw her deboard, he ran and held her with his wide arms and big hands. "I missed you something terrible." He kissed her, gently at first, but with more energy as her fellow travelers left the platform. "You look so beautiful."

Sally said, "I couldn't wait to get here. I don't like being away from you."

"Me neither."

Jake whistled to a carriage driver, who loaded Sally's trunk and other luggage and helped her into the seat. The couple bundled themselves in a wool blanket while riding through town to their company house on Washington Avenue. Once in a while he reached beneath the blanket and touched her.

The carriage stopped in front of a Victorian home with a stone stairway leading to a large door of glass, brass, and polished wood. Sally asked, "Is this where we stay? It's so large for two people."

"Yes. This will be our home until the first saw milling season is behind us." He showed the carriage driver where to put Sally's belongings and tipped him. Jake closed the door, turned to his wife, and said, "How 'bout if I take the afternoon off?"

"I hoped you would. Now where were we?" She kissed with persistence and longing until Jake guided her to the bedroom. After making love, they sat in the parlor and talked until midnight, when they shared themselves again. In the morning on his way back to work, Jake realized they'd never had dinner.

Construction came to a halt in late fall due to bad weather, so Jake worked on logging contracts. Rather than purchase timbered land, he solicited local loggers with access to pine on private land. Those contract loggers made deals with property owners to kick back a share of the profits from harvest. That seemed better to Jake than buying large tracts of land. With this arrangement he didn't need to invest as much in equipment or personnel since contractors would have their own wagons, sleighs, and work crews.

Eli told Jake to be careful about the wording in contracts since some loggers might fail to perform as promised. He said the mill should be especially wary of subcontracts let by loggers to friends or relatives. In some areas of the Midwest, he added, the subcontractors were lazy, deceitful, or lacked the equipment to complete the work.

Mr. Fred Linsey, a leader among contractors logging in the Saginaw Valley, didn't like the detailed legal language in Jake's contracts. So, a meeting was held in the partly finished office at the mill, even though the weather was cold and snowy. Jake and Thor stood before a small table in the middle of the office without heat or chairs. Snow had accumulated on the wooden floor in front of the windows, which did not yet have panes. Fred, followed by five associates, entered the room at ten minutes after the scheduled meeting time. Jake had a feeling they had staged the late arrival purposely to get control of the meeting. The six men huddled like a football team on the other side of the table.

Jake said, "Welcome to our mill."

Fred replied, "I represent myself and five others who might want to do business with your new mill here in town. This is Ralph Storey, Hank Schmidt, Kyle Tanzynski, Rudolf Truffenbacker, and Franz Zalinsky."

Jake reached across the table and shook each man's hand. "It's nice to see you all together at one time. I run this mill. This is my assistant, Thor." His co-worker reached across the table and shook everyone's hand. He smoothed his beard between each handshake.

"So here's my question," said Hank. "Why'd you require all logs to be delivered? You used to log. You know how much extra work it takes to load and move logs."

"Yeah, I know, but that's the rule."

"Whaddya mean? Why's it a rule?"

Jake said nothing.

"We've been talking," said Franz. "Some of the private land we rent is a long way from the river. Why can't we pile logs near roads and have your company tote them to the river? That way we'd only need skidding teams."

Kyle joined in. "Der's udder stuff, too. You say dat sticks must be fifty percent sound. That's not fair. Some mills take forty. Der's pine on Jeff Hale's place dat's so old it's dirty-five. Why can't I sell dat to you'se?"

Jake had trouble understanding Kyle, but tried to address his complaint. "That's the rule we're going to start with. After we get going, maybe things'll change. But for now, logs have to be fifty percent sound."

"You're stubborn," said Fred. "We're here to help. Let's start with easy specs and tighten 'em as the dollars flow."

Thor, who hadn't spoken yet, moved in front of Jake. He looked down at his boots, which shone brightly in the sunny room. "Gentlemen, I think you've made some good points. Our company is most concerned with the number of board feet you promise to deliver each month. As long as you agree with those figures and the penalties for not meeting your quota, maybe we can talk about adjusting some of the transportation and quality requirements."

Jake felt hurt. Here he was, trying to uphold orders from Royston Lumber Company while his friend was undermining his authority in front of new business associates. Why didn't he ask me first about changing the rules? Jake thought. He tried to regain his leadership in the discussion. "Of course, we'll have to check with our investors," he said.

"Well, said Fred. "We were going to question some of those cash penalties for missing a monthly quota, but...Whaddaya say, men?"

"I'm just glad we don't have to deliver every log to the mill," said Hank.

"How bout the rest of you?"

"I wanna cut dose logs on Jeff Hale's eighty acres," said Kyle. "I've been eye'n 'em for yars."

"Let's do it," said Fred.

Jake got several invitations to dinner at the homes of other sawmill owners in the Saginaw River basin. Although Sally encouraged him to accept those invitations, he was reluctant. What if someone recognized Sally from her previous jobs in Bay City? How would I explain being married to a former waiter girl?

Sally seemed to sense the reason for his hesitation. One night when they were discussing their social calendar, she said, "You know, I didn't want to return to Bay City. Maybe I just wanted to put the past out of my mind. Perhaps I was afraid someone would recognize me and I would embarrass you."

"Sometimes I worry about that, too." He was glad that she had brought up the subject.

"I thought about this on the train from Grafton. At one of the stops, I watched a well dressed gentlemen give a drunkard some money. I was close enough to hear their conversation."

"What did they say?"

"The rich man told the drunk to use the money for food, not whiskey. He said that he, too, had been destitute and craved alcohol but now was a successful businessman. He told the drunk to have hope and trust in God."

"What's that have to do with you coming back to Bay City?"

"The drunk answered, 'God would never forgive me for all the things I've done.' And then the rich man replied, 'That's the key to salvation. You must admit you've sinned.

You must accept Jesus as the Son of God, who came to earth and was crucified for our sins. Then you will be forgiven.'"

Jake was silent. He thought about Luke 7, which he had read in logging camp. He remembered the prostitute who had bathed the feet of Jesus and was forgiven. "All that...on the train?"

"Yes. When I got here, I felt forgiven. I felt glad to return to Bay City as a lady."

After their discussion Jake accepted all the offers to attend weddings, dinners, charity fund-raisers, and other social activities with fellow timber men. The couple went to the Opera House on several occasions and attended many Christmas parties in the mansions on Center Street and Washington Avenue. Neither Jake nor Sally cared if she was recognized because she was now a different person, redeemed and reborn.

When the Holiday season was over, Jake began to line up companies that were interested in buying finished lumber. He invited several purchasing agents to meet at the partly built mill. Signs were posted in storefronts and on telegraph poles in the countryside. Jake went to seven different lumberyards in towns near Bay City and Saginaw to invite representatives to the meeting.

The attempts to attract distributors worked. Ten men came to hear about lumber that might be available from the new mill.

Jake said, "We're kind of new in the business, so I can't guarantee the number of board feet for sale per month. What I'd like to do is get the name of your company if you're interested in buying lumber. Then, when we've got some finished boards for sale, I'd like to hold an auction. Is that reasonable?"

"Not for me," said a representative from a lumberyard in downtown Bay City. "The construction business is brisk. My company needs firm agreements on lumber volumes by grade. If our customers can't count on us, they'll go somewhere else." Four other men agreed and left the meeting.

The remaining five distributors talked about ways the auction would be held. One potential buyer south of Saginaw said his business was much less predictable, so they could handle some uncertainty of supply. "My company needs some assurance that we can at least be given fairly graded lumber at a reasonable cost. It wouldn't be right for you to sell everything to one high bidder and leave the rest of us high and dry. Can you at least offer the option of one-fifth the volume to each of us at the high bid? That way, we can go back home and try to sell our management on the price by grade."

Thor didn't like that arrangement. "What if we all agree on a price and then none of your companies fill orders? Then our new mill will be stuck with unsold lumber."

"This is too complicated for me," said the buyer. "Our company usually signs a contract to purchase so much lumber at an agreed-upon price by grade during specific months of the milling season. I've got to withdraw my interest at this time." He left the mill.

The remaining four men seemed nervous until Jake said, "Let's meet again in two weeks and see how we can solve this issue. In the meantime, please put the mailing address of your company on the paper I'm circulating."

That night Jake began drafting a letter to Mr. Bruce Royston explaining his dilemma and asking for advice on how to solve the issue. While describing the problem, he came upon a possible solution. What if I lobby the parent company to provide me a fixed amount of lumber, if needed, that could be resold to the lumberyards? If the new mill is successful in meeting the sales quotas, that lumber won't be required. If my mill can't meet the demand, Royston Lumber Company could ship me a specific amount of lumber. If we cut more timber than in our sales agreements, Thor and I will have the luxury of selling that surplus on the spot. He ripped up the letter and decided to visit Bruce in person the next morning.

A receptionist with long fingernails escorted Jake to Bruce's office. He explained the problem of getting lumberyards to handle the potential lumber to be produced by the new mill. He summarized his idea to have Royston guarantee the volume by grade available for sale.

"I don't see any problem with your suggestion. Just send me the quantity of lumber you need guaranteed, and we'll consider it done."

"Thank you, Bruce. This will help our mill get some good pine from private lands." The men shook hands.

"Now I've got something for you," added Bruce. "My father thinks you may have a knack for dealing with mill owners. He'd like you to work with others throughout Michigan, Wisconsin, and Minnesota. He suggested you attend an annual meeting of lumber men in Winona."

"I've heard that name before. Isn't Wenona across the river from Bay City?"

"No, I'm talking about Winona, Minnesota, not Wenona, Michigan. It's a city on the Mississippi River."

"That's a long way from here," said Jake as visions of river rafts and houses built on stilts came to his mind.

"Here's some background on two topics that will be discussed there." He handed Jake a file stuffed with papers and legal documents. "I'll be going, too, and will meet you there. Can you go?"

"I'll have to check with Sally."

"Please consider my father's suggestion. See if your wife can live without you for a couple of days."

"I've always wanted to see the Mississippi," said Jake, who suddenly thought about his grandpa floating on a barge down the Erie Canal. "Thank you for your help with the timber guarantees. I'm sure this plan will work. The line yard managers are concerned about us being a new mill with no production history."

"We're happy to see your´new mill ready for the spring. If you need anything else, just ask."

Jake left Bruce's office with a pile of papers to study. He thought, I've still got the wanderlust after all this time. Visions of steamboats and river ports filled his mind. He was going to see the Mississippi River!

The first white pine logs were delivered to Jake's mill near the end of April. Royston Lumber Company sent a crew of four men to train new millwrights in the use of saws and operation of the steam engine. The timing was perfect because Thor had hired ten men to start work on May 1 and another five to start on May 8.

Jake stood in his new sawmill and watched the first log sliced. He and other workers cheered as three men guided a wet log from the millpond up the conveyer belt. A sawyer, seated in a wire cage near the spinning saw, assessed the log's characteristics. He barked orders to two assistants who locked the log into the carriage. Those men dogged the log along the spinning saw, which sliced off a one-inch board along the entire length. Then the men pulled the carriage back to its initial position, and another slice was taken. After the rough boards were cut, they were moved to a trimming room, where sawed to specified lengths. Another team of men carefully stacked the lumber in high piles near the railroad tracks.

Jake laughed to himself when the men continued to sing ballads while they worked. This is just like Saturday night in camp, he thought.

One afternoon Sally walked downtown to shop for a new dress. She needed something nice for a dinner engagement at the mayor's house. Just as she turned off Washington Avenue, she saw a man on the other side of the street staggering from too much drink. She recognized the man's voice as he sang loudly in broken English, mixed with Polish. Yes, she realized, it's Sammy, my old customer and friend.

Without hesitating, she charged across the street and hugged him. "Sammy, it's me. Sally!"

The drunk wobbled as he backed away from her. "Sally 'da…'da…waiter girlie? You'se couldn't bees."

"Yes it is. I'm married now and started a new life. My husband owns a sawmill right here in Bay City."

"It is you. I'll be. And you're married?"

"Yes."

"So weeze can't go…to…your crib?"

"No. I don't do that any more. I'm a lady now. In fact, I probably can't ever see you again. I hope you understand."

"Good luck…my…waiter gurlie." He wobbled, started singing again, and staggered down the street.

Sammy hasn't changed at all, but I have, she thought. I'm different. My past is gone, behind me now. She skipped like a schoolgirl on her way to the dress shop. I really am forgiven.

It wasn't long before the mill was working a second shift as the loggers delivered more pine than even they had imagined. By July 1 the first boards were shipped by rail to line yards. There was no need to draw on the guarantee made by the parent company. Thor even offered to sell surplus lumber beyond the promised quota to each of the four yards. After the buyers saw the quality of the first shipment and the high standard for grading, the extra lumber was sold the first week it was offered.

The biggest problem at the mill was carelessness caused by worker exuberance. The men were so excited about meeting production goals they began having serious accidents. The first mishap occurred to Jon Peters who cut the ring and pinky fingers off his left hand. Jon later kept one of the pickled fingers in a jar near the circular saw and showed it to each new man who started at the mill. Jake could have stopped the gruesome initiation but decided it was a good lesson in safety and seemed to help Jon deal with his permanent affliction.

Jack Tumble was hit by a piece of metal buried deep inside the trunk of a pine tree when it was flung by the circular saw and pierced the skull of his forehead. A coworker said he saw brain matter ooze through a crack that was four inches long and one inch wide. Jack was given sick leave for three weeks and tried to recover from the resulting convulsions that seized his body every hour or two. His agony ended when an infection spread inside the wound. After the funeral, Jake held weekly meetings of all mill workers to discuss safety problems they saw and solutions they recommended.

Allowing any mill worker to stop the conveyer belt prevented some of the accidents caused by haste. Jake established a new rule that only the man who stopped the conveyer could turn it back on. Being able to stop the belt seemed to create a more relaxed atmosphere. The conveyer was rarely turned off, but workers felt less frenzied knowing they could stop logs if necessary.

After hearing that an exploding boiler had killed three workers in a Saginaw mill, Jake ordered the powerhouse's wall to be encased with a second row of bricks. His attention to safety was contagious. Workers learned to balance their desire for increased production and pay incentives with a high regard for safety.

Thor often became melancholy when he thought about Mattie. One time when he seemed especially depressed Jake said, "Why don't you take a few days off and go home to Grafton?"

"I had the same idea but didn't want to ask you for time off during the busy time."

"Ha. You'll work much harder once you have Mattie off your mind for a while. Now get out of here."

Thor was supposed to return in four days, but stretched his time off to seven. Jake started to worry about the welfare of his friend. Did he get to Grafton? Was he hurt along the way?

When Thor returned, he apologized. "I'm sorry, boss. We had such a good time. I didn't want to leave her behind."

"Thanks for coming back." Jake patted him on the shoulder. "The two of you will soon be together again."

The milling season ended when the maples turned red and orange. Jake's account manager tallied profits from the exceptionally good year and mailed a larger than expected check to Bruce Royston for the investors' share. There was so much money left over that Thor suggested each mill worker be given a bonus to be based on pay grade and number of hours worked. Jake agreed and distributed funds in cash at a ceremony to close the plant for the year. With their generous end-of-season bonuses, some workers purchased new winter clothes or upgraded their homes. A few boarded trains to visit family and relatives before heading to winter logging camps.

An argument ensued when Thor suggested the bonuses be extended to the logging contractors and line yard managers. Jake said, "We already paid those men good money. Why should they get bonuses beyond our agreements?"

"Because we need them to work even harder next year. The bonuses will make sure they come back to us instead of some other mill." He stroked his beard with his hand.

Jake shook his finger at Thor. "Yeah, but then next year they'll expect a bonus, too, and we have no idea what winter will be like. If there is little snow, there will be fewer logs to cut. All those men made lots of money this summer. Why fan their greed?"

Thor appeared frustrated. He snapped his suspenders and said, "Listen, these men worked hard this milling season. They helped us build this company and fill our bank accounts. They deserve a share of our success."

Jake, aware that he had offended his friend, compromised. "Okay, but let's just give a small bonus. That way we can thank them for helping us without making any lofty commitments for future years."

"Okay," said Thor. "I knew you'd do the right thing."

Thor used his own bonus to help with the cost of his pending wedding to Mattie. Jake took a thousand dollars and put the money into Sally's bank account as repayment for the capital used to start the mill. They gave the rest to Sam Granger, who built them a frame house three blocks from the Royston's estate in Bay City. The mansion was similar to others in Bay City with intricate trim, several stained glass windows, and cove moldings. It had Queen Anne architecture, included a gable, a second story balcony, a veranda, and ornamental shingles. It even had the third-story ballroom that Sally had dreamed about after dancing in the streets some time ago.

Once in awhile, Sally heard people in town refer to Jake as a baron—a timber baron or lumber baron. She wondered, why would they call Jake a baron? His family wasn't royalty. No famous person had knighted him or given him any kind of title. He'd never received a commission during the Civil War. How could he possibly be a baron?

She looked up the word in her dictionary and was surprised to find it meant a wealthy person of high social status. That couldn't be, she thought. Certainly, he's making lots of money. We've got several bank accounts. But we're not wealthy.

She continued to read the definition in the dictionary until her eyes stopped on the next word, baroness. So, if Jake is a baron, then I'm a baroness, she concluded. My title has changed from waiter girl to timber baroness. Maybe I like that, she thought. Yes, I do. I'm a timber baroness.

18

Jake Travels to Minnesota

Even with the excitement of a new marriage and success in financial and social affairs, Jake couldn't wait to see the Mississippi River. He intentionally spent more time with Sally as the date of the timber men's meeting approached. That way, he thought, she will object less to my leaving.

Jake met Bruce Royston on November 8 at the restaurant within Huff House, a three-story hotel in Winona, Minnesota. Henry D. Huff, the city's first businessman, had built the hotel on Fourth and Walnut Streets in 1855 to accommodate three hundred guests. Huff owned a flour mill that was destroyed in the fire of 1871. He started a railroad, which failed and lost a fortune in wheat speculation. Afterwards, he moved to Chicago but returned later to Winona, a disappointed and angry man.

Bruce placed a napkin in his lap and began talking about the upcoming meeting. "This place has been a center of logging controversy since the 1850s," he said. "There's been a lot of money made here, some by our company. Of course, a few firms went bankrupt because of power struggles between timber barons."

"I saw several large mills coming into town on the train. They looked prosperous," Jake said, recalling his long train ride from Kalamazoo to Chicago and the steamboat journey up Lake Michigan. Crossing Wisconsin required him to take several stagecoaches and trains. Finally, he rode the old Winona and St. Peter railroad, whose expansion to the South Western was stalled after the financial panic of 1873.

Jake felt nervous about crossing the swing bridge from the Wisconsin shore across the Mississippi to Winona. The bridge had collapsed on May 27, 1871, one day after construction was complete, under the weight of a freight train carrying quarry stone. It was rebuilt in January of 1872.

Bruce continued. "The pine comes from the Chippewa River Valley, north of us in Wisconsin and Minnesota."

Jake said, "I heard most of the fighting occurred over the Beef Sloughs."

"Yeah. That's an inlet off the Chippewa River three miles below Durand, Wisconsin. It flows for about twenty-five miles and then joins the Mississippi River. The Sloughs is like a delta with islands, lakes, and lagoons. It's a fine booming ground to hold and sort logs."

Jake's mind drifted to thoughts about Sally. Maybe I should bring home a gift, he thought.

The waitress took away their appetizers and returned with two bowls of clam chowder. Jake tried the soup cautiously because he'd never had it before. "So, why all the fighting between companies?" he asked.

"The local sawmills did everything they could to keep eastern investors away. They lobbied to pass legislation that discriminated against outsiders. The companies also bought as much land as they could around the mouth of the Sloughs."

"This tastes like fish," Jake remarked. "That's what it is. It's fish soup."

"Meanwhile," Bruce said, "the outsiders bought pine lands north of the Beef Sloughs and invested in new mills. Some investors lobbied the Wisconsin legislature and got a franchise to hold and sort logs at the Sloughs, against the wishes of local lumbermen from Eau Claire and Chippewa Falls."

Jake used his napkin and put it back in his lap. "Was your father involved in all this?"

"Oh yes. Our company's been part of the negotiations from the beginning. We helped finance the construction of booms that trap logs coming down the Chippewa and shove them into the Sloughs, where they're sorted and tied into rafts." Bruce shifted his position to one side while the waitress took away his soup bowl and replaced it with well-done steak, a baked potato, and steaming corn.

Jake's steak was rare. He said, "Do most of you easterners like your meat well done? How can you eat it that way?"

"I'd rather have mine cooked than raw like yours." Bruce laughed. "So anyway, several years ago, things were a mess on the river. The Big Log Jam occurred in the spring of 1869 when one hundred fifty million board feet of logs piled up behind a boom in Chippewa Falls."

"Did ya see it?"

"Yes. My father sent me to see if our company could help. The river was choked with logs for fifteen miles. Wood was thirty feet above the riverbank in some places." He waved for the waitress to refill his glass of red wine.

Jake said, "My friend Eli told me about a log jam he worked. Several men were killed when they blew it with dynamite. They even lynched the powder monkey." He pushed his fork into the potato, broke it up, and mashed it on his plate. "This potato is good, but a little dry. Would you pass the butter, please?"

"This jam took all summer to free. Hundreds of men worked with cant hooks day and night." Bruce cut his steak into several small pieces, like a mother would do when feeding her child.

"So what's all this have to do with our meeting tomorrow?"

"There's a little more to the story. That summer a man named Fred Weyerhaeuser came up to the logjam from Rock Island, Illinois. Many of the logs were his. They were stuck in the river hundreds of miles north of his sawmill." He sipped the freshly poured wine and blotted his lips, leaving a faint red stain on the white napkin. "The next year, Fred approached the promoters of the Beef Slough Company, who agreed to lease the boom for five years to Weyerhaeuser and his friend, Lorenzo Schricker from Davenport, Iowa. The agreement included a requirement that the lessors provide cash to improve the booming grounds."

Jake finished his steak and asked for another glass of wine. He felt full and was starting to notice the effects of the alcohol.

"The idea worked. Under Weyerhaeuser's leadership, the logging companies all met on December 28, 1870, at the Briggs House in Chicago. It was the first time so many men got together to discuss their common problems. Before, they'd just fought and bickered. As a result of the meeting, they formed a logging company and elected Schricker as president."

"I still don't get the connection with tomorrow's meeting," Jake said. He covered his mouth to conceal a yawn.

"Now, years later, this operation is making big money. Our treasurer has reported that the company's receipts well exceed expenditures. So, we're meeting to celebrate the success of our shared venture. There's some issues to discuss, but we're mostly getting together as colleagues and friends. My father thought you should come to meet some of the other lumber men with investments in the Midwest."

The waitress returned, cleared their plates, and offered them a choice of desserts. Bruce chose vanilla ice cream that had just been made that afternoon, while Jake selected the apple pie. Before retiring to his room, Jake thanked Bruce for the update. "If we have some time, can we go see the booming grounds and tour some of the mills?"

"I'll leave that to you. I'll introduce you to some of the owners. Maybe they'll invite you to see their operations. I'll see you in the morning. Sleep well, my friend."

Jake noticed that Bruce wobbled while walking toward his room. He smiled, recalling the long day, the heavy meal, and the many glasses of wine.

The meeting was held in a private banquet room a floor below the formal restaurant. Jake entered the smoke-filled room, aware that he wasn't dressed as well as the other men. Most wore jackets and ties. All held drinks and circulated between small clusters of men whose conversation got louder with each additional round. As promised, Bruce introduced him to several of the men. The first was William Stone from Philadelphia, who asked, "Don't I know you? Are you a member of the Yale Club?"

Jake didn't feel insulted. Being almost a full head taller than the other men helped give him an air of superiority that was more impressive than an Ivy League degree. "No, I didn't go to Yale. I know about lumber, though. I spent several winters with Emerson Logging Company in northern Michigan."

William wasn't intimidated either. "Perhaps I met you at one of Mr. Emerson's parties on his private steam ship?"

"No. I didn't work in the office. I cut pine in the woods."

"Oh, you poor fellow. In all that cold and snow?"

"I loved it. By the way, what do you do?"

"Contracts, my man. Contracts."

"Oh, you poor fellow. Lost beneath all those sheets of paper in a musty old office?"

William burst out laughing. Like a chess player that's been checkmated, he conceded, "Flareau, you're all right." He stared at one of four waitresses serving drinks to the gentlemen. "Enough about business. Do you see that slender one over there with the long legs?"

Jake felt uncomfortable talking about women. He stepped back and said, "Nice to meet you, sir. Let's talk again later."

He moved toward Bruce who introduced him to another lumberman. Jake met seven or eight of the influential men. Isn't it strange? he thought. Power comes with being tall. He recalled a painting of President Lincoln surrounded by shorter men, all listening with care to his words.

A stocky man with short hair banged on a coffee table in the center of the room. "We've got two items of business," he barked. "Let's talk about them now before the liquor takes away our ability to reason."

A young man with athletic build said, "Come on Harry, you never had an ability to reason—sober or drunk. Don't try to fool us."

When the laughter subsided, Harry presented the first of the agenda items. "Now that the Sloughs is a profitable venture, each company will benefit from increased supply. Mr. Weyerhaeuser has asked us to consider whether a committee should fix lumber prices or whether prices should fluctuate with competition. What do you think?

At least a dozen hands were raised. Men voiced several opinions ranging from support for shared prices to resentment over any regulation of free trade. It was decided that a committee be appointed to monitor, but not establish, lumber prices.

"Good, gentlemen. We did that in record time with no black eyes. Now, the second item may be more difficult. Our association has been asked to consider ways that new business can be created and encouraged at the Sloughs. One of the representatives at the State House seems to think we have too closed a group, like a fraternity house at college. He thinks we are keeping out newcomers instead of welcoming their investment capital. Any opinions on this one?"

The second topic was debated with jokes and cajoling. The audience groaned and cheered after each speaker presented his opinion. When the discussion was winding down, Jake raised his hand. "I'm new here as a representative from Flareau and Company, but I want to comment on the issue under consideration." He was surprised at how easily the words seemed to flow. He paused and looked around the smoke-filled room. Everyone was still, waiting for his suggestion. "It seems to me that the Beef Sloughs should be in public ownership. It's too important to be run only as a private profit-making venture."

This time there was no chatter after the suggestion. Each man was thinking hard, trying to digest and analyze what Jake had said. They were attempting to anticipate the potential consequences of public ownership on their company and its operation.

Bruce waved his hand and was recognized by Harry. "My associate from Bay City has made a very thought-provoking proposal. Obviously, this is the kind of idea that requires careful consideration. Let's make this an agenda item for next year's meeting. In the meantime, I propose we prepare a letter to the state representative and tell him he has gotten some bad information. Our association is open to new business and welcomes free competition."

"Hear, hear!" The men cheered and raised their glasses.

Harry pounded a gavel on the coffee table. "Meeting adjourned. Now, let's get down to some serious drinking."

After the discussion several men approached Jake and introduced themselves. Some agreed with his suggestion and made comments about ways the industry might tax itself to support pro-logging government officials who could regulate the Sloughs. Others disagreed with his idea, saying there was already too much government regulation of business. They all complimented him on the boldness of his idea and the fluency of his presentation. Jake felt like he belonged.

The next morning Bruce waited with Jake at the railroad depot.

"I'll give my father a good report of your participation at the meeting," he said. "Of course, we need some time to analyze your suggestion. If our board agrees with your idea, it will become a recommendation from Royston Lumber Company. Otherwise, the proposal will stand alone as a recommendation from Flareau and Company."

"I understand." Jake felt confused by all the attention given to his idea. "Please accept my apologies if I spoke without first consulting you. I was just thinking out loud."

"You did well. Don't worry. These things take time. Sometimes it takes several years for an idea to become reality."

The men talked about hunting, fishing, sailing, and many other topics during the two-day trip back to Bay City. They no longer talked about work.

When they arrived in town, Bruce said, "Please give my best to Sally."

Bruce boarded a carriage and waved goodbye.

Jake took the next carriage to his new home. On the way he thought about Sally. These business trips are very intense. I never seem to relax. I can't wait to see her smiling face and brown eyes.

Before long he saw the iron gate surrounding his house. He paid the carriage driver and climbed the stairs. Tired but happy, he yelled, "Sally, I'm home!"

His wife ran toward him, wearing a red evening dress, ruby earrings, and a gold bracelet. The stone fireplace inside their home was ablaze with cozy flames that took the chill from the late fall night.

She hugged him and said, "Oh, I missed you so. Please don't let them send you on too many of these long trips. I can't stand to be without you."

"I love you so," he said.

The couple kissed for several minutes. He slipped the strap down her right shoulder and put his lips on her soft neck. He smelled the sweet odor of her chestnut hair, mixed with his favorite perfume. Jake slid her, limp in his arms, to the Grecian davenport in the piano room beside the library. He placed her on the long sofa. She squirmed on the couch and kicked her feet to hurry him.

This is my partner in life, he thought. I agree with her. No more long trips.

19

Sally and Jake Visit Clayburg

Jake's mill prospered for several years. He and Sally got established in Bay City and gained a reputation for being charitable and generous. They gave money to the library and opera house, as well as to the indigent and sick. Thor also became a rich man, although he kept his simple ways. He still wore highly polished boots and suspenders, although now of fine European quality.

Mattie and Thor were married in the Monota home on the outskirts of Grafton. The little house, already too small for all the children, bulged with guests from town, as well as from the Bay City sawmill. It was a short ceremony, held in a cramped living room. The audience stood in a circle surrounding the couple and minister.

Sally smiled when she saw Mattie's shoes, carefully arranged beside the front door of the house. Her friend didn't wear a traditional wedding gown. Instead, she was dressed in a white muslin dress with forget-me-knot flowers embroidered on the shoulders and back. Beneath a hem of dainty lace, Mattie's bare feet were exposed. They curled and uncurled as Reverend Hughes spoke. Sally's eyes shifted to Thor, dressed in business attire. A silver-colored necktie of canvas gauze, the same material used to trim his hat, accented his suit. She smiled again when she spied his highly polished boots.

What a fitting ceremony, Sally thought. Mattie and Thor are being married in bare feet and boots. Maybe the real advantage of wealth and position is the freedom to express one's individuality. She felt Jake grasp her hand and squeeze it.

He whispered in her ear, "Remember our wedding? I'm glad we're together." He squeezed her hand again.

"Me, too. And that's because of Thor. I'll never forget the time he came to Bay City when your family was ill." She felt a tear form in the corner of her left eye. "He's a dear friend to both of us. I'm so happy for him and Mattie."

They stood, hand in hand, and watched the newlyweds kiss at the end of the service.

One day in November Jake received a telegraph from Bruce asking him to visit a sawmill up north in Clayburg, Michigan. The new mill, a subsidy of Royston Lumber Company, had unusually high overhead. Jake was asked to review the firm's cost and production figures.

He was excited about the possibility of seeing the Straits of Mackinac at the junction of Lakes Huron and Michigan. Clayburg was only a short distance from this historic site, where the French and English had traded with trappers and Indians for centuries. Jake thought about the Jesuit priests whom were missionaries there, voyagers' canoes laden with beaver pelts, and uniformed soldiers marching inside the timbered walls of Fort Michilimackinac.

Sally didn't want her husband to leave home. She asked, "Why don't you send someone else? You have your own sawmill to run, now. It's not fair." She flung her hairbrush across the counter.

"I asked the same question in telegraphs between me and Bruce." Jake picked up the hairbrush and handed it back to her. "I guess the Clayburg mill has some special problems." Jake wasn't sure what to say next. Just a few days before he'd agreed not to take any extended business trips, and here he was getting ready to leave again. He considered arguing that his company wouldn't exist if it weren't for the Royston family. What can I say? I've never seen her this mad.

Sally walked away to the bedroom with Jake following. She dumped the clothes from his suitcase on the bed. "I don't want you to go. Tell that to your rich investor friends."

Sally climbed the stairs leading into the attic and returned with Jake's old carpetbag from logging camp. "If you're going," she said, "then I'm going, too."

He rubbed his chin and considered his wife's suggestion. "What a great idea!" he said. "Let's get the fanciest hotel room, have expensive meals, and send the bill to Bruce."

"Now you're making sense," she said.

The couple made up and finished packing. Jake didn't like fighting with his wife.

Clayburg was an easy train ride from Bay City, except for a stagecoach detour around some inland lakes where rail service was not yet available. Travelers filled every available spot on top and within the stagecoach. Those who found no vacant place were destined to wait for the next coach and a later connecting train.

Sally and Jake enjoyed the time together. They noticed a change in late autumn scenery from the bare hardwood trees of southern Michigan to thick evergreen forests of the north. Some spots between northern towns had light snow on the ground and in the surrounding cedar and spruce trees. They told each other stories from their past about growing up together in Grafton.

While they waited at a depot for a connecting train, Jake told Sally about his grandpa's journey from New York to Michigan. "The hardest part wasn't yankin' the barge over shallow spots in the Erie Canal," he said. "It wasn't fighting mosquitoes in the swamps of southwestern Michigan. Grandpa's toughest times were on the Lake Erie when stormy waves almost sunk the steamship."

He reached in his pocket and took out the ten-dollar gold piece he had carried with him. "This was Grandpa's good luck charm. It's an eagle, dated 1839, the year he left New York State. I also inherited my grandpa's wanderlust."

Sally seemed hypnotized by the story. "I've seen you carry that coin everywhere, but I never knew why. So, that's why you like to move around and go to new places."

"Probably," he said. "I've just got the wanderlust."

She fumbled in her luggage beneath the depot bench. "Here's something I've got from childhood, too." Sally dropped the keepsake in Jake's hand.

He looked in his palm and saw the arrowhead he'd given her at the fire when they first met. "I remember. Even then, we talked about it being a good luck charm."

"Yes. It reminds me how terrible times can often bring good endings. The fire caused my mother to leave, but brought you into my life."

He said, "Isn't it amazing that we found each other? We're so different, yet so much alike. You come from a wealthy eastern family and my dad was a market hunter. I like change and new adventures, while you like to stay put."

"Yes, but we have similarities, too. We both want to help others."

"We both like nature."

"We also have good luck pieces that we keep near, no matter where we go." Sally tickled him.

The connecting train arrived in a cloud of hot ashes. Jake lifted their luggage into the passenger car and bolted up the stairs when Sally prodded his rear. Laughing and giggling, he waited for her in the last seat near a large window.

Along the way Jake observed with care the vast clearings, several square miles in size, filled with burned pine stumps. Some were spotted with abandoned houses and decayed sawmills, now too far from pine lands. In the horizon of a few clearings, he saw bleached ghost towns. In the foreground were hummocks of grass on barren soil. But everywhere, there were blackened stumps—the remains of once majestic forests.

The train pulled into the Clayburg station beneath a haze Jake first thought was fog. While they were deboarding, he noticed a strong smell of burnt wood and realized the blue-gray mist was smoke from forest fires.

When they arrived at the Regal Hotel in Clayburg, a man greeted them, took their baggage, and guided them to the registration desk. Jake watched Sally gaze at the winding staircase in the center of the lobby. She seemed to like the fancy hotel with brass doors and colorful drapes. She appeared even more excited when they were taken upstairs and ushered into the spacious suite with canopied bed and upholstered furnishings. A balcony, accessible through French doors from their bedroom, offered a picturesque view of the city below. It was clearly a sawdust town, with five mills, now quiet in December along a slow-moving river.

They made love gently that evening and fell asleep, nude, in each other's arms, exhausted after the long trip to northern Michigan.

In the morning, the couple had breakfast together at the hotel restaurant. Sally went shopping while Jake walked to the mill. He made it to the office a few minutes before his scheduled appointment and said to the receptionist, "I'm Jake Flareau, here to represent Royston Lumber Company. I believe I'm expected at nine."

"Oh yes, Mr. Flareau. Please come this way." She led Jake through a side door into a long hall with doors leading to executive offices.

As Jake walked toward the conference room, he heard a booming voice say, "Who the hell is this guy from Bay City. Does anybody know what he wants?"

That's a voice from the past, thought Jake, but he couldn't place it at first. When he entered the room, he saw a familiar person, sitting in a thick leather chair at the head of a long polished table. His black greasy hair swirled when he moved. It was Dietrich Krausse.

Eight men in business suits, each with a stack of papers and glass of water before them, sat at the table.

Jake thanked the receptionist and marched up to Dietrich. "I haven't seen you in years."

Dietrich shook Jake's hand. "So you're the bad guy from Bay City. I take it you work for Royston." His eyes darted from side to side as if he'd been caught doing something wrong.

"Is this your mill?"

"Yeah, we moved here from Kalamazoo." He turned toward his men and said, "This is Jacques Flareau, an old childhood friend of mine. He's damn good with an axe, boys. At least Royston sent someone who knows the woods.

Dietrich pointed toward the man on his right, who stood, snapped to attention, and introduced himself.

"I'm Charles Zudman," the man said. "The company attorney and senior vice president."

The second man rose. "Tom Penrose, Sales."

"Rob Enros, Procurement."

The rest of the men stood and introduced themselves one by one until all were standing except Dietrich.

"Okay boys. That's enough. Now, what do you need, Flareau?" He punched his fist into his palm. The men sat down. All of them dipped their pens in inkwells at the same time, preparing to take notes.

Jake straightened his tie and walked in a circle around the table. He studied each man carefully as if he was picking one as prey. "Your silent partner in Bay City has received some complaints about lumber grading. Let's start there," he said.

Dietrich slammed his hand on the table. "How we grade lumber is none of their damn business. They gave us money to build this mill and we send them checks each month. It's up to me, not them, to run the day-to-day operations of this plant."

Jake raised his voice. "Not so." He faced Dietrich. "They have a reputation in the lumber industry. Mr. Royston doesn't want to be associated with a dishonest subsidy. It might injure the family's good name. The parent company is sick and tired of getting complaints that you're cheating lumberyards. Now, what are you going to do about it?"

"Come on," said Dietrich, "if Royston wants to defend his good name, why the hell didn't he come here himself? Why'd he send a backwoods boy like you?"

The attorney spoke up. "Whoa, now," he said. "According to our original agreement, Zudman Brothers pays three percent on a note of 1872. There's nothing in the agreement about grading practices. In addition, many of these line yards alter lumber grades after boards are received. You've got no proof that our company is negligent. I'd suggest you give us complainants' names. We'll investigate this ourselves."

"Okay. Let's talk about legal issues." Jake moved in front of the attorney and waved some papers under Zudman's nose. "Mr. Royston wanted me to remind you of section 12.2 part (a) in the agreement, which reads as follows:

> The loan balance shall be due and payable within 20 business days if Zudman Brothers defaults on interest payments for three consecutive months or becomes involved in illegal or questionable business practices."

"Get out of here, Flareau!" screamed Dietrich. "If Royston wants to accuse me of breaking our agreement, tell him to come see me." He stuck out his long, skinny neck.

Two of the larger men stood to escort Jake out of the room.

Jake organized his papers. "It was nice to see you again, Dietrich. I'll find my own way out. Good day, gentlemen." He left the room followed by the two burly men.

When he got back to the hotel, Jake found Sally combing her hair in a looking glass. "How'd you do shopping?" he asked.

"Oh Jake, it's so nice to see all the new things they have for ladies. I bought a dress, some perfume, and a jeweled comb for my hair."

"Should we send the bills to Bruce?" The couple laughed together, then kissed.

"How'd your meeting go?"

Jake wasn't sure whether to tell her about Dietrich. She'd told him before not to mention his name. It might upset her, he thought. On the other hand, what if she finds out later that I'd met with him?

He said, "You'll never guess who runs the mill here in town."

"Who's that?" She stopped combing her hair and turned toward him.

"Dietrich Krausse, that's who."

"Oh no," she said. "You mean I'm here in the same town as that evil man? You're not doing business with him, are you?"

Sally felt her jaw tighten. She could taste the warm, salty flavor of blood and noticed she had bitten the inside of her mouth. A stinging sensation crept up her shoulders, burned along her collarbone, and tightened her neck muscles. Here it comes again, she thought. This time, she envisioned herself pushing Dietrich into a hole in the ground. He stood on tiptoes, leaping in the air but couldn't get out. Three wolves with yellow-green eyes and pearly white fangs surrounded him. The vision relaxed her clenched teeth and strained neck and quelled her uncontrollable urge for revenge.

Jake explained what they had discussed and how they got in an argument. "I'm going to recommend that Royston Lumber Company request the principal of their loan be paid within twenty days."

"Good. I hope you bankrupt him. He might as well get used to suffering. He's going to burn in hell. Flames will broil his skin and scorch his eyes, but he won't be given the luxury of death." She took her clothes from the dresser drawer and put them in the carpetbag. "Let's go home. This place is making me sick."

Jake put his belongings in the leather suitcase. "I agree," he said.

After paying their bill, the couple waited for the doorman to summon a carriage. He looked at Dietrich's mill looming above the town's buildings. "I'm going to finally fix that evil man," he told Sally. "I'm gonna put him out of business. I'll bankrupt him."

"Good. That's exactly what he deserves. He thinks about money and power all the time. Thanks to you, he'll have nothing left."

Jake watched the carriage driver load their luggage in a cloud of smoke from nearby forest fires.

Sally asked the driver, "Isn't it dangerous to have fires burning so close to town?"

"No, ma'am," the driver said. "There's no problem. Stumps have been smokin' around here since May. Folks did get a little worried when the Markey's barn caught fire. Several telegraph poles north of town caught fire, too."

"What's started all the fires? asked Jake.

"Farmers have burned brush from cleared land. Railroad men, building new tracks west of town, burned slash in long rows."

"Why doesn't the marshal stop people from burning?"

"Because most people don't get upset about fire. It's just part of the north country, like snow and wind." He unloaded their baggage at the train station.

All the way home, the couple talked about how satisfying it would be if Dietrich had to sell his mill, auction his personal belongings, and beg for menial work.

When Jake got back to his office, he sent a telegram to Bruce. It said:

> Zudman Brothers is cheating customers and Krausse is probably embezzling funds. I suggest you terminate the agreement of 1872 using provisions of section 12.2 and make their note due and payable.

The next day, he received a telegram in response.

> The board accepted your recommendation. I am sending an invoice, signed by my father, demanding a bal-

> loon payment from Zudman Brothers, payable within twenty days. Our attorney says you must deliver it in person to Mr. Krausse in front of at least two witnesses. Perhaps you should request the marshal to accompany you. Good work.

Jake was worried. Even Bruce must have sensed something about Dietrich's violent nature. He didn't want to return to Clayburg by himself. He also knew the marshal in Clayburg was handpicked by Dietrich. There was no way he could ask for assistance from Foster.

That evening, Jake said to Sally, "Royston's asked me to hand deliver the request for loan repayment. I'm leaving for Clayburg tomorrow morning."

He was exhilarated by her response. "Good. Go get him. He deserves everything you're going to do. Bankrupt that evil man. Take away all his money and power."

Jake shared her desire for revenge. "I'll fix him for you."

"Hey wait! Let me come with you. I'd like to be there when you serve the papers."

"Oh, Sally. He's mean and his men are thugs. They might hurt you."

"He's already hurt me. Now, it's time to hurt him back. I'm going."

"It's too dangerous. You should stay home." He raised his eyebrows. "I can take care of Dietrich."

Sally shook her head sideways. She raised her voice and said, "I'm going with you. Period. We're done talking about this. I've got to pack."

Jake knew he couldn't stop Sally now.

20

The Burning of Clayburg

Jake and Sally arrived at Clayburg's Regal Hotel late at night. The next morning they walked from the hotel to a restaurant on East Miller Road. The couple shared a full breakfast before going to Dietrich's mill. At the mill Jake said to the receptionist, "We're here to see Mr. Dietrich Krausse. I'm Jake Flareau and this is my wife, Sally."

The neatly dressed woman looked at a thick ledger on the edge of her desk. "I'm sorry. You don't have an appointment. Can I schedule you to meet with Mr. Krausse toward the end of the week?"

"No, we have to see him today. It's a legal matter."

"Let me see if I can squeeze you in. I'll be right back." She walked briskly down the hall into Dietrich's office. Returning, she said, "I'm sorry. He's in a meeting right now and is not sure when it will be over."

"We've got to see him right now," Jake said. "It will only take a minute."

She left again and came back with regrets. "He's very sorry, but they're closing a deal with some logging contractors."

Sally shifted her weight from foot to foot until Jake slammed his fist on the receptionist's desk. He said, "We've got some legal papers to serve. If he likes, we can return with the marshal."

Jake grabbed the papers and stormed down the hall with Sally behind him. When he flung the door open to Dietrich's office, Sally saw three men drinking whiskey and smoking cigars. Since none of them appeared to be logging contractors, she barked, "You liar."

Dietrich's grinned. "Well, well," he said. "It's my old girlfriend. I haven't seen you in years."

She stomped up to the desk where he sat. "It's nice to see you in your big fancy office for the last time," she said. "We're here to put you out of business."

Dietrich's men backed toward the wall. They appeared shocked to see a lady in a place of business and even more surprised to see her argue with the boss.

"Shut up, Sally," Dietrich said. His black greasy hair shone in the sunlight coming through a side window. "Women aren't allowed to talk in this room. Does your boyfriend have something to say to us?"

"I'm her husband, not her boyfriend," Jake yelled.

"You've got to be kidding."

Jake dropped the papers on his desk. "Here's the legal order from Royston Lumber Company." He smiled. "You have twenty days to repay the loan."

Dietrich scanned the document. His eyes seemed to fix on the signature. "How'd you pull this off? Royston's a powerful man. Why'd he take your advice?"

Sally interrupted. "Because Bruce knows you're a liar and a cheat."

Dietrich's associates inched slowly along the wall toward the door and one by one slipped out of the room.

When they were all gone, Jake said, "See, even your business friends know you're in trouble. They don't want anything to do with you. You're finished."

"Will cash help you forget this problem? Say twenty thousand dollars?"

"No." He frowned.

Dietrich said, "There's no way I can make that balloon payment. I'll have to sell everything I own."

"You should have thought about that before."

Sally said, "Jake and I are putting you out of business because you're an evil man." Her eyes glared.

"Well, then, if I can't have my mill then nobody else will get it." He stood and looked at the papers on his desk. "I'll take care of this problem my own way." Dietrich smashed his fist into his palm. "Now get out of here, you two, or I'll call the marshal."

On the way out, Jake said to the receptionist, "Please make a note of the time and date that I served papers to Mr. Krausse. If you don't, you'll be in trouble with my attorneys in Bay City. My wife and you are witnesses."

"Yes, sir. I made a note in Mr. Krausse's appointment book that you were here."

"That's not good enough. Add a comment that I demanded his loan be repaid within twenty days."

"Yes, sir." She sighed and made a note in the ledger.

Dietrich left the office and went to one of the woodsheds near the back of the mill. He dipped a ladle in a drum of kerosene used for lamps and poured it on several stacks of wood. He also splashed kerosene on the outside wall of the mill where none of the workers could see him. After tying a rag on a piece of lumber, he rubbed it in the fluid spilled beneath the drum, and lit the torch. Running around the back of the mill, he ignited the kerosene in a dozen places with his flame. The back wall of the mill and several piles of stacked wood were soon on fire. Dietrich smiled. That's right, he thought. If I can't have the mill, nobody will, especially Sally and Jake.

One of the mill workers smelled smoke, ran out the side door and saw flames climbing the side of the building. "Fire!" he yelled. "Hurry! Get some water!" Workers followed him outside and tried to extinguish the flames. Dietrich sneaked around the corner of the mill and walked away.

The fire spread quickly to the dry woods nearby. Dietrich saw a log in the woodlot glow like hot coals in a wood stove and then explode into flames. A foreman ran toward the log, kicked dirt on it, and extinguished the fire. Suddenly, more logs inflamed. He yelled, "Help! Fire! Fire!"

A young man carrying a bucket darted out the door and shouted, "Where?"

"Beneath the trees by the railroad track. The woods are on fire!"

Dietrich watched everyone run from the mill. Young men went to the pump, drew buckets of water, and emptied them on the flames. The wind grew stronger as if sucked into the clearing by the heat. The woodlot was soon packed with workers trying to extinguish the fire. Despite their efforts, flames jumped from the ground to the treetops and raced toward town.

A narrow flame popped through the back wall of the mill and jumped to the crest beneath the roof. Windowpanes broke when fire leaped through a glowing hole in the roof. Flames roared up the sides of the mill

Seeing the building turn into flaming rubble, Dietrich suddenly felt sick to his stomach. In his haste to destroy the mill, he had forgotten to remove his money from the safe in his office. He dashed by a line of men passing buckets from the nearby well and ran to the safe. He felt the heat of the fire on his arms as his fingers touched the dial. His nose burned from the searing gases. Smoke obscured his vision.

Sally and Jake had gone back to the Regal Hotel before the fire broke out. After eating dinner at the restaurant downstairs, they returned to their room and changed into casual clothes. Hearing a sound in the distance, Sally asked, "What's that noise?"

Jake replied, "Thunder, I think."

"It's more constant, like a waterfall."

"It must be the wind. Maybe a storm is coming." Jake peered out the hotel window and saw the mill illuminated by orange flames. "Sally, it's a fire. Come see!"

She looked out the window and grabbed his arm. "Hurry! Let's help put it out."

The couple ran toward the sawmill along with dozens of others from town. Marshal Foster stood near the mill, circled by a group of men. He pointed to some darkened spots on a map showing where the fire had passed and drew a large arrow to show the current wind direction. "It looks like the fire might move from here toward town," he said.

"We've got to put it out." The marshal asked volunteers to dig trenches. "Make firebreaks wherever you can."

Jake grabbed a shovel and began digging in the sandy soil.

Sally glanced back to the mill and thought she saw someone inside the frame of glowing timbers. She ran to get a closer look and saw Dietrich, still trying to turn the dial to the combination of his safe. "Get out of there!" she screamed.

"In a minute," answered Dietrich.

The smoke made it impossible to see the safe, let alone numbers on the combination lock.

At that instant the roof of the mill made a screeching sound and heaved.

Dietrich jumped.

Sally watched the roof buckle in two places. Hot sparks and flaming timbers crashed down on Dietrich. One of the larger rafters hit him on the thigh and pinned him to the ground.

"Get out!" Sally yelled.

"I can't!" Dietrich cried. "I'm pinned to the ground. The board's not very heavy but I can't lift it. I'm hurt."

Good, Sally thought, I can watch this evil man burn before my eyes. He deserves it. I've waited many years for this moment.

Dietrich continued to scream inside the torched office.

His pain made Sally feel remorseful. Maybe I should run into the burning mill and free him. I can't just sit here and watch a human being die. She squinted through the smoke and flames.

That's crazy, she thought. Dietrich deserves this. He's an evil man. She knelt on the ground.

Her conscience resurfaced. At times, I've been evil, too. She recalled some of her experiences in Bay City. I've had sex with hundreds of men for pay. I spent time in jail. I hurt my father by running away from home. She stood and took a few cautious steps toward the wall of flames.

Wait a minute, she thought. Many of those things happened because Dietrich raped me. It's fair and just that he dies like this.

Dietrich yelled, "Sally, help! Save me!" His voice seemed fainter.

His plea made her reconsider. Jake married me even though he knew about my past. He forgave me. So did my father and the people in Grafton. But how can I ever forgive Dietrich? He hurt me deeply.

It seemed like hours, but in a few seconds Sally resolved the conflict within her between revenge and forgiveness. She raced into the office and yanked the smoking board off Dietrich's thigh. He was right, she thought. The board isn't that heavy.

He staggered out the door and moved away from the burning mill. He coughed for several minutes until his lungs cleared of smoke. Exhausted, he collapsed on the ground.

"What about my money?" he said. "All my money is in that safe. The bills will burn if the metal safe gets too hot."

"Aren't you even going to thank me?"

"For what? I wish you had never come to Clayburg. Everything was just fine until you and Jake showed up."

Sally caught movement in the corner of her eye. She turned around.

"What are you doing?" Jake asked.

"I just pulled Dietrich out of the burning mill."

"You did what?"

"He was trapped inside when part of the roof collapsed."

Jake looked at the smoking rubble that used to be the mill. "You went in there to save him?"

"Yes."

"We better get out of here. It's not safe here." Jake tossed his shovel on the ground. "The marshal thinks the entire town may burn down. Everyone is running to the river. I've seen people with their hair on fire. Hurry! Let's go."

Sally and Jake ran, hoping the water would save them. Along the way, she saw a charred body near the livery. The face seemed melted and looked like it was covered with black tar. A few moments later she tripped and landed on a corpse. She recognized the body as that of the waitress at the restaurant. The dead girl had no burn marks or other visible signs of injury.

People were screaming. Sally heard husbands calling for their wives and mothers yelling for their children. She heard water splashing and people crying.

The river was shrouded in steam. Sally dived into the water, which cooled her warm body. A few minutes later she felt Jake's arm around her waist.

A few survivors huddled on shore, some wrapped in wet blankets. Most refugees from the fire sat near her in the river. Some, in deeper water, floated downstream between flaming logs.

Two hours later Sally no longer saw flames in the distance. Smoke settled into low spots in the horizon. She and Jake climbed out of the river and hugged each other on the bank. He took off his shirt and wrung it out. Others moved from the water to the shore when the faint light of dawn arrived. Sally rubbed her bloodshot eyes, but everything still seemed hazy. She was shocked by the vacant stares of people with blackened faces and arms, wandering the riverbank.

Jake, as if waking from a dream, seemed to realize others might need his assistance. He said, "I'm going back to town. Maybe I can help."

"Me, too," said Sally. "Please don't leave me here. I'm scared."

He hugged her. "Come, let's keep moving so we stay warm. The temperature's dropped at least forty degrees since the fire went out." He put his shirt back on.

"Okay. Don't walk too fast."

They moved silently through the black, smoldering trees toward Clayburg. The entire town was gone. Nothing remained except stovepipes and chimneys. Marshal Foster stood near the razed church and waved a stick at the crowd. "I know you want to salvage your belongings from the ashes," he called out, "but first we have a responsibility to the dead. We need to gather the corpses and list those missing. Then you can hunt for your personal belongings."

Everyone began sifting through rubble with blackened hands and shovels without handles. Bodies were carried to a makeshift morgue where the church had been. Some of the corpses were so charred that metal rings from the burned barrels had to be used to move them.

Sally and Jake walked away from the town and approached the mill. It was gone, nothing left but a blackened site. There was no evidence of human activity. Piles of ash remained where once were boards, stacked several feet high. The knee-deep sawdust was gone. Sheets of tin from the mill's roof were scattered amongst the smoldering rubble.

"Look here," said Jake. Several footprints in the ash led to a well by the edge of the clearing.

Sally moved toward the well, fearful of what she might see inside. She leaned over and looked down. First she saw long black hair and then a pink tongue, clenched in the teeth of a blue face. The head floated upright in circles. "My God!" she sobbed. "It's Dietrich."

He looks so pathetic, Sally thought. Here is the short boy that forced himself inside me. Look at him now. There's nothing frightening now about that blue face.

He must have stayed behind at the mill and tried to get the money from his safe. The fire must have gotten so hot, she thought, that Dietrich couldn't stand it. He must have dived into the well out of panic, begging for water to cool his seared skin. Sally put her hand on her stomach and felt dizzy.

Jake lowered a milling tool with metal hook into the well. He pulled out Dietrich's brown-yellow corpse and eased it onto a pile of ash. A wad of black hair framed his sunken but open eyes. Sally stared down at the crooked face. You finally got what you deserved, she thought. God did this to you. I forgave you, but He didn't. He did this to get even.

Sally was never the same after the fire. Maybe it was because Dietrich was killed. Perhaps it was because she forgave him and herself. Once back home, she had only one last vision. It came without warning when she was in the greenhouse watering some of her herbs.

Dietrich's face flashed across her mind. She remembered the time he came to the blacksmith shop in torn pants to help gather elderberries. She clenched her jaw and felt her neck muscles tighten.

Then a calm came over her as she envisioned his face when dead, a crooked mouth and frown staring up at her from the ground near the well. She sighed, knowing the conflict within her had finally been resolved. The years of torment were over. Her guilt had been replaced by a closeness to God and a feeling that all of this had happened for some reason.

One evening after coming home from the opera, Jake retreated to his library. Sally came from upstairs in her nightgown and opened the heavy wooden doors to the walnut paneled room.

Jake said, "Hey, I told you to knock first when you enter the library. This is my special hide-away."

"Oh, silly. I thought we shared everything."

"Then how come I have to knock to enter your greenhouse?"

They laughed and hugged each other.

Sally was a little upset that the room was not as tidy as it could be. Some books were piled horizontally on top of others that lay crooked on the shelves. The smell of stale pipe smoke also bothered her. She didn't say anything but collapsed into an upholstered chair facing Jake, who rummaged through his desk drawers.

"Is there something you want?" he asked.

"Yes, but I don't want to bother you." She noticed how good looking her husband was. The black hair on his chest spilled over the collar of his shirt.

"You're not bothering me. What would you like?" He closed the desk drawer and moved in front of her chair.

"Oh Jake, the opera was so wonderful tonight. Thanks for taking me." Sally loosened two buttons on her nightgown.

"You looked so refined. I love that dress you wore tonight." He leaned down and kissed her.

"I've come to ask if we could dance together in the upstairs ballroom." She stood and kissed him back.

"Of course, dear." Together, they climbed the stairs to the third floor of their mansion and danced to Sally's humming. She closed her eyes, forcing all other thoughts from her mind. She heard the music, smelled the fresh scent of Jake's cologne, and felt secure in the strong, powerful arms of her husband.

Minutes later the couple chased each other downstairs until they reached the bedroom. Sally's desire was overwhelming. She felt like she was going to explode. Their lovemaking was hurried, more intense than usual.

Afterwards, Sally felt a calm. Her muscles relaxed. She felt content, at peace with herself and the world. She rolled toward Jake and said, "There is something special I'd like to tell you."

"What's that?" he asked.

"I've missed three periods." She blushed.

"You mean we're going to have a baby?"

"Yes, dear. You're going to be a father."

Naked, Jake leaped out of bed and danced around the room.

"What will we name him?"

She replied, "How about Sam? No, that's too short. Maybe Harry. No, I knew a Harry who never bathed. Sidney? Alex? …"

"What if our baby is a girl?" asked Jake.

"Why don't we name her Mattilda, after Mattie?"

"That would get too confusing. How 'bout someone from the Bible, like Ruth?"

The couple discussed names until they fell asleep. When they woke in the morning, they continued the conversation and reached a consensus. If a boy, the baby would be named after Jake's brother, William, who had died from the ague. If a girl, they would name the baby after Lily.

"William Flareau II," said Sally as she descended the stairs.

"Or Lillian Flareau," said Jake.

At a landing halfway down the rug-covered stairs, the couple stopped. Jake put his arms around her and drew her close. She felt his heart beat. His warm eyes stared into hers for several minutes. Speechless, his lips touched hers. They were soft, warm, and moist.

"Sally I love you so. You've made my life complete."

"I love you, too."

The couple continued down the stairs and into the dining room.

Sally talked with Jake, oblivious to her past, content in the present, and hopeful of a blessed future.

The End

About the Author

Ed Langenau was born in Brooklyn, New York and grew up in suburban New Jersey. After he graduated from Rensselaer Polytechnic Institute and completed a tour of duty with the 25th Infantry Division in Vietnam, his outdoor interests led him to Michigan State University's graduate school. Dr. Langenau was fortunate to then be able to work as a wildlife biologist for the Michigan Department of Natural Resources in both research and management positions. After retiring, Ed published articles in *Michigan Out of Doors, Deer and Deer Hunting, Michigan Sportsman,* and other magazines. He then became interested in writing fiction with an outdoor theme. *Lumberjacks and Ladies,* his first novel, retains his trademark: blunt and colorful language mixed with well-researched information.